Reflection

OTHER BOOKS BY DIANE CHAMBERLAIN

Reflection

DIANE CHAMBERLAIN

HarperCollins*Publishers*

HarperCollins books may be purchased for educational, business, or sales promotional use. For information please write: Special Markets Department, HarperCollins Publishers, Inc., 10 East 53rd Street, New York, NY 10022.

FIRST EDITION

Designed by Caitlin Daniels

ISBN 0-06-017652-0

96 97 98 99 00 ❖/RRD 10 9 8 7 6 5 4 3 2 1

To Mom and Dad,
my favorite octogenarians

I am grateful to the following people for sharing their expertise and ideas with me during the writing of *Reflection:*

April (Read2Learn) Adamson, Judy Harrison, David Heagy, Mary Kirk, Don Rebsch, Ed Reed, Joann Scanlon, Cindy Schacte, and Suzanne Schmidt, along with the Mount Vernon Writers' Group and my teatime colleagues, the Online Book Group.

1

This was Helen's favorite part of the sonata, the slow, measured rise and fall of the notes, the yearning, pleading sound flowing from her piano. Her eyes were closed in concentration when she heard the low growl of thunder in the distance. She lifted her hands from the keys and looked through the window. Her eyes were still sharp enough to see that the wind was spinning crazily through the trees, baring the pale undersides of the leaves and bending the stand of volunteer bamboo nearly to the ground. It was only five o'clock on a summer afternoon—the Fourth of July, to be exact—but it was already dusk dark, that sort of darkness that made the woods look at once foreboding and inviting.

The sky above the trees suddenly pulsed with light, and thunder rumbled once more in the distance.

Helen loved a good storm, and she skipped the entire second movement of the sonata to begin the roaring, thundering third. It wasn't until the rain began in earnest that she remembered the tools in the garden. She'd planned to work out there again this afternoon, but the piano had seduced her on one of her trips through the house.

She rose slowly from the bench and walked into the kitchen and out the back door. She did not bother with an umbrella, and the rain felt fresh and cool on her face as she crossed the yard to the garden.

The scuffle hoe lay on the ground near the thigh-high shoots of corn. She picked up the hoe, then turned in a circle, hunting for the shovel and trowel, shaking her head when she spotted them in a tangle of weeds. Had those weeds been there a few hours earlier? They were popping up as fast as she could pull them these days. They raised their healthy green faces to the rain as she bent over for the trowel.

She walked to the edge of the bamboo, where Rocky was buried, and pulled a few weeds from around the boulder she'd managed to roll on top of the fresh grave. She'd nearly wrenched her back moving the stone, but she hadn't cared. The vet had come out to her house to put the terrier to sleep only the week before, and she was not quite over it yet. She missed the wiry body leaping on her bed in the morning for a cuddle. She missed the way he would lie at her feet, no matter where she went in the house. She'd wept and wept watching the vet dig the grave, as though all the losses she'd endured in her eighty-three years had been encapsulated in the death of the little dog. Rocky had been her family since Peter's death ten years earlier, becoming the object of her nurturing and the source of her affection. The loneliness in the house the past week had been a palpable force.

The trees whipped around her shoulders as she stood up from Rocky's grave, and thunder roared in her ears like a menacing animal lurking just out of sight. Something made her turn to look back at her house—that little miracle of wood and glass she and Peter had created more than sixty years ago—and suddenly the world turned white. Ice white. So cold it burned.

Pain, everywhere. Above her, pink and blue dahlias bloomed in the dark sky before dropping their petals in a shower of sparks. She lay still for several minutes, waiting for the petals to fall on her, wondering why she didn't feel them on her skin, until she realized it was fireworks she was seeing in the sky above her. Fireworks. The Fourth of July. The gardening tools. Weeds and rain.

She couldn't swallow. Couldn't hear. Shouldn't there be sound with fireworks? She tried to lift her head to see exactly where she was, but the muscles in her neck were frozen. Maybe she'd had a stroke. Oh, the pain in her chest, her head! Maybe she'd fallen and given herself a concussion.

She squinted as tiny gold fish wriggled across the sky, disappearing in a pale orange mist. She tried to remember. There'd been a storm. Thunder. The white light, sudden and blinding. She knew then what had happened, and she felt a keen sense of disappointment that the lightning had not simply killed her. It would have been a splendid way, a splendid time, to die. Her family was gone; the last of her good friends had passed away a few months earlier. She'd had a fine life. There'd been sorrow, to be sure, but she'd known deep and enduring love. Selfless love. She had known passion. And she had touched many lives.

Perhaps she would die after all. She could not get to the house, and it might be days before anyone came up here and found her. All right, then. She closed her eyes to the soundless spectacle of light above her and tried to will herself back into unconsciousness.

Too many clues in the attic.

The thought darted into her brain, and her eyes sprang open. The boxes in the attic. Why hadn't she taken care of them? She'd meant to clean them out long before now. She could not die yet, not until she'd gotten rid of them. She tried to lift her head again, wincing with the effort, finally giving up. Was the house behind her? To her right? Left? A dozen dahlias flashed in the air above her, and she stared at them numbly. Who would care enough to weed through those boxes? Even if someone did, would they ever be able to put the pieces of the puzzle together? Surely this was needless worry.

Closing her eyes against the exploding dahlias, she put herself in the hands of fate.

"Mrs. Huber?"

Helen opened her eyes to see a young woman at her bedside, and once again she had to struggle to remember where she was. Spader Hospital. She'd been there . . . how long? Days. She knew that much. The white light.

She squinted at her visitor, trying to remember why the visage of this woman struck fear in her heart. Oh, yes. The social worker. The one who wanted to put her in some sort of home.

"You're awake." The social worker smiled at her.

"I can take care of myself," she said, before the woman had a chance to start talking about the home again.

"I know." The social worker nodded, patronizing her. "I'm sure in time you'll be able to, but as we talked about yesterday, you're going to need some help for a while. You have a badly sprained ankle and wrist, as well as a concussion. And your blood pressure and heart rate are very unstable. You know what happens when you try to get out of bed."

Helen could not even sit on the side of the bed without the room spinning and fading to black. "You'd be surprised what I'll be able to do once I'm home," she said.

The social worker nodded pleasantly. "But at first you're going to need some help," she said. "Not for long. Not forever."

Helen stared at her, afraid. The woman had rosy cheeks, a too bright smile, brown hair shaped like a bubble. She was somewhere in her midthirties, too young to understand that once you allowed someone to take over, you would never have control of your life again. She knew the social worker saw her as a stubborn old lady, set in her ways, making life difficult for those who thought they knew what was best for her. Worse, she had overheard the woman—or maybe it had been one of the nurses—talking about her in the hall-way, saying something about her being "just an old woman who hap-pened to be married to an important man."

They called her "demanding," too. Every afternoon there was a thunderstorm, and she found she could not bear the noise, the light. She'd never been a fearful sort of person, but now the thick, swirling clouds of an approaching storm made her tremble. She'd insisted that the nurses move her bed away from the window and pull the shades.

"There's a wonderful home not far from where you live." The social worker spoke carefully. "It's expensive, but you can afford it, I'm sure." Obviously the woman knew that the royalties from Peter's music had left her more than comfortable financially, although no one would ever know it from the simple way she lived.

"I told you, no nursing home," Helen said firmly.

"All right." The social worker tried unsuccessfully to hide a sigh. "Let's look at some other options, then. Do you have any relatives who might be able to help out?"

Helen shook her head. "My only living relatives are a granddaugh-ter I haven't seen in nearly thirty years and a great-grandson I've never even met. They live way out in San Antonio. I wouldn't think of imposing on them."

"I understand. But let me just give your granddaughter a call. I'm sure she'd like to know your situation, and maybe the three of us can put our heads together and come up with an idea."

Helen started to shake her head again but changed her mind. She was curious about her granddaughter. She'd been cut off from Rachel since the girl was fifteen. There had been a few Christmas cards in recent years—enough to tell Helen about the grandson, Chris, and that Rachel was a high school teacher—but no other contact. Rachel would be in her early forties by now.

"Rachel Huber," Helen said. "My address book is at home, but you can try Information, I suppose. She's on some street that begins with an *S*, I think. Some Spanish name, in San Antonio. But don't you dare ask her to come here. I will not impose on that girl." She wondered if she should say more, if she should tell the woman the real reason Rachel should not come to Reflection, but decided against it as the social worker rose to leave the room, looking a little smug.

She was back within an hour, her pink cheeks aglow.

"Well," she said as she took her seat again next to Helen's bed. "You are in for a very pleasant surprise."

"What?" Helen eyed her with suspicion.

"I spoke with your granddaughter. I didn't ask her to come," she added quickly. "I promised you that. She suggested it on her own. She's a teacher, but she's taking this coming year off. Isn't that one of those meant-to-be coincidences? She said it would be wonderful to see you and Reflection again. I guess she grew up here?"

Helen stared at the woman, then held out her hand. "Give me her number. I'm going to call her and tell her not to come."

"She *wants* to come, Mrs. Huber. She was very sincere. Actually, she sounded enthusiastic, as if she'd been waiting for someone to suggest a way for her to spend the summer. When I told her you'd still be here for a few days, that we need to track down the cause of your vertigo and all, she said she would drive out instead of fly. She sounds like the adventurous type."

"But she has a little boy to take care of," Helen argued.

The social worker smiled. "That little boy is twenty years old and in college," she said.

Helen was speechless. Her great-grandson was already in college?

The social worker patted her hand. "I know it must be hard for someone who's been so independent to accept help, but—"

"That's not it," Helen interrupted her. "Just give me the number."

The woman reluctantly handed over a small piece of paper and, with a few words of advice on letting Rachel come, left the room.

Helen spent the evening trying to read, but it was hard to concentrate on her book with that scrap of paper resting on her bed table. Should she call Rachel, tell her it would be a mistake for her to come back to Reflection? But oh, how she wanted to see her granddaughter. What kind of person had Rachel grown up to be?

She picked up the piece of paper, studied it for a moment, then crumpled it in her hand. It might be selfish of her, but she would let her granddaughter come. She would let her think she needed her help. It would probably be a while before Rachel realized it was the other way around.

Rachel sat up in the strange bed, eyes wide, heart knocking against her ribs. The footsteps were still there, that rapid-fire *click, click, click* of someone in a hurry, but they were fading into the distance outside her motel-room door.

She lay down again on the damp sheets. She was in West Virginia, she remembered. Somewhere near Charleston. She'd arrived late the night before and barely noticed the nondescript motel room before falling into bed. For three days she'd lost herself in audio books played on the car's tape player. For three days she'd kept herself from wondering whether she was making the right decision in going to Reflection. She had avoided thinking about her reasons for leaving that little town, but she knew those thoughts were scratching to be let in. The hurried footsteps had brought them back to her far too easily.

It had happened on a Monday, that much she could remember. She knew she'd spoken to the police afterward only because her parents told her she had. She'd had to whisper, her father said, because she'd screamed for so long and so hard after it happened that she had no voice left. The police couldn't understand some of her breathless answers, and they made her write them down on small sheets of paper.

She remembered those pieces of paper. They were square, pink. Odd how her mind chose to save one memory and discard another. For the most part, the memories did not disturb her. She knew that they should, though. She had known that for a long time.

A town this small can't lose ten of its children in one fell swoop and go on unchanged.

Who had said those words? Over the past two decades they had played in her mind, coming to her at weird moments. She might be leaning over a desk helping one of her students with math, or folding the laundry, or making love to Phil. She did not know if the voice belonged to a man or a woman. Perhaps it had been one of the policemen, or someone else whose path had crossed hers during those few terrible days. Or perhaps, her therapist had suggested, it was her own voice she was hearing.

She remembered the rapid clicking of her shoes on Spring Willow Elementary School's polished hall flooring as she raced toward her classroom. Sometimes even now, if she were rushing somewhere and heard that staccato rapping of her shoes, panic rose in her throat and she would have to slow down, change her pace, make the sound go away. When it was someone else's footsteps, though, she had no choice but to wait them out.

She did not recall making the decision to go to her cousin Gail's in San Antonio after it happened. She knew from what her parents had told her that she herself had made the decision once Gail offered to take her in, but she had no idea what pros and cons she had weighed. Her mind had been numb, full of holes and blurry, dreamlike images that made no sense and carried no emotional weight. Was it fear that had driven her away from Reflection? She could not say. She had simply followed the advice of others blindly. It was all she had the strength to do.

Gail, who was seven years her senior, had insisted she be in therapy. Rachel could not remember the therapist's name or what she looked like, but she did remember some of the things the woman had said. For the first few sessions Rachel did nothing but cry. That was good, the therapist said. Let it all out. Rachel was ashamed to tell her that her tears were not for the children or even for her husband, Luke. Her tears were over Michael, the man she loved and would never be able to have.

"Ah," said the therapist. "You're transferring your pain over Luke and the children to a smaller loss in order to make it more tolerable." But the therapist was wrong.

Rachel did not intentionally evade the therapist's many attempts to get her to talk about the children. She simply could not remember them. The students were a blur to her, and she knew she had to keep them that way. She could not bring herself to take too close a look at them, to remember details like a smile, or blue eyes, or scattered freckles across an upturned nose.

She wondered whether the therapist had been disgusted by her unwillingness to examine what had happened, or if she had understood then what Rachel was only coming to understand now, twenty-one years after the fact. She had tucked her memories of the children and Luke into a neat little box in her mind, to be opened only when she was ready to deal with what she might find inside.

And she was ready now, or she would have to be. The call from the social worker had shocked her at first. Go back to Reflection to take care of an old woman who was essentially a stranger to her? But the timing of the call was serendipitous. Phil was gone. Chris was home for the summer but thoroughly involved with his friends. She'd taken time off, intending to get herself back in shape, physically and emotionally, after this difficult year. She could do that as easily in Reflection as she could in San Antonio. And so she'd said, "Sure, I'll come," responding with the same detached calm that always accompanied her thoughts of her hometown. It was as if she'd been expecting that phone call, waiting for someone to tell her it was time to go home.

She'd looked forward to the drive. It had been a while since she'd traveled on her own, and she found herself altering her route, intentionally getting lost, exploring places not on her itinerary. She'd brought her bicycle with her, and she took it off the bike rack a few times to ride through an intriguing town or speed along a path by the side of a river. She liked having time to think. Yesterday she'd come up with a way she could give something back to her hometown. She would contact the schools to see if she might be able to tutor students who needed extra help, on a strictly voluntary basis. The thought pleased her enormously, easing something inside her that had long needed easing.

It was quiet outside her motel room, and she got out of bed. This would be her last day on the road. She took a shower and dressed, then bought a newspaper in the motel's sundry shop before walking across the street to a restaurant. She ordered cereal and bananas, spreading the paper out on the table while she ate. She grimaced at the picture on the front page. Rwanda, again. The devastation in the refugee camps. Adults with empty eyes. Sick, starving children.

She had lived in Rwanda once, teaching in the Peace Corps in the early seventies. Even then the country had been in turmoil. She stared at the blank faces of the children. They could be the sons and daughters of children she had taught.

The cereal suddenly felt like rocks in her stomach, and she put away the front section of the paper in favor of the comics.

It was one o'clock when she pulled her car off the road at the crest of Winter Hill, and for the first time she felt certain she'd made the right decision in coming. She was not the superstitious type, but when she'd reached the Pennsylvania border a few hours earlier, the classical station she was listening to played Peter Huber's *Patchwork*. It was her favorite of her grandfather's compositions, and it felt almost as if he were talking to her, winking at her the way he used to do when she was small, saying, "Welcome to your home state, Rachel."

Everyone knew the story behind that particular piece of music. The idea had come to Grandpa one day when he was walking on Winter Hill and saw the patchwork of green-and-gold farmland spread out in front of him, as she was seeing it now, with the scrubbed little village of Reflection mirrored in the glassy waters of the pond.

Rachel doubted this view had been much different then. The barns and silos and farmhouses had been repaired and painted or in some cases replaced. But the three sky-touching churches had stood near the pond for a hundred years. The gray flagstone, the largest of the three, was the Lutheran church she had attended as a child. Across the street stood the Mennonite church, its white clapboard image perfectly re-created in the pond's mirror. She could not recall the denomination of the third church, the diminutive brick chapel, but from this distance at least it was as charming as the others. Reflection had been an old and crumbling little town even when Rachel was small, but from up here it was lovely, the sight of it comforting.

She'd been right to come. This would be a good summer. A healing summer.

In the distance, several miles west of town, the boxy shape of
Spader Hospital rose out of the trees. Rachel looked at her watch.
She had an hour before she was supposed to pick up her grandmother. She got back into her car and drove slowly down the hill
toward the town where she'd grown up.

Passing a farmyard, she noticed that the laundry line stretching
between the house and barn was hung with blue shirts and black
pants. An Amish family had lived in that house for as long as she
could remember. Still no electrical cables, no telephone wires in sight.
What had she expected? The Amish had endured in this area for two
centuries, their way of life virtually unchanged. Had she thought they
would succumb to modern times in the two decades she'd been
gone?

She began her tour on Water Street, the blue-collar neighborhood
in the southern part of town. The street felt narrower than Rachel
remembered it, almost claustrophobic, yet she felt buoyed by the sight
of it. The houses hugged the curb, and the steps of their wooden
porches sagged, but for the most part they were well kept and freshly
painted. Flowers and shrubs grew in every tiny exposed patch of earth
between the buildings and the street. Many of the houses were
duplexes. But there was one lone triplex, she knew, a few blocks
closer to the center of town.

She almost missed it. Someone had painted it robin's-egg blue, and
she found she could not quite remember what color it had been
when it was her home. Something neutral—beige or white or gray.
The blue was outrageous, but she liked it. She parked her car across
the street and studied the building. The two doors on the left were
close together; the third was set apart. Fitting. She'd never thought of
that before. The first door had belonged to her family, the second to
Luke's. Her parents had moved into the building within days of
Luke's parents, and pregnant Inge Huber and pregnant Charlotte
Pierce had become fast friends. When their children were born—a
girl to Inge, a boy to Charlotte—their mothers kidded that they
would marry one day. Rachel and Luke's future was set at their birth.

What a beautiful boy he'd been. Dark-haired, blue-eyed. Rachel could not remember a moment in her childhood that Luke had not been a part of, that she had not felt his nearness. They would bounce out their front doors and be pulled together as if they were magnetized. Even at ten, eleven, twelve, when most boys were avoiding girls as if they would suck the life from them if given the chance, Luke and Rachel had been inseparable.

Rachel hugged herself, grimacing against the nostalgia. After graduating from college, she and Luke had followed their mothers' plans and married. And Michael Stoltz had been their best man.

The Stoltz family had moved into the third apartment of the triplex when Luke and Rachel were seven years old. Michael had just gotten his first pair of glasses, and that about summed him up. He was a slender, gawky child, shorter than most of his classmates, annoyingly bright and adored by his teachers but not well accepted by his peers. Perhaps it was because Luke and Rachel lived so close to him that they saw something in him the other children missed. He was a valuable friend, and by the time Rachel was eight or nine years old, she and Luke could no longer imagine going off together without inviting Michael to come along. Still, although they were a threesome throughout elementary school, in high school no one ever doubted that the bond between Luke and Rachel was based on more than friendship. She and Luke would fix Michael up with a date from time to time, but nothing ever worked out for long. He was not bad-looking, but he was still skinny, and that combined with his bookishness made him invisible to the eyes of adolescent girls.

Where was Michael now? When she'd left Reflection, he'd still been in Rwanda with plans to teach in Philadelphia once he was out of the Peace Corps. And he was married to Katy Esterhaus, the one girl from their high school who could match him for brains.

With a shake of her head, Rachel turned the key in the ignition and started slowly up Water Street toward the center of town. She didn't dare think too long about Michael.

Ahead of her, the small, circular park that stood in the center of town came into view. The streets of the town fell away from the wooded circle like curved, misshapen spokes of a wheel. The park looked denser and greener than she remembered, and Rachel found herself averting her eyes from it as she drove past. Somewhere in that lovely little circle, scattered among the oaks and maples, stood ten weeping cherry trees, planted shortly after she'd left. Her parents had told her about the trees in a letter. She'd been living in Gail's apartment in San Antonio for a couple of months by that time, and she'd locked herself in the bathroom with the water running in the tub so that her cousin would not be able to hear her sobs. Her parents had also told her about the stone memorial erected in the park to make certain that no one, not her generation or the generations to come, would ever forget what had happened to their children.

Rachel drove through the center of town, past the old Starr and Lieber Bank building with its beautiful curved stone facade, past the huge Victorian house that served as the library. She came to the pond and immediately broke into a smile. Stopping the car close to the curb, she glanced at her watch again. It was too late. She would have loved to get out and walk around the narrow path circling the water. Huber Pond. Named after her grandfather, Reflection's major claim to fame.

The forest surrounding the eastern half of the pond had once been her playground, and it was as thick and dark as she'd ever seen it. She and Luke and Michael had loved those woods. They'd play for hours in them, building forts or pretending to be pioneers. Whatever game they played, it held an element of fear, because they knew that deep in the woods lurked the "bat woman," the odd, spooky woman who lived in a rundown, overgrown old cottage there. She was like the witch in Hansel and Gretel, they thought, eager to shove little children into her gaping black oven. They dared one another to visit her, jumped out at one another from the woods yelling, "Bat woman!" They threatened one another with being dragged to see her. But none of them ever ventured into that part of the woods, and sitting in her car, Rachel wondered if the woman had been a figment of their collective imaginations.

Even though it was getting close to the time she was to pick up her grandmother, Rachel felt compelled to get out of her car to look at the statue of her grandfather, set close to the edge of the pond. She had forgotten what he looked like. His heavy brows and round, wire-rimmed glasses gave his face a serious look. His beard and mustache were neatly trimmed. She was moved by the handsome bronze image of him. Peter Huber, 1902–1984. He had died eleven years after she'd left home, but she had not seen him since she was fifteen, in 1965, when her parents had forbidden her to have any contact with either of her grandparents. She'd bump into them from time to time in the little town, occasionally exchanging furtive hugs or pained greetings, but that had been the extent of her contact with them. She remembered her grandfather as a kind man, quiet and gentle. Even as a child, she'd imagined his quietness was due to the fact that his brain was always working, always creating. When he'd sit down at the piano, his house would fill with the rich, smooth sound of his music. She wished she could have known him from an adult's perspective.

She doubted she would have the chance to get to know her grandmother in that way, either. The social worker at the hospital had described her as quite frail and very depressed. Rachel's role this summer would be to care for a woman who was fading away.

As Rachel walked back to her car, she suddenly turned and did a double take. The sign next to the pond, which had read HUBER POND all the years she'd lived in Reflection, now read SPRING WILLOW POND. She stared at the sign for a long time. It made no sense. Why would they change it? It would always be Huber Pond to her.

Decker Avenue was the most logical street for her to take to the hospital, but it was home to Spring Willow Elementary School, where she had taught for all of six days before fleeing town, and she opted to take Farmhouse Road instead. She drove for several miles through farmland, the hospital poking its head up in the distance occasionally as she rounded curves and slipped over hillsides.

The attendant in the hospital parking lot told Rachel to leave her car at the curb in the circular driveway, since she was only picking someone up. She parked carefully behind a horse and buggy, a little awestruck. She'd grown up thinking that those buggies were a natural part of the landscape, but now the sight of one touched her. There were still people in the world staunchly committed to their principles.

Her grandmother's room was on the second floor, and she found the older woman sitting up in a chair, dressed in a midcalf-length blue denim skirt, a white blouse, and blue canvas shoes. She knew by the ready smile that her grandmother had been watching the door for her arrival.

"Rachel." Her grandmother lifted one arm toward her, and Rachel bent down to kiss the soft, cool cheek. The older woman gripped her hand as though she might never let go. There were tears in her eyes.

"Hello, Gram," Rachel said. She would not have recognized her grandmother. Helen Huber was still a pretty woman, with expressive blue eyes and high cheekbones, but her dark hair was now white and short. It was smoothed back from her face, which was terribly thin. She needed to eat. Good. Rachel had been in a cooking mood ever since school let out for the year, feeding herself entirely too well.

Gram turned her head, and Rachel noticed the delicate, fernlike pattern tattooed onto her cheek, slipping beneath the collar of her blouse. A burn. The lightning. She shuddered.

"How are you feeling?" she asked.

Her grandmother smiled. "My hearing's quite keen," she answered, and Rachel realized she had asked the question loudly. "And to be honest, I'm feeling achy and old and ready to go home. But I'm so, so happy to see you." Her lower lip trembled, moving Rachel to bend low for another embrace.

A nurse brought a wheelchair, and Gram shifted slowly into it. It was obvious that she was in a good deal of pain, and Rachel was immediately reminded of Phil's last few months.

"This is my little granddaughter," Gram said as the nurse pushed her through the hall to the elevator. Rachel walked at her grand-mother's side, holding her hand.

"Nice to meet you." The nurse smiled.

Once down at the curb, Gram gingerly transferred from the chair to the passenger seat of Rachel's car. The nurse handed Rachel a couple of prescriptions and a list of instructions.

"You were so good to come," Gram said as they pulled out of the hospital driveway. "Though it wasn't necessary."

"I'm pleased I had the time off." She glanced over at her grand-mother, at the feathery lines on her cheek. "Is the burn very painful?" she asked.

"What? Oh, this?" Gram touched her cheek. "No, not at all. They call it 'aborescent erythema.' It's not a real burn. It's from where the lightning followed the pattern of rain on my skin. They say it will fade away soon." She sighed. "The worst part is the dizziness. I've fainted a few times."

She talked a bit about what had happened, the work in the garden, the white light, and then she fell quiet. Talking seemed like an effort for her, and Rachel felt the strain of silence in the car. Chattering to fill the void, she told her grandmother about her earlier tour through town, past her old house, and the older woman listened, nodding her head occasionally.

"What is your husband doing this summer?" Gram asked finally.

"Phil died last October." Rachel kept her eyes on the road. "He had leukemia. He'd been sick for a while." She knew she hadn't mentioned Phil's death in her Christmas card. She hadn't seen the point.

"Oh, I'm very sorry," Gram said. She touched Rachel's arm. "How terrible for you."

Rachel acknowledged the sympathy with a nod. She missed Phil's strength and support. Their marriage had never been one of passion, but its foundation of friendship, caring, and tenderness could have sustained her forever. Eleven years her senior, Phil had been the principal in the school where she first taught after moving to San Antonio. She'd poured it all out to him during her interview, trying to keep a cool head, a professional demeanor, as she described what had happened in her classroom in Reflection. He checked her references, talked to professors she'd had in college, her supervisor in the Peace Corps. He believed in her, he said when he called to offer her the job, and she'd had a hard time not bursting into tears. She'd worked hard to prove him right in his assessment of her. She'd taken classes at night to get a master's degree in special education, and she had become a teacher other teachers turned to for guidance. For the last ten years she'd taught emotionally disturbed students and French on the high school level, and she'd won four awards in addition to being named teacher of the year in her school district two years ago. She owed Phil her self-confidence, her pride, and her ability to lay the past to rest and embrace the future.

A full three minutes passed before Gram spoke again. "I've been there, you know."

What was she talking about? "Do you mean San Antonio?"

Her grandmother actually laughed. "No, although I was in San Antonio once when Peter had to go there. Interesting city. But no. I meant I've gone through what you have. Taking care of a sick husband. Losing him."

"Oh, that's right. How did Grandpa die?"

"Kidney disease. It was slow, which gave us a long time to say good-bye but prolonged the suffering, too."

"Yes." Rachel had done most of her grieving for Phil while he was still alive, anticipating his loss. She had not cried once after his death, but felt his loss deeply, felt the unjustness of it. He'd had so many plans for the rest of his life. She'd withdrawn from her friends for several months, taking solace in food, parking herself night after night in front of the television. She was more than ready to change that pattern.

"Tell me about my great-grandson," Gram said.

"Well, his name is Chris, and he's twenty years old and a very talented, wonderful kid. He'll be a junior—a music major—at West Texas State this fall." She felt the little pocket of worry in her chest begin to mushroom again. Chris *was* a talented, wonderful kid, but this summer he'd hooked up with a group of neighborhood kids to form a rock band. He seemed obsessed with the band, his classical training forgotten. "Music is his first love," she said. "He's played piano and violin since he was small." Now, of course, he was playing keyboard, singing in a voice that scratched its way through songs possessing no discernible melody.

"You should have brought him with you," Gram said.

She had considered asking him, pulling him away from those new friends, but he never would have agreed to come. Besides, she would have been nervous about having him here. He knew very little about her past.

"Maybe he can visit for a few days later in the summer," she said.

"He's twenty, you say?" Gram asked.

"Uh-huh."

"He was Luke's boy, then, was he?"

Rachel jerked as though her grandmother had touched her with a live wire, and she could respond with little more than a nod. Yes, Chris was Luke's son, and he knew it, although he'd always called Phil

"Dad." Still, it shocked her to hear Gram say Luke's name out loud, as if it were not a dirty word.

She'd told Chris that Luke had died in Vietnam. During his junior year of high school, though, Chris took a trip with the San Antonio Youth Orchestra to Washington, D.C., and he'd called her from the hotel one night, nearly in tears.

"They don't have Dad's name on the Vietnam Memorial," he said.

It was the first time she had heard him refer to Luke as "Dad." It was jarring, but it touched her all the same, and she thought she was being given a little window into Chris's soul.

Rachel explained that Luke had actually died shortly after his return from Vietnam from injuries he had received there. In many ways, that was the truth. She was not the type of mother to protect her child from pain, yet she could not see what purpose would be served by spelling it all out to him. He never had to know. For a few weeks, though, he'd talked about campaigning to have his father's name added to the memorial, and Rachel was relieved when the idea died a natural death.

"Shall we go through town?" Rachel asked. "We have to get your prescriptions filled."

"There's a pharmacy and a grocery store right off Farmhouse," Gram replied. "We'll need some food. There won't be anything to eat at my house."

Rachel turned onto the road her grandmother indicated and pulled into the parking lot of a small supermarket, new since she'd left home.

"What would you like?" she asked her grandmother.

"Doesn't matter," Gram said. "But I don't eat meat."

Rachel had forgotten. No meat had been allowed in her grandparents' house. And they'd always worn canvas shoes, eschewing leather. They had been passionate about animal rights long before it was fashionable.

Rachel dropped the prescriptions off at the pharmacy and picked up a few bags of groceries, leaving Helen to rest in the car, all the windows open to catch the breeze.

After returning to the car, she put her purchases on the backseat next to one of her suitcases. "I stopped up on Winter Hill this morning to admire the view," she said as she pulled onto the road. "It's exactly as I remember it."

"Not for long," Gram said.

"What do you mean?"

"It's a big brouhaha," she said. "The owner has plans to develop it. They're going to put two big office buildings on this side of the pond, and more than a hundred tract houses will be built where the woods stand now."

"No!" Rachel felt the loss almost as if she'd never left town. "You won't be able to see the reflection of the church in the water, or—"

"Oh, that's not half of it," Gram said with disgust. "Imagine what sort of traffic a development like that will generate. And those roads are used by the Amish with their buggies. The Amish and Old Order Mennonites will move out of the area—they're talking seriously about it. They're being run out. Their cemetery butts right up to the woods. The houses will practically be in their burial ground. And then we'll have the golden arches and the colonel and his chicken, all of which Ursula Torwig, our new mayor, thinks will be wonderful. She's all for growth. People are fighting it. I've got my fingers crossed somehow it'll all work out." ·

"Who owns the property?"

"Do you remember the little cottage back in those woods behind Huber Pond?"

"Yes! I'm not sure I ever saw it firsthand, but the bat woman lived in it, right?"

"Bat woman?" Gram chuckled. "Marielle Hostetter, I suppose you mean. She owns it."

Marielle Hostetter. Rachel had not heard the name since her childhood. She pictured a child-eating old hag. "She's still living?"

Gram laughed again. "She's twenty-some years younger than I am. Only around sixty. But she was never *well*, exactly. Never quite right in the head."

"But she's shrewd enough to develop the land?"

"Well, I'm not so sure she is. She has two nephews, though, who seem to be running things. She's in a nursing home now, and the boys are handling her affairs for her. And *they're* shrewd all right." Gram let out a long sigh. It seemed to Rachel that she was about to say more, but then she leaned her head against the seat back, closing her eyes as though she planned to sleep, and Rachel decided to let the subject die.

She was eager to see her grandparents' house again. The triplex she'd lived in was close to the heart of Reflection, while the wood-and-glass house her grandparents had built for themselves was nestled in a patch of forest two miles outside of town. Rachel had loved riding her bike out there a couple of times a week to visit them, and nearly every Sunday she would go with her parents to Gram and Grandpa's for dinner. That was before the forced estrangement. Suddenly, her parents announced that Rachel could no longer see them. Her grandparents were involved in "illegal activities," they said, which could not be condoned. Nor could they put themselves and Rachel at risk by being associated with them. Rachel had felt very young and naive. Obviously, the whole situation was over her head. She couldn't imagine her smart and loving grandparents involved in anything criminal, nor could she understand her parents cutting ties with them so abruptly, regardless of what they'd done.

Twice Rachel had ridden her bike out to her grandparents' house after being told to avoid them. She'd hidden in the heavy woods and watched as young men drove in and out of the yard in their beat-up old cars or on motorcycles. Some of the men looked scruffy and scary, others were clean-cut, but none of them were more than three or four years older than she was. It saddened her—angered her really—that these guys had access to her grandparents when she did not. And what was going on inside the house? She hedged away from that thought, unwilling to accept the most obvious explanation—her grandparents had somehow gotten themselves involved with drugs. Her parents refused to discuss the matter with her.

"The less you know, the better off you'll be," they'd said.

Gram did not speak again until Rachel turned onto the winding, forested road leading to her house.

"Listen, Rachel," Gram said softly. "When your parents died, cartons of their belongings were delivered to my house. No one had an address for you at the time, or I would have made certain they were sent on to you. There were many boxes of things that I just didn't have time to deal with. It was ten years ago, when Peter was very ill.

So I had someone carry them up to the attic. They've been there ever since. You're welcome to go through them."

Rachel was intrigued by the thought. "What's in them?"

"I really don't know. They're on the north side of the house, the side that faces the vegetable garden. There are dozens of boxes up there, but the ones from your family all have your father's name marked on the side."

Rachel squinted at the driveway that cut through the trees. "Is this it?"

"That's right. Good memory you have."

Rachel turned the car into the driveway and drove up to the familiar contemporary-style house. A newspaper lay in a plastic bag on the front step, and Rachel smiled. "Do you still get the *New York Times* delivered on Sundays?" she asked.

"Absolutely," Gram replied.

Rachel's eyes were drawn to the bird feeders hanging from the eaves above the porch. More of them hung from the trees standing in the yard. "You still have all the bird feeders!" she said.

"I try to keep the birds out front here and away from the garden," Gram said. She pointed to the rear of the house. "You can just pull around back," she said. "If you like, you can keep your bicycle in the shed."

Rachel drove around to the rear of the house and came to a stop by the back porch.

"Oh, look at that mess," Gram said.

Rachel followed her gaze to the large square vegetable garden, overgrown with weeds.

Gram shook her head. "I'll have to give up on it for this year. I got everything in and growing, but when Rocky—my dog—got put down, I lost some of my steam, and now with this . . ." She waved her bandaged hand toward her well-wrapped ankle.

Rachel could see the tomato plants in cages, the row of lettuce nearly buried under a tangle of green. It had been years since she'd taken the time to plant a garden, and here was one already planted for her. "It looks salvageable," she said. "I'd enjoy working in it."

Rachel helped her grandmother out of the car. Gram had to lean against the car door, waiting out a moment of dizziness before she could tackle the steps leading up to the house.

Inside, nothing had changed. The two pianos, still nested together, reigned supreme in the living room, the huge window behind them filled with the green of summer. The old couch—could it really be the same couch covered in the same ivy-print fabric that she'd sat on as a teenager?—was plush and inviting. Floor-to-ceiling windows brought the outdoors inside, and those patches of wall not made of glass were lined with books. Rachel had forgotten that about her grandparents' house. Bookshelves adorned every room, even the kitchen and bathroom. And there was a library with a fireplace. She peered around the corner to try to see into that inviting room, but the angle wasn't right.

Rachel stroked her hand across the ebony lid of one of the pianos. Nothing had changed, and yet something seemed wrong, out of place. She couldn't put her finger on it.

"Let me make up your bed fresh for you," she offered.

Her grandmother looked at her. "I don't like people doing things for me," she said. "I'm not used to it. Makes me feel old and useless."

"It's temporary," Rachel said, although Gram did seem very old to her. And she knew that once the elderly started having physical problems, they could go downhill fast.

The linen closet was filled with white sheets, stacks of them, neatly folded, and Rachel enjoyed making up her grandmother's bed with them. The bedroom was only vaguely familiar to her; she had not been in it often. It was large and square, the furniture made of solid, unadorned pine. Two comfortable-looking chairs rested in front of a picture window, and a huge cedar chest sat on the floor at the foot of the bed.

Rachel helped her grandmother change into a nightgown and watched as the older woman carefully negotiated her way beneath the covers.

"Do you need a pain pill?" Rachel asked.

"No. I'm so tired I could sleep with an elephant lying on my head right now." She clutched Rachel's hand. "I feel like I'm dreaming that you're here," she said. Tears glistened in her eyes again, and Rachel leaned over to kiss her forehead.

"I'm really here," she said with a smile.

After leaving the room, Rachel made up the full-sized bed in one of the other two bedrooms, the one nearest Gram's so she would be able to hear her in the middle of the night. This room was filled with antique oak furniture, an anachronism in the contemporary house. Rachel put away her clothes, then found herself drawn to the aging books on the bedroom's wall of bookshelves. They must have been her grandfather's collection. Hundreds of books about composers, musical instruments, politics, and puzzles. She'd forgotten Grandpa's addiction to puzzles. Crosswords, cryptoquotes. You couldn't get him away from his puzzle books long enough for Sunday dinner sometimes.

She wandered into the living room again. She remembered the beautiful painting above the fireplace—Reflection wrapped in a winter snow, the view from Winter Hill. She shook her head at the thought of that view disappearing under a developer's bulldozer.

Turning to the piano, she swept her fingers lightly across the keys. She had tried to learn to play as a child. With Peter Huber for a grandfather, it seemed terrible not to be able to play his compositions. But whatever talent Grandpa had possessed had skipped her generation and landed in the genes of her son.

That's what was missing, she thought. Music. She didn't think she had ever been in this house when music was not playing, either on the piano or on a record.

She hunted for a stereo and was surprised when she opened an old armoire and found a compact disc player and a large collection of compact discs inside. Somehow she had not expected Gram to be quite so modern. But here they were, at least two hundred discs in their plastic jewel cases.

She pulled a few of them out. Lots of classical, lots of old folk— Pete Seeger, Woody Guthrie, Bob Gibson. There was a whole section devoted to various pianists and symphony orchestras playing Huber pieces, and Rachel wondered which were the best, which Gram would put on if she were awake. She rifled through them until she found *Patchwork* performed by the Academy of St. Martin-in-the-Fields, and she slipped the disc into the player and stood back to listen as the first few teasing, eerie notes filled the room. She smiled to herself. This was right. This was the way her grandparents' house should feel.

She went into the large, open kitchen and set an eggplant on the cutting board and began cutting it into slices. They'd have eggplant Parmesan for dinner. She had a garden to weed, a grandma to pamper, and beautiful music all around her.

She was very, very glad she had come.

3

Lily Jackson arrived at the Hairlights Salon at around eight and let herself in. She started a pot of coffee, then took the petty cash from her purse and put it into the register. She nibbled on her cinnamon-raisin bagel as she poured herself a cup of coffee. Leaning back against the counter, she took a sip.

This was her favorite time of day, when Reflection was just waking up and she had the beauty parlor to herself. She'd already been up for hours. Ian had helped her walk the dogs—there were five of them this week, too many for her to handle on her own. Then she'd helped him water the plants in his beloved greenhouse. She'd crawled back into bed with him, snuggling for a few minutes before getting up and rummaging through her closet for something to wear. She'd finally selected a long black skirt and vest and a white blouse. It was the only outfit she owned that would be appropriate for the funeral that afternoon.

She saw the same people every morning on her walk from home. Arlena Cash on her way to her job at the bakery, where Otto Derwich had already been working for hours, filling the streets with the scent of baking bread and cinnamon rolls. She saw Sarah Holland on her way to the bookstore and Russell Martin heading toward the post office.

She would often pass Sam Freed as he walked to his law office. Sixty-seven years old and one of Reflection's three attorneys, Sam walked the four miles into town every day. He had a ready smile for anyone he met along the way. People had always been fond of Sam, but he was particularly popular these days. Marielle Hostetter and her nephews had tried to retain him as their lawyer in their fight to develop their land, but Sam had flatly refused to take them on. People respected him for that.

Every morning Lily stopped in the deli for a bagel and a few minutes' exchange with the cluster of regulars—other shop owners and store clerks, a few secretaries and bookkeepers and bankers. The people who revved up the town in the morning. They always gave her a warm greeting, asking her about Ian or the dogs and occasionally offering or soliciting a few tidbits of gossip. She liked that the other business owners treated her as if she were one of them, even though she'd only owned Hairlights for a little over a year.

She'd been fired from the two other beauty parlors she'd worked at. She had a problem with authority, her bosses told her. That was not news to Lily. When someone told her what she should do, she felt an immediate urge to do the opposite. So she'd started her own beauty parlor. She'd needed to sweet-talk her way to the loan at the bank, and she'd worked on Polly for weeks before her friend agreed to split ownership of the business with her. But here they were, eighteen months later, with a healthy clientele and no one to answer to.

She glanced at the appointment book, then checked the messages on the salon's answering machine and jotted down the information on a notepad: two women requesting appointments, one cancellation, and an early-morning call from Polly's father—one of Lily's favorite human beings and the best veterinarian around. He took care of her foster dogs for free.

Polly, Marge, and CeeCee arrived at the same time, as Lily was setting up her station and drinking her second cup of coffee. Polly was Lily's age—twenty-eight—and CeeCee was twenty-three. They were singing "Love Shack" when they walked in the door, and Marge, who was nearing sixty and had the prettiest silver hair in town, looked ready to stick her fingers in her ears.

Marge gave Lily a hug and a kiss on the cheek, as she did every morning. She would tell anyone who would listen that Lily had saved her by stealing her away from the last beauty parlor she had worked at. Marge was a boon to business. She brought in the older customers, who loved having someone close to their age do their hair.

"Your dad called," Lily said to Polly.

"Thanks." Polly turned to CeeCee. "You took my blow dryer again."

"You shouldn't have gotten such a good one, then." CeeCee filled her spray bottle at the sink.

Polly reached for the phone and dialed, while Lily straightened the pile of magazines on the square, glass-topped coffee table.

Polly suddenly turned toward Lily, her mouth open, eyes wide. "You've got to be kidding," she said into the phone.

Lily stood up from the magazines to look at her, and Marge and CeeCee stopped what they were doing.

"God, she has her nerve." Polly gave a raised-eyebrow look of disbelief to her coworkers, and the three of them completely abandoned their tasks and waited for her to get off the phone.

Polly finally hung up and put her hand to her mouth. "You will not believe this," she said. "Dad called Helen Huber to check up on her. You know, he put her dog to sleep a few weeks ago, and then she got struck by lightning and was in the hospital and everything?"

The women nodded, eager for her to get to the point.

"So he called to see how she was, and she said she's doing fine, that her *granddaughter* got into town on Wednesday and is taking good care of her."

"Her granddaughter?" CeeCee looked astonished. "You mean . . . Rachel Huber?"

"One and the same," Polly said.

The air in the room suddenly seemed very warm, and a gray haze slipped across Lily's field of vision. She felt as if she might pass out if she didn't sit down. She steadied herself with a hand on the counter.

"She came back." Marge uttered the words softly.

"She's out of her mind," CeeCee said. "I was doing Sue Holland's hair a few weeks ago, and we were talking about her husband—you know how crazy George is—and she was saying that he's actually a pussycat, that he's hated only one person in the whole world and that's you-know-who."

"Maybe she'll stay all summer," Polly giggled. "Then she could lead the Reflection Day ceremony in September."

"She won't survive here all summer," said CeeCee.

"If she has any sense at all, she'll stick close to Helen's," Marge suggested. "Maybe no one would have to know she's back, then."

No one pointed out to Marge the obvious flaw in her thinking: Once a piece of information had made its way into Hairlights, it was as good as known by everyone in town.

"Maybe she'll apply for a teaching job." CeeCee laughed.

"Yeah," said Polly. "My sister has way too many kids in her fourth-grade class. Maybe Rachel could take over teaching for her."

CeeCee howled as though this was the funniest thing she'd ever heard, and Lily walked toward the rear of the beauty parlor and through the open door to the supply room, where she leaned against one of the shelves and waited for the gray haze to lift. Gradually, she became aware of their voices, nearly whispering now, and she cocked her head to listen.

". . . your insensitivity," Marge was saying. "How do you think those kind of jokes make Lily feel? And here she is, getting ready to go to her uncle's funeral today and all, and you're joking about—"

"You're right," Polly interrupted her. "We were terrible. I completely forgot."

"It's not like something you think about every day," CeeCee said. "I mean, Lily's so well adjusted and everything."

"I don't think we should talk about Rachel Huber in front of her again," Marge said.

Polly and CeeCee muttered words of agreement.

"All I can say," Polly said, "is that this town's going to chew her up and spit her out in little pieces."

Lily took a bottle of shampoo from one of the shelves and left the supply room. At her approach, the other women immediately busied themselves at their stations.

"Tomorrow's my mother's birthday," Polly said. "I thought I'd get her that striped skirt in the window of Daley's."

"Oh, no! I love that skirt." CeeCee fluffed her short, dark hair in the mirror. "I wanted to get it."

"So get it," Polly said. "You and my mother don't exactly attend the same social events."

Lily stopped in the middle of the room. "I think she has guts coming back here," she said.

They all turned at the sound of her voice.

Polly approached her, touched her arm. "I'm sorry we were joking about her before," she said. "Really, Lil, I wasn't thinking."

"Me neither," CeeCee said.

"She has guts," Lily repeated. "And I hope no one gives her a hard time."

It was nearly three-thirty by the time Lily and Ian left her aunt's farmhouse after the funeral service and headed toward the cemetery for the burial. Lily had not been close to her uncle, but she'd felt a certain obligation to be there, to represent her side of the family, and she'd found the service moving in its simplicity. She'd had trouble concentrating on the words of the people who spoke about her uncle, though. Her mind was too clogged with thoughts about Rachel Huber.

Ian eased the car over one of the gentle crests in Farmhouse Road, and Lily shut her eyes at the blinding intrusion of sunlight through the windshield. She pulled down her visor and then could see the long processional of buggies ahead of them, a sinuous black snake stretching between their car and Reflection. Ian began riding the brake, and Lily wondered if they should have gone ahead of everyone else to the cemetery. But then she would have felt even more set apart from the others. As far as she knew, she and Ian had been the only people at the service to arrive in a car.

Ian glanced over at her. "It's slow going, but I think it's better this way," he said. "Makes you feel more like part of the family, doesn't it?"

She smiled. "Yes." She had long ago stopped marveling at her husband's ability to read her thoughts. Ian was a magician—a professional magician—and there were times she was convinced he possessed powers other human beings did not.

Ian eased up on the brake a little. "Do you wish you'd known him better?" he asked.

Lily sighed, thinking of the reserved man, her mother's brother, whose body lay in a pine coffin in the horse-drawn hearse at the front of the procession. "I'm not sure how knowable any of my Amish relatives are. They've always treated me kindly, but I am my mother's daughter, you know."

"Ruth the Rebel," Ian said with some glee. He loved hearing about the adolescent adventures that ultimately led to Ruth Zook's excommunication from her family's Old Order Amish church and to the shunning he considered barbaric. Lily had tried to explain to him that shunning was not punishment but rather an incentive to bring those who had strayed back into the fold—although she knew her mother's interest in the fold was nonexistent. Ruth was still alive, living in Florida. She would not have cared about attending her brother's funeral even if she had been allowed to do so.

"I bet she was like you," Ian said. "Wild and crazy. I can't picture you Amish, no way, no how. You're too rowdy. Too earthy."

She smiled. Lily could not imagine her mother wild and crazy, either, although at one time she must have been, at least by Amish standards. Ruth had been baptized into the church at the age of sixteen, a devout and pious girl, according to all who knew her then. But she'd met a sweet-talking Mennonite clerk in the dry-goods store and had quickly gotten pregnant with Lily and her twin sister, Jenny. Unrepentant, she was excommunicated and banned by her community and family. Lily wished she'd known that spirited girl. Ruth had become a sad woman, soured on life.

The procession reached the more congested section of Farmhouse Road, and the cars of tourists and locals stopped to let them pass. A few people got out of their cars and aimed their cameras at the long line of buggies.

The woods surrounding Spring Willow Pond were on their left, a lush, cool oasis in the sea of farmland. The road hugged the forest for nearly a mile, and since they were traveling at a snail's pace, Lily could see deep into the woods.

"Do you think they'll leave any of the trees?" she asked.

"Not many," Ian said. "Too expensive. The more trees they knock down, the more houses they can put up and the more money the Hostetters will have in their greedy little pockets."

Lily looked away from the woods, not wanting to think about their transformation from heaven to tract housing. She turned the air-conditioning up a notch, adjusting the vent so that it blew into her face. The heat had to be unbearable in those buggies.

Ian followed the buggies onto narrow Colley Lane, the woods still on their left, the Amish-Mennonite cemetery with its rows of unadorned headstones on their right. He pulled off the road onto the left shoulder, parking in the shade of the trees, and they got out of the car and walked across the street to where everyone was gathering.

A dozen children immediately surrounded Ian, trotting along next to him as he and Lily walked toward the crowd. Ian grinned at Lily. He'd been playing with the kids before the service, stunning them silly with magic tricks. With his dark ponytail and magician's charisma, he'd been an immediate hit, earning himself a group of little followers.

When they reached the outskirts of the crowd some of the children walked over to their parents, but a few stuck close to Lily and Ian, standing quietly. Lily watched as four men carried the coffin, supported by two thick poles, to the open, hand-dug grave. She could see the backs of the men rounding as they lowered the coffin into the ground. Then she heard the thumping sound of dirt as the pallbearers began covering the coffin with earth.

Jenny was buried in this cemetery. Lily glanced toward the far corner, near the woods, where her sister's plain headstone backed up to the trees. She'd always taken comfort in the thought that Jenny was cradled in the protective green of those trees. *The more trees they knock down, the more houses they can put up,* Ian had said. Lily turned her attention back to her uncle's grave.

Midway through the burial, the men stopped and took off their hats, and a man standing near the side of the grave read something in German. Lily glanced around her. Meticulously manicured farmland surrounded the cemetery on three sides, and across narrow Colley Lane the forest provided a tall, thick shield from town. What would happen when the developers came? She tried to imagine the woods replaced by houses, built tightly together, each looking like its neighbor. No privacy for these mourners then. No privacy for the dead. Children would play on Jenny's headstone. Lily's eyes burned. These people would not fight well for themselves. It was up to others to fight for them, others like Michael Stoltz. She trusted Michael to know what to do. Everyone was counting on him.

She and Ian declined the invitation to return to Lily's aunt's house for a meal. Ian gave hugs to the children, promising to teach them a trick or two the next time he saw them, and then they were off, driving away in the only gas-powered vehicle lining the shoulder of Colley Road.

The dogs greeted them when they got home. Lily let them knock her over in the hallway of the small house she and Ian had been renting since they married five years ago. She didn't bother to get up, just lay there on the floor, getting stepped on and licked and nuzzled, and laughing for the first time all day.

Through the blur of gold and black and white fur, she saw Ian drop to the floor next to her.

"My woman's laughing!" He joined the dogs in their affectionate attack, tickling her until she was breathless. "We are extremely happy to see our woman laugh again, aren't we, fellas?"

Lily lifted her arms through the crush of dogs to put them around Ian's neck. She pulled the leather band from his ponytail, and his straight black hair fell on her cheek. "I love you," she said, raising her head to kiss him.

Ian frowned at her. "Something's bothering you, chickadee. Something more than your uncle."

"How can you possibly know that?" she asked. "I'm lying here laughing, for heaven's sake."

"Yeah, you're laughing, but right here"—he touched the space between her eyebrows—"is this teeny tiny little line that you only get when you're upset about something. Or have a bellyache. Do you have a bellyache?" He slid one of his long-fingered hands under her skirt until it came to rest on her stomach.

She shook her head. "No. I wish it were that simple."

Ian's expression immediately sobered. "What is it?"

Lily sighed. "I found out something this morning," she said. The floor was growing uncomfortable, but she liked Ian's nearness and the warmth of the dogs at her head and side. "Rachel Huber is in town."

"Whoa. Damn." Ian let out his breath. "Is she just passing through, or what?"

"I'm not certain. She's here to take care of Helen, and I don't know how long Helen will need help."

"Whoa," Ian said again. He sat up and leaned his back against the wall.

Missing his closeness, Lily reached for his hand. "It's not anything to get all worked up about, I guess," she said. "It just took me by surprise this morning. Shook me up a little."

"Sure it did." He nodded. Ian had moved to Reflection as an adult. He did not have the memory of September 10, 1973, ingrained in his mind as most residents of the town did, and Lily never treated that date as if it were significant. Yes, she closed Hairlights on Reflection Day last fall—it wouldn't have felt right to keep it open when all the schools and other shops were closed—but otherwise she pretended that the second Monday of September was just another day on the calendar. She did not even attend the Reflection Day observance anymore. But she knew that Ian understood how she felt.

"Can I help you somehow?" he asked. "What can I do?"

She touched his cheek. He always wanted to fix things for her, but some things were beyond repair. "I don't know," she said. "All I know right now is that she shouldn't be here. She shouldn't have come. People are"—she shook her head—"no one's ever forgiven her."

"Have you?"

"Yes. Absolutely. I never blamed her in the first place."

Ian leaned over to kiss her. "You're a good woman, Lily Jackson."

They cooked and ate together, then took the dogs down to the small park near their house. They let their own three dogs run loose but kept the two foster dogs on leashes. She didn't trust them yet. Too many foster dogs had taken off on her. Maybe tomorrow she'd give them a chance.

She was tired when she climbed into bed that night, but she couldn't sleep. She listened to Ian's even breathing for more than an hour before finally getting up and slipping on her robe. In the second bedroom, she stood on a chair to reach high into the closet for the old photograph album. She carried the album into the living room and turned on the light in the corner.

The pictures she wanted to see were in the middle of the thick album. Spring Willow Elementary used to take class photos every year in each grade. There was her kindergarten class, 1971, nineteen little students squinting into the sun, and Mrs. Loving, looking far too old to be managing a classroom of squirmy kids. Lily had been the squirmiest of them all. Her problems with authority had started very early. She was standing right next to Mrs. Loving, and it appeared that the teacher was gripping her arm, probably in an attempt to get her to hold still long enough to have the picture taken.

On the end of the front row stood Jenny. The other children had refused to believe that she and Jenny were twins. Twins were supposed to look alike, they argued. Lily had been very blond, while Jenny's hair was fine and dark and straight. Lily had been tall; Jenny tiny. And Jenny knew how to hold still. She was the good twin, no doubt about it. The twin who got all "excellents" on her report cards, while Lily's cards were covered with handwritten messages of doom and frustration from her harried teachers.

Her class had been reduced to eighteen in the first grade because Danny Poovey's family moved to Lancaster. The first-grade picture had been taken indoors. Miss Lintock stood with the boys in the back row. All eyes were wide, giving the children surprised expressions. Lily knew the name of every child in the picture, and she went over them, categorizing each: living, dead, moved away. Jenny wore a startled look in this picture, as though something had frightened her, and the image brought tears to Lily's eyes. She wished she could pull that little girl from the photograph and hold her close, tell her that everything would be all right. A year after the picture was taken, Jenny and nine other children from that class had died, and in their collective sense of powerlessness, the citizens of Reflection had pinned responsibility for their deaths on the children's young second-grade teacher, Rachel Huber.

There was no picture of that second-grade class. Pictures had been scheduled to be taken in late September, and no one even thought to suggest taking a picture of that diminished class of children once the tragedy had occurred. There were no other class pictures in the photograph album, either, although Lily supposed they had been taken. She'd asked her mother about that once, and her mother had replied that she did not want those reminders in the house. Lily had wanted to say, "But you still had a child in those pictures." Of course she didn't dare. Her mother had, after all, lost her good twin that day.

4

Helen rested her head against the back of the green Adirondack chair. She was slightly winded and dizzy from the effort of walking out to the porch from the bedroom. The cane she was using was more a nuisance than a help.

Rachel appeared next to her chair. "Are you comfortable?" she asked. "How about one of those little pillows for the small of your back?"

"A pillow would be very good," Helen said, and she watched as Rachel stepped back inside the house. She was getting accustomed to asking for things, to accepting the help Rachel offered so freely. It had been hard at first, but she'd gradually come to the realization that her granddaughter truly enjoyed taking care of her and the house.

From the Adirondack chair, Helen kept an eye on the sky. It was blue, a little hazy, with just a few clouds. Good. Safe for one more day, she thought. She was growing idiotically fearful of storms.

Rachel returned with the pillow, and Helen leaned forward to let her granddaughter slip it behind her back.

"Do you like polenta?" Rachel asked as she sat down on the porch swing and opened one of the household's vegetarian cookbooks on her knees.

Helen nodded. "All that stirring, though. It's been a long time since I made it."

"We'll have it tonight."

Rachel had been with her for four days, and Helen could feel the life returning to her house. The young woman had cleaned the windows and opened them up to let in light and air, making Helen feel less trapped by her invalidism—even though every time she passed the piano she stared in frustration at the keys and her wrist throbbed. Rachel went for bicycle rides and long walks, which Helen envied, and returned with armloads of wildflowers to scatter throughout the house in the collection of old vases. Rachel was not a vegetarian, but she was eating like one, and cooking like one as well, and Helen found her own appetite returning. It had been a long time since she'd eaten so well.

Sometimes when they were sharing a meal at the kitchen table Helen would study Rachel's face and see John, her son, in the younger woman's features. The light brown hair, large gray eyes. The narrow, slightly Roman nose and sharp cheekbones. The similarity pained her, and she didn't allow her gaze to rest for very long on her granddaughter's face.

Helen had initially blamed her daughter-in-law, Inge, for driving the wedge between John and his parents. At some point, though, she'd had to admit to herself that the estrangement had been John's decision. He had simply rebelled against them, as most children do, she supposed. She and Peter had raised him a liberal-thinking Quaker, and he'd turned into a narrow-minded Lutheran. He became conservative, bigoted. She and Peter disgusted him, he'd said, wounding her deeply. Fortunately, John and Inge did not seem to have ruined their lovely daughter. Helen could discern no hint of intolerance in Rachel.

She could see a sadness in her, though. The girl was still grieving, she thought. Still trying to adjust from being married to being alone. Only time could help with that.

She and Rachel did not talk much. Oh, they talked about food and the garden and the house and the birds and the wildflowers. But they never touched on anything of substance. A few times Helen considered bringing up the past, but Rachel seemed so guileless—almost naive—that Helen could not find a suitable opening for the conversation. Rachel would talk occasionally of going into town, and Helen would find ways to discourage her, but at some point she would have to let her go. She didn't know what would happen in town. Perhaps nothing. Perhaps no one would even notice her. That was unlikely, though. Strangers stood out in Reflection. Besides, people already knew she was there. Marge had called the day before to ask Helen how she was doing and had told her that customers in the salon were talking about Rachel being in town. Marge trimmed Helen's hair every month or so, and Helen knew what Hairlights was like. News traveled quickly anywhere in town, but you could double the speed if you started it out in the beauty parlor.

"I got the weeds out of the corn this morning," Rachel said suddenly, pointing toward the garden. "I hope I can finish the rest of them by tonight."

"I could hire someone, Rachel. I hate for you—"

Rachel leaned forward from her seat on the swing, resting one strong hand on Helen's arm. "I'm enjoying it, Gram. Really, I am. We've got a problem, though." She looked out to the yard. "You're not getting enough light back here."

"Ah, yes." Helen had forgotten about that. She'd meant to have the trees pruned before she planted this year but had never gotten around to it. Suddenly, she felt the devil slip inside her skin. She could barely contain her smile as she turned to her granddaughter. "Maybe you could call Michael Stoltz for me," she said. "He does tree work and general handyman things in the summer."

The color rose to Rachel's face more quickly than Helen had anticipated. "Michael Stoltz?" she asked.

"Yes. You and he were friends when you were children, weren't you?" She knew how deep that friendship had gone. She and Michael had spoken about it more than once over the years.

"Yes, we were." Rachel gazed at the garden, her cheeks a feverish red. "I had no idea that he still lived around here, though."

"He came back after Katy—his wife—got her medical degree. She wanted to practice here. Do you remember, her father was a doctor in town when you were growing up? Doc Esterhaus?"

Rachel nodded. She looked dazed.

"So Katy took over the pediatric part of his practice when he retired, only right now she's on some kind of special voluntary service program with the Mennonites. She's in Russia, I think it is. And Michael's the minister at the Mennonite church."

The cookbook slipped from Rachel's knees to the floor of the porch. "He's *what*?" She reached down for the book.

"A minister."

Rachel shook her head, as though Helen must be mistaken.

"He's very well thought of in town," Helen continued. "He's heading up the organization that's trying to block Marielle Hostetter from developing her land, though I don't hold out much hope for him. She won't talk to him. Won't talk to anyone except her nephews and her lawyer."

Rachel didn't seem to hear her. "Michael's a minister," she repeated. "Do they have any children?"

"A boy, eleven, or maybe twelve by now. I'm quite sure he's stayed with Michael instead of going with Katy. I don't recall his name. My memory's not what it once was, I'm afraid."

"Michael wasn't Mennonite growing up. He was . . . I don't think he was raised in any faith. Does he wear plain clothes? Use a buggy?"

"Oh, no." Helen laughed. "Only the Old Order Mennonites still use buggies. Some of them buy cars, but only black cars, and they paint the chrome on them black. But Michael's church is very liberal."

Rachel looked down at the cookbook, running her fingers over the cover. "I'm having trouble remembering which denomination is which," she said slowly. "It's a peace church, isn't it?"

"Well, they all are, all the plain sects. And they believe that a church should be made up of adults who belong out of choice rather than being baptized into the faith as infants. The Amish and some of the Old Order Mennonite groups still dress plain and shun electricity and higher education. But for the most part, the modern Mennonites go on to college, and they're very active in various relief programs."

"It fits," Rachel said.

Helen thought she saw tears in her granddaughter's eyes, but they only shimmered there for a moment.

"Michael was a conscientious objector during Vietnam," Rachel said.

"I know. I remember him speaking on the steps of Town Hall." Helen remembered that speech very well—almost verbatim—but if she told that to Rachel, it would open up questions she didn't feel

like answering. "He's still good at speaking, I hear. Gives a good sermon."

Rachel laughed. "I just can't picture it."

"So, would you like to call him about the trees, or would you
rather I did it?" Helen asked.

"I'll call him," Rachel said. "Tomorrow." She returned her attention to the cookbook, flipping through it with a slow, even rhythm,
but Helen was certain her granddaughter did not see a single word
printed on those pages.

The attic stairs looked rickety, but they felt solid beneath Rachel's
feet as she climbed them. Fumbling in the dark, she found the light
switch. The small attic was crammed with stacks of boxes. The air was
warm and stuffy. She fought her way through the field of cartons to
reach the window, and it was several minutes before she got it open.
She was perspiring from the effort, but the cool night breeze was
worth it.

Putting her hands on her hips, she looked around. Which side did
Gram say her parents' boxes were on? North? Which way was north?
She spotted the name John on the side of a box against the far wall.
Picking up an old metal footstool, she walked over to the north wall
and sat down.

She'd been putting this off since her arrival at her grandmother's,
but now that she knew Michael was here, that she might see him, she
knew she could no longer avoid the memories. It had been so easy to
do exactly that here in Gram's wonderful house—this refuge from
reality. Miles from town and a thousand miles from San Antonio, she
might as well have been on another planet. That first day when she'd
seen her old triplex and thought about Luke and Michael seemed like
months ago. But Michael was here, and that changed everything.

She bent over to open the first box and felt the waistband of her
jeans cutting into her stomach. She'd already lost a pound or two, but
still, this extra weight was tenacious and repulsive. She was at least fifteen pounds heavier than she had been the last time she'd seen
Michael, when she was twenty-three.

So what? She growled at herself in disgust. He's married. And he's a
minister. She was still having trouble getting used to that notion. What

would he think of her being a Unitarian? She'd joined that church years ago so that Chris could have some sort of religious education. It had been the only denomination she could find that didn't require her to believe in something.

The box was full of leather-bound appointment books that must have belonged to her father. They looked thoroughly unfamiliar. Three cryptic journals, filled with dates and places written in strange handwriting, were tucked into the side of the box, along with two framed photographs of her grandparents. Helen and Peter Huber, looking handsome, the way she remembered them from her childhood. Digging further, she found a slightly blurry, unframed photograph of a young woman, fully clothed in a dress, shoes, and hat, jumping from a rock into swirling water. Rachel studied the picture closely. Was it Gram? She couldn't tell, but the image brought a smile to her lips.

She pulled out a few loose pieces of paper and saw that they were sheets of music, handwritten. It suddenly dawned on her that she was not sorting through one of her parents' boxes. She turned the box this way and that, looking for her father's name to no avail. Carefully, she piled the appointment books and journals and photographs back into the carton, leaving out the picture of the leaping woman. She stopped to take one last look at the sheets of music. Even though she could make little sense of them, they fascinated her. The scribbled manuscripts were undoubtedly early versions of her grandfather's compositions.

She folded down the flaps on the top of the carton and slid it across the floor to the south wall before turning to tackle the boxes marked with her father's name.

The first two boxes held carefully wrapped Hummel figurines, her mother's treasures. Rachel had nearly forgotten how every spare inch of shelf or table space in their house had been covered by knick-knacks. The third box held a tarnished silver tea service.

Had her parents saved anything of hers? Any memorabilia? She had left everything behind when she'd fled from Reflection, taking only some clothes. It had never occurred to her to take any other possessions. Least of all, memories of her husband.

Her parents had left town shortly after she had, settling in another part of Lancaster County. They'd come out to San Antonio three times, once for her wedding to Phil and twice to visit. They'd died together in an automobile accident a number of years ago. Rachel hadn't learned about their deaths until two weeks after the funeral, when someone managed to unearth her address from her parents' files. Only then did she realize that her mother and father had continued to feel the need to keep her whereabouts a secret.

The fourth box was filled with her things, and she shivered as she pulled out the objects, one by one. High school yearbooks. A few ancient Beatles albums. Two shoe boxes marked "Rachel" on the top in her mother's handwriting. Inside were pictures Rachel had taken over the years. Plenty of her dog, Laredo, and plenty of Luke and Michael when they were kids. She pressed her hand to her mouth. So long since she'd seen an image of either of those boys. She glanced through the pictures quickly, intentionally refusing to study them.

Beneath the second shoe box was her small white wedding album, wrapped in clear plastic. Rachel and Luke. Their names were embossed in large gold letters on the front of the book, and beneath it in smaller type, June 9, 1972. She rested her hand on the album, hesitating a moment before opening it.

When she finally lifted the cover she was immediately plunged into that long-ago day, truly one of the happiest of her life. She looked at the pictures of her glowing face, of Luke in his uniform, his smile warm and full of love. No hint in their faces of what was to come. That day had been her last taste of innocence. How she'd trusted the world back then. How easily she'd made the decision to spend the time Luke would be in Vietnam in the Peace Corps. She'd had to fight to go. She had not been married when she'd applied, and the Peace Corps did not like to take just one member of a married couple. But they had invested enough in her training by then that she could persuade them to let her go. It had been the luck of the draw that she and Michael had ended up in the same village together. Katari needed two teachers, male and female and French-speaking, and she and Michael requested—and were fortunate enough to receive—the same assignment.

People had chastised her for not staying home while Luke was serving in a dangerous war. She should be available to meet him if he could get leave, they'd said. But she'd never been the type to sit home. Growing up with two boys as her best friends had made her adventurous and independent. She'd been excited about going to Africa, and besides, it would make the time go faster.

In a few of the wedding pictures she thought she could detect a hint of sadness in her face, evidence of the long separation she and Luke were about to endure. There was such love in Luke's eyes, and in hers. Love and certainty. There had never been any doubt, in her mind or his or in the minds of people who knew them, that this marriage was right. Yes, they were young, but they were meant to be together.

She was stunned by Luke's resemblance to Chris. Luke had been twenty-one in these pictures; Chris was now twenty. So close in age, so obviously cut from the same exquisite cloth. After she'd left home, Rachel had possessed only one picture of her first husband, a wallet-sized snapshot of him in his uniform. Now, to suddenly see Luke from all these different angles—the easy, handsome smile, the expressive blue eyes—was overwhelming. She stared at his face, holding the pictures into the light, searching for a sign that the dark side lurked inside him even then. But she saw nothing of the kind. Whatever had turned Luke into a dangerous man had come from outside.

Michael, their best man, was grinning in every picture, delighted by the happiness of his two closest friends. Sometime during college, Michael had completely shed his gawkiness. He was still slender, but there was beauty in the structure of his face, and he'd grown into one of those men who looked better with glasses than without. Katy Esterhaus had been his date, but she was in only one picture. She was staring into space, blond and squinty-eyed behind her own thick glasses. Rachel had always thought an undiscovered prettiness lurked behind that studious demeanor. She wondered what Katy looked like now.

Two months after the wedding Luke was in Vietnam, and Rachel and Michael flew together to Zaire, then Rwanda, where they spent the next year working side by side in an impoverished, muddy village, teaching and learning and growing. She'd had some anger at Luke during that year for not attempting to become a conscientious objector, as Michael had done. She'd tried to understand Luke's feelings of patriotism. He'd clung to them despite the fact that by 1972 many people doubted the legitimacy of the war. His letters were few and slow in coming, though full of love for her and caring for Michael.

Gradually, though, the tenor of those letters began to change. Three months after his arrival in Vietnam, he wrote of killing someone, and she knew he'd been crying as he'd written those words. But a few months later his letters offered no sense of sorrow or remorse—no feeling at all—when he described the bloody details of the war he was fighting. She felt him hardening with each letter she received. She'd read them to Michael, usually after they'd had dinner together in her small cinderblock house, which had more space and light than his.

" 'Yesterday we managed to ambush this group,' " she read from one particular letter. " 'It was a challenge, but we got them. Some kids were in the way and got hurt. It was too bad, but one of those things that couldn't be helped.' "

She raised her eyes to Michael's after reading the letter, and he said quietly, "What's happening to him?" She shook her head slowly, without speaking, afraid of the answer to that question. Luke was becoming a stranger to her.

She was changing, too. Something happened when you existed side by side with another person for a year, in hellish conditions, doing the sort of work that made you cheer together over the smallest successes, that made you cry in pain together over life's injustices. Neither she nor Michael had ever experienced an existence in which death and suffering and unfathomable poverty were an accepted—and expected—part of daily life. Something happened when that person you'd known forever was suddenly your one link to your past, to your *real* life, to your sanity. When that person was so fine a human being, so life-embracing. When you watched him make children learn who had not been learning, or help a man dig a grave for his youngest son, or drive the frantic mother of a malaria-stricken baby fifty miles to the nearest hospital. Something happened. And one day she looked over at Michael and felt a slow, subtle twist of pain in her chest, and she knew she'd crossed a line between loving him as a friend and loving him as something more.

And then, of course, the fear began. Fear that those feelings would grow inside her until she could no longer control them. Fear she would never be able to stop thinking about him when she lay in her bed at night. As bad as the fear was, though, the guilt was worse.

They'd been working together for five or six months when she realized that Michael felt it too. It was during her second bout with malaria. Michael stayed with her through the night, bathing her with the coolest water he could find to bring the fever down. In the morning he made her strong tea she could barely touch, and he sat on the edge of her bed, stroking her face and arms and neck with a damp cloth. It was Sunday; neither of them were expected to teach that day, and so they talked. Oh, they always talked, but this time was different.

"I was watching you with Mbasa yesterday," he said, referring to the mother of a three-year-old boy who had disappeared sometime during the night. Mbasa had been hysterical when Rachel found her down by the stream. "You sat with her all day," Michael said, "and you were so comforting to her. You knew just what to say. I was . . . in awe."

He turned his face away from her then, and she knew. He didn't want her to see the raw emotion there, but she heard in his voice the same tenderness she felt for him. A tenderness pure in and of itself but touched with longing.

"Michael," she said, reaching her hand up to his cheek. "Do you love me?"

"Of course I do. I've loved you and Luke since I was a kid—" He stopped himself. "That's not what you mean, is it?"

She shook her head.

"Yes, I love you, and it scares the shit out of me."

She wept then, too weak to hold in the feelings that had been churning inside her during the past few months. She told him how much she loved him, how paper-thin her memory of Luke had become. Luke wrote her letters of death and killing and violence and anger, while Michael seemed the embodiment of serenity and compassion.

"Listen to me." Michael wrapped his hand around her wrist. "What you and I are feeling is wrong, Rachel. I'm not saying we're bad for feeling it. I think it's normal after what we've been through together, but we can't give in to it. Luke is going through something terrible, something so bad that you and I cannot even imagine it. We know he's a good guy, right? He has a good heart. We have to remember that. Remember when he found those kittens behind the high school and practically cried when the vet said they had distemper and had to be put down?"

Rachel furrowed her brow, the memory vague through her fever.

"We're in this bizarre situation," Michael continued. "Luke's a million miles away, and his letters sound like someone else wrote them, and so it's almost like he doesn't exist anymore. And then you and I are working together every day, in this kind of . . . emotional setting, and we're horny as hell, right?"

She smiled and nodded.

"The whole mess is a recipe for disaster, and we're going to have to fight it."

She was relieved. At least she would no longer be alone in the battle.

From that day forward, they did not touch. Where they had been easy with their hugs and casual pecks on the cheek, they now behaved as though they were separated by an invisible wall.

In March, Luke was among the last soldiers to leave Vietnam, and Rachel received permission to fly to San Francisco to spend a week with him before his transfer to Fort Myer in Virginia. The week with her husband did nothing to ease her fears. She had no sooner greeted him in the airport than a teenage boy with long hair and holes in his jeans walked up to Luke and spit on the front of his uniform. Within seconds Luke had flattened his assailant to the floor. Rachel stepped out of the way, alarmed by the hatred in her husband's eyes and by his focused and furious attack on the terrified boy.

Luke didn't leave his anger at the airport. He covered it up with silence, but she could see it clouding his eyes when he looked at her. One night he told her he no longer had any respect for Michael, or for anyone who would shirk his responsibility to his country. She was trying to formulate a reply when he fell silent again, and he remained that way for the rest of their week together. Luke's body was with her in San Francisco, but his mind was still back in Vietnam, and Rachel returned to Katari and Michael with guilty relief.

She decided to leave Rwanda and the Peace Corps after only a year, partly because she seemed to have no resistance to malaria and partly because Luke's time in the military would be up in August and she felt honor-bound to be with him. Although he was now in Virginia, his letters still seemed full of anger and an odd, unsettling paranoia.

She was due to leave in July, while Michael stayed behind to begin his second year in the Peace Corps. Katy Esterhaus was coming to Katari to visit him the following week, and Rachel was glad she would not be leaving him entirely alone. She planned to go back to Reflection, where she would find an apartment and inverview for the teaching positions she'd applied for through the mail. Then on August 2 she would pick Luke up at the airport in Philadelphia. They would have a month to get to know each other once more before she had to start teaching and Luke began his search for a civilian job.

She could not eat or sleep as the day of her departure neared. Although she and Michael had not acted on their feelings, she still felt weighed down by guilt. What if being with Luke again did not undo her yearning for Michael? She tried to forget the week she'd spent with the angry stranger in San Francisco. She had made a commitment to her husband, and she was determined to honor it. She had loved him her entire life. Maybe the distance she'd been feeling from him had been nothing more than self-protection. In case he'd been killed, she'd shielded herself from loving him too much. Surely when they were together again in Reflection she would once again feel her deep love for him.

She was packing when Michael came into her cinderblock house. Her suitcase was on her bed, her back to the door, and she did not realize he was there until she felt his arms circle her from behind. She did not even start, as though she'd been expecting him to come, to embrace her this way. He buried his lips against her neck, and she leaned back against him. His hands pressed flat against her rib cage, just below her breasts, and she closed her eyes when he moved one hand underneath the hem of her shirt. He slipped his hand up to her bare breast. She held her breath as he pressed his palm against her, running his thumb across her erect nipple, and she knew that if she didn't stop what was happening right that minute, it would be too late for both of them.

"Michael." She drew his hand away gently and pulled herself from his arms. "We can't."

Michael sat down on her bed and looked at his hand as if he could still feel the weight of her breast on his fingers. He shook his head, raising his face to her. "We've been saints, Rachel," he said. "They should canonize us."

"I'm really proud of how we've handled this whole situation," she said. "We don't have anything to be ashamed of." But she did feel ashamed. Not for what had just happened, but for the thoughts of Michael that were always with her, for those moments in her bed at night when she would stroke her own body, imagining her hands were his. Never Luke's. She would try to conjure up images of her husband, but he remained an elusive stranger in her fantasies.

Michael's eyes were red. "I don't want you to leave," he said.

She sat down next to him, pulling him into her arms, into a quiet, pained embrace.

"I love you," he said finally.

"I love you, too," she whispered.

"I don't think I'll ever feel this way about anyone else. Maybe it's wrong for me to say that, but I want you to know it." He straightened his shoulders, seeming to get a grip on himself. "And I want you to go home and be a terrific wife to Luke. Make him happy, 'cause he's been through some shit over there, all right?"

"Yes, okay," she said. "I guess it's good you'll still be here, and that we won't get to see each other for a year."

"Uh-huh." He didn't sound any more convinced than she did.

"And that Katy's coming."

He nodded. "Right. And by the time I get home, we'll all be back to normal and you'll look at me and say to yourself, 'What the hell did I see in him?'"

Rachel closed the wedding album and leaned against the bare attic wall, wiping her damp cheeks with her fingers. She had not seen Michael again after that night. He had taught the following day, and someone else had taken her on the long drive to the airport.

She had desperately wanted things to work out with Luke, but everything was against her. She was in love with a man she could not have, while her husband had turned into someone she could never love again.

5

Michael Stoltz drove through the falling darkness. He had one last stop to make before he'd be through for the night. He checked his watch in the overhead light of the car. He had less than an hour before he was to meet Drew back at his house. He hoped Amos Blank would not be a tough sell.

He'd collected thirty-one signatures since noon, stopping at farms and Amish-run shops. The petition was straightforward. It asked the board of supervisors to deny Marielle Hostetter's proposal to develop her land. The shortsighted planning commission had already approved the proposal, despite the impact study, which showed—in his opinion, anyway—the variety of ways in which the town would suffer because of the development. So the petitions were important. Michael already had two hundred signatures on the petition he'd passed among other residents of Reflection, but getting the plain sects to sign was a different matter.

He turned into the long driveway of the Blanks' farm. The stretch of macadam bisected a wide expanse of moonlit pasture, and the white farmhouse itself was bathed in a welcoming glow. Michael parked close to the house and got out of his car.

A dog, a mixture of collie and shepherd, barked from the porch, and a child peeked out from behind the dark shades in one of the front windows. Michael waved, laughing as the shade quickly dropped back into place.

The dog ran down the steps, its barking intensifying as Michael walked toward the house.

"Hush," he said, and the dog's tail began to wag. He sniffed the back of Michael's hand and trotted along next to him to the front steps.

Michael did not have to knock before Amos opened the door for him.

"Come in, Michael." Amos sounded as if he'd been expecting him.

"Thanks." Michael stepped into the wide, open living room. It was lit by a propane-gas lantern on the mantel, tinting everything in the room with a warm gold hue.

Michael held up the tablet. "I have a petition with me—"

"I know what you have," Amos said. "I've heard. Sit."

Michael heard the clatter of dishes from the kitchen as he took a seat on the sofa. He could smell cabbage, and something else. Ham, probably. Biscuits. He hoped he was not interrupting the Blanks' supper. The little girl he'd seen at the window peered around the frame of the living room door. She was big-eyed, and her hair was parted in the middle and pinned tightly back from her face. Amos said something to her in German, and she disappeared, giggling.

Michael turned his attention back to his host. "The petition simply states our concerns about allowing the Hostetter development to take place." He attempted to hand the tablet over to Amos, but the other man made no move to take it.

"I don't know that it's something we should get involved with." Amos stroked his long graying beard. He was probably no more than forty-four, Michael's age, but he looked at least ten years older.

"Well, you can look at the other signatures. Thirty-one of them just today." He named some of Amos's neighbors. He did not tell him about those who would not sign. The Amish were divided on this—not in the sentiment that the land should remain as it was but on how strong a stance they should take. Nonresistance was a fundamental tenet both of their church and his own. Still, it was important to let those in power know their objections, important to be counted.

"I'll tell you something I don't understand," Amos said.

"What's that?"

"I've heard that Drew Albrecht is doing this with you—getting names and such." He motioned toward the petition.

Michael knew where this was going. Drew himself was a builder. It was hard for people to believe he could have any sincere concern about rampant growth taking over Reflection, but Michael trusted Drew's sense of loyalty to the town. More important, Drew was able to connect to the business community in a way he himself could not. Similarly, his being a minister gave him the sort of credibility among the Amish and Old Order Mennonites that Drew could never hope to achieve. Whether or not a farmer chose to sign the petition, Michael knew he had the man's trust.

"That's right," he said. "And it's true Drew's a builder himself. But I can assure you he has Reflection's best interest at heart."

Amos narrowed his eyes at Michael. "And your cousin? What's she make of this work you're doing?"

Michael smiled. "I don't know," he answered honestly, although he could certainly guess. His cousin was Ursula Torwig, the growth-oriented mayor of Reflection. "Ursula and I have never agreed on much."

Amos tightened his lips, then reached for the tablet with a sigh. He held it toward the light to read the names, nodding his head. The lantern hissed softly from the mantel as he read, and the tablet cast a shadow across his white shirt and black suspenders. Finally, he accepted the pen Michael offered him and signed his own name at the bottom of the list.

"There's going to be an extremely important public hearing on September sixth at the Starr and Lieber Bank building." Michael took the tablet back and stood up. "It will give people an opportunity to voice their concerns before the board makes its final decision. We can arrange rides for any Amish who want to go."

"We'll see," Amos said as he walked Michael to the door.

Once in his car, Michael set the petition on the passenger seat and drove slowly up the long driveway to the road. He cut through the heart of town to his own neighborhood. Drew's car was parked in front of the house, but no one was in it. Jason must have let him in.

He found his friend in Jason's bedroom, engrossed in a game of chess.

Jason looked up at his father. "Just a couple minutes, Dad," he said. "I've almost got him."

Michael stood behind his son's chair and rested his hand on Jason's shoulder. The boy tolerated the fatherly gesture for close to ten seconds before shrugging his hand away, and Michael sat down on the edge of the twin bed.

Drew wore a weak grin as he ran a hand through his thinning, pale hair. He had on one of his many Hawaiian shirts, this one red and blue, and he leaned his elbows on the table as he studied the board. Only a few white pawns rested near his elbow, but Jason had amassed a small army of black pieces on the other side of the board. They were reflected in the boy's glasses, a shifting black blur when he moved his head. For the first time Michael noticed the unruly length of his son's dirty blond hair. Katy would have a fit if she could see it.

Drew pursed his lips at the board as he hesitantly moved one of the black rooks toward Jason's white battalion. "I want you to know, Jace," he said, "that I used to let you win at this game to boost your confidence."

"Nah." Jason slipped his queen into position. "Checkmate."

"Drat." Drew sat back in his chair, shaking his head at Michael. "Your kid has no mercy."

"Wanna play again?" Jason asked him.

"I'm sure he'd love to, Jace." Michael stood up and squeezed his son's shoulder. "But we've got work to do."

Jason put on the lonely, hangdog expression he'd been wearing since Katy left for Russia and began putting away the chessmen.

"I'll get you next time," Drew warned as he left Jason's room. He followed Michael into the family room, where he picked up his own stack of petitions and sat down on the sofa. "Is Jace making any friends at computer camp?"

Michael shook his head. "None that I hear about. He complains nearly every morning about not wanting to go." He wondered if the camp had been a mistake, if he should give in to his son's pleas to stay home. It hurt him to see Jason's isolation; he remembered his own too well. Jason had the same skinny, four-eyed look to him that he'd had, that same nerdy intelligence that set him apart from other kids his age. Michael had told Jason that he'd been the same way and that he understood how it felt, but the boy only responded with an indignant, I-don't-know-what-you're-talking-about look.

Katy regularly fed into her son's denial. "You're making a problem where there isn't one," she'd tell Michael. But Katy was wrong. He knew the pain of an isolated child when he saw it.

"I got thirty-two signatures," Michael said.

"Hey, that's great!" Drew looked surprised. He hadn't thought any of the Amish would sign. "I got fifty-seven. I'll tell you, though, there's a fair amount of support for the other side among business owners."

"Well, you were talking to people who stand to profit. Any signatures we get from them are a bonus."

"True, but we still have to face the fact that there are a lot of people who are honestly convinced that Ursula's right. They think the economy needs the boost."

"Dad?" Jason appeared in the doorway.

"Yes?"

"Please, could we get cable, Dad? Everybody else has it, and they're always talking about stuff that's on it, and I don't know what they're talking about."

Michael sighed. This was Jason's new ruse. When he wanted something these days, he acted as though his lack of it was the cause of his social problems. "Sorry, Jace," he said. "Cable's out." Just what they needed. A few dozen more mind-numbing television programs in the house.

Jason made a sound of exasperation as he trod back down the hallway to his room.

"He's been like this ever since Katy left," Michael said. "He misses her a lot. Needs a ton of attention. Thanks for playing chess with him." He straightened the papers on his lap.

"My pleasure." Drew grinned. "Only wish I could beat the kid."

"You want something to drink?" Michael offered, and Drew nodded.

He was taking two bottles of club soda from the refrigerator when the phone rang. He picked up the receiver.

"Michael?" It was a female voice, and he struggled unsuccessfully to place it.

"Yes?"

"This is Rachel Huber, Michael."

Michael set the bottles on the counter. This was the one voice he had never expected to hear again. He could barely find his own. "*Rachel*," he said. "I don't believe it."

She laughed, and although her laughter was deeper now, richer, the familiarity of the sound made him smile. "I'm at my grandmother's," she said. "She had an accident and—"

"Yes, I heard. How is she doing?"

"All right. She's not much of a complainer. I'm just here to help her out while she's laid up."

Michael's thoughts were so wild and jumbled he could not put them into words. Rachel was here, a few miles from where he stood. He thought about kicking Drew out of the house, getting in the car, and driving over to Helen's. How good it would be to see her.

"Michael?" Rachel asked. "Are you tongue-tied?"

"I can't believe you're here," he said. "I want to see you. Right now." He grimaced. *Get a grip.*

Rachel laughed again. "Well, how about tomorrow? Maybe I can drop ten pounds by then."

He smiled. "Have you gotten chubby?" He tried to picture her with some weight on her slender frame and felt the thoroughly unexpected stirring of an erection. He should not see her. Not with Katy gone. It would be a mistake.

"Chubbier than I should be," she said. "The main reason I'm calling—or I guess one of the main reasons—is that my grandmother has some trees she needs pruned back to let light into the garden and she said you sometimes do that sort of work in the summer. Would you have time?"

"Sure." His mind raced. That would be best. He would see her in the safety of Helen's house, Helen's presence. "I can come over Saturday morning."

"All right, great. I'm looking forward to seeing you."

"Rachel?" He squeezed his fingers around one of the bottles on the counter as he plowed headlong into dangerous territory. "Look, I don't want to have to see you for the first time in twenty years while I'm pruning trees. Were you serious about tomorrow? Can you get away for a bit late in the afternoon? Could we meet someplace?"

"Yes." She sounded as if she'd been waiting for the suggestion. "Where?"

"Spring Willow—" He stopped himself. She would not know what he was talking about. "Huber Pond?"

"Oh, yeah," she said, her voice rich with nostalgia. "On the grassy part where we used to hang out?"

"That's right," he said. "How about four-thirty?"

"I can't wait," she said. "I'll see you then."

He got off the phone, uncapped the bottles of club soda, and walked into the family room.

Drew looked up at him and set the petition on the coffee table. "What put that grin on your face?" he asked.

Michael handed him one of the bottles. "Guess who's in town?"

Drew shrugged.

"Rachel Huber."

Drew sat back in his chair. "No joke," he said. Michael recalled that Drew had moved to Reflection in his twenties and so had not known Rachel personally. Of course he would know about her through rumor, though. Through legend.

"We were so close." Michael sat down and took a swallow of club soda. "We did everything together as kids. And we were in the Peace Corps at the same time. Lived in these old cinderblock shacks. Well, actually, *mine* was a shack. Hers was a little better. They figured that, since she was a female, she should have the more substantial building to live in." He was rambling. He looked down at the bottle in his hand. "If she hadn't been married"—he shook his head—"things would have turned out differently."

There was a crease between Drew's eyebrows. "You'd better watch it, Mike. I mean, with things being rocky between you and Katy, you're ripe for getting yourself into trouble, wouldn't you say?"

Michael had told Drew—and only Drew—about the problems between himself and Katy. Anyone else in that tight little town would have been shocked to know that all was not well with the preacher and his doctor wife.

"I'm only going to pay a visit to an old friend," Michael said.

"Well, have a good time, then." Drew stood up abruptly, his soda untouched, and he slipped the sheath of petitions under his arm.

Michael looked up in surprise. "You're leaving?"

"Yeah. I forgot I have some things to do at home." His jaw was tight, and with the ferocity of a punch to the stomach, Michael remembered that Drew had indeed known Rachel Huber after all.

He stood up to touch his friend's arm. "Drew, I'm sorry. I just realized. I completely forgot about Will."

Drew shrugged away the apology. "Hey," he said. "It was a long time ago. Rachel was a very green, brand-new teacher then. I'm sure she's grown up by now. I'm not the type to hold a grudge forever."

Michael followed him to the door, silently berating himself for his insensitivity. Drew made his good-bye brief, turning his head away quickly but not before Michael saw the pain in his eyes. Drew never spoke about Will. It made it easy to forget he'd ever had a son. For the first time Michael realized that, while the past twenty years might have dulled Drew's pain, they had not killed it.

He closed the door and could hear the radio playing in Jason's room. He straightened the pile of papers on the coffee table, then walked down the hall to spend some time with his lonesome son.

6

The rumbling was faint at first, so faint that Helen managed to convince herself it was something other than the ominous growl of distant thunder. She sat in her library, trying to read, wishing Rachel would get home from her run to the grocery store. The store closed at ten, and it was after that now. She could not be much longer.

Outside the library window the woods were suddenly, briefly illuminated, every leaf drawn in perfect detail, and Helen gasped. There were too many windows in this house. Too much glass. She knew the rules: Avoid water. Don't use the phone. And stay away from windows.

She closed her book and stood up slowly, on guard against the black curtain that often fell over her vision when she rose too quickly from a chair. Favoring her ankle, she walked out into the little hallway between the library and the living room and leaned against the wall of that small haven. No windows here. Yet she could still see the flickering white light as it ricocheted off the walls around her.

She folded her arms across her chest, feeling very foolish. A fearful old woman, that's what she was. Her body had changed on her completely in the last few weeks. It was no longer reliable. She ached when she got up in the morning, staying stiff for hours. The pain deep in her muscles was constant some days, intermittent on others, but always close enough to remind her of her frailty, her vulnerability. She could fall asleep instantly, any moment of the day, although her sleep was void of dreams, like death. She was constantly thirsty. Jumpy, too. Her body jerked to attention each time a twig snapped outside the window. Her wrist was improving, but it still throbbed from time to time, and she feared she would never again be able to play the piano, never again be well. Was this how she would spend the rest of her days?

She'd been reading about lightning. She'd never been superstitious in her life, but she'd asked Rachel to buy some potted herbs for her to grow on the kitchen windowsill: rosemary, Saint-John's-wort, opine. They would protect a house against a lightning strike, the books said. She did not tell Rachel why she wanted the herbs, and the girl, unable to find opine on her first try, substituted thyme. Helen sent her out again, this time to a nursery in Lancaster, fabricating some plausible reason why she needed opine. She could not tell Rachel the truth about such silliness.

She jumped at the sound of the front door opening.

"I'm home!" Rachel called out.

The thunder and lightning had joined forces now, occurring in unison, and Helen could barely bring herself to leave the sanctuary of the windowless hallway and walk into the kitchen.

Rachel was already unpacking the two bags of groceries.

"You're soaking wet." Helen averted her eyes from the light show outside the window.

"Feels good." Rachel was still wearing a smile. No doubt that smile had not left her face since the phone call to Michael an hour or so earlier.

"What are you doing, still up?" Rachel asked.

"Reading." She wanted to say she would go to bed now, but her feet were frozen to the floor. She wondered how Rachel could seem so unaware of the riot of light and sound going on around them.

A sudden crack of thunder exploded above their heads, and Helen let out a cry. She stepped back against the wall, her cheeks hot with embarrassment.

Rachel had been about to put a box of cereal in the cupboard, but she stopped her hand in midair. "This storm's terrifying you, isn't it?" she asked.

Helen could only nod. There was a soft tickle of tears in her eyes.

Rachel set the package of cereal on the counter. "Let's go to my room," she said. "We can close the blinds in there and get cozy." She stepped forward and put a gentle arm around Helen's shoulders, turning her toward the door. Helen forced her legs to move, feeling like a small child in the protection of someone far stronger, far braver.

Once in the guest room, she sat down on the bed while Rachel closed the blinds and turned on the night-table lamp.

"I feel so foolish," Helen said. "I used to adore sitting out a storm. The wilder, the better."

"Anyone who's been struck by lightning would be crazy if they didn't have a healthy fear of storms, Gram."

"I suppose." She felt far better already. The drawn blinds barely let in the flashes of light from outside, and the sound of the thunder was beginning to recede. Her eyes lit on a photograph propped up against the books in one of the floor-to-ceiling bookcases. "Is that . . . ?" She pointed to the picture, and Rachel followed her gaze.

"Oh." Rachel picked up the photograph and sat down next to Helen on the bed, holding out the picture for her inspection. Sure enough, it was the old picture of her jumping into the swirling Delaware River. "I meant to ask you about this," Rachel said. "When I was looking through the cartons in the attic, I accidentally opened one of yours first and found this picture. Is this you?"

For a moment, Helen couldn't answer. Rachel had been in her boxes? How much had she seen?

"Yes," she said, struggling to give the picture her full attention. "It was taken on my eighteenth birthday. We had a picnic at a park near our house in Trenton, my sister Stella and a few girlfriends and myself. And it was hot. So I decided to cool off."

Rachel laughed. "Fully dressed?"

"I had a wild streak in those days. I wasn't afraid of much." She'd had no sense of limitation in her youth, and no fear of risk. At the age of twelve she'd driven a friend's car down the steep, icy hill in their Trenton neighborhood; at fifteen she'd beaten a neighbor boy swimming across a narrow point in the river. And as often as she could get away with it, she'd sneak into New York against her parents' wishes and finagle her way into Carnegie Hall, through back entrances accidentally left open or by telling tall tales to the ushers, in order to hear her favorite musicians perform.

Rachel took the picture from her hands and rested it on her own knees, studying it closely. "I know so little about you," she said quietly. "I didn't even know you'd lived in New Jersey. What was your family like?"

Helen leaned back against the wall. "My father—your great-grand-father—fancied himself a writer," she said. "He was a bright man, but brilliance doesn't put food on the table, unfortunately. He wrote a great deal, primarily philosophizing about the politics of the time. Very dense reading. But he never sold a thing. I don't think he cared, though. He just had to get it all down." She looked at her grand-daughter. "He was crippled, you know."

"No, I didn't know that."

Helen nodded. "His legs were mangled in an accident when he was a boy. So there wasn't much he could do in the way of work. My mother played the cello and the piano. She came from money, but her family disowned her when she took up with my father. She cleaned houses. That was how we got by."

Rachel was leaning forward, listening intently.

"Our dinner-table conversations centered around politics and music. Mother taught me to play the piano. I adored it and longed to study music myself, but I could read the writing on the wall. My mother's arthritis was bad and getting worse by the day, my father couldn't work, and I was the oldest of four children. Once I got out of school, I knew I was going to have to find a job to support my family."

"So how did you ever meet Grandpa?"

"I'm getting to that," Helen said. "I found a job in New York, doing secretarial work in the school of music at Columbia University. I was determined to be as close to music as possible. They gave me a room on campus, and I sent the little pay I made home to my family."

"And Grandpa taught at Columbia, right?"

"That's right. He'd studied composition in Paris, and I was fasci-nated by him and tormented him with questions." She recalled fol-lowing him around campus, making a nuisance of herself. Peter Huber had had many admirers. His good looks had been arresting and elegant, but it had not been not his physical attributes that had attracted her. She'd been drawn to his talent, to his wealth of knowledge about composition. He'd finally invited her to have dinner with him. They'd talked through the entire meal, barely touching their food, and she'd felt a deep and enduring friendship taking root.

"He took an interest in me," she continued. "Not a romantic interest, but he could see how much I loved music, how keen I was on learning, and he thought I should have that chance. And so—" Helen thought carefully about what she would say next. "Your grandpa's family was quite well off."

Rachel nodded.

"And so he offered to put me through school."

"He did? I had no idea."

"Well, I couldn't take him up on the offer because of my family's needs, so Peter took care of them as well."

Rachel frowned. "You mean, he—"

"He sent money to my family every month. He bought my father braces for his legs and saw to it that he had the best care available. He made sure my mother didn't have to work and could stay home and take care of the family."

"Why?" Rachel asked. "Why would he do all of that?"

"Because he was the world's most generous and kindhearted man." Helen's lower lip trembled, and she knew her eyes had filled with tears.

"He must have loved you very much." Rachel rested her hand on Helen's arm.

"He thought I had talent," Helen said. "That I was worth the investment. Anyhow, we were married a year or so after that."

"Was he much older than you?"

"I was nineteen, he was twenty-seven. He was only beginning to make a name for himself. He was thoroughly wrapped up in music, as I longed to be, and we also shared a commitment to social issues, which had been ingrained in me from my father."

"I'd forgotten about that." Rachel set the photograph on the night table. "What year did he win the Nobel Peace Prize?"

"It was in '63. The only accolade he ever showed up to accept."

Rachel smiled.

"He was not too popular with the government back in the fifties, though. 'An inconvenient artist,' they called him. They balked at giving him a passport because they thought he was affiliated with Communist organizations." Helen smiled sadly. That had been a difficult period, in many ways. She had been suffering from the deepest depression of her life. She wondered if Rachel had any memory of the sad, quiet, distractible grandmother she'd been during the girl's early years.

"Anyhow," she continued. "Peter was very fortunate. His fame gave him the opportunity to have some political influence, and that was of tremendous importance to him."

"I've been prowling through his books." Rachel gestured toward the bookshelves. "Every one of them is either about music or politics. Except for the puzzle books."

Helen laughed. "Too bad he hated the military. He would have been an excellent cryptographer. He certainly loved his puzzles."

"So what about you, Gram?" Rachel asked softly. "Did you ever get to finish school?"

"No. I planned to, but I got pregnant with your father and that took care of that."

"Oh, but it sounded as though you really wanted to learn. You had promise."

"Well, I did continue to learn, though not in quite so formal a fashion. Peter taught me all he knew about music and composition. But we're talking about the 1930s, Rachel. There was little encouragement for women to be composers in those days, and tremendous pressure to be good mothers. So that's what I set out to be. A good mother."

Rachel shook her head. "Doesn't seem fair," she said. Then she scooted to the far side of the bed, leaning back against the wall to face her. "When did you and Grandpa move down here?"

"Well, Peter grew up here, you know that, don't you?"

Rachel nodded.

"At one time, his family owned a major part of the land around the town. They lost much of it during the depression. Their family home was over by the Jensen farm. Peter and I were living in New York, but we visited his family quite often. Even though I preferred the city at that time, I fell in love with this area down here, and of course Peter always had a soft spot in his heart for it. He needed that mixture—the stimulation of the city and peacefulness of the country. So in '33, his parents gave us this ten-acre plot, and we built this little abode on it."

"'Thirty-three!" Rachel exclaimed. "I never realized this house was that old. It seems so contemporary."

"Well, it's been remodeled a few times over the years, but back then people around here thought it was a bit out of place. They just chalked it up to the fact that Peter was an artist, an eccentric. He's the one who designed it, putting in all the glass. I've always loved the windows, how they bring the woods right into the house." She looked ruefully toward the closed blinds. "I'm not so thrilled with them anymore in the middle of a thunderstorm, though." The thunder was nothing more than a distant grumble now, and she could smile about it, shudder in mock seriousness. She sighed. "I missed living in the city," she said. "I missed the concerts and plays and museums and excitement. But I was a wife and mother. It was time to give up my wild streak."

"You gave up a lot for Grandpa," Rachel said, and there was a touch of indignation in her voice. "Your education. Your own career."

Helen looked down at her hands. For a moment she couldn't speak. "You and I are from different generations, Rachel," she said finally. "It makes it hard for us to understand each other, I guess. I would have given up anything for Peter. I could never have paid him back for all he did for me." With another sigh, she gripped the bedpost and got to her feet. The black curtain threatened her vision but lifted quickly. She smiled at her granddaughter. "Thank you for being so caring tonight."

Rachel looked up at her from the bed. "You're welcome. I enjoyed our talk. And I'm sorry if what I just said upset you."

Helen whisked away the apology with the sweep of a hand. Then she motioned toward the picture on the night table. "May I?" she asked.

"Of course."

Once in her own room, Helen felt very tired. It had been a long night, with too wild a mix of emotions. Fear, warmth, comfort, regret.

She put on her nightgown, crawled under the covers, and turned off the night-table lamp. In the darkness, Rachel's words came back to her.

You gave up a lot for Grandpa.

Helen reached up to turn on the light again. She lifted the photograph from the night table and examined it closely. She could see the excitement in the young woman's face, the love of life.

Rachel did not know a fraction of what she had given up.

7

Rachel parked her car on Water Street and walked toward the center of town, past the Starr and Lieber Bank on the corner, past the old gingerbread-trimmed library, which looked as though it could use some new paint. She was beginning to perspire in her long-sleeved shirt and white pants. She'd originally dressed in shorts but changed her mind after seeing herself in the full-length mirror. Too much flesh for a meeting with a minister.

She stopped in front of the Mennonite church. It was larger than she remembered it and very white and plain against the green back-drop of the woods. The narrow arched windows were clear-paned, and a tall steeple pierced the summer sky. A perfect reflection of the church was mirrored in the still water of Huber Pond. Rachel shook her head with a smile, still unable to grasp Michael's connection to the building.

She shifted her gaze to the small brick chapel next to the Mennonite church. United Church of Christ, according to the sign on the front lawn. Across the street, her old Lutheran church was low and broad, its gray flagstone and red door pretty and welcoming. The last time she'd been in that church had been for her wedding.

There were twenty churches in Reflection. The statistic from her childhood slipped into her mind as she walked past the pond toward the row of shops along Main Street. Twenty churches, three banks, three schools, and one exceptional bakery.

Halper's Bakery was still there, right in front of her. She stepped through the door, wondering if she would find the brownies of her childhood inside the old glass cases. Sure enough, they were there, looking exactly as they had when she was a teenager. She'd often stop here after school to buy brownies for the boys and herself. They were flat, dense, and dark brown, topped with a thick slab of chocolate icing. Pure decadence.

She was the only customer in the store, and she smiled at the gray-haired woman who was busy behind the counter. "Two brownies, please," she said.

"Be right with you, honey." The woman was arranging sugar cookies on a tray. Her hands were gnarled and painful-looking.

The alcove above the cash register was mirrored, and Rachel grimaced at her reflection. She tugged at her hair. She'd left San Antonio too quickly to get a perm, and her light brown hair hung uncertainly in that limbo between curly and straight.

The woman walked around the corner of the glass case toward the brownies.

"I noticed they changed the name of Huber Pond," Rachel said. "I haven't been here in a while."

The woman glanced up at her as she opened the rear of the case. "They changed it a long time ago," she said.

Something in her voice warned Rachel not to pursue the subject. She looked down at the brownies. "I used to buy these brownies all the time when I was a kid," she said. "They were sinful. I'm so glad to see you still make them."

The woman had picked up a sheet of tissue paper, but she stopped short of reaching into the case. Instead she cocked her head at her customer, eyes narrowed behind clear-framed glasses.

"Are you Rachel Huber?" she asked.

"Yes, I am," Rachel said, surprised.

The woman's features suddenly changed. Her nostrils widened, her lips paled and tightened. She started to reach for the brownies again, then seemed to change her mind. She set down the sheet of tissue paper, closed the door to the glass case, and walked quickly toward the rear of the little shop, where she disappeared behind a swinging door.

Rachel stared after her, perplexed. After standing there for a moment, she called out, "Excuse me?" but there was no response. She was about to leave when a young girl—a teenager—stepped through the swinging door.

"You wanted brownies?" The girl brushed a strand of blond hair from her eyes.

"Yes." Rachel pointed toward the case and noticed that her hand was trembling. "Two of them, please."

The girl extracted the brownies from their tray and slipped them into a bag, which she set on the countertop.

Rachel handed her a five-dollar bill. "Is she all right?" She nodded toward the swinging door and whatever room lay beyond it.

"She will be." The girl did not look at her as she rang up the sale. "Just got upset for a minute." She handed Rachel her change, then shrugged awkwardly, the lock of hair spilling into her eyes once more. "Maybe you shouldn't come in here again," she said. Then she turned on her heel and walked through the swinging door before Rachel had a chance to respond.

She left the bakery, her step now less light and unencumbered. She walked over to the pond, past the statue of her grandfather and onto the path that circled the water. The path dipped into the woods and then opened onto a small grassy area. Michael was sitting on a bench, and he stood when he saw her emerge from the woods.

She felt the grin spread across her face as she neared him. He had put on weight—not much, just enough that no one would think of him as scrawny any longer. His brown hair was touched with gray and receding slightly. The angles of his face were still clean and sharp, and even at a distance she thought she could see the warmth in his eyes behind his black, wire-rimmed glasses. He was wearing khaki shorts and a black T-shirt, and she suddenly felt silly for her hot and conservative attire.

They reached for each other as she neared him, and for more than a minute they stayed locked in a wordless embrace. Rachel did not want to let go. Her body shook with the effort of holding in tears, and she suddenly knew why her love for Phil had felt as if something were missing: her heart belonged to this man.

"Michel," she said, although she had not thought of him by that name since their days in French-speaking Rwanda. For that year she had called him nothing else.

His laughter was soft against her cheek. "No one's called me *that* in a while," he said.

When they finally pulled apart, Michael smiled as he brushed the tears from her cheeks with his fingertips. "Let's sit," he said.

She nodded, reaching into her purse for a tissue. "This bench didn't used to be here." She sat down, turning so she could look at him.

"No. They put it up a few years ago. I instigated it, because I love to sit here when I'm writing or reading. My office is right there"— he motioned toward the church on the other side of the pond—"so it's very convenient."

She pulled one of the brownies from the bag and handed it to him. "What do you write?" she asked.

He took the brownie from her, grinning. "Haven't seen one of these in a long time. Thanks." He took a bite, licked a crumb from his finger. "Sermons, mostly," he said.

Rachel shook her head. "I can't believe it, Michael. When my grandmother told me you'd become a minister, I thought she must have you mixed up with someone else." She slipped a piece of brownie into her mouth. It was abysmally rich, almost inedible.

"It was hard for me to believe at first, too."

"How did it happen? Whatever—"

"We can get to that in a minute," he interrupted her. "I want to hear about *you* first. Catch me up on everything. Are you teaching?"

She nodded. "High school. Special ed. And a little French."

"I'm glad to hear that." He looked relieved. "I worried you might have quit after . . ." He shook his head. "It would have been such a loss."

"No, I could never give it up. I love it." Teaching had become the strongest force in her life, her core. "I'm going to be one of those teachers who's still at it long after she should be."

"That's the spirit," he said.

A silence slipped between them. There was so much to say. She wasn't certain where to begin.

"I wish we hadn't lost touch after I left," she said finally. "I was desperate to talk to you after everything happened, but you were still in Rwanda, and I felt as though I shouldn't try to get in touch with you because of Katy. Because you'd gotten married. I didn't feel as though I had the right to . . . you know."

He nodded. "I wish you *had* gotten in touch with me. I tried to get your address from your parents and grandparents after you left, but your parents refused to tell anyone where you'd gone. They were extremely protective of you. And Helen and Peter didn't know."

She was surprised to hear him call her grandparents by their first names, as though he knew them well.

"I know you started writing to Helen at Christmas a few years ago," he continued. "She was really pleased by that. I thought once or twice of asking her for your address then, but I didn't want to stir up the past for you."

She nodded. He'd probably been right not to contact her. She slipped the rest of her brownie into the bag, and he followed suit.

"How did we ever eat these things when we were kids?" he asked with a smile. "We must have been indestructible."

Rachel cleaned the chocolate from her fingers with her tissue, her eyes on the still water of the pond. "So this isn't Huber Pond any longer," she said.

"It's been Spring Willow for a long time," Michael said. "The town council voted to change the name around the time you left."

He didn't say it. He didn't have to. Rachel knew she'd been the cause of that change. The name Huber, once so respected, had lost its positive association overnight.

She looked past him into the black-and-green mesh of the trees. "I love these woods," she said.

"Did Helen tell you about the Hostetters' plan to raze this piece of land?"

"Yes, and she said something about you trying to stop it."

He shook his head, mouth tight. "I'm trying, but I'm not too optimistic."

"It's the bat woman, right? Remember how afraid we were of her?"

He gave a short laugh. "Yeah, and we were right to be. We just didn't know what it was we had to fear." He looked at her with a question in his eyes. "Did you ever know why she was the way she was?"

Rachel shook her head.

"I don't think I found out till I moved back here, so you probably never heard the story. She was shot in the head when she was four years old, by her mother, who then turned the gun on herself."

"*What?* Oh, that's some kind of rumor."

"No, it's the truth. She suffered mild brain damage. She was raised by her father, who died when she was twenty or so, and she managed to live by herself until last year."

"Why would her mother have done that?"

"I don't think anyone knows the answer to that question."

Rachel felt a wave of sympathy for the woman she'd viewed with such disdain. "So now she and her nephews are planning to make some money off the land, huh?"

" 'Some money' doesn't begin to describe it. They will be quite wealthy." He looked up at the steeple on the other side of the pond. "My poor little church is going to be surrounded by office buildings."

Rachel followed his gaze to the church. "I can't imagine it," she said.

He suddenly smiled. "Remember the time you fell through the ice?"

Her eyes darted to the section of the pond near the gazebo. The boys had tricked her into skating over there, knowing the ice was thin where the sun bathed it all day. She'd gone in. Gone under, actually. She could still remember looking up at the translucent ice above her head. She had not felt panic. She'd been mesmerized by the way the ice filtered and curved the light from above. Michael and Luke had panicked, though. She'd stayed under so long that by the time they'd pulled her out they were frantic, and full of apologies.

"I got you guys back plenty of times."

"Yeah. You were a vengeful little thing."

They reminisced awhile, the thoughts flowing easily, about children who no longer existed. The fishing expeditions. Floating on inner tubes down the stream that cut through the woods. Riding their bikes out to the eerie, cavernous quarries. They'd been so young. So sure of the safety and predictability of their world.

"You know what was hardest for me?" Michael leaned forward, elbows on his knees. "The bond was always so strong between the three of us that I felt like we were one indivisible unit. A team. I knew you and Luke were destined to be more than buddies—I knew that from the start—but even when you guys started dating in earnest, you still included me in so much that I never felt left out. But when you finally got around to having sex, I was suddenly on the outside."

Rachel laughed. "Well, come on, Michael, what did you want?" She was relieved that she did not have to tiptoe around such delicate topics merely because he was now a man of the cloth. "We told you every graphic detail." And they had. She and Luke had only been fifteen at the time, and making love had seemed the logical evolution of their relationship. It was calculated, premeditated. They'd made love for the first time close to where she and Michael were sitting, in these woods behind the pond, and they had told him their plans. Afterward they described to him, in clinical terms and at great length, exactly how it felt. Like Masters and Johnson, educating their public.

"The three of us had a bizarre relationship," Michael said.

"I know, and I'm so glad. It was a wonderful way to grow up, having you two around all the time."

Neither of them spoke as a sparrow flitted across the surface of the lake, dusting the water lightly with its feathers. The reflection of the white church quivered in the ripples for a moment before coming into focus again.

She wondered how far, chronologically, they would take their reminiscence. How far was safe? "Is there anyone left in town from high school?" she asked.

"Let's see." Michael stretched out his long legs, his tennis shoes white against the grass. "Not many. Oh, you know who's still around? Becky Frank. She's a loan officer at the Starr and Lieber branch in Bird-in-Hand. You were good friends with her, weren't you?"

Rachel pictured the bubbly redhead instantly. "Fairly good," she said. "I'd like to see her. Is that still her name? Do you think she's in the phone book?"

"Let me call her and have her call you, all right?" Michael suggested quickly, and Rachel agreed, although it seemed like an unnecessary step in the process.

"So, tell me about your son and your husband," he said.

So that was how they would handle the difficult years, she thought. Skip over them, at least for now. She was relieved, not quite ready to dive into that pain.

She told him about Phil, how he'd hired her when she arrived in San Antonio, what a fine, supportive husband he had been. Michael frowned as she talked about his long illness and his death.

"I miss him a lot," she spoke softly. "I wake up in the morning sometimes and forget that he's gone, and then reality suddenly whacks me on the head." She smiled. "I can't quite get used to the idea of being single again. Not an easy adjustment to make."

"No, I'm sure it's not." Michael shook his head. "You've been through more than your share of trauma, Rache."

"Oh, I've had plenty of good times, too." She didn't want to give him the impression her life had been filled with sorrow. She told him about the teaching awards she'd won, about the trips she and Phil had taken over the years. She told him about the bicycle race she and Chris had competed in the year before.

"Really?" He looked surprised. "I was in a race last year, too. Came in close to last, but I had a great time."

"You never were particularly competitive," she said.

"Or athletic." He laughed. "But I love cycling. Maybe we could go for a ride together someday."

"That'd be great. I have my bike with me."

"You said your son was in the race with you?"

"Uh-huh." She began talking about Chris, about his achievements and his good-heartedness, but her mounting concerns about her son quickly got in the way. She suddenly realized how much she missed being able to talk to Phil about Chris. It felt good to have a chance to air the problems.

She'd spoken to Chris on the phone that morning, listening to his enthusiastic recitation of everything the band was playing, feeling, thinking. She'd tried to listen patiently, but when he told her he was considering skipping school this coming year to play with the band instead, she lost her cool. They argued for several minutes without resolution until he told her not to worry about it; he hadn't made up his mind yet for sure. Later in their conversation she heard something in his voice she had never heard before. Concern. Was she okay, he asked her? Was she lonely? Her twenty-year-old son was worrying about her. She'd been touched. It made her miss him more than she already did.

"He looks like Luke, Michael," she said quietly. "He looks exactly like him. I was looking through my old wedding pictures last night. Luke was only twenty-one in them, and Chris is twenty, and God . . ." She shivered, blinked against the surprise of tears. "It really shocked me to see the resemblance."

"Do you have a picture of him?"

"At my grandmother's. I'll show you when you come over."

Michael talked about his own son, Jason. Jace, he called him, who was going into the seventh grade and loved computers. "You think you've got worries with Chris." He shook his head. "Jace is me, thirty years ago. Awkward, skinny, unpopular. The big difference is that I had you and Luke. You two really saved my life, you know that?"

"Oh, you would have eventually come into your own."

"I don't know about that. I hope you're right. I hope Jace will blossom one of these days. Poor kid is the product of two nerds." He laughed. "You don't know how many times I've lain awake at night wondering how I could conjure up a couple of friends like you two for him. I was very lucky." He took her hand, squeezing it lightly before letting go.

"All three of us were," she said.

"I need to spend more time with him." Michael wore a faraway look, the expression of a man who was not certain he was doing a good job with his son. "I work late a lot, and the Pelmans—our next-door neighbors—let him stay over there in the evening when I'm gone. They have a grown son who's into computers, and he and Jace have a great time together. Jace gets along extremely well with adults." Michael took off his glasses and rubbed the bridge of his nose before putting them on again. "I'm going on a church trip with him for a few days, starting tomorrow. It's with one of the youth groups, and they'll be spending a week and a half in Philly helping to refurbish some low-income housing. Jace asked me to go with him, which I think is a pretty good indicator of how out of it he is socially. I can only stay the first couple of days, but I hope by then he'll be feeling more comfortable. He's never been away from home that long, and he seems very needy since Katy's been gone."

So Michael would be gone for a few days. Rachel swallowed her disappointment. "Tell me about Katy," she said.

He clasped his hands together and raised them above his head in a slow stretch. "Oh, boy," he said. "Katy. Where do I begin? In some ways, she's the best thing that ever happened to me. She's the reason I ended up here." He nodded toward the church. "As a minister, I mean."

Rachel drew her legs up onto the bench. "Tell me," she said.

"Well, after everything happened, with you and Luke and the children and . . . everything, I really fell apart. I felt as though I was to blame."

"You? How could you possibly have been to blame?"

"Because of the letter."

She sucked in her breath. She had completely forgotten. "But you married Katy before anything happened," she said.

"Yes, I did." He looked at her. "And you know why I married her, don't you?"

She could picture the black handwriting in that brief, terrible letter. "I know what you said in your letter, but—"

"No buts. I wrote that I married her to forget you, and that was the truth. I did love her, in a way, but I hadn't seen her during that entire first year in Rwanda. I was so down when you left, and suddenly she was there. She looked great. Seemed wonderful, and I needed her. There were so many things I'd wanted to express to you and couldn't, and suddenly Katy was there and it was safe to . . . love her, I guess. It was very impulsive of us, getting married. Her parents were furious." He smiled at some memory. "So anyhow," he continued, "she changed her plans and stayed with me until November. She skipped the beginning of medical school for me. Though I have to say, life in Katari didn't suit her too well." He laughed. "She didn't know how I felt about you, of course . . . Does this bother you? Me talking about this?"

Rachel shook her head, although little slivers of glass seemed to be crackling just below the surface of her skin.

Michael continued. "Katy knew we were close friends, of course, and she probably guessed I felt more for you than that. I don't know. We never talked about it." He shook his head. "She's not a talker. I guess that relieved me at the time. I didn't have to deal with anything. But it's made our marriage a little bit difficult."

Rachel could see him carefully selecting his words.

"So, Katy was there in Katari when I got the word about Luke and the kids in your classroom. I was devastated. I couldn't make any sense of it. How could something so terrible happen to so many good, innocent people?"

He stretched again, and Rachel waited tensely for him to continue.

"Well, Katy was raised in a Mennonite family—I don't know if you remember that."

"Yes, vaguely."

"She essentially took me on as a project, I think." He chuckled. "She could see I was ripe for conversion. She taught me how to pray. It took a long time, but I eventually began to feel some solace in prayer. In God."

Rachel said nothing. He was moving into unfamiliar terrain.

"I thought about you so much," he said. "I worried about you. I wondered how you'd ever be able to find peace for yourself after going through something like that."

"It was hard," she said in a whisper.

"Are you still Lutheran?"

She shook her head. "Unitarian, if anything. A heathen."

He smiled. "You live a good life, Rachel. A thoughtful life, whether or not God's a conscious part of it. I can understand the doubts of others. I'll never stop questioning, but I do believe there's a God—a powerful love greater than anything I can comprehend."

"It must feel very comforting to have that sort of faith."

"It is." He nodded, then continued. "So, when I came back to the States, Katy and I lived in Philly. I was teaching there and Katy was in school, but we came down here every Sunday. She got me going to church. Got me to talk to the minister and, more important, to one of the elders, Lewis Klock, who's a wonderful man and still with us, thank the Lord. I finally began to find real peace. The whole situation with Luke still didn't make sense—I don't think it ever will—but through faith I found a way to cope with it. And I was very attracted to the Mennonites, especially to their commitment to relief work and their pacifist philosophy."

Rachel nodded. "That makes sense."

"I became consumed by it, and eventually I realized that I wanted to be a minister. I wanted to make it my life's work."

"Wow." She smiled. "So you went into the seminary?"

"Uh-huh. In Harrisonburg. Then I came back here." He looked over at his church again. "This is a terrific congregation. The most progressive Mennonite church in the area. Most of our energy goes into relief work of one sort or another. We're gathering supplies to send to Rwanda—well, to the refugee camps in Zaire—in a month or so."

"Really?" She wanted to ask him about Rwanda. She wanted to know if his heart ached when he saw the pictures of suffering in the paper every morning. If anything, she guessed it would be worse for him than it was for her. She had seen the need over there when she was in the Peace Corps, but she'd also recognized her limitations. Michael, on the other hand, had never allowed limitations to color his actions. He gave away his small allowance each month. He'd buy medicine for a sick child or food for a hungry family. He gave away his clothes, his time, his energy. Gave and gave and gave. He fit in well in Katari, better than she did, because the villagers were a generous people. The village reminded him of Reflection, he'd told her once. Everyone caring about one another, like one big extended family.

"Teaching would never have been enough for me, Rache," he said. "Now I get to do all the things I love to do. I can still teach, but I can also write, and study, and speak, and counsel, and I can help people all over the world." Michael's eyes had taken on a glow as his voice rose with enthusiasm.

Rachel touched his hand. "I'm so glad, Michael," she said. "I think Katy's been good for you."

He looked at her as though he'd never had that thought before. "In some ways, yes, but . . . I don't know how much to say. I don't talk about this. I belong to a support group through the church—Mennonites are very big on support groups." He smiled. "But I can't tell them what's going on with Katy and me. Sitting here with you, though . . . we used to tell each other everything, didn't we?"

"Yes, but please don't feel as though you have to—"

"No. I want to. I don't get to say much of this out loud. I've let one of my friends, Drew, in on a little of it because sometimes I think I'm going crazy." He plucked a blade of grass from the hem of his shorts and flicked it into the air. "Things aren't wonderful between Katy and me," he said. "She's ambitious and intelligent and beautiful and a terrific doctor, but she's one of those people who keeps some distance between herself and everyone else, you know what I mean?"

Yes, that was the Katy she remembered. "Even with you?" she asked.

"Even with me. And with Jace, too. She's not at all demonstrative. Not warm. She's always been that way, but even more so lately. Before she left for Moscow, she said she wasn't very happy anymore, although she couldn't really say why. I tried to persuade her into going to a counselor with me, but she refused. She said the few months' separation would be good for us. We'd each get a chance to think things through."

"How long has she been gone?"

"Three weeks, and we've only talked on the phone a few times since she left, although she's spoken to Jace more than that. She comes back in October." He folded his arms across his chest. "It scares me. I want my marriage to survive, but I want it to survive in a better form, and I'm not sure Katy can change. Or that I can. And divorce is not an option."

"Because of your religion?"

He nodded. "There are no divorced Mennonite ministers. I'd lose everything. There are very few divorced people in the congregation as a whole, and depending on their circumstances, they're either tolerated or subtly shunned." He let out his breath. "So now you know the unpleasant truth about the minister and the doctor. Everyone thinks Katy and I are this very bright, very noble couple who has it all together. They don't know that when we go home at night, we don't talk." He winced as if the words cut him, then looked at her with a weak smile. "Didn't mean to dump all that on you, old friend."

She touched his arm. "I'm glad you felt like you could," she said.

"Enough of that topic," he said abruptly. "How is Helen doing?"

Rachel looked toward the gazebo, where the sun was dipping behind the latticed roof. "She's doing quite well. A little easily spooked by thunder and lightning, but who can blame her?"

"No kidding."

"And speaking of my grandmother"—she looked at her watch—"I'd better get home to her. I'm playing the role of master chef this summer."

He smiled at her. "I bet you're good at it. I'll never forget the culinary talent you displayed with that boar in Katari."

She groaned. She had wanted to make a feast for her neighbors, and she'd tried spicing up the precious meat, a gift from a neighbor who could ill afford it, with Italian seasoning. She and Michael were the only ones who would touch it.

"Michael," she said slowly, "when you see the newscasts or the pictures from Rwanda in the paper, how do you feel?"

He looked into her eyes. "Helpless," he said. "Like something inside of me is dying and I can't do anything about it."

"Me, too," she said. "Tell me what your church is doing. Can I help, even though I'm not a Mennonite?"

"Of course you can. I'm not sure they've actually started gathering things yet. I can put you in touch with Celine Humphrey. She's one of the elders, and she's in charge of the program."

"Good. That would be wonderful. And you know something else I want to do while I'm here?"

"What's that?"

"Tutor. On a voluntary basis. Can you tell me who to contact to find some potential students?"

He hesitated, and she was surprised by his lack of enthusiasm.

"I can take the kids nobody else wants," she added. She'd taught classes filled with those kids for the past ten years. "So, who should I call?"

Michael told her the name of one of the counselors at the high school. "She's there this summer," he said. "You should be able to reach her between nine and two without any problem."

"Great." She stood up, and Michael fell into step next to her as she started walking toward the street.

The path dipped into the woods once again, and Rachel ventured to ask him the question that had been gnawing at her for the last couple of hours.

"Who's the woman who works in the bakery?"

"Arlena Cash?"

"Gray-haired? Has arthritis in her hands?"

"Uh-huh."

Rachel pursed her lips. "When I bought the brownies, she asked me if I was Rachel Huber, and when I said yes, she disappeared into the back of the store. Left me standing there. Finally a girl came out and sold me the brownies. She said I should probably not come into the store again."

Michael nodded, his eyes on the path. "Definitely Arlena. Her son was in your class."

Why hadn't she guessed? "Was he one of the ones who . . ." She could not finish the sentence.

"Yes," Michael said. "And Otto Derwich owns the bakery. His son Jimmy was in your class, too. Jimmy's all right, though. Some injury to his foot, but he's a record producer in England and doing okay." He rested his hand on her back. "Maybe you'd better forget about the brownies while you're in town."

She turned to face him in the middle of the path. "It never occurred to me . . . I was only thinking about myself, coming back here. I thought that maybe being here could heal *me*. I'm still haunted by what happened sometimes. But I'd forgotten there'd still be people here who were hurt by it all. It was so long ago." Her voice had risen, and she was glad they were in the cover of the woods.

Michael put his hand on her arm. "It's true it happened a long time ago, but this town has never been able to forget."

"What if I talked to them? To Arlena. And to Mr. . . . . Derwich, is it?" She could not place the name from that long-ago classroom. "What if I told them how sorry I am? I never had the chance to do that when it happened, Michael. I left so quickly. They probably think I feel no remorse. And . . ." She looked up at the canopy of trees above them. "Oh, God, I was rambling on in the bakery about the pond or the brownies or something completely inane. I wish I'd known she was one of the mothers. I need to be able to talk to her and tell her—"

"Listen to me, Rachel." Michael held her by the shoulders. "There's something you need to understand. Arlena Cash is not the only one. She's the tip of the iceberg." He spoke carefully, his eyes cutting into hers as if she might be too slow or too thick to get his point. "Yes, it was a long time ago, but just as you're still haunted by it, so are they. The mothers are everywhere. The fathers, too. My friend Drew is one of them. And there are sisters and brothers, and cousins, and people who knew people. This is a tiny town. Everyone was touched in some way, and you were the logical scapegoat. You can try talking to them, one on one, but the truth is, I don't think they'll give you the chance."

She swallowed her shock. He sounded so stern that she couldn't help but wonder if he blamed her, too. "What can I do?" she asked.

He shook his head. "I don't know. I don't think there's anything you can do at this point. Just realize that some people here might not welcome you with open arms."

She lowered her head, squeezing her eyes closed as he pulled her close to him.

"I'm sorry," he said softly.

She drew away from him with a long sigh. "Well, thanks for the warning, I guess."

They started walking again, and the woods quickly fell behind them as the path neared the street.

"Where's your car?" he asked when they reached the sidewalk in front of the Mennonite church.

She pointed toward Water Street.

"I'll say good-bye here, then. Tell Helen I'll be over Saturday. He leaned over to kiss her cheek. "I'm very glad you're here, Rachel."

You and Gram may be the only people who are, she thought to herself as she hugged him quickly. Then she turned and started walking toward her car.

8

Lily was late getting to the salon on Wednesday morning. One of the dogs—she didn't have a clue which one—had gotten sick on the living room carpet, and she'd taken the time to clean it up before leaving. By the time she'd reached the salon with her bagel from the deli, Polly and Marge and CeeCee were already there, and the coffee was hot.

She poured herself a cup. "Anyone check the messages yet?" she asked.

"I'll get them." Polly pulled a pad and pen close to the answering machine and pressed the play button.

"My name is Rachel Huber." The voice rose from the machine, and all four women froze to listen. "I'd like to make an appointment for a perm. Is there any chance of getting in either today or tomorrow?"

Rachel Huber left her number, and Polly clicked off the machine. "Okay," she said. "Who takes her?"

"Marge should probably do it, since she does Helen," CeeCee suggested.

"I'd really rather not," Marge said. "I know too many people who'd call me a traitor."

"Well, I don't trust myself to do a decent job on her," CeeCee said.

Lily leaned against the counter, sipping her coffee, watching her coworkers. She knew they didn't consider her to be in the running.

"I think we should draw straws," Polly said.

"Don't bother." Lily reached for the appointment book. "I'll take her."

The women stared at her in stunned silence.

"You don't have to do that, Lily," Marge said. "None of us actually has to take her. We can call her back and say we're booked."

"Don't do it," Polly was looking at Lily as if she were a wounded animal. "Why put yourself through that?"

Lily lifted the receiver from the phone and began to dial. "We are not booked up," she said to the other women. "And she's a paying customer who's entitled to an appointment. I'm going to give her one."

The voice that answered matched the voice on the answering machine.

"Is this Rachel Huber?" Lily asked.

"Yes, it is."

"Rachel, this is Lily Jackson from Hairlights Salon. I have an opening at two today. Can you make it?"

"That'd be perfect."

"All right. See you then." She hung up the phone and shrugged at the pained disbelief on the faces of her coworkers. "Done," she said. "Now let's get to work."

She was blow-drying Diana Robinson's hair when Rachel Huber arrived. CeeCee and Marge exchanged looks across the heads of their customers, and Polly cracked her knuckles, like she always did when she was anxious about something.

If Lily had not been expecting her, she never would have recognized her second-grade teacher. Lily could barely remember what "Miss Huber" had looked like—she'd only had her as a teacher for six days—much less imagine how twenty years had altered her. Still, she had no doubt at all that the woman standing at the reception counter wearing denim shorts and sporting a fading perm was Rachel Huber.

She watched Polly check her in, hand her a Styrofoam cup of coffee, and usher her to a seat in the small waiting area. Rachel sat down and pulled a magazine from the coffee table onto her knees, and Lily felt the slow tease of nausea. Maybe this wasn't such a great idea after all.

She finished Diana's hair, then steeling herself for what lay ahead, stepped over to the waiting area.

"Rachel Huber?" she asked.

The woman looked up, and Lily was struck by the ready smile, the open, trusting face. She was a little overweight and her features were imperfect, but she was still quite attractive. It was impossible not to feel the warmth in that smile.

Lily reached out her hand, thinking that her former teacher was going to look even better once she'd gotten her hair into shape.

"I'm Lily Jackson," she said.

"Hello, Lily." Rachel stood up and shook her hand.

Lily led Rachel back to her station, the eyes of her coworkers burning into her all the way.

She stood behind the woman, looking at both their faces in the brightly lit mirror. She could see the difference in their ages clearly, could imagine they had once been teacher and student. But nothing in Rachel's face frightened her. She sometimes still had nightmares about that day, but those dreams did not include the face she saw reflected in the mirror.

"So, what can I do for you?" Lily asked.

"I'm overdue for a perm." Rachel lifted her hair from her neck and let it fall. "I live in San Antonio and usually get it done every five or six months, but it's been about eight now. I left in a rush and couldn't get it taken care of."

Lily ran her fingers through the thick, light brown hair. "Yeah," she said. "This is one heck of a dead perm."

Rachel laughed.

"How much curl do you want?"

"I usually get quite a bit, but I'm ready for a change," she said. "What do you think?"

"How about a body wave?" Lily suggested. "We'll trim off the old ends. And bangs would look great on you." She held some of Rachel's hair over her forehead. "Don't you think? Just little feathery ones."

"Go for it." Rachel smiled, and Lily liked her spirit.

She cut Rachel's bangs, then took her into the back room to wash her hair. They had a shampoo girl on Saturdays when they got busy, but most of the time the stylists did all their own work.

"How's your grandmother doing?" she asked as she worked the suds into Rachel's scalp. "She comes in here about once a month. She's a kick."

"She's doing okay."

Rachel described Helen's injuries, and Lily shuddered, imagining what it would be like to feel lightning cut through you.

"She's the one who recommended you guys," Rachel added.

"How's she making out without her little dog?" Lily asked. "Rocky? Was that his name?" She was better at remembering the names of her friend's dogs than she was the names of their children.

"Right. After Rachmaninoff. She doesn't talk about him much, but I know she misses him. It's got to be so awful when you get to be that age and your friends are dying off. I think Rocky was a good companion to her."

"I take in foster dogs. If you ever think she's up to having another pup around, let me know and we'll find her one."

"Maybe when she gets stronger," Rachel said. "I had to leave my own dog in San Antonio. My son's watching him, so I know he's all right, but I still miss him."

Rachel Huber missed her dog. This woman was okay. "What kind of dog do you have?"

"Boxer. His name's Phoenix. He's cuddly, though. Not the usual boxer personality."

"All dogs are cuddly at heart." Lily sat her up, dried her off, and walked her back to the station, where she began wrapping Rachel's hair around white and purple rods. Rachel asked her questions about the foster dogs, Lily's favorite topic.

"My landlord thinks I only have two dogs." Lily laughed. "When she comes over, I have to hide the others."

"Well, if you ever need help with that, give me a call," Rachel offered. "You can hide the dogs at my grandmother's, and she and I can get our needs for canine affection met."

Rachel sounded as if she meant it, and Lily liked her better than ever.

She snipped the top off the waving lotion and began saturating the rods. She hoped Rachel was not aware of how blatantly Polly and CeeCee and Marge were watching them, as if they were waiting to see what Lily would do with this perfect opportunity for revenge at her fingertips.

"You're just here till Helen's on her feet again?" Lily asked.

"I'll probably stay till the end of the summer," Rachel answered. "Although I could stay longer if I have to. I'm a teacher, but I'm taking next year off."

She was still teaching. Lily felt a little jolt. For some reason, she hadn't expected that.

"Reflection must be quite a change after San Antonio," she said.

She thought she detected a second's hesitation before Rachel answered. "Yes, but I know Reflection pretty well. I grew up here. On Water Street."

Lily nodded. "I know," she said quietly. "Do you still have some friends here?"

"Well, at least one. A guy named Michael Stoltz, who—"

"Michael!" Lily said. "He's a friend of yours? He's the minister of my church."

Rachel smiled into the mirror. "I hadn't seen him in a long time. It surprised me to discover he'd become a minister."

"Oh, he couldn't be anything else. He's so great. He married my husband and me. And he headed my youth group a billion years ago. He was so cool." It had been her last year in youth group and Michael's first year as a minister. She had adored him, even had a crush on him for a while. She could talk to Michael about anything. He was one of the few adults in her life who hadn't locked horns with her. He'd encouraged her questioning, her belligerence. "I cut his hair," she said. "His wife's, too. Everyone adores Michael—except for a few diehards who don't think he should have been allowed to be a minister, since he wasn't raised in a Mennonite family. Did you go to Reflection Junior-Senior High together?"

"Uh-huh. And college. And we did the Peace Corps together, too."

"No kidding? I'd forgotten he was in the Peace Corps."

"Yes. We were in a little village in Rwanda together." Rachel began talking about the work she and Michael had done overseas, and Lily knew very quickly that Rachel's feelings for Michael went beyond friendship. And Katy was out of town until October. Her mind clicked with the possibilities. She'd bet Rachel could get Michael laughing again. It had been a while since she'd seen a genuine smile on the minister's face.

She'd never understood that marriage. Michael was outgoing, a real people person. Katy was . . . hard to describe. Nice enough, certainly. Well respected. "She's so damn *pleasant*," Ian had said after meeting her for the first time, his voice conveying disdain. "Pleasantness" didn't mean much to Ian. Katy would sit in Lily's chair and read a magazine so she didn't have to talk. She was polite, but she maintained a cautious distance. Never divulged a single personal detail. But it didn't matter. Other people did it for her.

Lily was not a gossip by nature, and she took some pride in that fact, but people told her things. People simply sat down in her chair and, as though there were truth serum in the coffee she gave them, began to pour things out to her. That was why she knew something about Katy she had no right to know. She knew something even Michael didn't know.

"How long have you been married?" Rachel asked.

"Five years. I met my husband at a party where he was performing. He's a professional magician."

"You mean that's his job? Full time?"

Lily laughed. "That's exactly what my mother said when I told her about him."

"Sorry."

"It's fun. He loves what he does, and he's really, really good at it." She was suddenly aware of how quiet it was in the salon, although everyone was working. CeeCee, Polly, and Marge were too busy listening in on her conversation with Rachel to do much talking with their own customers.

"Ian's really smart," Lily said. "I mean *incredibly* smart, especially in math. He got scholarships to college and everything, but he only went a couple of years because he discovered magic. It's what makes him happiest. That and plants. He added a greenhouse onto our rental, and he's always out there with his little green babies." Ian would have liked to have some real babies, but the thought gave Lily a chill. Children were entirely too fragile.

Rachel sighed. "I need to hear this, I guess. My son, who could have a brilliant future ahead of him as a classical musician, is now talking about dropping out of school to play in a rock band."

"Let him." Lily squeezed Rachel's shoulders. "Everybody's got to find what makes them light up in the world. Ian positively lights up when he does magic. Math never had that effect on him, believe me. Michael Stoltz lights up when he preaches. I light up when I'm around my dogs. What about you?"

"Teaching," Rachel said without hesitation. "I teach kids who have trouble learning. When I reach one of them . . . well, it makes me realize there's nothing I'd rather do."

For some reason, Rachel's words brought tears to Lily's eyes. She stopped working for a minute to look at her former teacher's face in the mirror. "Okay," she said, recovering quickly. She slipped a plastic cap over Rachel's hair and turned the knob on her timer. "Time to let these set up."

An hour later Rachel's hair was unwrapped, cut, and ready to dry. She sat in front of the mirror and patted her thighs. "I need an aerobics class," she said to Lily. "Do you know where I might find one?"

"Everybody goes to the classes that meet in the basement of the Lutheran church." Lily lifted her hair dryer from the counter. "There's a couple of them every day of the week." She wasn't certain, though, how welcoming Rachel would find those classes.

Once it was dry, Rachel's hair looked soft and light. The perm lifted the color, made it shine. Lily was impressed with her own handiwork, and Rachel was clearly pleased.

They walked together to the counter, where Rachel pulled out a charge card. Lily ran it through the scanner, then handed her the form and a pen. She made a quick decision as she watched Rachel sign her name.

"I was in your class," she said.

A startled look crossed Rachel's features. "Oh. Lily. Yes, I remember a Lily. Your last name was . . . Wright?"

"Yes. It's Jackson now. I was your troublemaker. My twin sister, Jenny, was the quiet, studious one."

Before Rachel could respond, Lily squeezed her hand. "People might be hard on you here," she said. "Be strong."

9

Rachel put the last of the breakfast dishes in the dishwasher and turned to see a rueful expression on her grandmother's face.

"I'm so sorry everything's falling on your shoulders," Gram said from her seat at the table. "I hate this helplessness."

"I don't mind at all." Rachel closed the dishwasher and began wiping the countertop with a sponge.

They were waiting for Michael to arrive. This was the morning he was to prune the trees, and Rachel could not keep her eyes from her watch as she cleaned the kitchen. He had called her twice from Philadelphia during his stay with his son's youth group, and they'd talked for nearly an hour each time, enjoying again the instant, comfortable intimacy they'd shared on the bench by the pond.

He was often on her mind. No, *often* was too refined a word to describe the persistent nature of those thoughts. She thought of him ceaselessly, and it frightened her. It had not been long enough since she'd lost Phil. She felt weak and needy and vulnerable. Or maybe she simply had too much time on her hands and too little else to think about.

What did she want from him? She asked herself that question as she lay in bed at night, listening to the rhythmic croaking of frogs through her open window. She wanted his friendship for the summer. Someone to talk to, laugh with. And she didn't want to lose contact with him, ever again. She would stay in touch with him for the rest of her life.

She wanted more than that, and she knew it. And she was wrong to want it, just as she had been wrong to want it in Rwanda in 1973. If she could resist it then, when she'd been younger, more impulsive, and deprived of physical love for a year, surely she could resist it now. Besides, it was not being offered to her. She had made a great leap in her mind from a simple trip down memory lane on a park bench to becoming the lover of a man who was married and a minister. Yes, she had entirely too much time on her hands.

Gram rose unsteadily to her feet. "I'm going to pick out some music for the CD player and then do my ankle exercises," she said.

Rachel reached out to help her, but the older woman waved her hand away.

"I'm all right," she said. "The dizziness just lasts a second or two now." She limped into the living room, cussing at her cane.

Rachel smiled. Her grandmother had been a surprise. Somehow, Rachel had expected this summer to be almost a retreat. Time alone, to think and heal. But her grandmother's presence was constant. Gram was a living, breathing, dynamic human being.

And what on earth had Rachel expected? She had not given this trip east much thought. The social worker had called; Rachel had seen the opportunity. Taking care of her grandmother was simply part of the deal. Before this trip, if anyone had asked her whether she loved her grandmother, she would have answered that she did. But love in that context was a flat little word. Her memories of Gram had been too sketchy to elicit much in the way of real emotion. In her mind the older woman had been reduced to little more than a stereo-type, an image the social worker had reinforced. She'd expected to find a slightly crotchety and very ill old lady. But Gram was not easily pigeonholed, not the sort of person you could ignore as you went on about your business. Ignoring Gram would be like ignoring herself.

Rachel constantly found herself reflected in her grandmother. Gram's yearning to be surrounded by beautiful music was the same as her own. They could both sit contentedly on the porch for hours doing nothing more than watching the birds flit in and out of the trees. They shared a love of the garden, of watching things sprout from the earth and grow green and strong with promise. Rachel understood her grandmother's frustration at not being able to get down and dig in the earth with her. The older woman would watch her, though. She'd sit on the porch and watch her pull weeds and pinch back the tops of the basil plants.

That her grandmother felt trapped by her infirmities was all too obvious. When Rachel started bringing flowers into the house, it was as if she'd given her grandmother the stars and the moon. Gram would hobble from room to room just to look at them. That's when Rachel decided to take her out. First they drove, traveling through the farmland, Gram opening her window fully to breathe in the barnyard scent Rachel remembered from her childhood but had not yet adjusted to as an adult. They drove through neighboring villages, Gram telling her about friends from the past who had lived on this street or that. Rachel slowly realized that, although her grandmother had a wealth of acquaintances, her close friends, her intimates, had all died, many of them within the past couple of years.

It wasn't until they were preparing to take their second such drive that Rachel seized upon the idea of a wheelchair. She found a rental place in Lancaster, picked up the wheelchair, tossed it into the trunk, and took it along on their drive. Once they reached the wooded area where she had gathered many of the flowers for the house, she pulled out the chair, helped Gram into it, and wheeled her—with effort— down the packed-earth path through trees and fields and the muted colors of summer wildflowers.

The path was a little bumpy, but Gram insisted she didn't mind. They were very quiet as they moved through the woods, quiet enough that they saw a fox when they rounded one bend, and a deer and her fawn when they rounded another. At one point Gram reached up to squeeze Rachel's hand where it was locked around the handle of the chair.

"This is a gift, Rachel," she said. "Thank you."

And at that moment the flat little word *love* took on more dimensions than Rachel could count.

She wanted to ask her grandmother about people's reactions to what had happened in her classroom, but there seemed to be an unspoken agreement between them to keep things light. That was probably good. Gram's home could remain her refuge.

The hairdresser, Lily, had shocked her when she'd admitted to having been in her class. Rachel had remembered the little girl instantly, even though her twin sister and the other children in the class remained a blur. She remembered Lily because from day one she'd known that child was going to be her challenge. A little blond devil. If she asked the class to do something, Lily would argue against it, or simply set about doing something else. Rachel even recalled discussing her with one of the more seasoned teachers on the staff. How do you deal with a recalcitrant seven-year-old? Now Lily was the lovely, chatty, capable, and kind owner of a hair salon. Rachel had liked her immediately. She was one of those people who offered instant comfort, instant trust.

People might be hard on you here, Lily had said. Rachel had thought of the incident in the bakery and had nearly opened her mouth to tell Lily what had happened. But that would not be fair, she thought. Lily had lost her sister in that classroom. *Damn.*

Since that day in the bakery, though, no one had said a negative word to her. She'd gone into town three times, twice to the grocery store and once to the music store on Main Street. The grocery store was large, and she'd had a pleasant sense of anonymity there. She'd talked with the cashier about the artichokes she was buying, explaining how to cook them, how to eat them, relishing the everyday nature of the conversation. The cashier had been as friendly as she could be. Of course, she hadn't known Rachel's identity. Maybe that wouldn't have made a difference. Lily had known, and she had not cared.

In the music store she'd bought five CD's of contemporary music she wanted to share with her grandmother. The cashier, a middle-aged woman, had not been particularly warm, but neither had she been rude or told her not to come back. Still, Rachel had felt her face burning with irrational guilt the whole time the sale was being rung up, and she paid with cash rather than her credit card so the woman would not discover who she was.

Gram had loved the music, and from the kitchen Rachel could hear that she had selected one of the new CD's to play this morning.

It was nearly nine-thirty when Michael arrived. Rachel was straightening her bedroom when she heard him call through the front screen door, "Any Huber women here?"

She walked into the living room and opened the door for him. He was wearing that grin, the grin she'd loved as a child and adored as an adult.

"Hey," he said. "How's my favorite heathen?"

"Good." She smiled. "And how was Philadelphia?"

"Excellent." He touched her arm lightly as he stepped past her to buss her grandmother's cheek. The older woman had hobbled into the room on her cane.

"How you doin', Helen?" he asked. "Where's that chair Rachel said she got you?"

"In the car. I'm not going to use it in the house, for heaven's sake. That thing scares me." Gram shuddered. "Every time I get in it, I have to get myself right out again just to prove to myself I'm not stuck in it for good. Do you know what I mean?"

"Hmm." Michael nodded. "I think so."

"If I ever get to the point where I can't get out, promise me you'll come over and put me out of my misery, all right?"

Rachel started to laugh, but Michael's serious expression stopped her. "I'd do whatever I could for you, Helen," he said.

There was a bond between these two people, Rachel thought. Somewhere over the years their paths had crossed with some meaning she did not understand. She felt insignificant at that moment, unconnected to either of them.

Michael turned his attention to her. "If I see one more piece of drywall ever again, it'll be too soon," he said.

"How was it?" Rachel asked.

"Good experience," he said. "The kids are working hard. They're getting to meet the families they're helping, and I think that really makes the difference." He winked at Gram. "But I'm ready for a little outside work now."

Gram raised her cane in a salute. "I'm going to get my hat and sit out on the porch to watch you do it," she said.

Rachel offered to get the hat for her, but Gram shook her head and walked back to her bedroom. Michael followed her with his eyes. "She's getting around better than I expected," he said.

Rachel looked at him curiously. "You two seem to know each other very well," she said.

He nodded. "Yeah, we do."

"How?"

"She hasn't told you?"

She shook her head.

He glanced toward Gram's bedroom. "Well, everyone in Reflection knows everyone else," he said.

Rachel did not think that was the complete answer. Michael went outside to set the ladder in place, and Rachel opened all the front windows of the house so they could hear the music as they worked in the yard. The second CD—*Patchwork*—was playing by the time she got out to the garden. Michael was already standing on the ladder, working on one of the higher branches, and Gram supervised them both from her roost on the porch. It was difficult for the three of them to talk with the physical distance between them, but it didn't matter. The music poured over them, and Rachel felt a complete sort of contentment. Her hands in the earth, two people she loved close by, her grandfather's music putting her into a trance.

They took a break from the yard work around eleven. Rachel had made lemonade and her mother's poppyseed bread, a recipe she'd kept tucked away in her memory all these years. She'd picked the very last of the strawberries from the garden, and she and Michael nibbled on them as they sat on the porch steps, their backs against opposing posts so they could look up at Gram.

"So, Michael," Gram said, "how is the land fight going?"

"Don't know. The hearing is September sixth, and we're trying to get as many people to show up as we can. Drew and I have been collecting signatures—by the way, I have the petition in my car if you're willing."

Gram nodded. "Of course. I wish I could be out there pounding the pavement with you. Let me know if there's some way I can help."

"Even got quite a few people from the Old Order groups to sign."

"Are you catching some flak about having Drew Albrecht in on this?" Gram asked.

"A bit, but I think it's a plus to have a developer on our side against the Hostetters."

Rachel shaded her eyes as she looked up at her grandmother. "Michael said Marielle Hostetter was shot in the head by her mother." She waited for confirmation of the bizarre story.

Gram looked out to the trees, and it was a minute before she answered. "Yes," she said. "Her mother went a little crazy one day and shot Marielle, who was four at the time, and her husband, and then herself. The husband lived of course, just got the bullet in his arm, which put a long break in his career as a painter."

"Why do you think she did it?" Michael asked.

"Who knows what would make a woman do a thing like that?"

"I didn't know Marielle's father was a painter," Rachel said.

"Oh, yes. A very bright and talented man. You know that painting above the sofa?"

Rachel pictured it instantly, the view of snow-wrapped Reflection from Winter Hill. "That's his?" she asked.

Gram nodded. "Yes, it is. He gave it to Peter. They were friends, the two eccentric artsy types in the community. He would be appalled to see that piece of property ruined. It inspired most of his work." She looked down at Michael. "Your cousin must be thrilled, though."

Michael groaned. "Don't rub in my relationship to her, all right, Helen?"

"I don't get it," Rachel said. "Who's your cousin?"

"Ursula Torwig," Michael said. "Our mayor."

"Oh!" She had not made the connection. The country cousin, they used to call her. Ursula's family had lived outside of Reflection on a pig farm. "Wow. She's come a long way."

"Too far, if you ask me," Michael said.

Gram yawned and rose slowly to her feet. "Well, you two, I think I'm going to take a short nap."

Michael stood up to help her into the house, but she brushed his hand away.

"Do you want a pain pill?" Rachel offered.

"No, thanks. I want a nap, that's it."

Rachel followed her into the bedroom and closed the curtains against the bright sunshine.

"Oh, I forgot to give Michael the check," Gram said, once she'd settled herself beneath the covers. "It's in my purse in the kitchen. I made it out to the church, of course. He'd never take it for himself. Will you give it to him, please?"

"Sure."

She found her grandmother's purse in the kitchen, but the first thing her hand touched when she reached inside it was a clear plastic bag. She drew the bag out to see that it contained sprigs of dried herbs. She sniffed them and knew they were cuttings from the herbs Gram had asked her to buy. Odd, she thought as she slipped the bag back into the purse. Was it a superstition of some sort, or did she simply like the scent?

She found the check and carried it out to the porch, handing it to Michael as she took her seat against the pillar again.

"Thanks." He didn't bother to glance at the check before sticking it into his shirt pocket. "How about a bike ride tomorrow?" he asked. "It would have to be late in the day. Sundays are busy for me."

"I'd love it." She hugged her knees in anticipation. She hadn't ridden in several days.

They talked about their bikes for a while, and she quickly realized that he was as fanatical about cycling as she was. They had even bought the same top-of-the-line model.

"I didn't realize a Mennonite would have such fancy material possessions," she teased him.

He laughed. "Oh, we have them all right. We just feel guilty about it."

"Do you have a TV? A VCR?"

"Absolutely. And more photography equipment than any human being has a right to."

"Really?" Her mind started clicking. "Do you do your own developing?"

"Black-and-white, yes."

"Maybe you can help me, then," she said. "Someone donated all this photography equipment to my school. There are cameras and enlargers and trays and chemicals and all sorts of stuff. I think it would be great to use it with my special-ed kids, but I don't know how."

"Then this summer you will learn." Michael smiled. "I use the darkroom at the high school. I have a key, so I can get in whenever I want. Do you have a camera with you?"

She shook her head.

"You can borrow one of mine. It'll be fun." He grinned at her and leaned forward. "So," he said, "when was the last time you went to Hershey Park?"

She smiled at the quick flood of memories. She could smell the park, the cotton candy and french fries, the oil they used to grease the rides. "It must have been . . . '69? With you and Luke and . . . some girl. Katy, maybe."

"Maybe, though she and I didn't date that much in high school."

Rachel had been to Hershey Park too many times to count, but she doubted she had ever been there without Luke.

"Can we go?" she ventured.

"I think we have to. It's changed a lot since you were last there, though."

"Should we wait until Jason gets back and take him with us?" she suggested. "I'd love to meet him."

"No." He spoke with such force that she jumped. "You and I know we're just friends, Rache, but Jace is sort of . . . vulnerable right now. He misses Katy. He's not going to be comfortable seeing his dad strolling around with another woman."

She nodded woodenly, trying to make sense of the sudden hurt in her chest. When she spoke, she selected her words with care. "I don't like feeling as though our friendship is something we have to hide," she said.

He let out a sigh and picked at a splinter jutting from the top step. When he looked up at her, his grin had been replaced by a serious expression. "I need to be careful, Rache. Both because I still have feelings for you and because of how people would perceive seeing me with another woman while Katy's out of the country, even if that other woman is just an old friend."

She closed her eyes and leaned back against the post, knowing she had to give words to the uncomfortable thought creeping into her head.

"Just tell me," she said, "reassure me, that your not wanting to be seen with me has nothing to do with the fact that I'm Rachel Huber."

He understood immediately. "Of course not, Rachel."

She looked down at the porch floor, running her hand lightly over the wood, back and forth. After a minute she asked, "Would you like to see a picture of my son?"

He brightened, either very pleased by the idea or relieved at the change of topic. "Yes. Go get it."

She went into her bedroom and pulled three loose photographs from her night-table drawer. She'd brought the recent pictures with her, taken of Chris at his birthday party in May.

Out on the porch again, she handed the pictures to Michael. She sat down next to him on the step so that she could see them over his shoulder.

Michael looked at the first photograph, and Rachel felt his body tense. She knew why. After seeing those pictures of Luke the other night, she knew how startling the resemblance was between father and son.

"Oh, my God." Michael could not seem to take his eyes from the picture. "My God," he said again, shaking his head.

She heard him swallow as he took off his glasses and wiped his eyes with his fingers. Her own tears were close. She dared to rest her hand on his back, her cheek on his shoulder, and she was relieved when he put his arm around her waist.

"Whew," he said finally. He shook his head again at the picture. "Oh, man. Makes me miss Luke something fierce."

"The pre-Vietnam Luke."

"That's the only Luke I knew."

Michael studied the second photograph, then the third. "He has a ponytail?"

"Just a little wisp. And an earring."

He laughed as he removed his arm from around her. On cue, she lifted her head from his shoulder and shifted a foot or so away from him on the step.

"You're lucky you have him." He handed the pictures back to her.

"Yes, I know."

He gave her a weak smile, then looked out at the garden. "Well," he said, "I'd better get back to the trees."

She watched him walk across the yard and climb the ladder before she lowered her eyes once more to the pictures of Chris. Michael's reaction to the photographs had touched, but not surprised, her. She doubted anything he did could surprise her. She'd known him far too long. And she knew him very well.

10

Lily loaded Mule and Wiley and the three foster dogs into the back of her van. The dog-adoption service had found homes for two of the dogs she'd had the week before, but they'd quickly brought her two more. Huge animals, these new ones, and she did not particularly trust the two males together. They snarled at each other as they sat in the back of the van, and Lily changed her mind about the seating arrangement. She took the shepherd mix out of the back and placed him in the passenger seat before setting off.

She'd gotten out of work early for a Saturday afternoon. She did not particularly want to spend her free time on the task ahead of her, but she felt as if she had little choice. She wished she could talk to Ian about it. Ian knew all there was to know about her, but he didn't know about this. She'd decided a long time ago that it wouldn't be fair to tell him, to make him carry that burden. So she'd made the decision to drive out to Fair Acres today on her own. She could take the dogs with her. Make it a real outing.

Fair Acres was fifteen miles from town, through farm country. She had to slow down twice to circumvent buggies plodding along the edge of the road, but otherwise the drive was easy. Pretty. She kept the air-conditioning blowing. The dogs were clean, but still, you put five furry bodies in an enclosed space on a warm day, and it could get kind of gamy.

She'd never been to Fair Acres, although she'd driven by it several times. As she neared the wide front gate, she wondered if she should have called first. Would Jacob Holt be home? He'd retired out here three years ago, after working as a school principal for most of his long career. He'd been the principal of Spring Willow Elementary when she was a student there, then he'd transferred over to the junior-senior high just as she was entering the ninth grade. In his retirement speech, he'd talked about how he'd always longed to be a farmer. It was his dream, he'd said in that deep, bellowing voice.

The gate was open, and a curved wrought-iron sign that read FAIR ACRES formed an arch above it. Lily drove up the driveway toward the farmhouse. Her palms were sweating.

She parked around the side of the house and walked up the porch steps, where she knocked on the wood trim of an old screen door. The porch was bright in the afternoon sun, making the inside of the house look dark and shadowy through the screen. She knocked again, and after a moment someone appeared in the shadows, walking slowly toward the door. An elderly woman. She'd forgotten that Jacob Holt lived with his mother.

The woman waited for Lily to speak.

"Hello," Lily said. "I'm looking for Mr. Holt?"

"He's in the barn yet," the woman said, and even with those few words Lily could hear the Pennsylvania Dutch accent.

"Thanks," she said. "And do you think it would be all right if I let my dogs out here? There are five of them. They won't bother the farm animals." At least she hoped they wouldn't.

"Ach." The old woman smiled. "Leave 'um run."

Lily walked back to the van and opened the door for the dogs. Thrilled with the sudden freedom, the wide spaces, they began running in wild circles around her, making her laugh as she started walking toward the barn. The pasture on her left was dotted with cows—Black Angus—grazing lazily, and a chicken scooted across the driveway, just out of reach of the dogs.

The wide barn doors were open, and she stopped outside, peering into the darkness, the powerful smell of hay and manure filling her nostrils. "Mr. Holt?" she called.

"Around here." The voice came from somewhere to her right. She walked around the corner of the barn to find him working on his tractor.

He raised his head at her approach and stood up straight, wiping his hands on the rag hanging from the pocket of his overalls. She was struck by how young he looked—younger than he had at his retirement ceremony. His skin had a healthy glow, and smile lines crinkled at the corners of his eyes. He was not smiling right now, though. Not at all.

"Lily," he said, his eyebrows arched in surprise.

"Hi, Mr. Holt." Even though she'd known Jacob Holt for most of her life, she would never have felt comfortable calling him by his first name. "You look terrific," she said. "The farming life agrees with you, huh?"

"Sure does. Should have retired years before I did."

Mule suddenly bounded around the corner of the barn and jumped up on the old principal, his huge front paws flat on the man's chest. Lily cringed, but Mr. Holt laughed, burying his hands in the dog's long black coat. "Whoa, boy," he said. "Aren't you a beauty? And there's more of them!"

Lily turned to see Wiley and the foster dogs tear around the corner toward them, the two males snarling at each other.

"I hope you don't mind that I brought the dogs with me," she said. "I asked your mother, and she—"

"No, that's fine." Mr. Holt was down on his haunches, patting, stroking, getting his face licked, and laughing. She'd never known he was a dog lover, a fact that only muddied her already conflicted feelings about this man.

She watched him play with the dogs for a moment, then drew in a breath. "Rachel Huber's in town," she said.

Jacob Holt looked up at her, his face dark and unreadable in the shade of the tractor.

"Just for a while," she continued. "She's nursing her grandmother."

Holt got slowly to his feet, wiping his hands on his overalls. "I heard Helen took a lightning strike," he said.

"Yes."

He nodded as though the conversation was over and turned his attention back to the tractor, reaching deep inside the hood. Was that it? Wasn't he going to say anything else?

"People are talking," she said. "I'm afraid they're going to be mean to her."

He frowned at the workings of the tractor, tugging at something that refused to come free. He was ignoring her, pretending she wasn't there. Hoping she'd go away, the way he surely had to wish Rachel would go away—leave Reflection and never return.

"Mr. Holt?" Lily dug her fingers into the thick fur behind Mule's ears. "I want to—"

"Lily." He straightened his spine again. "It's water under the bridge. Leave it alone."

She was tempted to argue, but what right did she have? It was one thing for her to make a decision that would affect her own life, quite another to do harm to his. And maybe he was right. Maybe she would only be making things worse.

Mule nudged closer to her, trying to get her hands moving, his fur trapped in the tight confines of her fists. "Don't you ever . . ." she began, then stopped herself with a shake of her head. "Sometimes, when I'm by myself, I remember what happened, and I feel so . . . *alone* with it. Kind of like it's this weight sitting on my chest, and it's so heavy I can't breathe."

He was not listening. His attention was riveted on his tractor.

"Doesn't it ever get to you?" she asked. "Don't you feel any guilt?"

"Guilt?" He looked up at her. "Over what?"

She could not respond. He knew. He knew perfectly well over what.

"Leave it alone, Lily," he said again. "That's the best advice I can give you."

He pulled the rag from the pocket of his overalls and wiped it across his forehead before dipping his hands back into the tractor again.

Lily studied his face a moment longer before turning to go. Maybe it was only her imagination, or maybe the angle of the sun had shifted while she'd been standing there, but she could have sworn that the lines in his face had deepened in these last few minutes, that his skin had taken on a faint gray hue. She could have sworn that Jacob Holt had aged ten years in the space of her visit.

11

It was Sunday morning, and Michael sat at the desk in his church office, putting the finishing touches on his sermon. The scent of the freshly baked bread resting on the edge of his desk made him hungry. He'd found the wrapped loaf sitting outside his office door, along with a bag of ripe tomatoes and a few ears of corn—one of the special benefits of serving in a community where farms were abundant.

His office was in the basement of the church. The ground sloped away from the corner of the building, allowing the large room to have several good-sized windows and a sunny interior. The walls were lined with his treasured collection of reference books. He could easily lose himself in here.

He'd come into the office very early that morning, as he did every day of the week. He liked to spend some time in the sanctuary, where the dawn light fell warm and soft across the pews. It was his quiet time for prayer. Usually he prayed for other people in his life, for members of his congregation, for his family. Today, though, he had prayed for himself. He'd asked God to guide him in his relationship with Rachel, so that his friendship with her would bring harm to no one. He'd asked for the wisdom to know how much time together was too much.

Then he'd come down here to his office for those few final minutes of solitude before the hectic activity of Sunday began. The church service would be followed by Sunday school, after which he would visit a few of his parishioners who were either hospitalized or homebound. Then he had promised to make an appearance at the fiftieth-wedding anniversary celebration of two longtime members of the church. He loved the whirlwind pace of a typical Sunday. It would be nice, though, to end the day with a bike ride with Rachel, especially with Jason still in Philadelphia. He missed his son badly.

He was jotting notes in the margin of the sermon when his gaze fell upon the green flyer stuck in the corner of his blotter. He held it into the light from the window. It was an announcement of the September 6 hearing, and he knew it had been designed by one of the teenagers in the youth group, Donna Garry, who must have left it on his desk the night before. She'd done a good job, adding a border of trees around the information to remind the reader exactly what would be lost if the land were developed.

He hoped Donna would be in the Reflection Day ceremony this year. It was the Mennonite church's turn to plan the program, and he'd volunteered to take responsibility for it. He had an ulterior motive in doing so, but as the day neared, he realized he might have made a mistake in taking it on. There was little more than a month left until Reflection Day, and he hadn't even met with the kids yet. The thought made him groan out loud. He was not looking forward to putting together a program for an event he detested—the forced remembrance of an ancient tragedy. For Rachel's sake, he hoped she would be gone by then.

There was a terrible snag in Reflection's makeup, he thought, a fatal flaw. The town simply could not let go of the past. He knew people who could not drive by Spring Willow Elementary without remembering. He knew people who still heard the sobbing, the keening that had filled the school yard that long-ago September morning.

One of the kids in the youth group had asked him whether he knew Rachel. Her mother had said she'd seen Rachel in town, "walking around like she belongs here."

"She *does* belong here," he'd replied. "This is her hometown, just like it's yours."

"Most people really don't want her here, though," the girl had said.

I do, he'd thought. People had blown Rachel's role in what happened way out of proportion, he told the girl. Although he'd always wondered about that himself. If he'd had a child in Rachel's classroom that day, he wasn't certain he could have forgiven her, either. When Jason was in the second grade, he'd thought about it almost daily. What would it be like to send your child off to school in the morning and never be able to see him or touch him again? Would he hold the teacher responsible? Yes, he probably would.

He gave up on the sermon, setting it aside as he turned his chair to face the window. He could see the pond, and he laughed out loud at the sudden memory of Rachel, Luke, and himself dragging a big old crate to the water's edge, hopping inside, and setting sail, only to have the crate break apart when they'd reached the pond's center.

So many memories. Having Rachel in town brought them all to the surface. Yet there was one memory he did not like; it had haunted him most of his life and now seemed to leap up at him when he least expected it. Why was it that all other pain seemed reduced by the years, but the pain of humiliation could make you wince long after its occurrence?

He'd only been thirteen at the time, and somehow the basketball coach had talked him into playing with the school team that season. He was no athlete, and everyone knew it. He was the only kid on the team who wore glasses guards.

He was playing in a game late in the season when, during the last tense moments of a tied score, he managed to make a beautiful basket—for the other team. No one would talk to him in the locker room afterward, and the only conversation directed toward him at the after-game party was in the form of taunts.

The party was held at one of the player's houses, a beautiful ranch-style home with an indoor swimming pool. Everyone went swimming, and two of his teammates tackled him in the pool, leaving him trunkless. There was no way he could get out of the pool in that condition, but no one seemed to care.

Katy was there. Twelve years old, new to public school after years in Mennonite classrooms, and every bit as gawky as he was. She was trying hard to fit in with the popular crowd, even smoking a couple of cigarettes that night. She had been nice to him during the previous few months, and so when she walked past him on the side of the pool, he asked her if she would get him a towel. She glanced in his direction, a haughty look of scorn on her face, and turned her back on him to talk with another boy.

It was Rachel who eventually rescued him. She'd been in another part of the house, and when she finally entered the pool room and discovered what had happened, she quietly brought him a towel. Later he overheard her calling the two boys who had taken his trunks "inconsiderate, weasel-brained pigs."

He and Katy had never talked about that day. Probably she had forgotten about it. After all, it had not been her humiliation. And he had forgiven her. He preached forgiveness; he'd had to learn to live it as well.

But forgetting was harder, and there were still times when he would look at his wife and remember the expression on her face that day when she turned her back on him.

With three churches so close together, parking was a problem. Rachel found a place on the side street by the bakery and walked the two blocks to the Mennonite church. She set a quick pace, trying to mask her anxiety. There were other people on the street, and she was certain they were eyeing her.

She felt like a fake, as if everyone could tell that she was not a regular churchgoer. She attended Unitarian services once in a while, but church was certainly not a large part of her life. She remembered Michael talking about how much prayer meant to him. She'd prayed when Phil was sick, although she was not certain to whom or what. But the praying itself was a comfort. It was something to do, giving her some control in a situation where she had very little. She could not say, though, that she possessed faith. She envied the solace Michael had found in his faith after Luke and the children died.

She had almost reached the front door of the church when she heard someone call her name, and she turned to see Lily Jackson walking toward her. Next to her was a tall, slender man, his dark hair pulled back into a ponytail. Lily's magician husband, no doubt.

"Hi, Lily," she said, relieved to find a familiar, welcoming face. People definitely had their eyes on her, either because she was a stranger to the church or because they recognized her. It didn't matter. Lily was obviously taking her under her wing.

"Come sit with us," Lily said.

"I'd like that. Thank you."

"This is my husband, Ian. Ian, Rachel."

"Ah, the lady with the boxer!" Ian grinned at her, and she grinned back, liking him immediately.

"That's right." She shook his hand.

"That's the way Lily identifies people," he said. "You could have told her you won a Pulitzer or were a mud wrestler or met your husband on top of Pike's Peak, and all she'd remember is what kind of dog you have."

Lily gave him a mock roll of her eyes and took Rachel's arm. "Have you been to a Mennonite service before?" she asked, walking with her through the open doorway.

Rachel shook her head and lowered her voice to a whisper. "My first time," she said.

They found seats in a pew about halfway to the front, and Lily sat between Rachel and Ian. Rachel glanced at the program one of the ushers had given her. Lots of hymns, a few committee reports, and then the sermon, to be delivered by "Michael."

She whispered to Lily. "Just 'Michael'? No 'Reverend'? No last name?"

Lily smiled. "No reverends here," she said. "This is probably going to be less formal than you're used to."

It was. Less formal even than a Unitarian service, with its chalice lighting and subtle rituals. The church itself, with its white walls and dark beams, was quite plain. There were no icons or adornments, no stained glass. The service began with several hymns, all sung a capella. None of them were familiar, but she muddled through them anyway, aware of Lily's high, clear voice next to her. After the singing, a tall, dark-haired woman took the microphone and talked a little about Rwanda.

"Celine Humphrey," Lily whispered to her. "She's one of the elders."

Rachel thought she remembered Michael mentioning the woman's name. The Mennonite Central Committee was planning to send supplies and volunteers to the refugee camps, Celine said. She asked people to put together layettes and health kits, and to gather old blankets and clothing.

When Celine had finished speaking, a man dressed in khaki pants and a blue short-sleeved shirt spoke at length about the Peace Tax Fund. Then a teenage girl took the microphone and talked about her youth group's trip to Bolivia. While the girl was talking, Rachel noticed Michael sitting in a chair a short distance from the pulpit. How long had he been there? She could not see him clearly from where she sat, but it looked as if he were wearing a shirt and jacket. No tie. Certainly no clerical robes.

He suddenly laughed along with the congregation at something the girl said, and Rachel tried to return her concentration to the service, but it was difficult. She had not told him she'd be here, and she wasn't sure if her presence would please him or not.

There was another set of hymns, after which Celine Humphrey read from the Bible. Finally, Michael rose from his seat and stepped up to the pulpit.

"No robes?" she whispered to Lily.

Lily smiled. "Uh-uh."

"Just one of the guys, huh?"

"You got it."

But he was not just one of the guys, and that was quickly apparent. He began by telling a story, and she recalled the last time she'd heard that deft, open, engaging quality in his voice, that quiet dynamism. It was the same voice he'd used to deliver his conscientious-objector speech on the steps of Town Hall. He would never shake the rafters with that voice, but he didn't need to. It was the only sound in the church.

He was talking about communication, and he told a parable of a young man who bought a suit for his wedding, discovering only the night before the ceremony that the pants legs were three inches too long. Heartsick, he realized he had no choice but to wear the pants legs rolled up at his wedding, and he went to bed discouraged. His grandmother couldn't sleep, thinking of her grandson's dilemma, and in the middle of the night she got up, cut three inches from the pants, and hemmed them. His mother, equally concerned, got up an hour later to do the same thing, and shortly before dawn, his sister did likewise.

Michael drew the story out, working his audience like a master comedian. Lily giggled, and Rachel could see smiles on the faces around her as Michael finished his tale.

"A little communication would have saved the groom a wealth of embarrassment," he said. And then he immediately dove into another story, and this one Rachel knew well.

"When I was twenty-two years old and working in Rwanda, I was excited about learning Kinyarwanda, the language spoken in the village where I was teaching. I thought I was doing pretty well with it. I was even dreaming in Kinyarwanda. But sometimes words alone aren't enough for meaningful communication."

Rachel knew what he was going to say, and she didn't want to hear it. She tightened her grip on the program in her lap.

"One night, very late, a man I'd never seen before came to my home. He said to me in Kinyarwanda, 'You have a car. You can take me to Kilgari. I need to go there.' Kilgari was the nearest large town, quite a distance away."

It was three hours away, Michael. Tell them it was three hours away.

"I did have a car," Michael continued. "A very beat-up old Jeep I'd bought for fifty dollars. I had no desire to drive this stranger into town in the dead of night. I told him he'd have to wait a few days until I made a trip into town. Then he could come with me. I loved being able to say all that in Kinyarwanda, and I began talking to him about other things. The village, the children. I kept on talking, playing with my new language, my new toy. I would have said I was communicating quite beautifully in this man's native tongue, and I was feeling very smug about it. But I didn't understand the culture yet. I didn't realize that these people were too polite to interrupt me, and I went on for about an hour and a half, until finally a friend came over."

Rachel bit her lip. She had been that friend.

"I loved an audience then as much as I do now, and I continued my one-sided conversation with the gentleman who wanted to go to Kilgari. Finally, my friend noticed something I had missed. She said to me in English, 'Something is very wrong here. Look at his eyes.' I looked at the man's eyes then and saw what she had seen. There was a tear in the corner of his eye. Suddenly, I could see everything. He was bursting with grief and anxiety. It had been there all along, but I was too busy talking to listen to the signals he was giving me. And I asked him, 'What is it? Why are you unhappy?' And then he told me. 'My wife is dying,' he said, 'I brought her here. She's behind your house. I need to get her to the clinic in Kilgari, but you won't take me. You just want to talk.' 'Why didn't you tell me?' I asked, but I knew he had been trying to tell me all along. I was hearing him, but I wasn't truly listening."

He went on to describe the terrible middle-of-the-black-night trip to the clinic and the woman's brush with death. And then, suddenly, he was talking about the Bible. Reading it was not enough, he said. Unless you really *listened* to Scripture, you would not be able to understand it. He continued, talking about communication with God, but Rachel could not concentrate on what he was saying. She was still in Rwanda, sitting in the back of his Jeep, surrounded by three people in anguish: the feverish woman whose head she held on her lap, the husband awash with his feelings of helplessness, and Michael, quietly blaming himself for the woman's deteriorating condition.

When Michael had finished, he took his seat again and another hymn was sung.

Then Lily whispered to her. "They're going to pass the micro-phone now, and people will get up and talk about something good—or bad—that's happening in their lives. It's also the time that new people can introduce themselves."

Rachel widened her eyes at her. She wanted to ask, "Do I have to?" but Lily had already turned her head away.

A woman near them stood up and accepted the microphone from the usher.

"I wanted to thank everyone for their support last week after Patricia's accident." Heads nodded, and the woman continued. "She's doing real well now, and the doctor says she'll be home sometime this week."

The woman sat down again, and the microphone was passed to two more people while Rachel fretted over what to do. She did not want to draw attention to herself. *You did nothing wrong,* she thought. *Stop acting as if you did.*

She stood up. The usher walked toward her pew and handed her the microphone.

"I'm Rachel Huber," she said, and she caught sight of Michael's look of surprise, followed by his smile. "I'm visiting your church today, and I've enjoyed being here very much."

She sat down again, trying not to read anything into the silence as the microphone was passed to a man on the other side of the aisle.

In front of the church after the service, she parted from Lily and Ian and approached Michael, who was standing by the front door, greeting his parishioners. He reached his hand toward her, and she shook it.

"Why didn't you tell me you were coming?" he asked.

"Didn't know until I got up this morning. It was impulsive. You were wonderful," she said. "So human. Nothing like the ministers I've known in my life."

She realized she was still holding his hand, and she let go.

"And you had guts introducing yourself like that. I'm glad to see you haven't lost your pride." He waved to someone standing behind her. "I want you to meet Celine," he said.

The dark-haired woman walked up to them, accompanied by a much older man.

"These are two of the church elders," Michael said. "Celine Humphrey and Lewis Klock. Lewis and Celine, this is Rachel Huber."

"Hello." Rachel shook their hands. The eyes of the gray-haired man were kind and affable. She remembered his name from her conversation with Michael in the park. He was the elder who had influenced him to become a minister.

"Rachel and I were in Rwanda together," Michael said.

"Oh, yes." Celine appraised her. Her eyes were as cool as Lewis's were warm. "Michael mentioned you might want to help us when we get rolling with the supplies?"

"Yes, I would."

"Well, give me a call in a couple of weeks. We should have some work for you then, if you're still interested."

"Thanks. I'd like that." Rachel wondered if Celine treated everyone with that air of indifference or if her coolness was intended for her alone.

A few other people began approaching Michael, reaching out to shake his hand, and she thought she'd better leave.

"I need to get back to Gram," she told him. "See you tonight?"

"Around six." He flashed her a quick smile as he reached for the hand of one of his parishioners, and as Rachel turned away, she could not miss the raised eyebrows, the look of curiosity, on Celine Humphrey's face.

By the time Michael brought his purple-and-teal bicycle over to Gram's, Rachel was dressed in her serious bike shorts and ready for a ride. They left Gram contentedly reading in the library and rode cautiously down Winter Hill and out into the countryside. They kept to the back roads, where farmland surrounded them and the hum of their tires and the buzz of cicadas were the only sounds.

They were well matched, Rachel thought. Michael was in the lead, and their pace was smooth and steady. After an hour, they stopped at a shaded picnic table along the side of the road and unpacked their food.

Michael had brought along a loaf of potato bread made by someone from his church and a wedge of cheese; she'd brought peaches and bottled water. After taking the food from his knapsack, Michael pulled out a camera and handed it to her. "Better take some pictures before it gets too dark," he said. "We can develop them in the high school darkroom in a few days."

She took the camera from him and stood on top of the picnic table, snapping the shutter at silos and barns, cows in a pasture, a lone, twisted oak in the field nearby. Michael offered advice on composition, and she tried to hold his words in her memory so she would be able to pass them along to her students.

She sat down after a few minutes and leveled the camera across the table at him. He smiled tolerantly as she snapped away. His face was cast in light and shadow, the line of his jaw sharp. Splinters of gold flickered in his hazel eyes, and she tried to imagine what those eyes would look like in the finished black-and-white photograph. She suddenly felt very impatient to see it.

She set down the camera and cut another slice of bread. "I love riding on these country roads," she said.

Michael swallowed a bite of his peach. "Me, too. I wish I could get Jace to ride with me, but he has zero interest. And Katy doesn't even own a bike. Did you and Phil ride together?"

The question saddened her. "A little," she said. "Before he got sick. But not in recent years." In the last few years she'd ridden alone, welcoming the solitude. Those outings had been her only escape from the pall of illness that had settled over their house. "I liked to go out on my own and just ride. See where I ended up."

"You were always the one with wanderlust when we were kids." Michael set the blade of the knife on top of the cheese and cut off a slice. "You'd read about places you wanted to go and dream up ways to get there."

"Yeah, and I finally got just about everywhere I wanted to go. We did a lot of traveling before Phil got sick. The only place I haven't been where I'm still longing to go is Norway."

He stopped the slice of cheese halfway to his mouth. "You're kidding," he said. "That's where I want to go."

"No." She eyed him with mock doubt.

"Really. I saw this poster one time in—"

"Of the fjords? And a little village?"

"*Yes*. How did you know?"

"Because it's probably the same poster that made *me* want to go there." She laughed. "It's on the ceiling in my dentist's office, and I stare at it while he's drilling away, wishing I were there."

"It's hanging on the wall of Lewis Klock's study." He shook his head. "There's something about that picture that draws you in. That's the mark of excellent photography, I think. The picture should tug at you."

"I'll tell that to my kids." She cut a sliver of cheese from the wedge. "How about you?" she asked. "Have you gotten to travel much?"

"Barely at all. Our schedules don't lend themselves very well to travel."

"Phil and I were lucky, having the summers and holidays off. Plus, money was never a problem. Phil came into our marriage with a fortune inherited from his grandparents."

"Is that how you can afford to take a year off?"

"Yes, although there was such an obscene amount of money, I couldn't bring myself to keep it. I have enough for a good retirement and to get Chris through school. The rest I gave away."

"Gave away?"

"Donated. To the Leukemia Research Foundation and a few other charities." She'd enjoyed the process of picking and choosing the charities she'd wanted to help. "I talked to Chris about it first, to make sure he didn't feel cheated out of an inheritance. But Phil had left a good chunk to him directly, and Chris really shocked me. I honestly expected him to buy a car or something extravagant, but he put the better part of the money in savings and did what I did with the rest. Donated it." Chris had selected all animal-related charities. PETA. Friends of Poultry, or some such thing. He'd been a vegetarian since he was old enough to think for himself. "I was really proud of him," she said.

"You set the example."

"I guess."

"I did the same thing with the money my parents left me," Michael said. "Not that there was that much. But once I'd set some aside for Jace, I gave the rest to the church. To the relief fund." He smiled at her, a rueful expression on his face. "Oh, Rache," he said quietly. "I'm really getting scared."

The skin on her arms tingled at the tone of his voice. "Of what?"

"Of having you here." He touched the back of her hand, lightly, briefly. "Things were pretty intense between us once. I haven't forgotten that. And it's been wonderful, being able to talk with you again. So easy, like we've never been apart. We have so much history together." He began rolling one of the peaches around on the table with his palm. "And if our history were all we had in common, we'd probably be all right. But it seems as though we share some of the same interests *now*, in the present, as well. The same values. We both love biking. We both want to go to *Norway*, for heaven's sake. We both gave away our inheritances. We understand each other without even trying. We love each other, and we have since we were kids. At least I assume . . . ?"

She nodded. She was full of love for him.

"And it feels dangerous, that sort of . . . bond we have," he continued. "That intimacy. It's what I want to have with my wife, and I know that's impossible. I talked to Katy the other night, and when I told her you were in town, I felt as if I were admitting to some guilty little secret." He straightened his back with a sigh. "I touched on this when we talked yesterday at Helen's, but I think the problem's growing by the minute. What I'm trying to say is, that while I want us to be able to do some things together this summer, I feel a need for extreme caution." He looked at her, eyebrows raised, to see if she understood him.

She understood very well. "Tell me how I can help?"

"Just be patient with me, please. If I say I don't want to see you on a given day, or don't want to have to explain you to Jace, or whatever, please understand that it's not you, it's me."

"All right," she said. She thought back to seeing him at church that morning. "Did I make a mistake at church today when I said I'd see you tonight?"

He smiled again. "Well, you did prick up a few ears," he said.

"Sorry." She would have to be more careful.

Yet, as they put away the food and climbed back onto their bikes, she felt relieved that she was no longer alone in wanting someone she could not have.

12

Mayor Ursula Torwig sat in her small office on the second floor of the old Starr and Lieber Bank building and rested her eyes on Spring Willow Pond. She was spending more and more time these days sitting and staring at the pond, imagining how it would look when the two big office buildings went up. They would be sleek, glassy structures, and the reflection of the pond would play in their expansive array of windows. Just three stories high, nothing too big. She couldn't understand the fuss everyone was making about the buildings. Some people clung to the status quo, even when it meant their economic decline. She loved Reflection as much as the next person, maybe more. She loved it enough to try to make it the best it could be, and she was certain that someday people would get used to the change. People would come to view the development as the center of a prosperous small town. And her office would be on the third floor of one of the new buildings, instead of this crummy little borrowed space in the bank. She would have a view overlooking the pond.

The plans were spread out on her desk. She pulled them out at least once a day, unable to get enough of them. The curving streets, the hundred spanking new houses. The development would provide an enormous boost for the town's economy. She'd be remembered as the mayor who turned things around for Reflection.

Drew had said that to her once. She'd awakened to find him watching her, to feel his hand resting on her hip. "It's going to be great, Urs," he'd said. "Someday this town's going to thank you. They'll put a statue of you right next to ol' Pete's."

They were going to win. The opposition might have greater numbers, but she had most of the businesses and developers on her side, and they were far more powerful. Plus, they made up the board of supervisors. What did the opposition have? Some citizens, a few Amish farmers who wouldn't fight for themselves if their lives depended on it. She did not care about alienating the Amish. They didn't even vote.

She was surprised Michael had gotten into the fray, but then, her cousin had always been a thorn in her side. She'd heard him speak once. He'd been talking about how he came to be a minister, how he'd struggled to find answers to the many problems in his life, and she'd sat there seething. *Right, Michael, you had it so rough.* Her family had eaten pork and beans every night, while his ate steak off good china. He'd grown up in town, with his own bicycle, and his own car, and he'd had the know-how to keep himself out of Vietnam. *She'd* gotten up at four every morning to do the chores on her family's pig farm, coming home right after school to finish up. She'd feared that her clothes carried the smell of the farm around with her, and she'd been too embarrassed ever to have friends over to her house.

She'd worked hard in high school, knowing it was her only way out. Between chores and homework, she'd slept very little and played even less, but she'd graduated at the top of her class, two years behind her cousin. She'd attended the local college, all her family was able to afford even with the scholarships. And now she was mayor. The thought made her smile. *You've come a long way, baby.* She glanced over at the empty space above the pond and saw the glittering new building that would house her office.

Someday soon, she thought. Someday very soon.

13

Rachel was combing through the pile of Brussels sprouts in the produce section of the grocery store when she noticed the young man stocking the lettuce. She saw him in profile one moment, then nearly head-on as he reached into the carton at his side. He was close to thirty, she guessed, with thick, dark blond hair, cut short except for a small wisp of a tail at the back of his neck, like Chris's. He had handsome features—high cheekbones, straight nose, strong chin—except for one thing: his face was lined by a patchwork of scars that cut across his cheek, down his chin, above his eye. Her hand froze above the Brussels sprouts as she stared at him. The poor man. Had he been in an accident? Or—her heartbeat quickened at the sudden distressing thought—could he possibly have been in her classroom?

He glanced up at her, and she quickly returned her eyes to her task, embarrassed she'd been caught staring. People must stare at him all the time. Children must worriedly ask their parents if the same thing might happen to them. What a burden to carry that face, so unabashedly handsome beneath the cobweb of scars.

She finished gathering her produce, aware every minute of the young man's presence. Suddenly, he looked at her again, a head of romaine in his hand.

"You're Rachel Huber, aren't you," he said.

"Yes," she answered, and then she knew for certain where he had gotten those scars. She clenched her hands around the handle of her grocery cart. "Were you in my class at Spring Willow?"

"Do you need to ask?"

She reached out to touch his hand. "I'm so sorry," she said, as he pulled his hand away from hers. "So terribly sorry."

He set the romaine on the pile of lettuce and began cutting open another carton. "I was one of the lucky ones, so they tell me," he said. "Seems like you were actually the lucky one, though, huh? Conveniently out of the room when it happened?"

"What's your name?"

"Kenneth Biers."

"Kenneth. If there were some way I could go back and change that day, I'd give up the rest of my life to do it." She was not lying. Her eyes burned with the truth behind the words. She wished there were some way she could have that chance.

He smiled a smile that said he did not believe her.

"If there's ever any way I can help you, please let me know." She could hear the emptiness in that offer and was not surprised by his derisive snort as he shook his head and returned to his work. For the first time, she regretted having given Phil's money away. It could have been used here, to help people like this young man.

Slowly, she pushed her cart away from the produce section and started down the dairy aisle. She was clinging to the cart, her knees rubbery, and the edges of her vision blackened briefly. This must be how Gram feels half the time, she thought to herself. Weak-kneed and dazed. She could not faint here, could not draw that attention to herself. "I'm sorry," she said again, to the air. *It wasn't my fault*, she wanted to say. She'd been a victim, too.

She finished her shopping with a wooden concentration, considering all the while the possibility of returning to the produce section and talking again with Kenneth. She turned her cart in that direction a few times but couldn't make herself go to him. What could she say? She was afraid to see his face close up, to feel what the mother of that young man must feel each time she set eyes on him. His mother must relish having someone to blame.

Once outside the store, Rachel unloaded her groceries, all the while imagining that the few people in the parking lot were staring at her. She was getting paranoid. She drove out of the lot, but instead of turning onto Farmhouse Road toward her grandmother's house, she turned right, toward town. She drove resolutely into the heart of Reflection, parked her car in front of the library, and in spite of the perishables in her trunk, walked over to the small circular park in the center of town, across the street from Huber Pond.

The park was deserted, and she felt an odd relief as the oaks and maples and birch trees closed behind her, making her less visible to the rest of the world. Yet she knew it was not relief this park had to offer her. As she slowly walked among the trees, she counted the weeping cherries, not stopping until she'd found all ten of them. At the tenth, she turned in a circle, her eyes searching for the stone memorial that had to be nearby. There it was, a sloping, symmetrical arc of fieldstone. She walked toward it slowly. Bouquets of cut flowers, some dried and dying, others fresh as though someone had brought them only minutes earlier, had been propped up against the memorial. At the peak of the stone arc was a bronze plaque.

In Remembrance of the Ten Children of Reflection Lost to Us on
September 10, 1973
That We May Never Forget

A list of the children's names followed: William Albrecht, Fredric Cash, Ruth Kitchin, Annie Paris, Patrice Rader, Jennifer Wright, Julia Shouse, Gary Feldman, Jacob Geyer, and Thomas Pike.

A list of strangers, Rachel thought. Too many names over the years. And these ten. Had she even known when she'd fled town which children had died? She could not remember. But she had to remember.

She straightened one of the bouquets of flowers that had fallen onto its side, then took a seat on a nearby bench.

She had been twenty-three years old when she returned home from the Peace Corps, leaving Michael behind her in Rwanda. She interviewed for several jobs and was offered the position at Spring Willow Elementary. Then she found an apartment and her father spent the weekend before Luke was to arrive helping her move her things from the old triplex into the even older one-bedroom apartment. Her mother talked to her about Luke, about how excited she must be to see him after all this time, and her father joked about how no one would bother them for a full week. Longer, if they liked.

"You kids just get to know each other again," he said. "We'll have plenty of time to spend with you later." She loved him for his understanding, but she could not explain to him that it didn't seem to matter to her. She could not rid her mind of thoughts of Michael, of her last memory of him, his hand cradling her bare breast. She couldn't tell her parents that she felt no longing to spend time alone with her husband, that she wished with all her heart that she did.

She met Luke in the Harrisburg airport, and he hugged her hard. He was still handsome, although his body had changed. He looked thinner, but when she embraced him she felt the hardness of him beneath her arms, as though all softness had left his body and the muscle that remained had grown taut and tight. He felt like a stranger, but he whispered into her ear as he hugged her, "Beautiful lady," and that sounded like the Luke she knew.

He was protective of his luggage, checking the bags, wanting to be sure he left nothing behind. He carried three pieces, she carried two as they walked out to the car, and when she set one of the suitcases down to fumble in her pocket for the parking ticket, he grabbed her arm.

"Keep your eye on it!" he snapped, pointing to the suitcase. The bag was so close to her, it almost rested against her leg, and she knew then that the Luke who had left her a year earlier was not the Luke who had returned. He seemed as angry, as tightly wired, as he had been during their painful week-long visit in San Francisco. Maybe worse.

He was quiet in the car.

"Are you tired?" she asked, wondering if that was the reason for his silence.

"Not really." He was looking out the window, watching Pennsylvania roll by, and the silence mounted between them.

This was ridiculous. Her oldest friend, and she could think of nothing to say to him.

"I've missed you," she tried, although it was not quite the truth.

"You, too." He smiled at her, but it was a quick smile. Forced.

What could she say? She could not begin to sum up her experience of the past year any better than he could his. Focus on the present, she told herself.

"I think you'll like the apartment," she said.

He turned to look at a passing motorcycle. "Sure," he said.

Another few minutes passed.

"Everyone's looking forward to seeing you," she tried.

He let out a short, disdainful laugh, and she looked at him in confusion.

"Everyone's so protected here, you know?" he asked. "I mean, it's a shitty world out there, and I've seen the most fucked-up parts of it."

She tightened her hands on the steering wheel, unaccustomed to hearing Luke swear.

"Reflection kind of feels like Disneyland to me now," he said. "You grew up your whole life here, like I did. You can't know what kind of fucking shit there is in the world when you're—"

"I just spent a year in an impoverished, destitute region in Africa, Luke." She felt angry, patronized. "I know it wasn't like what you had to go through, I know I wasn't in that kind of danger, but please don't talk to me like I've been living in an ivory tower."

He pounded a fist on the dashboard. "Pull this damn car over to the side of the road."

"What? Luke—"

"Pull it the fuck over!"

She quickly put on her turn signal and slipped as carefully as she could out of traffic and onto the shoulder.

"Turn it off."

Her fingers shook as she turned the key in the ignition.

"You don't have any fucking idea what I'm talking about, do you?" he said. "Fine. You've been in Rwanda. You've seen people suffer. But did you kill anyone, huh?" He grabbed her arm, tugging her toward him. "Huh? Did you? Did you watch your buddies get blown away? Watch their legs fly off? Feel one of their bloody, unattached hands whack you in the face?"

She shook her head. She felt sick. Her arm hurt where he was squeezing it.

"Well, then, let me tell you, girl. You were in the Garden of Eden compared to where I was." He let go of her and sat back in the seat, pointing ahead of them on the road. "Let's go," he said.

But she couldn't move. She was crying, hugging herself, her arms across her chest. She raised one hand, touched him tentatively on his forearm. "Luke, I don't want to start out like this. This is supposed to be a happy time, seeing each other after so long, finally getting to live together."

His face was red, and he slumped down in the seat. "I'm sorry," he said, but he didn't look at her. He pulled his arm from under her hand to scratch his head. "You've got to expect this. You can't expect me to come home after what's happened and be like I was when I left."

He looked at her now, and she thought she detected a trace of the man she'd known for so long.

"It helped me while I was in 'Nam and at Fort Myer to know I had you back home," he said. "To know we'd gotten married, that I had a wife. That I could come home and we could start a family and maybe be normal." He swallowed, his Adam's apple bobbing in his throat. "That's all I want now, Rachel. To have a normal life. I used to think that sounded boring. Now it sounds better than anything else."

"We'll have it." She leaned toward him, kissed him. His eyes glistened, and she felt the old, welcome love lift her up. She put her arms around him. "People will admire us for our normality," she said.

He smiled at that, an old Luke smile. "Take me to Pennsylvania Dutch country, Rachel," he said. "Take me home."

There were moments in the next few weeks when she caught glimpses of the boy she'd grown up with, the boy she'd loved as a brother, as a friend, as a man and a lover, but they were too few to ease her mind, and too weak to counterbalance the changes that were far more apparent in him. He had nightmares. He awakened nearly every night, sweat soaking the sheets, and she felt guilty that she had not paid the extra money it would have cost them for an air-conditioned apartment. She bought a window unit for the bedroom, but still the nightmares continued, the damp, alarming awakenings, and she knew it was nothing as simple as the heat that was disturbing him. Sometimes he was crying when he woke up in the middle of the night, sometimes he was yelling, words Rachel could not understand. Once their landlord called to complain about the noise, and Rachel knew that normality was a long way off.

He was rough when he made love. She'd had no other lover, ever, and she had treasured the tenderness he'd always shown her as they'd learned to give each other pleasure. Now, though, he was fast, plowing into her as if he were angry with her. Sometimes she felt as if he hated her. She began to wonder if he'd come to hate women in general. He referred to women on the street as "'bitches" or "cows." He told her about the prostitutes in Vietnam, or the women the soldiers would rape. He told her those things without judgment, and she could not be sure if he condoned them. He might even have been speaking about himself as one of those men, but she was too afraid of the answer to ask him.

He had weapons, and that was something else she couldn't ask him about. Had he bought them? Stolen them? She awakened in the middle of one air-conditioned night to find him sitting in the living room, dressed in his uniform, cleaning his rifle. He had the rifle, some grenades, a knife. He bought books on weapons, read them at meals. She was afraid, of what was happening to him and to their young marriage, but she was not afraid of Luke himself. Occasionally, he scared her when he yelled at her or grabbed her roughly, but she had known him too long, too intimately, to truly fear him. Even when she saw him lovingly working on his rifle, she only tiptoed back to bed, confused and worried but not concerned for her physical safety. Slowly, though, the love she had felt for him over the years was turning to pity.

He needed help. That was clear, but he refused to seek it. She called the military counselor at Fort Myer, who said they'd had no problems with Luke down there. He gave her the name of a psychiatrist in Lancaster and encouraged her to get Luke to see the man, but Luke's resistance was strong. He had no problems, he said.

The one person Rachel needed right then was Michael. Not for herself—she would put her own need for him aside. She needed him for Luke. Together they could help him. The three of them had been there for one another all their lives. As September neared she toyed with the idea of somehow getting in touch with him. Maybe he could get to a phone. Maybe he could even come home. Surely this situation was akin to a family emergency. Luke needed his old friend. And she needed Michael to see what was going on, to tell her she was not going crazy. She could no longer judge what was appropriate behavior and what was not. She would not recognize normality if she saw it.

But she held back from trying to get word to Michael and was quickly swept up into her new teaching job. Luke himself was unemployed, although he looked for work almost daily. He had his own degree in teaching, but it was September and schools weren't hiring.

During Rachel's first week at Spring Willow, Luke appeared at the school twice. Once she didn't even know he was there. She learned later that he had simply roamed through the halls dressed in camouflage, saluting anyone, child or adult, who crossed his path. The second time, he came to her classroom and loudly offered to tell her students about life in battle. The children were wide-eyed at the sight of a real soldier in their midst. The boys were wild with questions; the girls—with the notable exception of Lily Wright—were shy in their awe.

"You have to leave, Luke," Rachel told him.

"But they want to talk with me, don't you, kids?" he said, and he was right. Frightened or fascinated, they were captivated by the presence of the handsome soldier.

"We'll have you come back when there's more time," she bargained. "Right now we're in the middle of a lesson."

She finally got him to leave with that ruse, but she knew this couldn't continue. She put in a call to the psychiatrist, setting up an appointment for Luke for the following Thursday. She didn't know how she would get him there, but she knew there was no alternative. Clearly, he had to go.

The following day, a Friday, Jacob Holt called her into his office. The principal was ordinarily a kind man whom she had liked very much during her interview. He had become principal the year after she'd left Spring Willow Elementary as a student, so he'd been there for quite a while by then. She was not aware of how stern he could be, but she didn't blame him at all for his concern. She shared it.

"If your husband comes on school grounds again," he said, "I'll have to call the police."

She could not bear the thought of humiliating Luke by having him carted away by the police. It was unthinkable. Surely things weren't *that* bad. "It won't happen again," she said. It was Friday; she had the entire weekend to work on Luke, to persuade him to take the appointment she'd made for him the following week. "I promise you he won't show up here again."

Luke was not home when she arrived at the apartment that afternoon. She was afraid he was at the local bar where he'd been spending too many afternoons lately. She got the mail from the mailbox—one letter, the handwriting unmistakable. Michael. She did not even go up to the apartment before sitting down on the steps to read it.

Dear Rachel,

I'm writing to tell you that Katy and I were married on Saturday. I know that must be a shock to you; I'm still a little shocked myself. I love you very much—too much—and I will always cherish the time we had here together, but you and I both know nothing can ever come of it. I will be honest with you and only you—I am marrying Katy to forget you. She is staying on here with me for a while. Quarters are tight as you know, but we'll manage. I hope one day you and I can sit together and reminisce about Rwanda without any sadness or regret. And I hope you and Luke are finding your happily-ever-after. I love you, Rachel.

Michael

The letter burned her fingers. She set it on her knees and stared into space, aching with loneliness. Something made her turn her head to the right, and she spotted Luke walking up the street toward the apartment. Quickly she folded the letter and crammed it into her purse.

He was not drunk, but he had been drinking, and he wanted to make love. Or have sex. It no longer seemed like lovemaking to her, and all she could picture when he was inside her and she was enduring him, nothing more, was Michael touching Katy, kissing her, loving her. She cried when Luke fell into a sex-and-alcohol-induced sleep next to her. She wept loudly, knowing he would not wake up. She felt hatred toward him.

Saturday, she carefully planned her approach. "I made an appointment for *us* with the therapist in Lancaster," she said. "*We* need help."

Maybe if she made it sound as if she didn't think it was Luke who had the problem, he would go.

"You have to work," he said.

"I'll get a substitute."

"Don't bother," he said. "I'm not going. That's not the way I do things. No one in my family's ever gone to a shrink, and I'm not going to be the first one."

"No one in your family has ever been through what you've been through," she countered.

"I'm fine."

She studied her hands. "The principal called me in yesterday to tell me you can't come on school grounds any longer. All right? I could lose my job."

"I thought you wanted me to come talk to your kids about what it was like in 'Nam."

"Maybe later in the year," she lied. "Right now we have to placate Mr. Holt. Okay, Luke? Promise me you won't show up at school again?"

"If I could find a fucking job I'd be okay."

"I know."

They talked about his job search. He was still looking for a few hours each morning, but the time he started drinking seemed to be getting earlier each day. She did not dare confront him with that worry, and she tried to keep off his back for the rest of the day. It was easy. Her thoughts were still consumed by Michael's letter.

On Sunday she broached the subject of counseling again. She needed his commitment to go with her.

"For me," she said. "Please do it for me. *I* need to go. I'm having trouble adjusting to . . . things. For my sake, please come with me."

That tack seemed to work. He finally agreed, and she knew that Luke still cared about her, still wanted things to work out between them. She relaxed after he made the agreement, and they enjoyed that afternoon in a way they'd enjoyed nothing in a long time. They put air in the tires of their old bicycles and rode out into the countryside. They had a picnic on Winter Hill.

When they arrived home, she took a long bath while he went to the grocery store. At least she thought he was at the store. She was getting out of the tub when she realized he would have had to go into her purse to get the car keys, and she was trembling as she opened the bathroom door.

He was sitting in their bedroom, waiting for her, the letter balled up in his fist. She had a towel wrapped around herself, and she pulled it tighter.

"What happened with you and Michael in Rwanda?" he asked.

She started for the closet and her robe, but he was up instantly, grabbing her arm, twisting it behind her until she cried out.

"What happened?" he growled, his face close to hers.

"Nothing!" She tried to wrench her arm free, but he held it fast, forcing her to the edge of the bed.

"This letter doesn't sound like nothing. He says he loves you, the fucking bastard."

"He means as a friend, Luke. He—"

Luke smacked her across the side of her face with the back of his hand, and she fell to her elbows on the mattress.

"Tell me," he said. His hand rested hard on her chest, inches from her throat. She could feel her heart pounding, squeezed between the mattress and his palm.

"Luke, honestly, there isn't anything to tell. We were close friends when we went—you know that, you know all three of us have been very close all our lives—so that's all it was. We got to be even better friends, but that's all—"

"You fucked him."

"No, I did not. We did not. I never touched him."

"Lying bitch." Luke held her down with one hand and undid his belt buckle with the other, unzipped his fly. "I'm gonna fuck that coward right out of you," he said. He pushed the towel above her hips and wedged himself between her legs. Her flesh resisted him for a brief second before he forced his way into her. She choked with the pain, digging her nails into his shoulders with each dry, wrenching movement of his body, and she was relieved when he came quickly.

He was sobbing, holding on to her, and she was surprised by her own reaction. She wept for him, no longer afraid. She clutched him to her, stroking his hair. Somewhere inside him was the boy who had been her best friend. He was still in there. He had to be. What had happened to him was not his fault. With help, the old Luke would reappear. Thursday. Her hopes were pinned on Thursday.

"It'll be all right," she whispered to him, but her voice seemed to snap him back to his anger.

He leaped up from the bed. "*What* will be all right?" he asked, a look of suspicion, of paranoia on his face that sent a cold chill up her arms. Suddenly she knew she had to get away from him.

She stood up slowly, beginning to dress as she spoke. "Everything," she said, reaching in her dresser drawer for her underwear. "Thursday we'll go to the counselor and—"

"And you'll lie to him like you're lying to me. You have to tell the truth in those places, Rachel. You have to tell what really happened with you and my onetime best friend."

She pulled on her jeans and T-shirt before speaking again. "I'm going to my parents for the night," she said carefully, pulling a small overnight case from the top shelf of the closet.

"What the hell are you talking about?"

"I think we need to be apart tonight. We're both very upset, and I think it would be good if—"

Luke picked up the crumpled letter from the floor, stretched it open and began to read. " 'I love you very much,' " he read, " '*too* much' . . . I am marrying pig-faced Katy to forget you." He looked up at Rachel, the rage reddening his cheeks once again, and she quickly threw her makeup bag into the overnight case and closed it up. "Does that sound like an innocent man to you?" he asked. "You expect me to believe that he was in love with you for a full year and didn't touch you? I'm going to kill that bastard, that's what I'm going to do. I'm going to blow his fucking dick off and then put a bullet in his brain."

She left the room, and he didn't try to stop her. But she heard him call down the hallway, "And then I'm coming after you, Rachel!"

She was sick in the car, retching, but her stomach was empty and nothing came up. In the rearview mirror she could see the red welt on her cheek where he'd hit her, and her arm and shoulder ached from being twisted. She took a minute to rummage through her overnight case for some concealer, which she spread liberally on her cheek.

When she reached her parents' house, she told them only that she and Luke had had a fight and she wanted time away from him. Her mother tried to counsel her about sticking by her husband, working it out instead of running away, but Rachel barely listened.

In the morning she spent twenty minutes working to conceal the bruise on her cheek. She'd heard about women whose husbands beat them up, but she never thought she would be one of them. Those men were brutes, though, not like Luke. On the dresser in her old bedroom was Luke's high school picture. Where had that beautiful, clear-eyed boy gone? Could he ever come back?

The eighteen seven-year-olds in her classroom were full of themselves that morning. Her seasoned colleagues had warned her about Mondays. The kids were wild, wound up from the weekend, and it took her a good half hour to get them settled down and working. Even then, little blond Lily Wright was up every few minutes, sharpening her pencil, asking to use the rest room, trying to engage her classmates in conversation. On the other side of the room sat her dark-haired twin, Jenny, working quietly. She would probably be Rachel's best student. She had to remind herself these two were related. After Lily got out of her seat for the fourth time, wandering over to the pencil sharpener with her already sharp pencil, Rachel called her over to her desk.

The girl stood in front of her with innocent eyes.

"It's hard for you to sit still sometimes, Lily, isn't it?" Rachel asked.

"I don't know what you mean," the girl said.

Rachel sighed. She glanced at the clock. Ten-thirty. In a half hour, she could take a break. She'd call Luke, make sure he was all right.

"There are rules in this classroom, Lily," she said. "I think it's especially hard for you to stay in your seat, and I understand that, but you still have to stay there. It's a rule."

"But I need to sharpen my pencil."

Rachel looked past the little girl, through the window and out to the street, and what she saw struck horror in her heart. Luke was crossing the street toward the school. He was dressed in camouflage, which only made him stand out more than he would have otherwise, and his rifle was strapped to his shoulder. He was clutching something small close to his chest, and her first panicky thought was that he was carrying one of his prized grenades.

She stood up suddenly, startling Lily, who jumped away from her as if expecting to be hit.

Was he planning to hurt her? Scare her? Just talk to her? Or was this simply another of his unscheduled visits to the school, the visit that would cause Jacob Holt to call the police? She hoped the principal couldn't see Luke's approach from his office window.

"Children!" She clapped her hands together. "Listen to me. This is very important. All of you need to find your favorite book, or something to color and your crayons, and go into the cloakroom." She pointed to the doorless opening of the cloakroom at the rear of the room. She would get the children out of sight. Keep them safe in there.

The children looked at each other without budging.

"It's a game," Rachel said. "Let's see who can get settled in there most quickly."

"Stupid game," Lily muttered to herself as she sauntered, slowly, back to her desk. Rachel had an urge to kick her.

"Come on, come on!" Her heart was starting to race. She could see Luke disappear around the far outside corner of the building.

The children caught her fever. They were up now, racing into the cloakroom, giggling, allowing the weekend wildness to reemerge. Lily was last to go. Rachel had to drag her by the arm, more roughly than she would have at any other time.

"On the floor!" she commanded them, and enjoying the weirdness of the situation now, they obeyed. "Open your books and read. Now stay here. I'll be right back."

She tried to keep her face calm, moving deliberately as she passed back through the classroom. She grabbed the key to her classroom and locked the door on her way out. But after she turned the key, it jammed, and she spent precious seconds struggling to remove it. At least, though, Luke would not be able to get into the room. With any luck, she would be able to intercept him before he even reached the building.

Which door would he come in? Surely he wouldn't want to go past the principal's office. She raced down the west hallway toward the back door of the school and pushed the double doors open in one forceful motion. Once outside, though, she couldn't see him anywhere. She ran around the side of the building, looking toward the street, toward the playground. All was still. *Oh, God, oh, God.* Where was he?

She ran into the building again and straight into the boys' room. Empty. Then she ran, breathless, back toward her classroom, the clicking of her shoes on the floor the only sound. But as she neared the turn in the hallway, she heard Luke's voice.

"Where is everybody?" he asked.

She thought she heard the deep boom of Jacob Holt's voice in reply, and just as she turned the corner, a blast filled the world with sound and silver light that threw her back against the wall.

But even from there, she could see that her classroom had been turned into a battlefield.

14

The parking lot for Hershey Park was crowded for a Monday night, but Michael managed to find a space close to the entrance. Rachel was quiet—she hadn't said more than ten words on the half-hour drive—but he could sense her astonishment, nevertheless.

"It's changed a bit, huh?" he asked.

"Mmm. Makes me sad."

He felt a bit sad himself. Being there made him miss Jason more than he already did. He loved seeing the park through his son's eyes.

They paid the entrance fee and walked through the gate.

"This part is new," Rachel eyed the little buildings of the Tudor village that made up the front portion of the park. "This used to be the picnic area, didn't it?"

"Uh-huh."

They walked slowly around the park, Michael pointing out the changes, trying to make a game out of remembering what ride used to be where, but Rachel did not seem to care.

"You're quiet tonight," he said finally, as they strolled around the carousel.

"Sorry. Yes," she said. "It was a hard day."

"Do you want to sit down for a while? Talk?"

She nodded, and he led her to a bench near the Mill Chute, far enough from the ride that they wouldn't get splashed by the cars spilling into the pool of water.

She slouched down on the bench, her legs straight out in front of her on the ground. "I went to the little park in the center of town today, where the memorial is," she said. "I'd seen a guy—a young man—in the grocery store with a scarred face, and I knew he must have been in my classroom."

"Ken Biers."

"Yes. I think it hit me graphically for the first time why so many people hate me."

"Hate's a strong word, Rachel," he said, although he knew the word accurately described the feelings of some of the town's citizens. He'd been pleased when Lily and a few others had treated Rachel kindly at yesterday's service.

"I ruined so many lives. If I hadn't been the teacher in that classroom, nothing would have happened." She looked up at the Mill Chute as if noticing it for the first time. "Mill Chute's different," she said.

"Yes." He touched the back of her hand. "Go on, Rache. Tell me about the park."

She drew in a breath. "Well, I forced myself to remember everything. I haven't really thought about it for so long. It's too overwhelming. It depressed me terribly, Michael. I feel like I'll never be able to lift myself up from these thoughts and feelings again." She looked at him. "It seems like people hold me personally responsible, as if I'd thrown the grenade instead of Luke."

Michael nodded as he listened. This was a conversation he'd been dreading but one he knew they needed to have. "You left town so quickly after it happened that you missed the aftermath," he said. "I don't blame you a bit for getting out as fast as you could, though. It was probably the only thing you could do. But it makes it hard for you to understand." He leaned forward, elbows on his knees. "See, everyone had their own idea of how you should have handled things differently. People didn't like the course of action you took. They said you left the kids like sitting ducks in that little cloakroom."

There was a deep line across Rachel's forehead, and she twisted her hands together in her lap. "I didn't really know what to do," she said. "I had all of about two seconds to figure it out—"

"I know." He pried her hands apart and held one of them on his thigh.

"I thought I was keeping them safe and out of sight back there."

"And I'm not saying that wasn't a smart thing to do. I'm just saying that when something like this happens, people step back and think to themselves, well, if only she would have done thus and such, the kids would be all right."

"Done *what?*" Rachel asked. "What could I have done differently?"

He hesitated before speaking again. "Well, some people said you should have sent one of your students to Holt's office to let him know what was happening while you stayed behind with the rest of the class. Others thought you should have gotten all the kids out of there. Taken them to another classroom. People were most upset that you left the children alone."

Rachel let go of his hand to knot hers together again. "I thought I could intercept him," she said.

"And if you had locked the classroom door when you left, that probably would have worked."

"I *did* lock it," Rachel said, "Only the key jammed and I guess the lock didn't catch. I thought it did. At least I tried to lock it."

"Trying doesn't count in the eyes of a bereaved parent," Michael said. He knew he was speaking harshly, but he wanted her to know, to truly understand. "And they don't believe you anyhow. No matter what you did, it wouldn't have been right, or enough. They needed a scapegoat, and you were it. Your leaving so abruptly made you look particularly guilty. And when Holt told everyone that you'd promised to have Luke committed the week before but didn't follow through with it, that was the final straw."

The line in her forehead deepened. "I don't know what you're talking about," she said. "I never told him I'd have Luke committed."

"Holt told everyone that he'd met with you and told you that Luke was a danger to the community and he was going to have him committed. He said you agreed that he was dangerous, but that you would take care of it yourself that weekend."

Rachel looked confused. "I never said I thought he was dangerous. I didn't think he was. I told Jacob Holt I'd keep Luke from coming on school grounds again, and I said I'd get him help, which I was planning to do. He said something about the police—" She shook her head, pressing her palms to her temples. "God, maybe I did say that. I don't remember it at all, but . . ." Her voice trailed off.

Michael watched a car full of screaming teenagers plunge into the water. Then he took her hand again, because he knew what he was about to say was going to hurt her. "I understand how people feel," he started, "because I loved you and I would have trusted you with my children completely, and yet even *I* wondered if you could have done something different that day."

She turned her head away from him.

"I'm sorry," he said.

"Well." She let out a long sigh of resignation. "Who are the others? Who else is still in town who was hurt by what happened? You said your friend's son was one of them?"

"Yes, Drew's son, Will." He shifted on the bench. "There's Arlena and Otto in the bakery, and Russell Martin over at the post office was one of the kids. So was Sarah Holland—she works in the bookstore, and she's also badly scarred. She and Ken look like products of the same syndrome."

"Oh, God." Rachel shook her head.

"Lily Jackson, who you've already met and who lost her sister. There's a woman who teaches the sixth grade at Spring Willow who was also one of the kids. Her family moved away right after it happened, but she came back a year or so ago because she felt that she never got to deal with it. She thinks that being here is the best way to confront her fears. Very courageous lady." Michael went on to talk about the parents of the children whose names were on the memorial. They were farmers, teachers, shop owners, and the groundskeeper for the park. A couple of them worked in the bank, another in the dry cleaners.

Rachel shook her head. "There are so many," she said.

"Yeah. And Reflection can't let go of it. The second Monday of each September is called Reflection Day," Michael continued. "It's set aside to remember what happened."

"You mean, it's an annual thing?" Rachel asked. "Still? After twenty-one years?"

He nodded. "Yes. Schools and shops are closed, and the youth groups in the different churches alternate taking responsibility for presenting some sort of memorial program for the community. They hold it in the high school auditorium."

"What kind of program?"

"Mostly readings. The kids read personal essays or poetry. On three themes, basically." He let go of her hand to count them off on his fingers. "How precious children are to a community; how they need to be treasured and protected. How insane war is. How it can turn the healthiest, most popular kid in a high school into a"—he picked his words carefully— "deeply disturbed individual."

"What's the third theme?" Rachel asked.

He pursed his lips. He should have told her there were only two. "The third theme is the responsibility of an individual to put the greater needs of the community above his or her own needs. "

"I don't get it," she said.

Michael sighed. "There are people who think you left your classroom to save your own skin, Rachel."

She pressed her fist to her mouth and looked toward the Mill Chute. For a second she didn't speak, then she folded her arms across her chest, hugging herself as if she were chilled. "What do you think?" she asked.

He touched her arm. "No," he said, "I've never thought that."

"What can I do? How do I begin to make it up to everyone?"

He shook his head. There was no way.

"If people would only talk to me," she said. "I'm not a monster."

"I know that, Rache."

She let out a short laugh. "And I thought I could pay everyone back with a little free tutoring. Wake up, Huber. Well." She pulled herself together, sat up straight. "I appreciate you telling me all of this. Everything makes a little more sense now."

"I'm in charge of the Reflection Day program this year," Michael said. He sounded confessional.

"You are?" There was a tone of surprised betrayal in her voice.

"Yes, and I'm glad it's my turn, because it's been too long, and I want it to end. I want the theme this year to be that this is the last . . . damned Reflection Day, and I'm going to try to make that a reality. "

She took his hand, her touch gentle yet electrifying.

"You want a lot for Reflection, don't you?" she asked quietly. "You want to heal all its wounds. You want to save it from physical destruction."

She was right. He adored his hometown. "I hope I have more success with ending Reflection Day than I'm having with stopping the developers," he said.

"It's not going well?"

"David against Goliath. We'll have to see."

Rachel made a derisive sound. "You know, I still don't understand how Marielle Hostetter came to have so much clout," she said. "She's the last person I would have expected to be able to wield power over Reflection."

"I know. Life's strange sometimes."

"Why doesn't someone talk to her directly?" she asked. "Doesn't she have a sense of loyalty to the town?"

"I've tried talking to her, believe me. She'll only communicate through her lawyer."

"I think it's worth another try. Maybe I could get through to her."

He laughed. "You?"

"Yes. I'm sort of an outsider. Maybe I won't put her on the defensive the way you or someone else who's intimately involved in the situation would. And her father and my grandfather were friends, Gram said. Maybe that would give me an in with her."

He squeezed her hand. "I know you'd like to find a way to help, Rache, but that won't work. She won't talk to you. It's hopeless." There might be some way to save Reflection from the bulldozers, but he was 100 percent certain that talking to Marielle Hostetter was not it.

They sat quietly for a moment. Rachel gently rested her head on his shoulder, and he cursed the pleasure her nearness gave him. He remembered seeing her in church the day before. What a rush of joy he'd felt, discovering she'd come to the place that meant so much to him. A second emotion, following close on the heels of the first, was fear for her. She seemed so vulnerable and brave when she stood to introduce herself. He'd felt love for her then. Love that went way beyond the love he was entitled to feel.

"Well, we're a fine duo." Rachel broke the silence. "Here we are at Hershey Park, practically crying on a bench. "

"You ready to have some fun?" he asked.

She nodded and stood up.

"Speaking of fun," Michael said as they began walking, "the Fun House is gone." He pointed to the spot where it had been. A new ride, the Falcon, stood in its place.

"Oh, the Fun House was the best," Rachel said.

He could see the three of them on that crazy floor, screaming, freeze-framed at different ages. Seven. Ten. Twelve. Fifteen. Eighteen. Their voices changing, needs changing, relationships changing, but always the three of them moving like a unit. The images made him sad.

"What about Laugh Land? Is it still here?"

He shook his head. "Liability. They can't have those walk-through things anymore."

"That place terrified me when I was a kid."

It had terrified him, too, with the dark narrow hallways that hid the jumping things, the hands that grabbed you when you least expected it, the cobwebs that hung over your cheeks, the floor that slipped out from under your feet. When they got older, though, the darkness had been an escape from the light outside. Luke had had a friend who worked at Laugh Land, and he'd told them about a door in one of the dark hallways. On the other side of that door had been a small black room where they could stay unnoticed for hours, making out, Luke and Rachel at it hot and heavy on the floor, Michael with whomever he had managed to talk into going out with him that night.

"Remember the dark room?" Rachel laughed, reading his thoughts.

"Very well." He smiled.

They went on only a few of the rides; their inner ears were not what they had once been, but it was fun. They were anonymous here, Michael thought. In two hours he had seen no one he knew; Rachel could be a woman without a past.

She stopped at one of the concessions to buy a T-shirt for her son. Michael waited on a bench, watching her. In his mind's eye, he still saw her as twenty-three, and it gave him a jolt to see her objectively, from a distance. She was a forty-four-year-old woman. He wasn't certain whether a passerby would consider her pretty. He only knew that when she turned her head, when she smiled at the cashier, he felt the same twist of longing he'd felt two decades earlier, watching her teach a class full of Rwandan students.

She laughed at something the cashier said, then glanced over her shoulder at Michael and waved. No, she wasn't pretty. She was beautiful. And he was in deep trouble.

She walked over to him and pulled the T-shirt from the bag to show him the design. He barely noticed the shirt. He wanted to touch her. He wanted the dark room in Laugh Land. So he put his hands in his pockets and began walking again.

"How's your stomach?" she asked, pointing toward the old roller coaster. "We forgot to ride the Comet."

He groaned at the sight of the huge wooden network of twists and turns. "Haven't been on it since I was a kid."

"Come on." She took his hand, and against his better judgment he allowed himself to be led over to the ride.

They settled into the first car. This was probably the only time they'd ever sat together on this ride, he thought. The cars were two-seaters; she would always have ridden with Luke.

They climbed up the track slowly, and then the turns and drops began without letup. The speed and force of the ride pressed their bodies together, and as far as Michael was concerned, the ride was over far too quickly.

He put his arm around her as the car slowed to a stop, and she let her head fall back on his shoulder. Her hair was sweet-smelling and soft against his cheek, and he suddenly knew he had to get away from her.

"That was great," Rachel said as she reluctantly climbed out of the car. She reached for his hand to help pull him out.

"Michael!"

He turned to see Sean Howe, one of the boys from the youth group, waving at him. Sean was walking with his mother, Mary, whose husband was a member of Michael's Friday night support group.

"Hey, Sean, Mary!" He let go of Rachel's hand and waved back, smiling but shaken, the memory of Rachel's body pressed against his own instantly exorcised. He was relieved when Sean and his mother made no move to stop and talk.

How was he going to handle being in that support group Friday night? He would probably sit there in silence. He could not possibly divulge to his fellow Mennonites what he was feeling these days, what he was struggling with. That had to remain between him and God—and right now he wasn't letting God in on much of it, either.

The wind stolen from his sails, he was glad it was not too early to suggest leaving. They walked out to the parking lot. He felt a little sick and knew the queasiness was caused by more than the rides. He was quiet in the car, relieved that Rachel seemed content to listen to the radio, her head against the back of the seat, eyes closed. They didn't speak at all during the drive to Helen's, but he could feel the lure of her next to him increasing with each passing mile.

He pulled into Helen's driveway and around to the rear of the house.

"Want to sit on the porch for a while?" she asked.

He looked at the porch, seductive in the moonlight, and shook his head. "I want to call Jace before he goes to bed." He couldn't look at her directly.

"Well, we'll see you and Jace tomorrow night?"

He nodded, wishing he had not already accepted the invitation for them to join Rachel and Helen for dinner on Jason's first night home.

He got out of the car and walked her up to the door.

"It was fun, Rache." He leaned over and pecked her lightly on the cheek.

She looked at him quizzically. He tried to smile, batting her chin teasingly with his fist.

"See you tomorrow," he said.

He knew she was watching him as he walked back to his car, and he could still see her face as he drove home through town, his entire body flooded with longing.

He was dreaming about Rachel and the dark room when the phone rang. Rachel had been sitting on the floor of the room, her face barely visible in the darkness, and she'd been reaching for him, touching his leg, his thigh. He fumbled, half asleep, for the receiver.

"Michael?"

It was Katy. He raised himself to one elbow. "Hi," he said.

"I'm sorry. I know it's the middle of the night there. I've just been feeling . . . oh, a little low, I guess, and I felt like talking to you."

It was not like Katy to admit to feeling "a little low," much less to want to talk about it. He sat up against the headboard, trying to push the dream from his head. "What's going on?" he asked. Was she crying? He couldn't tell. The sound was muffled by distance.

"Oh, not much. I just wanted to hear how you're doing."

"I'm all right." He realized guiltily that he didn't want to tell her what he had done tonight. *No good, Michael. No damn good.*

"I've been thinking about what you said." Katy's voice was definitely thick. Weepy. "You know, how we need to find a way to start fresh? I guess the only choice we have is with a marriage counselor. I hate the idea, but I don't know any other solution."

Michael saw Rachel as she'd appeared in his dream, reaching out to touch him. He shook his head to clear it.

"Michael? Are you still willing to do that when I get back?" Katy asked.

She was hurting. She wasn't saying it—she didn't have the skill to say it—but he had no doubt at all that it was pain he heard in her voice.

"Of course I'm willing," he said, although his heart no longer craved the resolution of their problems.

"Maybe I'm just homesick," she said. "Maybe I'll feel differently about this tomorrow. This trip is way too long. I miss Jace."

"He misses you, too. We'll call you when he gets home tomorrow." He noticed she did not say that she missed *him.* Or that she loved him. He wasn't surprised. Sometimes she could write those words in a card or a letter, but she had never once said them to him out loud.

"Tell him I can't wait to talk to him, all right?"

"All right." They said good-bye, and he hung up the phone. He stared at the ceiling, the dark room trying to creep back into his head. *No.* He had a wife, and he had a son who needed them both, needed them together. He had a reputation to protect, a congregation that had faith in him, a town that depended on him.

And so he could have Rachel only in his dreams.

15

The phone rang as Rachel was finishing her English muffin.

"Stay there." Gram stood up and reached for the wall phone. "I'm already done."

Gram was doing well, Rachel thought. In the last couple of days she was hobbling less, refusing to use the cane, and she seemed antsy, anxious to be up and active. She was doing her ankle exercises every spare minute, it seemed.

"Hello, Michael," Gram said into the phone, and Rachel was surprised at the relief she felt. She wasn't sure why Michael had become so distant toward the end of their time together the night before, but it had left an icy feeling in her bones. She'd felt so close to him last night, and she'd had a good time, at least after the initial hour of difficult conversation on the bench by the Mill Chute. She'd truly had fun, for the first time in too long.

She touched her napkin to her lips and rose from the table.

"Take it in the library," Gram said. "I can clean up here."

In the library, Rachel sat down on one of the big faux-leather wing chairs facing the window and drew the phone onto her knees. "Hi," she said, and she heard the click as her grandmother hung up in the kitchen.

"Hi. How're you doing this morning?"

"Good. I really enjoyed last night."

He was quiet a moment, still distant, and she bit her lip.

"I need to talk with you," he said finally.

"We can carve out some time when you and Jason come over tonight," she suggested. "Or would you rather stop by now?"

"No. Let's just talk on the phone. And part of the reason I'm calling is to tell you we can't come to dinner tonight. I'm really sorry. I hope that doesn't mess up your plans."

"Did something come up?"

"No. Nothing came up." He sighed. She could picture him running his hand through his hair. "Oh, Rache," he said. "I wish things were different."

"What do you mean?"

"I mean that last night was a mistake. I can't do that again. Go out with you. Be that close to you. The temptation's too strong. It's too risky. I think you and I are both dangerously needy right now."

She squeezed her eyes closed, knowing she had not helped matters any by holding his hand, putting her head on his shoulder. But that closeness had felt so good. "I think I understand," she said.

"And I want to spend some time with Jace, just the two of us. He's been gone so long."

"Of course."

"And one other thing," he continued. "I got a call from Katy in the middle of the night. If she'd asked me what I'd done last night, I probably would have lied to her. I don't lie. That's not me. I can't live that way. And I felt guilty when I saw that mother and son from my church."

"You don't have anything to feel guilty about. We haven't done a thing except share a friendship."

"I've done more than that in my mind," he said.

That made her smile. She only wished those thoughts did not cause him pain. "But doesn't it make you an even better person if you can have that sort of thought and not act on it?"

He laughed. At least she thought he did.

"No, I don't think that makes me a better person, Rache," he said. "Anyhow, Katy has been thinking about our marriage, apparently. I mean, really thinking about it for a change. She said she wanted to work on it, that she's willing to go to a counselor with me when she gets back." He sighed. "Déjà vu, huh? You and I have to be as saintly as we were in Rwanda, okay?"

"Okay." She spoke softly.

"The danger was there last night, wasn't it?" he asked.

"The danger was there," she admitted.

"I won't have an affair."

"No. I don't want that either."

"I know you're not intentionally trying to tempt me, but you can't help it. Your *existence* is a temptation. Having your body pressed against me on the Comet is a megatemptation. Sometimes just talking to you is a temptation."

She understood completely, although she didn't want to. She wanted to deny that being with him set up a yearning in her. But when he'd start a sentence with the words "Do you remember . . ." he might as well be touching her. There was an intimacy in those memories, in reaching back through time to something they'd both shared and treasured.

"I know what you're saying," she said. "And I know that all you can offer me is friendship, and that's absolutely wonderful in and of itself. We've operated on these terms before, remember? We can do it again." She didn't dare remind him how difficult those terms had proven to be for both of them. "But . . . is that why you're not coming over? I mean, do you feel as if you need to avoid me?"

"Frankly, yeah." He laughed. He had to be glad this conversation was behind him. "Let's put a little time between last night and the next time we see each other, all right? I need it, Rachel. I know I said I'd teach you how to develop the pictures this week, but can it wait awhile?"

"Of course." She hesitated a moment. "Michael, is this the kind of thing you would pray about? Pray for guidance or whatever?"

"You'd better believe it."

She tried to imagine the comfort that would bring, turning her problems over to someone, something stronger than herself.

"I might try it myself," she said with a smile. "Wanna come over and teach me how?"

He laughed again. "The devil incarnate, Rachel," he said. "That's what you are."

Helen loaded the dishwasher and, on a whim, swept the floor. She was doing splendidly. It had been days since she'd needed a pain pill.

Her ankle was stronger, the dizziness rare, and her wrist was healing nicely. Soon she might be able to play the piano again. Each time she walked through the living room, the keys seemed to grin at her. Taunting. Waiting.

She walked into the living room to turn on the stereo, and soft piano music filled the air. She could hear Rachel talking on the phone in the library as she walked into her bedroom. There she picked up the book she'd been reading for the past couple of days and took a seat on the upholstered chair near the window overlooking the garden.

She'd read seven books since the accident, and she was going to need a new supply soon. A few she'd be able to get at the library; the rest she'd already ordered from the bookstore.

She turned at a knock on her open bedroom door.

"Can I come in?" Rachel asked.

"Of course."

Rachel sat down on her bed, and Helen shifted in the chair to face her.

"Thanks for cleaning up," Rachel said. "You really shouldn't, though. Doesn't it bother your wrist?"

Helen set the book down on her knee. "Not at all." She thought of telling Rachel that she barely needed her help any longer, but the last thing she wanted was to see her granddaughter leave. And the truth was, each time it stormed outside, she needed Rachel's nearness as much as she'd ever needed anything in her life—even with the herbs in the house, which she was coming to rely on to a ridiculous degree. She'd put some cuttings from them in her purse so she would have them with her always.

Rachel looked out the window, and Helen suddenly realized that her granddaughter wanted to talk. To *really* talk. This time Rachel did not have the garden on her mind, or which CD to play next, or what birds she'd seen on her last walk through the woods.

"What is it, Rachel?" she asked.

"Michael and Jason aren't coming for dinner tonight."

"Oh?" Michael *had* sounded rather serious when she'd answered the phone.

Rachel looked at her directly. "Michael's uncomfortable spending time with me."

Helen nodded. Of course he was. "Why is that?" she asked, all innocence.

Rachel looked down at her hands as if trying to decide how much to say. "When we were in the Peace Corps together, we became very close."

"Ah," Helen said, as if that were news to her. "You fell in love."

Rachel nodded. "But I was married to Luke at the time, and so we . . . we *acknowledged* our feelings for each other, but we never acted on them." She glanced at Helen as if trying to discern whether or not the older woman understood what she was talking about.

"You did not become lovers." Helen hoped her bluntness would rid Rachel of her trepidation in speaking so openly to her.

Rachel shook her head. She was studying her hands, knotted together in her lap. "No. And when I got back here . . . well, you know what happened then, and I guess Mom and Dad sort of spirited me away and I sort of let them—"

"You must have been in shock, Rachel." Finally, the poor girl was talking about it. "You probably didn't have much of a choice but to let someone take over for you."

"And then I lost touch with Michael. Until now. This summer. And now—"

"Those old feelings are still there."

"Yes, but now *he's* married, not to mention a minister."

"He married the wrong woman."

Rachel looked up from her hands, a stunned expression on her face. "Well, I don't know about that. She helped him find his faith."

Helen shook her head with the certainty of her convictions. "She's the wrong woman for him. I've known that for a long time."

Rachel narrowed her eyes at her. "What do you mean?" she asked. "And how do you know Michael so well?"

Helen moved her book from her lap to the small table at her side. "I know all about you and Michael in the Peace Corps," she said. "After Michael got back from Rwanda, he came here to see if we knew where you'd gone. We didn't, of course. He was very upset. He told Peter and me about how close the two of you had gotten. He said he'd always loved you, even when you were just kids, but he never did anything about it because it was so obvious that you and Luke were going to end up together."

Rachel lowered her eyes at this, as though Helen had exposed too many of Michael's secrets.

"He cried, sitting there in our living room," Helen continued. "We cried, too, because we knew how it felt to lose you. We'd already lost you years before, when your mother and father cut us off from you."

Rachel's eyes glistened. "I never understood—"

Helen waved her comment away before it could turn into a question. She would not get into that now. "Michael told us he married Katy to try to make himself forget you. Love doesn't work that way, of course, and he was quickly figuring that out, but it was too late. If I'd known where you were, I would have told him to tell Katy he'd made a mistake and go find you. Claim you."

A small smile passed across Rachel's lips at Helen's choice of words.

"Katy was young. She would have gotten over it. Just like she'll get over it now if Michael chooses to—"

"*Gram.*" Rachel's head darted up. "I couldn't. I couldn't do that to another woman. And Michael wants to keep his marriage together. He *has* to. It hasn't been a great marriage, but Katy called him last night from Moscow and said she wants them to go to a marriage counselor when she gets back. And he loves being a minister. It's his life. He's passionate about it. But he couldn't be a Mennonite minister if he were divorced." She shook her head. "There's simply no way to—"

"You know." Helen shifted in her seat with a sigh. "I admire that you want to be true to your values, but some things in life are too precious to let slip by. You and Michael are soul mates. You have been all your lives. Can you just walk away from that? Some things are worth fighting for."

Rachel shook her head, clearly appalled by Helen's disregard for the bond between Michael and his wife. "Yes, I can walk away from it. I have to. Maybe that's hard for you to understand because you were lucky the first time, Helen. You and Peter were . . . soul mates, as you say, and you didn't have to hurt anyone to be able to be together. I can't—"

"Peter and I were never soul mates, Rachel," Helen said quietly. "Not at all."

Rachel frowned at her. "I thought—"

"Peter and I loved each other dearly. We respected each other, and I was tremendously grateful to him for all the help he gave me. But we did not have the sort of . . . bond of the heart that you and Michael share. And that's just too precious to let slip by. Your marriage to Phil—am I right in guessing that also lacked something?"

Rachel looked briefly defensive, but she answered honestly. "Yes," she said, "but all marriages lack something. Our marriage was good, though. I was content."

"And with Michael?"

Rachel smiled wistfully. "I think it could have been different with Michael."

"Don't give up then, Rachel."

"Gram, you're asking me to hurt people. To hurt *him*. He doesn't want this. He wants to stay in his marriage. He wants to feel good and honorable about himself."

Helen slumped slightly in her chair. Rachel was right, and she was being entirely too interfering. It was so easy to disregard Katy Stoltz. Katy was a bright woman, respected and depended upon by Reflection's parents, who knew they could call her in the middle of the night with a feverish child. But still, Katy had never elicited in Helen much in the way of warmth or concern.

Rachel stood up. "I have to say this, Gram." She smiled. "You have been and continue to be a big surprise to me. And I love you for caring so much." She bent over to kiss Helen's cheek before leaving the room.

Helen picked up her book from the floor and turned to face the window again. The sunlight was full on the garden now. She could see the healing wound in the side of the maple where Michael had severed a branch.

They were meant to be together.

She shook her head to clear away the thought. She would have to let go of their dilemma. It was not hers to solve. Besides, she reminded herself, she had not done a terribly good job of solving her own.

* * *

Helen had been twenty-six years old and the mother of a six-year-old
son when, at Peter's invitation, pianist Karl Speicer visited the house
in Reflection for the first time. Karl had been born in Germany and
spent his teen years in England before moving to New York at the
age of twenty-one. His accent was impossible to place. Helen was
instantly drawn to his rich voice and its quirky intonation.

Many other musicians and composers had visited them since they'd
lived in Reflection, but the moment Karl—or Hans, as she came to
call him—stepped inside her house, Helen knew it was destined to
become his haven. It was late spring, and she had opened all the windows so that the forest and the sky seemed a part of the house itself.
Hans walked from room to room, looking out at the trees, stroking
the wood paneling, and she saw the delight in his eyes as he drew in
deep breaths, filling his lungs with air that was clean and welcoming.

He looked over at her and Peter after his self-led, uninvited tour of
the house. "I feel as though I've come home," he said.

"I can see that." Helen smiled. She did not mind the proprietary
nature of his words at all.

Peter put his hand on Helen's back. "I knew you'd love it," he said.
"You'll love the town, too."

Hans stretched his arms out as if to encompass the house and the
trees and country air. "Can I bottle it up? Take it back to the city with
me?"

"No," Helen said, "but you may visit as often as you like." She had
known him less than five minutes, and yet she felt certain she would
not tire of this houseguest.

Indeed she did not. The following day, while Peter worked at perfecting a new sonata—one he'd been developing for several weeks—
Hans and Helen and Johnny wandered around town. She liked to be
away from the house whenever Peter worked on a piece. Peter was
the dearest soul, but he made her nervous when he was "perfecting"
something. Sometimes he didn't know when to leave well enough
alone.

Hans was attracted to the Pennsylvania Dutch influence in and
around the town, and he was fascinated by the Amish. He loved talking to those shopkeepers who still spoke German, and they enjoyed

his genuine interest, nearly forgetting about their other customers. In the very first store they visited, the elderly shopkeeper excitedly hugged him, mistaking him for an old friend he'd known in Germany named Hans Schulmann. Helen laughed at the idea of dark-haired Karl Speicer being a Hans. She teased him, calling him Hans for the rest of the morning, but by noon that was who he had become to her.

That afternoon they built a tree house.

They'd had lunch with Peter in the kitchen, after which Hans said he wanted to go for a walk through their woods. She and Johnny accompanied him. They'd been walking for a short while when Hans spied an enormous oak, two broad branches set perpendicular to its trunk. He immediately suggested the tree house to Johnny, who was enthralled with the idea. So was Helen, and the three of them drove into town to buy the lumber they would need.

Johnny soon tired of the work. Helen took him into the house, where Peter agreed to make him dinner and put him to bed, and so it was actually Hans and Helen who did most of the building. They worked into the night and through the following day as well. And they talked. He told her he had never done anything like this before. "Never built a thing in my life," he said. She wouldn't have guessed. He was careful, yet inventive, and he seemed to have great confidence in what he was doing.

He told her how much he admired Peter. "I became a pianist to play the sort of music Peter's producing," he said.

"I want to hear you play," she said, and she was surprised by the hunger in her voice. She watched his hands as he hammered, as he sanded boards. He did not treat his hands as though they were delicate instruments in need of protection, as many pianists did. Yet, with their long, quick fingers, they looked as though they could dance gracefully across the keys.

The little tree house rose up around them, and they closed themselves in as night fell, working by lantern light. Helen did not care about the aching in her shoulders, the stiffness in her knees. The space was small, and she could hear Hans's breathing, feel his nearness. Even when they were not speaking, she felt connected to him by a network of thoughts, and she knew that she was feeling what some people called chemistry. Something she had never felt before. She loved Peter; she was quite clear in her mind about that. She adored him, but her blood had never surged at his closeness, as it was doing now. She had never felt the longing to stay up with him all night, talking with him, wanting to touch him. No man had ever had that sort of power over her, until this night.

When they returned to the house, they found Peter still hunched over the piano. Helen was eager to have Hans hear the piece on which her husband was working, but Peter was not yet ready to share, and so she made her guest a glass of iced tea and sat with him out on the porch.

"I've never lived outside a city," Hans said. He was mesmerized by the noisiness of a summer night in the country, closing his eyes to listen to the frogs, the cicadas, the crickets. When he had finished the tea, Helen got a flashlight and led him out to the lane behind the house. They walked in darkness all the way to the creek, where she shone the flashlight on the bullfrogs, which darted away from the intrusion.

Hans spotted the rope that had long hung from a tree at the water's edge, and he swung out over the water with a whoop. Helen sat on the bank, laughing, wondering how he had any strength left in his arms after the work they'd done on the tree house. When he joined her on the bank, she began telling him about the sonata on which Peter was working. She told him about the introductory flourish that heralded the principal themes. She hummed the biting scherzo for him, and Hans listened quietly.

"Peter never told me you knew anything about music," he said when she had finished.

She felt a stab of betrayal. "And just how does Peter present me to the rest of the world?" she asked.

"He says you're a wonderful wife and mother. Very supportive of his career." Hans took the flashlight from her hand and shone it into the dark water. "He never said how beautiful you are though."

Taken by surprise, she could think of nothing to say.

"I'm sorry," he said, turning off the light. "I didn't mean to embarrass you. It's just that it's impossible to look at you and not think about it. I'm astounded Peter never mentioned it. But then, Peter is a different sort of man, isn't he?"

"How do you mean?" She agreed completely but wondered exactly what would make Hans say that.

"Well, he's devoted to his work. And consumed by political issues. Not the type to be swept off his feet by beauty in a woman."

That was true. Peter had never seemed interested in her for her looks. He'd liked her mind, her talent, her convictions. He had certainly never told her she was beautiful.

"He's very lucky," Hans continued. "He can travel around the world and come home to a wonderful family. I hope I'm as lucky someday."

The following morning Hans fashioned a seat for the old rope swing, using leftover lumber from the tree house. He and Helen took Johnny and one of his friends to the creek for a picnic, leaving Peter behind at the piano. The children swung for hours, propelling themselves into the water, while Hans and Helen talked on a blanket.

At supper that night Peter announced, with a smile and a toast, that he was nearly finished with the sonata. It needed just "a few final touches," he said. He was so relaxed that after the meal he pulled out some of his books on ciphers and codes, and he and Hans bowed their heads together over them in the library while Helen cleaned up. She remembered Peter telling her that Hans shared his fascination with ciphers, and she could hear them in the other room, giggling like children as they competed in solving various puzzles.

When Peter returned to the piano, Helen and Hans walked back to the creek and the swing. Neither of them said a word, but it seemed understood between them that on this warm spring night they were going to behave like ten-year-olds.

The first fall from the swing into the cold water left Helen gasping for breath, more from laughter than anything else. The fully clothed plunge felt like something from her past, the reemergence of her wild side, locked inside too long. When she and Hans were thoroughly soaked and chilled, they sat down on the grass in the moonlight, laughing and talking, and it was several minutes before Helen realized that her white blouse had grown nearly transparent. It clung to the skin above her breasts, and she could see that Hans was trying to keep his eyes from drifting in that direction. She was ashamed of herself for wanting him to look.

Back in the house, Peter was aglow with accomplishment. He smiled indulgently at their soggy disarray. "Change your clothes," he said. "I'm finally done."

Helen changed quickly, excited to hear Peter play the sonata. Downstairs, she and Hans pulled chairs close to the piano and listened. Except for the piano lamp, the lights were off, and Helen closed her eyes as the music filled the room.

Beautiful, Peter, she thought. *You've truly mastered it.*

Hans applauded when Peter lifted his hands from the keyboard at the sonata's conclusion. "Perfection," he said. "Stunning." He stood up from his chair and, with a nod of assent from Peter, lifted the music from the piano. Taking a seat in front of the second piano, he began to play. He was a spectacular sight reader, and the new composition, by now so familiar to Helen, took on fresh meaning in his hands. The entire room seemed altered. The furniture, the rugs, the wallpaper, the pianos—all were ghosts of themselves, faded and warm in the dusky light. The trees outside the huge windows were jade green; they hugged the screens as if trying to get closer to the music. She saw Peter's small smile of satisfaction as he listened, but she knew he did not feel the intense emotions she was feeling. She could barely breathe.

She stood up quietly and slipped out the front door, holding the screen behind her so it did not make a sound as it closed. On the porch the music swirled around her, and she sat down in one of the wicker rockers and wept.

16

Summer-school classes were out for the day, and only a few kids were in the central corridor of the junior-senior high as Rachel walked toward the counseling office. The smell of the school had not changed in the twenty-six years since she'd been a student there. She breathed in the mix of scents: cafeteria, perspiration, and some other, nameless scent that seemed to emanate from the walls and the floor. The peculiar bouquet brought back nothing but good memories.

The counselors' office was where it had always been. She asked the receptionist if she could speak with Mrs. Reagan, and almost immediately a young woman appeared in the doorway. Her purple-framed glasses matched her dress.

"I'm Mrs. Reagan," she said. "May I help you?"

Rachel shook the woman's hand. "I'm Rachel Huber." She did not miss the quick look of surprise from the receptionist, but the name seemed to mean nothing to the counselor. "Michael Stoltz gave me your name. I wanted to talk with you about possibly doing some tutoring."

"Oh." The counselor smiled. "Come in, please."

Rachel followed her into a small cubbyhole of an office and took the seat she was offered.

"I'm a special-education teacher in San Antonio, and I'm here for the summer," she began. "I work mainly with emotionally disturbed students, and I'd like to do some tutoring while I'm here. On a voluntary basis."

"You're kidding." Mrs. Reagan slipped off her glasses and leaned forward, elbows on her desk. "You want to tutor the toughest kids in the school system for nothing?"

Rachel smiled. "Yes, I do." She rattled off her list of credentials and handed the counselor a slim folder. "I brought a few reference letters with me."

The woman looked through the letters. "This is great," she said. "I can think of a couple of kids right off the top of my head who are really struggling this summer." She picked up a pen and a sheet of paper. "All right. Let me get your phone number. Your name again is"—she looked at the top of one of the letters—"Rachel Huber?" The smile abruptly left her face.

Rachel could not stop a sigh. "I'm afraid it's just dawned on you who I am," she said.

The counselor slowly set down her pen. "You're right, and I'm not quite sure what to say." She rolled the pen on her desk with the tip of her finger. "I personally think it would be wonderful to have someone with your credentials working with our students, and I'll talk to the parents of the kids I have in mind, but you have to understand. It's a bit . . . delicate. I'm not sure how they'll respond."

"I do understand." Rachel stood up, deflated. She suddenly wanted her old life back. She wanted Phil and Chris with her. Phil would hold her and let her rant and rave about the easy dismissal of her offer. Chris would hug her and tell her he loved her—well, at least the younger Chris would have done that. "Let me give you my phone number," she said to the counselor. "If their kids really need help, I hope they won't pass up the opportunity."

"I hope they won't, either." Mrs. Reagan replied. She wrote down Rachel's phone number, then stood to shake her hand, and Rachel had the feeling that the woman herself bore her no ill will. Yet as she left the office, she was quite certain she would not be hearing from the counselor again.

She got into her car and began driving up Farmhouse Road, her hands tense on the steering wheel. She'd thought things had cooled down. She'd had no more run-ins with anyone, and while people did not treat her with warmth, they were not hostile toward her, either. She'd shopped in town this week, taken books out from the library, and picked up Gram's order from the bookstore, where she'd seen the young clerk with the scarred face, Sarah Holland. Sarah had been in the rear of the store, and Rachel had gotten only a glimpse of her, but that had been enough. She had not been entirely comfortable on those outings, but she refused to become a prisoner in her grandmother's house out of fear that people disliked her.

The only place she could not bring herself to go was Halper's Bakery. On Wednesday she'd summoned up her courage and walked to the front door of the building, thinking she would talk to Arlena Cash directly, offer her sympathy. But there had been several customers in the store, and so she'd walked right on past. She had wanted to see Arlena alone. And yet was that fair? What right did she have to try to talk to the woman when she was captive in her own shop?

She could have stayed on Farmhouse Road as she drove home from the school, but she turned onto Main Street and cut straight through the heart of Reflection instead. She knew full well that she wanted to see the Mennonite church. Stupid decision. There was a pocket of loneliness in her chest that had been with her for days, and thinking about Michael could only make it worse. The week had been long and difficult, knowing he was nearby but unreachable, untouchable.

She kept her eyes on the road and her foot on the gas pedal as she drove past the church. Would she have to go the rest of the summer without seeing him? It had to be his choice. He was the one with too much at stake.

The pocket of loneliness had become a cavern by the time she reached her grandmother's house, and she went straight into the library to call her son. She sat down in one of the wing chairs and dialed the phone.

"Hi, honey," she said when he answered.

"Mom, God!" he said. "You don't have to keep checking up on me."

She had called him twice this week, more than she called him when he was away at school.

"I'm not checking up on you," she said. "I simply miss you. Okay?"

"Okay. Sorry." How could he argue with that? "But we're practicing right now. Can I call you back later?"

She could hear the music in the background. Music and laughter, and she fought the urge to lecture him once more about returning to school in the fall. Each time she spoke to him she hoped to hear him say that he had come to his senses and couldn't wait to get back. Instead, he would talk about the parties or clubs the band had on its performance schedule.

"Well," she said, "I just wanted to invite you to come out here for a few days before the summer's over." *Please come, Chris.* She wanted to see him, even though she knew that if he came, she would have to tell him everything. Everything about herself, about his father. But it was time he knew it all, and she thought it would be best for him to learn about it here.

He did not sound particularly enthused by the invitation, however. "I have to stay here to take care of Phoenix," he said.

"The Lawtons would look after him, I'm sure." Her next-door neighbors loved her dog.

"I'll think about it," he said. "But we have a lot of work lined up."

"It might be your only chance to meet your great-grandmother." She hoped that didn't sound as if she were laying a guilt trip on him.

He sighed. "I can probably come for a couple of days, I guess. Not sure when, though."

"*Yes,*" she said, more than pleased. "You just let me know your schedule."

Her only real concern with having Chris in Reflection was that he might be treated poorly. He was, after all, Luke Pierce's son.

She was making dinner for Gram and herself when her former high school classmate Becky Frank called.

"Michael told me you were in town," Becky said, then added with a laugh, "like there's anyone who doesn't know."

They talked for a few minutes, and when Rachel said she was looking for an aerobics class, Becky suggested they meet at her class on Monday night and then have dinner together afterward. "They have a shower in the ladies' room," she said, "so we'll be all set."

The call pleased Rachel, giving her something to look forward to, and she found herself humming as she returned to her cooking.

After dinner she and Gram settled down in the living room with a couple of books. Rachel had dealt with the loneliness this week by throwing herself into caring for her grandmother—cooking, straightening the house, gardening. Gram was enjoyable company. She could talk about books or music, and she loved their drives through the country. She was able to walk a bit now, and Rachel more often than not pushed an empty wheelchair down a country path while Gram walked beside her.

"We need some music," Rachel said when she'd gotten a few pages into her book.

"We do indeed," Gram said.

Rachel began loading a few CD's into the CD player. She accidentally hit the disk skip button, and a couple of notes—just a couple—sounded before she pressed the stop button.

Gram looked up from her book. "Prokofiev," she said. "Concerto number three in C major."

Rachel withdrew the cartridge and looked at the label on the disk. Gram was right.

"I'm impressed," she said. "Try it again." She shuffled the CD's and let another few notes play.

"Haydn," Gram said before Rachel had even taken her finger from the stop button. "*The Passion*. Symphony number forty-nine in F minor."

Rachel eyed her grandmother with curiosity. She loaded ten CD's in the player, relaxed on the sofa, and using the remote, shuffled the music. She'd play a few notes, and Gram would gleefully guess the composer, the piece, the movement, and throw in a few esoteric facts about the creation of the work as well. She was extraordinary. It was a one-sided game of course. Rachel could not play, nor did she know if her grandmother was right most of the time. But the older woman obviously loved the diversion, testing her brain, her memory, and impressing the hell out of Rachel.

Chris would be good at this game, too, Rachel thought as she pressed the buttons on the remote. *I can probably come for a couple of days*, he'd said. She smiled to herself. She could not wait to have her wayward son here with her in her grandmother's house, where he would be surrounded by the classical music he had once embraced, as well as by Peter Huber's gentle, benevolent ghost.

17

"So." Drew leaned back from the coffee table where he'd been jotting down notes for their next press release about the Hostetter project. He looked over at Michael on the sofa. "You about ready to eat?"

"Sounds good." Michael moved a pile of flyers from his lap to the sofa and stretched. They'd been handing out the flyers about next month's hearing since one-thirty, on the street and in shops, talking to anyone who would listen to them. It was nearly six now, and his stomach was growling.

Drew stood up. "I'll get the coals going, and you can doctor up the steaks if you like. They're in the fridge."

He left the room, and Michael read over the notes for the press release one more time. They were trying to keep the story alive in the papers, and so far they'd done a good job of it. This particular release was about the cultural-impact study, which decried the Hostetter plan for the hardship it would place on the plain-sect communities in and around Reflection.

He stood up slowly and walked over to the hearth. Drew had built the house himself, and it was full of intriguing architectural touches, like the thick slab of wood jutting from the stone fireplace. It was not the mantel itself, though, that had attracted Michael's attention, but rather the lone framed photograph resting on it. A young boy with an impish grin, a splattering of freckles across his slightly upturned nose. A hint of mischief in his blue eyes. Michael had seen the picture of

Will a few dozen times before, but it sent a new wave of sadness through him now that Rachel was in town.

Drew was not much for sharing confidences, but on one occasion—after he'd had a few beers—he'd told Michael that his marriage had started to disintegrate after Will died. His wife became depressed to the point of attempting suicide, and she was in and out of hospitals for a year or so. When she started getting better, Drew had his own bout with depression, as if he'd avoided dealing with his own grief until she could handle hers without him. Ready to enjoy life once again, his wife could not tolerate Drew's black moods, and one day she simply packed up and moved out. They'd been divorced nearly ten years now, and as far as Michael could tell, Drew seemed thoroughly disinclined to remarry or even to develop a strong, close relationship with a woman. He dated women Michael thought of as "companions." Drew would go to the movies with them, or out to dinner. He'd probably had a sexual relationship with one or two of them. But he seemed to be a thoroughly confirmed bachelor.

"Marriage didn't do much for me," he'd said that night when he'd had too much to drink. "Gave me a son, took him away. Gave me a wife, made her crazy. Doesn't exactly inspire me to do it all over again."

Michael got the steaks from the refrigerator, brushed a little steak sauce on them, and carried them out to the yard where Drew was stirring the coals in the flagstone barbecue. Michael handed him the plate, then picked up a bottle of club soda from the picnic table and twisted off the cap.

His mind was still on Will's picture. He couldn't imagine losing a child. Much as he'd missed seeing Rachel this week, he'd thoroughly enjoyed the rare uninterrupted time with his son.

"So," Drew said as he slapped one of the steaks on the grill. "What's it like having your old comrade in town?"

It was a moment before Michael realized that Drew was talking about Rachel, not Jason. He took a swallow of soda. "Pretty rough," he said as he leaned against the wall of the barbecue. The stone was cool through his shirt. "I'm trying not to see her for a while. I haven't spoken to her in a week. We were getting too close."

"Really?" Drew looked at him from under hooded brows. "Just how far did things go?"

The question took Michael by surprise, and he laughed. "Nowhere you're thinking of," he said, then shook his head. "We were twenty-three the last time we had a hankering for each other. You'd think it would be easier to deal with—or at least less frustrating—at forty-four."

Drew laughed. "Yeah. I know what you're saying."

"I don't mean to imply that it's just physical," Michael said quickly. "It would actually be easier if it were." He could resist a purely physical attraction, he thought. So black and white. So clearly wrong. It was all the other things Rachel offered him that he found difficult to resist.

Drew gave him that hooded look again. "Are we talking the *L* word, or do we just plain want to jump her bones?" he asked.

Michael laughed again, awkwardly this time, and dropped his gaze to the soda bottle in his hand. "Not sure I can talk about this," he said. He'd intentionally skipped the support group on Friday night, but he really should go this week. He wished he could open up in there, use the group the way it was meant to be used. "It's both, I guess. We have a lot in common, and I've loved her since we were kids. I've just been able to forget that fact for the better part of the last two decades. Having her around makes it difficult."

"Listen, Mike." Drew peeked at the underside of one of the steaks, lifting it with the long tines of a barbecue fork. He stood up straight and looked Michael in the eye. "I know you and I don't exactly think alike on this sort of thing," he said. "I can't relate to the whole element of religion that's so important to you. But . . . why don't you just go for it?"

Michael groaned. "It's not that simple, and you know it. Not that neat and clean."

"You have this annoyingly refined sense of right and wrong, you know it?"

"Yes, I know it. And 'going for it' would fall into the 'wrong' category. Unforgivable. I have no right to see Rachel when I know it's putting my marriage at risk."

Drew shook his head. "Why are you beating that poor old dead horse? You and Katy have nothing together anymore. You told me that yourself and—"

"Wait a minute." An unexpected tide of panic welled up in Michael's chest. For a moment, he regretted ever having spoken candidly to Drew about his marriage. "If nothing else, we still have Jace."

"Yeah, but you're a grown-up, you know? And so's Katy. You need more than a kid to make you happy. And Jace would survive if you split up." Drew took a long draw on his beer. "You know, in all the years I've known you, I've never heard you say one really positive thing about Katy?"

Michael started to protest, but Drew interrupted him.

"Oh, you talk about how sharp she is, or about her professional accomplishments and all, but I've never gotten the sense that she makes you happy."

Michael felt the wave of panic again. Drew was right. "It's not just Katy that stops me," he said. "Not just my marriage."

Drew turned the steaks over. "You're trapped, you know that, Mike?" He looked at him. "I mean, there've been times when I've envied you because you always seemed to know just where you fit in. You're always so calm and . . . I don't know, at *peace* with yourself and your religion and all. But it's got you trapped, doesn't it? You can't do anything—"

"I don't feel that way," Michael argued. "I've never felt trapped." At least he'd never felt that way before.

"It's not really like you'd be doing something behind Katy's back." Drew could not seem to shut up. "You told me the two of you were viewing this time as a separation."

"Well, that's changed."

Drew eyed him, the fork poised in the air. "What do you mean?"

"I got a call from her the other night. She was upset and said she wanted to work out our problems when she gets back."

For the first time in too many minutes, Drew seemed to have nothing to say. He turned the steaks over again, unnecessarily. "She was probably just in a mood," he said finally. "PMS or something. Feeling lonely."

"Well, I don't know what prompted it. All I know is that I can't pretend I don't have a wife."

"Let me just say two things." Drew sat down on top of the picnic table. "I need to get this out, okay? Then I'll quit bugging you."

"Do I have a choice?" Michael asked wryly.

"No, you don't." He held his index finger in the air. "First of all, I personally think that you and Rachel should do whatever you damn well please."

Michael started to protest, but Drew cut him off. "I know you think I'm some sort of amoral pagan," he said, "but I'm just giving you my opinion. Whatever you do, though," he leaned forward, "you'd better keep it private. Friends or lovers, you've got to keep this thing under wraps."

"What are you saying?"

"I'm saying I've heard some dirt already. People have seen the two of you together, and people don't like her. Whether that's fair or not is beside the point. They just don't. And right now, with the land fight and all, you need to keep people's respect. This town worships the ground you walk on, but no one's so blinded by admiration for you that they won't see what's happening. You need to keep your credibility in shape."

People were talking about him behind his back. "Who's saying things?" he asked. "What have you heard?"

"Just . . . couple of guys on the crew. Russell over at the post office. Those who aren't saying it are thinking it. This town is too small and you're too visible and Katy is too well thought of. You don't need a scandal right now, Mike, so do what you want with Rachel—I personally think you should ball her brains out and have a good time doing it, and you should forget about your wife who said with her own two lips, 'I'm treating this like a separation,'—but whatever you do, don't get caught at it."

The steaks were done. He and Drew ate dinner on the picnic table, an unusual silence between them. Michael steered any conversation away from Rachel, away from Katy, but those thoughts gnawed at him all the same and he found he could hardly eat.

"Hey, I tore something out of the Sunday *Washington Post* for you," Drew said when they had nearly finished.

"What's that?"

"It's in the kitchen. An ad for the National Symphony. They're doing an all-Huber concert on . . . not this weekend, but the next one, I think. The nineteenth? Thought maybe Rachel and her grandmother might be interested."

"Yes, thanks. I'm sure they would be." And so was he, although he had Jace to think about. Jace and so much more. Still, he could picture himself and the two women making a weekend of it in D.C. Away from Reflection. Away from any gossip.

He left Drew's house earlier than he'd planned and drove directly to the church. He did not go downstairs to his office. Instead, he walked into the empty sanctuary, leaving it dark except for the light in the foyer, and sat down in one of the center pews.

He loved the elegant simplicity of this church. Through one of the tall narrow windows he could see the half-moon in the blue-black sky, and although they were not visible, he felt the nearness of the forest, the pond. He closed his eyes, and the inside of his eyelids held a dark memory of the half-moon.

I've gotten too smug, Lord.

He had lived a holy life for so long that it felt effortless to him. It *had* been effortless. It was easy to be righteous when there was nothing to tempt you away from that path. Rachel had been the cause of his failing when he was younger. His weakness. He'd wanted something he could not have. And here she was back again, like a test.

Is this a test, Lord? If it is, I need your help to pass it.

There were people in the church who had not wanted him as their minister because he had been raised outside the faith. He was raised with worldly values, they argued. Worldly ideals. He could slip too easily. Until now, he'd thought they were mistaken.

Grant me humility, and please help me to remember all those for whom I'm responsible.

"I personally think you should ball her brains out."

Michael jerked to attention, eyes open. Outside the window, the moon was a sharp white sickle in the sky, and it was a moment before he could shift his eyes from it and return his focus to his prayer.

Please give me the strength to fight temptation.

He sat quietly in the empty church an hour longer, words of prayer burning like a blister on his tongue. For the first time, though, he had the feeling that no one was listening.

18

Rachel's palms were damp as she parked her car in front of the small, brick United Church of Christ. She turned off the ignition and looked across the street at the Lutheran church. She was to meet Becky Frank there in five minutes, at seven o'clock, but she couldn't bring herself to get out of the car and stand in front of the church to wait. Women—and an occasional man or two—walked up the broad sidewalk toward the church's red door, carrying their gym bags, laughing and chatting together. As courageous as she'd been lately about going places, being seen, she did not want to wait awkwardly among those strangers.

She spotted the red hair first. Becky walked up the sidewalk of the Lutheran church and, once she'd reached the door, turned to face the street. She glanced at her watch, and Rachel got out of her car and waved.

Becky met her with a hug. "You look great!" she said. "Haven't changed a bit."

"Right." Rachel smiled. "Although I can say the same about you and mean it sincerely." Except for the finest of lines in the fairest of skin, Becky looked about seventeen. Her distinctive red hair was still cut in the pageboy that had been dated even in high school.

They entered the church foyer, and Becky led her down the stairs to the basement and into a large room with a hardwood floor and low ceiling. Several women and a couple of men were milling around, a few of them stretching, a few engaged in conversation. All of them wore curious expressions as Rachel and Becky entered the room. A couple of them greeted Becky warmly.

"This is my friend Rachel," Becky said to the women closest to them.

The women nodded at Rachel as Becky rattled off their names, but there was no time for anything more than introductions before the thirtyish blond instructor started the music.

It was a good class, strenuous enough to let Rachel know that she was still not back in shape in spite of her bike rides but not so taxing that she couldn't keep up. The instructor was the peppy type whose enthusiasm was contagious. She had everyone clapping and smiling, and by the end of the forty-five minutes Rachel felt flushed and happy.

In the spacious but cramped ladies' room she and Becky showered and dressed along with a half-dozen other women. Rachel wondered if they knew who she was. Several of them seemed friendly; a few others did not even look in her direction. Typical of any group, she thought.

Becky seemed to know them all well. She talked to the women about their kids and their jobs, while Rachel remained uncharacteristically quiet. She would usually try to join in the conversation of a group like this, but here she was afraid of stepping over boundary lines she couldn't see.

She was slipping on her sandals when one of the women asked her how her grandmother was doing. So they *did* know who she was.

"She's recovering very well," Rachel said with a smile—probably a bit too wide, but the woman's simple show of concern cheered her. "Thanks for asking."

She and Becky were heading for the door of the rest room when the woman called out, "I hope you'll come again," and Rachel was so heartened by that invitation that she barely heard the rush of whispering that followed them out the door.

"That's Dina," Becky said as they climbed the stairs to the main level of the church. "I work with her at the bank. She's a good friend."

They walked a few blocks to a small Italian restaurant on a side street. "It's my favorite," Becky said as she pushed open the glass door. "Not exactly elegant, but the food's good."

The restaurant was little more than a small, square room. Eight tables, half of them filled, were packed close together and covered with the requisite red-and-white-checked tablecloths. The fluorescent lighting overhead was too bright, and the posters of Italy on the walls were faded, but the smells from the kitchen held promise.

"I enjoyed that class," Rachel said once they'd sat down. She could still feel the rush of endorphins.

"Isn't it great?" Becky shoved her menu to the side without opening it. She obviously knew what she wanted. "Suzy's been the instructor for about three years, and she's the best I've ever seen. The manicotti's to die for, by the way."

They both ordered manicotti, then dove into catching each other up on the twenty-six years since high school. Becky had gotten married a couple of years after graduation, moved to Massachusetts, and had two children. She and her husband had divorced five years ago. "He found someone else." She shrugged. "It was hard at first, but looking back, I don't think we'd ever really been right for each other. And then I moved back here." She unwrapped her straw. "This town . . . While you're growing up here, you're thinking, 'I can't wait to get out of here.' Once you've been away awhile, though, you can't wait to get back."

Rachel pondered that thought. "It's the view from Winter Hill," she said. "Whenever I thought of Reflection, that was always the first image in my mind."

"Michael said you were widowed?" Becky asked gently.

Rachel nodded. "Twice." She grimaced. Why did she say that?

Becky wrapped her hands around her water glass. "I'm so sorry about what happened with Luke, Rachel," she said. "It must have been a terrible time for you."

"It was. Thanks."

"I still think about it sometimes. About Luke. He was such a neat guy. I think about how much he must have changed to do something so terrible. How hard that must have been for you."

Rachel nodded. "The war turned him into someone I didn't know." She felt freed by the way Becky refused to tiptoe around the topic. "He became . . . unpredictable."

"And I know that some people are upset that you're here. You're their scapegoat."

That word again.

"I just want you to know that everyone doesn't feel that way," Becky continued. "It's good for you to do things like taking this class. You're a legend in this town, just like your grandfather, only for different reasons. Twenty years have passed, and there are very few people here who remember the real Rachel Huber. They only remember the pumped-up myth of the teacher who . . . you know . . . who blew it, they think."

Rachel tried not to wince at Becky's choice of words.

"The only way to counteract that reputation," Becky continued, "is to let people get to know you. Michael told me about all the awards you've won as a teacher. People need to hear about that. I'm taking it upon myself to spread the word. Hope you don't mind."

Rachel smiled. "It means a lot to me to know that everyone doesn't blame me."

"Hell, no. Just a few people who still need someone to pin their unhappiness on. I don't give them the time of day."

Their meal arrived, and they ate and talked like the old friends they were, Becky bringing her up to date on nearly everyone from their high school class as well as their teachers and the school secretaries and cafeteria workers. By the time they left the restaurant it was dark outside, and Rachel felt fully satisfied. She'd had a good workout, good food, and good company.

She said good-bye to Becky on the corner, then walked the block to her car in front of the United Church of Christ. She slipped her key into the lock on the car door.

"Rachel?"

She turned at the sound of Michael's voice. He was walking down the sidewalk in front of the Mennonite church, his features barely visible in the darkness.

"Are you just getting out of work?" she asked.

He stopped on the sidewalk, the car between them, and glanced back at his church. "I guess you could say that. Where were you? In the library?"

"No. I took the aerobics class with Becky. Then we got some dinner."

He looked truly pleased. "That's great. I'm glad to see you out and about."

"I'm glad to see you, period. How's Jason?"

"Good. We've had a terrific week together." He looked out toward Huber Pond, and she saw the war going on inside him. She knew the instant he lost it. "Do you have time for a cup of coffee?" he asked.

She smiled at him. "I want to, Michael, but are you sure it's a good idea?"

"Probably not." He grinned his Michael Stoltz grin. "But let's do it anyway."

He didn't need to talk her into it.

They walked to the small café next to the bank. Brahms Café, it was called. The walls were decorated with musical instruments and pictures of composers, Peter Huber included. After feeling so welcome in the aerobics class, Rachel walked into the café without so much as a twinge of anxiety.

"You can sit anywhere, Mike." The waitress glanced at them, then did a double take when she realized who the preacher was with. Rachel felt the woman's eyes burning a hole in her back as she and Michael walked toward a booth.

An older man passed their Formica-topped table as they were sitting down. He shot a look at Rachel, then nodded at Michael. "Michael," he said, and Michael returned the greeting.

Rachel waited until the man was out of earshot. "Maybe this wasn't such a good idea after all," she said quietly.

Michael shook his head, let out a sigh. "Drew just lectured me, not more than a couple of hours ago, about not being seen with you. So what do I do? First chance I get, I suggest we go out in public."

"Oh, Michael," she said in frustration. "We're not doing anything wrong."

"I know that. And I refuse to act as if we are."

The waitress appeared at their table. "Rice pudding?" she asked Michael.

He nodded. "And coffee." He looked at Rachel. "Have some dessert?"

She shook her head and looked up at the waitress, who immediately averted her eyes. "Just decaf," she said.

The waitress called to an older couple standing by the front door and seated them in the booth across the aisle from her and Michael.

"Hello, Mike," the silver-haired woman said as she and the gentleman settled into the booth.

Michael nodded. "Hi, Marge. Dow." He hesitated a moment before adding, "Do you know Rachel?"

Marge nodded. "We met at Hairlights. This is my husband, Dow."

"Oh, yes." Rachel remembered the woman as one of the hairdressers in Lily's salon. "Nice seeing you again."

Marge and her husband lost themselves in their menus, and Michael gave Rachel a rueful smile. "Well," he said softly. "We might as well have rented a billboard to announce we were going to have a cup of coffee together. Marge is rather notorious for spreading the word."

"I really like Lily."

He nodded. "Lily's terrific."

"She gives me hope. She seems to symbolize something . . ." She hunted for the words. "She endured the tragedy, and yet she's so alive and strong and well adjusted and . . . she doesn't seem to blame me." She was aware of speaking softly, just in case she could be overheard by Marge, but the older woman and her husband seemed engrossed in their menus.

Michael nodded, but she got the sense he didn't entirely agree with her rosy picture of the young hairdresser. "Yes, she's adjusted well, and she's not the type to blame anyone for anything. She's a very forgiving sort of person. It's something the church teaches—to forgive—and Lily's a good example of that. But she still has a wounded side to her. She probably won't let you see it, but it's there."

"How do you know?"

"When she was in high school, she was in the youth group at the church, and she talked to me a lot about her sister. About the guilt she felt over having survived when her sister didn't. It's common knowledge that she's afraid to have kids. Afraid of losing them."

"Oh. Poor thing." Rachel pursed her lips. She had wanted to believe that Lily had somehow been spared the tenacious suffering that had so many people in its grip.

"Hey, take a look at this," Michael said with an abrupt change of topic. He pulled a newspaper ad from his pocket. "Drew gets the *Washington Post*," he said, laying the ad flat on the table and turning it so she could see. "What do you think?"

It was a large ad for the National Symphony Orchestra, and it was a moment before she understood. "An all-Huber program!" she exclaimed. "Oh, I've got to take Gram."

He smiled. "And me, too, all right? If I can figure out a way to swing it. I thought we could get a couple of rooms near the Kennedy Center and stay overnight. It's too far to drive back that late."

The happiness she'd been toying with all night suddenly flowered again. She wished she could tell him how much she wanted that time with him, how much she'd missed seeing him this week. But she couldn't. It might scare him as much as it scared her.

She studied the ad as he talked about the logistics of getting tickets. There was a picture of the pianist who would be performing with the orchestra that night. Karl Speicer. A handsome man, though quite old. At least in his seventies, judging from the picture. His hair was white, and he wore an engaging smile. The name was vaguely familiar. "I think Gram has some of this guy's recordings," she said. "He plays a lot of my grandfather's compositions." She looked up at Michael. "I'm so glad you saw this. Gram's going to be thrilled."

The waitress appeared with the rice pudding and coffee.

"How are preparations going for the hearing and all?" she asked.

"All right. We handed out leaflets today and talked it up. I think we'll have a good turnout. Just hope we can get some of the Amish to show up." He ate a spoonful of pudding before speaking again. "I spoke with the student leader of the youth group this morning," he said. "We're going to meet Friday to start planning the Reflection Day observance. I talked to her about gearing our presentation toward making this the last Reflection Day." He smiled. "She was a bit shocked at first, I think. I mean, she's only seventeen. There's been a Reflection Day every year of her life. But we talked about it, and I think she understood my reasoning. She actually sounded excited about it by the end of the phone call. That's the good thing about working with teenagers. They're rebels at heart. They enjoy thumbing their noses at an institution."

Rachel frowned into her coffee. The whole Reflection Day concept struck her as bizarre and destructive. "When is it again?" she asked.

"September twelfth. It's always the second Monday of September."

She supposed that she, better than anyone, should remember the second Monday of September. She hoped she would be back in San Antonio by then. "Well," she said with a sigh, "the one aspect of Reflection Day that I *do* like is its focus on the cost of war."

"Yes. So do I." Michael slowly finished his pudding. He set his spoon in the empty bowl and looked at her squarely. "I've always felt terrible that I wasn't around when Luke got back. That I wasn't there to help him. And you."

"You had an obligation in Rwanda, Michael. Besides, you didn't know anything was wrong until it was too late."

He lowered his eyes to the ad on the table, pushed it around a bit with the tips of his fingers. "Vietnam," he said, shaking his head. "You know, I've been to Washington a dozen times in recent years and still can't bring myself to go to the Vietnam Memorial."

She could see the pain inside him. Still, after all these years.

"You were so wise to recognize you couldn't fight," she said. She pictured him standing on the steps of the Town Hall, facing a small crowd of protesters as he asserted his status as a conscientious objector. He'd said he was unable to accept violence as a solution to any problem. "When I heard you speak that day, it was the first time I had any doubts about my feelings for Luke," she admitted. "I admired you for taking that stance. And that speech you made . . . I cried."

Michael smiled at her. "Do you know who was responsible for me being a conscientious objector?" he asked. "Do you know who helped me write that speech?"

She shook her head. "Who?"

"Your grandparents."

"*What?*"

"You wondered how I know your grandmother so well. That's how. Both Helen and Peter helped me figure out what to do about the draft. When I decided that I could, with good conscience, be a C.O., they helped me obtain that status, which wasn't too easy, considering I didn't belong to any church back then. Peter spent hours with me, helping me put my feelings into words."

Rachel was stunned. She leaned back in the booth and stared at her old friend. She would have sworn she'd known all there was to know about him back then. "Why didn't you ever tell me about that? I didn't even know you knew them. *I* wasn't even allowed to see them myself, and there you were, spending hours upon hours with them." She heard the hurt in her voice even before she felt it.

"It was very important that as few people as possible knew what Peter and Helen were up to."

"What do you mean, 'up to'?"

"They were very well known among the draft-age men—boys—throughout the county. You know what pacifists they were. They would have done anything to keep guys from going to fight. Anything, legal or not. And most of what they did wasn't. They harbored AWOL soldiers, they drove draft resisters up to Canada. They doctored medical records, gave advice on how to flunk physicals, and counseled and nurtured C.O.'s like myself. Remember Bobby Mullen?"

Rachel nodded at the name of one of their high school classmates.

"They altered his medical record to make it look like he had a bad knee. They fixed Darren Wise's record so it looked like he had high blood pressure, and they gave him pills to take before his physical to make sure his B.P. would be consistent with his records."

In spite of her shock, Rachel couldn't help laughing. "So that was their terrible crime," she said. "That was why my parents turned their backs on them." She could imagine her father's outrage over her grandparents' blatant disregard for the laws of their country as they struggled to save young men from the fate Luke had suffered.

"Why didn't they help Luke?" she asked.

"They would have, willingly, but he wasn't interested. I dragged him over to their house one time, and he was disgusted by the scam. He felt it was his duty to fight. He told me I was taking the coward's way out." Michael's voice broke slightly on the last word, and Rachel reached across the table to cover his hand with her own.

He drew his hand away from under hers, slowly but deliberately, and for a moment neither of them spoke.

Rachel blinked back tears. She shouldn't have touched him. Not with Marge sitting right across the aisle from them.

"Oh, Rache," he said. "I'm sorry."

She felt the twist in her heart and shook her head. She didn't want to cry here.

Michael leaned forward. "I've been doing a lot of thinking and praying," he said. "A lot of soul-searching. I'm coming to understand some things that are hard for me to face up to."

"Like what?" Her voice came out in a whisper.

"I thought I'd turned to faith as a way to deal with Luke's death, and the loss of the children, and all those things that didn't make sense and hurt too badly to live with. Katy and the church made me feel safe and settled and forgiven. I thought I'd found answers, but I realize now that what I actually found was a way to . . . escape." He looked out the window. The Mennonite church stood less than a block away, its steeple piercing the night sky. "I'm so insulated now," he continued. "I'm insulated from everything that can cause me a moment's unrest. It was so hard not acting on my feelings for you back in the Peace Corps. A terrible moral dilemma for me. Well, now I'm very protected from having to make moral decisions. The rules and constraints on me are very clear, and I thought I was way beyond temptation. But then here comes Rachel, like a test."

"I don't want to be viewed that way, Michael." She was not certain if it was hurt or anger she felt over the use of the word *test*. "It makes me into an object—the evil seductress—instead of an old friend who cares about you. Who wants only good things for you."

He stared at her for a long moment, his eyes warm behind his glasses.

"You're right," he said. "I keep doing this, don't I? I keep looking for a nice, neat way to understand my life. If you're a test, then I can resist you. If you're just a good and caring friend, it makes it harder."

She smiled. "You make it sound like you're the only one with a moral code. I've got one, too, you know. It's not elaborate and complicated. It's very simple: I would never move in on another woman's man. All right?"

He laughed. "I'm making this more difficult than it has to be, is that what you're saying?" He put a few bills on the table and stood up, nodded to her to join him.

They walked in a comfortable silence to her car, but she knew better than to give him a hug before getting in. Still, once she was in the car and watching him walk down the road, she felt the tightening in her belly and all the other shades of desire she'd been fighting all week. How easily that old feeling of guilt-edged longing could be brought to life again. Maybe this was a test after all.

19

Helen was sitting at the piano, picking out the melody of a song with her good hand, when she heard Rachel's car in the driveway. She abandoned the piano and sat down on the ivy-upholstered sofa, opening a book on her lap. It was a minute before she heard the car door slam, another before she heard her granddaughter's footsteps on the porch.

"Have a good time?" she asked as Rachel walked in the door.

"I can't believe Mom and Dad kept me away from you just because you were helping guys beat the draft." Rachel dropped into a chair.

Helen smiled. So Michael had told her. "Well, I guess what we were doing seemed like a terrible thing to your parents. It would have seemed like a terrible thing to a lot of people, had they known. Your mother and father thought they were putting you in jeopardy by letting you spend time with us. Besides, we always had a house full of boys. They wouldn't want you over here." She told herself she wasn't lying. Those *were* the reasons for the estrangement. At least in part.

Rachel looked toward the empty fireplace, and Helen turned her book facedown on her knee. There was hurt in her granddaughter's face. After all this time.

"We thought we were doing something that was very important," Helen said. "Very necessary. I would never have given up the ability to have my granddaughter in my life if I didn't think what I was doing was critical."

Rachel nodded. "I understand."

"It was a difficult period of my life." Helen raised her hand in the air and discovered it was trembling. She lowered it quickly to her lap. "I thought John—your father—would get over it. I never thought he'd cut you out of our lives for good. Forgive me, Rachel."

"I don't think there's anything to forgive. It was just unfortunate. But I'm glad you did what you did. I'm proud of you for that."

Helen was touched. "We felt good about it," she said. "We were taking action instead of sitting around complaining." She smiled to herself. "Peter got himself arrested a few times," she said.

"Really?" Rachel nearly smiled. "And how about you?"

"Only one time for me." She set her book on the end table, folded her hands in her lap. "So," she said, "I didn't know you were going to see Michael tonight."

"No, neither did I. We bumped into each other in town and went out for a cup of coffee. Oh! Guess what?"

"What?"

"Michael and I are taking you to Washington, D.C., on the nineteenth to hear the symphony perform an all-Huber concert."

It took a moment for Helen to absorb what Rachel was saying. "An all-Huber concert?" she repeated.

"Yes. They're doing *Patchwork* and *Lionheart* and the Second Concerto. What do you think?"

"Who?" Helen leaned forward. "Who's doing it?"

"The National Symphony."

"No. I mean who's the pianist?" She held her breath.

"Oh. It's Speicer, I think. Karl Speicer."

The living room did a delicate spin, and Helen clutched the arm of the sofa. Rachel was immediately on her feet, dropping to her knees in front of her.

"Are you all right, Gram?"

The room snapped back into place, but her no-longer-trustworthy heart was beating hard against her ribs. "Yes," she said. "Yes, I'm all right. But the date. The date of the concert. I'm not sure it's going to work out."

Rachel frowned, leaning back on her heels. "Do you have other plans?"

Helen shook her head.

"Don't you want to go, Gram? We thought it sounded like something you'd enjoy."

Yes, she wanted to go. She just did not know if she could survive the pain of being in that audience. She nodded weakly, resting her hand on her granddaughter's arm. "We'll go," she said. "And you're right. It's a wonderful idea."

20

Lily leaned against her van where it was parked in front of Hairlights. She sipped the coffee she'd brought from home as she waited for Rachel. It was six in the morning, and the new sun cast a pinkish glow on the small buildings and deserted streets of Reflection.

Rachel had brought Helen into Hairlights the day before to have Marge cut her hair. Lily chatted with them about the farmers' market held on Thursday mornings near Leola, and when Rachel expressed interest in going, Lily suggested they go together this morning. There were those who thought she was crazy. Notably Marge and Polly and CeeCee. And she herself was not sure whether her attraction to Rachel was pure or perverse. Given the facts of history, Lily should want to avoid the woman. Yet she felt drawn to her.

Rachel had talked about the aerobics class while Helen was getting her hair cut. The class was great, she'd said, just what she needed. Rachel truly seemed unaware of the stir her presence in the class had created, and the resentment. Lily had heard that Ellie Ryan had even dropped out. But then, Ellie was a notorious hysteric, a prima donna. She hadn't even lived in Reflection back when everything happened. But she did attend the Mennonite church, and Lily guessed that was the real source of Ellie's discomfort with Rachel Huber.

There were rumors about Rachel and Michael, more each day. They'd been fairly gentle rumors at first. Someone had seen them together at Spring Willow Pond. Someone else had seen them riding their bikes. Nothing sordid. But in the last day or so there had been a notable burst in both quantity and tenor.

Marge said she'd seen them together in the Brahms Café Monday night. "They are in love," Marge said with typical Marge-like certainty. "They were in a deep—*very* deep—conversation, unaware of anything around them. At one point, she was crying." Coming from Marge, the story had to be taken with a grain of salt. Marge could make a soap opera out of Sesame Street. But the rumors made Lily squirm nonetheless.

She was worried about Michael. She'd told Ian that she wished Michael were not human. Ian, of course, completely understood her meaning, although she doubted anyone else would have. All she meant was that she *needed* Michael. She needed him as her minister. The church needed him, and the community needed him. And so the fact that he was vulnerable, fallible—that he was *mortal*—frightened her, now more than ever. If he was indeed spending time with Rachel, as he appeared to be, the danger was real. Rachel was the warm, cuddly type. You just had to watch her for half a second to know that. You just had to see her brush a strand of her grandmother's hair from her cheek, or see the gratitude in her eyes when Helen explained that it had been Polly's veterinarian father who had found her lying, lightning-struck, in her garden the night of the Fourth of July. Rachel had touched Polly's arm then, and Lily grinned at the love-hate war she saw going on inside her business partner.

Rachel Huber had warmth to spare, and Katy Stoltz was as cold as Spring Willow Pond in the dead of winter. And very absent. In a different world, Lily would have loved to see Michael and Rachel together; in the real world, though, the cost would be too great for all of them.

Michael's sermon on Sunday had been about forgiveness. It was one of his best, she thought. Ian said it was magic, his highest compliment. But everyone knew what Michael was really saying behind his soulful delivery of parables and Scripture. Everyone knew he was talking about Rachel and Reflection, and Lily felt the congregation tighten up as the sermon progressed. Not everyone thought it was magic.

She saw Rachel turn the corner by the bank building, and she waved.

"I feel sorry for all the people who are still in their beds and missing out on this." Rachel called out. She raised her arms to encompass all of the town in its pink-and-gold early-morning glory.

"I know what you mean," Lily said. "This is my favorite time of day." She reached through the van window and pulled out a thermos. "I brought extra coffee. Want some?"

"I'd love it," Rachel said.

Lily poured the coffee into a plastic mug and handed it to her.

"I've got a little addiction," Lily admitted as she poured a second cup for herself.

"Oh, well. As vices go, you could do worse."

They got into the van, and Lily apologized for the dog odor, if there was any. She doubted her ability to tell anymore.

"I probably wouldn't notice if there were, either," Rachel said. "Eau de Rover's the customary scent at my house."

"You'll have to come to the charity show I'm working on for the ASPCA," Lily said.

"When's that?"

"The twenty-fifth. I'm working on some dog acts, and Ian's going to do his magic. It'll be tons of fun."

"Sounds like it," Rachel said.

They rode in silence past the Amish-Mennonite cemetery. Lily threw a quick glance in the direction of Jenny's tree-shaded grave, as she always did when she drove by, and Rachel suddenly asked, "What do you think would happen if I went to see Marielle Hostetter? Talked to her about the land?"

Lily laughed. "You'd be wasting your time."

"Maybe," Rachel said with a shrug. "Couldn't hurt, though."

Lily didn't argue with her, although she couldn't imagine how anything could be gained by talking with Marielle.

She turned at the next intersection and, with the cemetery safely behind them, shifted the conversation back to dogs and the ASPCA show for the rest of the drive.

The farmers' market was bustling, as usual. They parked in the huge dirt lot and walked toward the stands. The market was half inside a huge warehouse and half outside. Lily and Rachel walked among the outside tables laden with fruits and flowers, vegetables and breads and jellies.

"Meats and cheese are inside," Lily said.

"It's overwhelming," Rachel said, clearly pleased. "I wish we had something like this where I live."

The market was usually a social event for Lily, a chance for her to catch up on the lives of her friends and neighbors. The vendors would tease her, chat with her, pester her to buy their produce. But today was different, and Lily knew it was because of the company she was keeping. There was no denying it. She felt the coolness like a chill in the air, slipping around her shoulders, making her shiver. The only saving grace was that Rachel seemed oblivious to it all. She moved from stand to stand with a smile on her face, a greeting for everyone, accepting the stoic responses of the vendors in return. She didn't know any better.

"Oh, Lily." Rachel pointed toward a table stacked high with corn. "I have to take a look over there."

Lily automatically looked to see who was selling the corn. No one she knew. Rachel should be all right. She turned back to the stand in front of her and started filling a bag with peaches.

"How are you today, Sally?" she asked the woman standing behind the table.

"All right." Sally spoke through tight lips. She took the bag from Lily, set it on the scale. "See you've made a new friend," she said as she marked a price on the bag.

It was rare for Lily to be at a loss for a response, and she hesitated long enough to swallow those that might be sarcastic. Sally had her reasons for disliking Rachel. Sally had her pain.

"Yes," she replied simply. "I have."

"How long's she going to be here?" Sally had her eyes on Rachel, who was handing a few dollar bills to the man behind the corn.

"Probably just for the summer." Lily counted out some change and dropped it into Sally's palm. "Just until her grandmother is better."

"Long enough," Sally said.

Barbara Jasper suddenly appeared at Sally's side, having left her own vegetable stand to get in on the gossip. "Just here for the summer, you say?" she asked Lily.

"Probably."

"My sister said she's having an affair with Michael Stoltz."

"No!" Sally looked shocked. "He would never!"

Lily rolled her eyes. "Come on, you two. Of course Michael's been seen with her. They went to school together. Their families lived in the same triplex. They grew up like brother and sister, for heaven's sake. Give me a break."

That seemed to shut them up, at least until Lily had walked away and was out of earshot. She bought a few more things, and although people seemed a little stiff with her, it might have been her imagination. Maybe she was the one who was on guard.

She searched the market for Rachel and spotted her walking in the direction of the tomato stand tucked into the shade of the warehouse. Uh-oh. George Holland's stand. Could be trouble.

Lily darted through the crowd as unobtrusively as possible until she reached Rachel's side, but she was a second too late to cut her off.

Rachel smiled at her. She was already carrying a few sacks of produce in her arms, and she pointed toward George Holland's beautifully arranged tomatoes. Mr. Holland himself was nowhere in sight. "Aren't these gorgeous?" Rachel asked her.

"Yeah, they are," Lily replied.

Mr. Holland suddenly appeared from behind the corner of the building.

"Hello, Lily!" He spoke so jovially that she knew no one had told him she was traveling with Rachel Huber today. But then his eyes fell on Rachel, who was holding one of his tomatoes to her nose. He looked at Lily again, eyes narrowed, glaring.

"You bring her here?" he asked. "To my stand?"

Rachel looked at him in surprise, then at Lily.

"Not specifically, Mr. Holland. But yes, I brought her to the market."

Rachel spoke, her voice uncertain. "I'm Rachel Huber," she said unnecessarily. "Was there . . . did you have someone in my class?"

"His daughter." Lily spoke for him.

"I'm so sorry," Rachel said.

Mr. Holland grabbed the tomato from her hand, throwing it into the garbage can at his side. It landed with such force that seeds flew through the air and splattered on his white apron. Rachel looked as if she were about to speak again, and Lily gave her a little shove.

"Go, Rachel. I'll catch up to you."

Rachel seemed rooted in front of the tomatoes. "I'd like to talk with you," she said to Mr. Holland. "I'd like to understand—"

"You shouldn't have come back," he said.

"Go, Rachel." Lily prodded her. She wasn't sure who she wanted to protect more, her unjustly accused second-grade teacher or her old neighbor, whose pain she understood well because she shared it.

George Holland leaned close to Rachel. "I've been saving a bullet for you," he said.

For one brief moment, Rachel's eyes registered their shock. She glanced at Lily, then turned on her heel and walked away.

Lily looked at Mr. Holland. His face was as red as his tomatoes, but the color faded quickly, and he seemed to deflate before her eyes like a balloon stuck with a pin. He leaned his beefy hands on the table and sighed.

"I shouldn't have said that," he said. "Just took me off guard, seeing her here. How can I treat her decent, Lily, you tell me that? How do *you* do it? *Why* do you do it? What would your mother say if she could see you walking around here with the schoolteacher, eh?"

"It was Rachel's tragedy, too," Lily said, but he didn't seem to hear her.

"At least my Sarah's still alive," he continued. "Pretty ruint, I'd say, with the scars and all. But alive. Your Jenny . . ." He shook his head.

Lily looked to the spot where Rachel had disappeared in the crowd. "Maybe I was wrong, bringing her here. She wanted to see the farmers' market. I was coming today; it seemed logical. But . . ." She sighed. "Maybe it was a mistake. I'm sorry I got you upset."

"She put Arlena Cash in the hospital, you know."

"What do you mean?"

"I mean, Arlena's been sick ever since that day she looked up and saw the schoolteacher standing in the middle of her store. Went in the hospital with chest pains Tuesday."

"That might have happened anyway," Lily argued.

Mr. Holland cocked his head at her. "I look at you, Lily. You're a beautiful girl. Full of life. And I think about Sarah. She used to be beautiful, too. Men would have fought over her. She should be married and have little ones. She deserved that. I can't look at you without thinking about *my* little girl."

Lily stepped forward and wrapped her arms around George Holland's bulky mass. "I'm sorry," she whispered. He was the proverbial salt of the earth, this man. Everyone here was. She'd known most of these farmers all her life, and she loved them all. They were good people who would do anything for her, for each other. Good people who, in this one regard, had grown bitter, full of venom.

When she pulled away, she saw the sheen of tears in Mr. Holland's eyes.

He didn't look at her. He busied himself opening up one of the small paper sacks on the table. "Two wrongs don't make a right," he said. He put three tomatoes in a bag and handed them to her. "Give these to the schoolteacher," he said. "Tell her it was just too much, seeing her here like that."

"All right," Lily said softly. She turned around.

"And Lily?"

She looked back at him.

"Tell her I haven't owned a gun in ten years."

Lily gave him a smile. "I will," she said.

She'd been wrong to bring Rachel here, she thought as she walked back to the parking lot. People were still too unforgiving, and Rachel was too trusting. Rachel tromped around the farmers' market, around town, with a courage borne of ignorance. She stepped into the fire not knowing it could burn. She had probably seen more of the world than Lily had, but she still did not understand this little corner of it.

She found Rachel sitting inside the unlocked van, the door open to catch the breeze. Lily climbed into the driver's seat, leaving her own door open as well. Rachel's eyes were rimmed with red.

"He said for me to give you these." Lily handed the bag to her.

Rachel peered inside. "Why?" she asked.

"He regrets what he said. And he said to tell you he doesn't even own a gun."

A half-smile crossed Rachel's face. "You've been very kind to me, Lily."

Lily hesitated. "I'm sorry. I'm sorry people think the worst of you. But I understand how they feel."

Rachel nodded. "You did lose your sister," she said.

Lily's tears surprised her, and she turned her head to look out the open door of the van. "We weren't alike in any way," she said. "Not in looks or anything. But there was a connection between us. It went way beyond anything conscious." Sometimes even now she would hear the word *twin*, taken totally out of context—"Where's the twin to this sock?"—and feel a sharp pain south of her breastbone.

"I don't remember Jenny well," Rachel said. "I remember you though. You were going to be my challenge for the year."

Lily smiled. "I was every teacher's challenge."

"Now I've learned to nurture that trait in my students. Instead of being afraid of it I try to help them use that creativity. But with you it scared me. I was too new. I didn't know what to do with you."

"You weren't the only one. I can't recall any teachers I had who nurtured that side of me."

They were both quiet for a moment.

"I remember your husband," Lily said softly. "I can picture him very clearly. I'm not sure if that's because I truly remember what he looked like or if it's just that I've seen his picture so many times over the years. I thought he was very handsome." She suddenly recalled seeing a bloodstained shred of Luke Pierce's camouflage shirt on the corner of Rachel's desk after the explosion. Another shred on the ledge below the chalkboard. The visual images were still sharp and clear, too clear, and the heat of the van suddenly seemed to press all the air from her lungs.

"Oh, God," she said, her hand to her forehead.

"Are you all right?" Rachel asked.

"Yeah." Lily pulled the van door closed. "Let's get out of here."

She drove out of the parking lot and onto the street, trying to focus her eyes on the sunlit fields stretching out on either side of them, but all she could see were those bloody pieces of cloth.

Secrets were insidious, she thought. They started out easy to hold on to, but while you weren't looking, they turned as caustic as acid. And it was the person keeping them who was first to feel the burn.

21

Michael was eating at his desk, as he usually did before the support group meeting on Friday nights. He was not looking forward to the session. He no longer felt comfortable meeting the eyes of his congregation, as though people might be able to look straight inside him and see—what? He was guilty of nothing. Yet he was carrying guilt around with him like a sack of rocks he could not put down.

He felt safe with the youth group. He'd met with them today to talk about the Reflection Day observance, and he'd felt like his old self with them. Comfort and self-confidence coursed through his body with such jubilance that he knew how sorely he'd been missing those qualities in himself lately. He'd gotten into a long philosophical discussion with the kids about the meaning of Reflection Day, about Rachel's role, about what it meant to be human and fallible. The hope for Reflection lay in this generation, he thought. These kids had no memory of their own about what had happened that day. They could make up their own minds as to how to address the situation. He did his best to empower them, to let them know this was something important they could have a say in. Once they acknowledged that much of their resistance to doing away with Reflection Day had to do with losing a school holiday, they embraced the concept of making this year's observance the last one.

"It's not up to us, though, is it?" one boy had asked.

"No," Michael said. "It's not up to us. But we can influence it. We'll have to do a good job. We'll have to be convincing."

"Hi, Michael." Celine appeared at his office door. She wore a smile he could not read. "It's almost seven-thirty."

He nodded, touched his mouth with his napkin. "Be right there," he said.

Celine disappeared, and with a reluctant sigh, Michael stood up to face the unknown.

There were seven people in the group, but two were missing that evening. Next to Celine sat Ian Jackson, who like Michael had come to the Mennonite faith through marriage rather than being raised in a Mennonite family. Frank Howe sat on the other side of Celine. He was the father of the boy Michael had seen at Hershey Park when he'd been with Rachel. Next to Frank was Ellie Ryan, probably the least liberal of his congregation. She had moved from Bird-in-Hand to Reflection and always made a point of the fact that she was merely trying the Reflection church on for size. Even though she'd been part of the congregation for two years now, she had not yet pulled both feet in the door.

"Hey, Rev." Ian moved his chair to open the circle and let him in. No one in this church called him Reverend, except Ian. And with Ian he knew it was a term of affection. He'd met the young man five or six years ago, when Lily drew him into the church. He'd counseled the couple before they got married, and what always stuck in his mind was Ian's answer to his question about how they met. Ian had been doing volunteer work at the ASPCA when Lily came in to exercise the dogs.

"I watched her for a while," Ian had told him, "and then I said to myself, 'Ian, this woman is like a greenhouse.'"

"A greenhouse?" Michael had asked.

"Yes. She has a purpose, she's efficient, yet she's warm to the point of giving off heat and she's so open you can see clear through her."

Michael had known right then that those two were a match. Since that day, every time he saw Lily he could not help but picture the clear glass and warm confines of a greenhouse.

Although none of them were assigned to lead the group, he or Celine usually got things rolling. Tonight it was Celine.

"Let's check in," she said. "You want to start, Frank?"

Frank drew in a breath. "Well, things are better with Sean," he said, referring to his son. He must have talked about Sean at the last meeting, the one Michael had missed.

"He caught Sean smoking," Celine said to Michael.

"Well, I didn't make a big deal out of it, like you all said," Frank reported. "And it's all blown over. I don't think he'll be doing it again." He looked at Ian, who took the cue.

"I'm doin' good," Ian said. Ian was almost always "doin' good." He rarely had anything urgent to report, although occasionally he'd talk about his longing for children and Lily's fear of having them. "Nothing major going on." He nodded to Michael.

"Well," Michael said. "Jace really misses Katy." He realized the instant the words left his mouth that he always used Jace in here. Jace was the one worry in his life he was willing to present to the world. He could not see himself discussing his other concerns with the group. Some role model. He was playing a game. But it was to protect the others, wasn't it? How would people feel if they thought their minister did not have his act together? Let them think he had an unhappy, troubled son. He held Jace up to them like an offering. The realization took him aback, and it was a moment before he continued. "This separation is hard on him," he said.

"When's Katy due back?" Ellie asked.

"Mid-October." He'd spoken with Katy the night before, and she had returned to her cool and guarded self again. It was as if a different woman had made that tearful, middle-of-the-night phone call to him. Michael turned to Ellie, wanting to get the spotlight off himself. "And how was your week?" he asked.

Ellie offered some response, but he didn't really hear her. Nor did he pay much attention to Celine when she checked in. He was waiting for what he knew was coming, and after a moment or two of silence, it began.

Frank shifted in his chair. "We talked about your situation last time, Michael," he said. "You weren't here, and we had some . . . some bad feelings about talking about it without you, but we had to. It was pressing on us. I guess we were all hoping it would just go away. But it hasn't."

"No," Celine said gently. "No. The whole situation seems to have intensified this week."

"I'm not sure what you mean by 'the situation.'" He would volunteer nothing until he had a clear definition of what they were talking about.

"This is almost exactly what happened at my last church," Ellie said. "When the minister starts to lose his . . . his *integrity*, it filters down through the congregation. I don't want to see that happen here."

The skin beneath his shirt collar felt very warm. "Please explain what you mean, Ellie. What do you mean, I'm losing my integrity?"

"That's a little strong, Ellie," Ian said.

"We want to give you all our support, Michael," Celine said, leaning toward him. Celine had once wanted to be a minister, but family commitments had gotten in her way. She had become an elder instead, and she was excellent in that position, but Michael was not accustomed to having her in control. He did not like this sudden reversal of roles.

He sighed. "You're talking about the rumors," he said.

"Rumors based on fact," Frank said.

"We're not here to judge Rachel Huber—or you, Michael," Celine said. "We want to help you. You're very important to us."

He was trapped. He leaned forward himself, elbows on his knees. "Please listen to me," he said. "I've known Rachel since I was seven years old. She was one of my best friends. If she were a man and I was spending time with him, no one would be batting an eye."

"If people saw you with your arm around him like they have with Rachel Huber, they'd be batting an eye for sure," Frank said.

Ian made a disgusted sound. He was head of the tolerance committee and didn't take well to homophobic sentiment, but Michael was too struck by Frank's words to notice anything else. Someone had seen him with his arm around Rachel? He could not even remember doing that—at least not in public.

"That's irrelevant," Ellie said. "She's not a man, and she's not just anyone. You know, I lived in Bird-in-Hand when the incident happened with the kids in her classroom, and I was just twelve. It seemed like it was happening far away, and also since I went to a Mennonite school, I felt sort of protected, like it couldn't possibly happen in my school. When I first moved here, I had a fleeting thought about it. You know how everyone around here equates Reflection with that tragedy. I understand you were good friends, Michael, but many people are distressed. They feel like you're not only betraying Katy, but the church as well."

"I'm not . . ." His voice was too loud. He worked to lower it. "I'm not betraying anyone," he said. "Too much is being read into this."

"I've been getting a lot of calls," Celine said. "So have the other elders. People are calling totally out of concern and love for you. Some people think that having Katy away this long has been hard on you, having to deal with Jace alone and everything. This is the first time you and she have done any voluntary service separately, isn't it?"

"Yes, but—"

"Please, Michael, for our sake as well as your own, nip this thing in the bud."

"There is nothing to nip." He wanted to be back in the safe and boisterous confines of the youth group.

"Look, Michael," Frank said, "you've been seen all over the place with her, and not just looking like friends, either."

He sat up straight and tried to smile. "There are reasonable explanations for all of this, but I don't like being put in the position of having to defend myself against rumors."

"Maybe it'd help, though, Rev," Ian suggested gently. "I mean if you just addressed the whole issue up front, maybe—"

"Your wife is making a sacrifice," Ellie interrupted. She had tears in her eyes. "She's thousands of miles from home and her family, helping people who need her desperately. Even if your relationship with Rachel Huber is completely innocent—which I'll tell you frankly, Michael, no one believes—you need to end it."

The meeting seemed to drag on forever. He tried to explain the tenor of his relationship with Rachel. He tried to discount the rumors. He tried to engage the others in helping him put an end to unfounded concerns, all the while knowing that he was being no more honest with them than he was with himself.

Celine came into his office after the meeting, as he was getting ready to leave.

He looked up from his desk.

"I'm sorry, Michael," she said. "We had to address it. It's gotten too big, and I'm very concerned. I see you every day, and I see you holding it in, whatever 'it' is. You don't look at me. Sometimes I've noticed that you have trouble concentrating on whatever it is we're talking about. You stare off into space."

He looked at her sharply. "Do I?" he asked.

She nodded as she sat down. "Can you talk to one of the other elders, maybe? How about opening up to Lewis? You know how much he loves you."

"If I feel it's necessary, I'll talk to him."

She sat down and rested her hands on his desk. "I hope that, even if you're not willing to admit what's going on to us, at least you're admitting it to yourself," she said. "That you're trying to work this through for yourself."

He looked across his desk at her and felt himself giving in. "I am," he said softly, and he felt the sudden shift of power in the room. He had been her mentor until this moment.

"I've looked up to you," she said gently. "You've always shown me that tough things could be handled in a way consistent with our faith. And now . . ." She shook her head. "You know what it would mean, don't you? If you let your marriage fall apart?"

"My marriage is not going to fall apart. My marriage—" He could not remember what he'd been about to say. There was a blank in his mind where his marriage should have been.

"Aside from the personal element, the professional consequences are immense."

"Celine, please. I'm not going to let that happen."

"You have a responsibility to us, Michael. "

"I know that."

She stood up and smiled at him. "All right," she said. "Enough for now. Good night, Michael, and God bless."

She left the room, and he stared at the empty doorway for a moment afterward. He must be as transparent as a greenhouse himself, he thought. How else could so many people know what was in his heart?

22

The nursing home in Lancaster seemed better than most, cleaner and cheerier. The smell was antiseptic but not unpleasant, and a huge bouquet of flowers graced the coffee table in the empty front room. Rachel guessed that Marielle Hostetter had the money to put herself in a decent place.

She tracked down a receptionist who told her to "chust seat yourself dawn" while she looked for a nurse. Rachel sat down on the sofa behind the coffee table with its exuberant bouquet. It was Monday afternoon, and she had not told anyone about this visit. Michael and Gram were bound to try to discourage her, and she was determined to make this effort. Granted, the thought of saving the land through simple persuasion of its owner seemed far-fetched at this point, but it sounded as though no one had tried in a while. It could hardly hurt.

The receptionist walked past the door to the waiting room, and Rachel looked at her watch, wondering if they were going to let her in. She pictured Marielle Hostetter's room under guard.

Suddenly, a round-faced woman appeared in the doorway. "You here to see Marielle?" she asked, an expectant smile on her face.

"Yes." Rachel stood up.

"Great. I'm her nurse. Follow me." She led Rachel down a long corridor to an open door at the end. Standing in the doorway, she bellowed above the sound of a TV, "You have company, honey!" Then she turned to Rachel. "Go on in," she said. "Let me know if you need anything."

The nurse disappeared down the hall, and Rachel stepped into the doorway of the small bedroom. A woman sat in a large recliner, a few feet in front of a television set on which a game show was playing. The television audience roared, and the woman laughed along with them. She seemed completely oblivious to Rachel's presence.

"Ms. Hostetter?" Rachel took a step into the room, but the older woman didn't turn her head from the TV.

Rachel walked up to the chair and stood at an angle, near the television. "Ms. Hostetter?" she asked.

Marielle looked up at her, then back at the TV. "This is *Wheel of Fortune,*" she said. "My favorite."

What did that mean? Did she not want to be interrupted? Rachel was intrigued by her face. It was—there was no other term for it—misshapen. As if someone had pulled on the corners of a square of putty until it took on this altered, injured look. Along one side of her forehead ran a deep red scar, and Rachel shuddered at the memory of how she'd gotten it. She had never seen this face before. Not in the woods, not anywhere. She would not have forgotten it. Despite its oddness, though, it was not the bat woman's face from her imagination. This woman looked harmless.

"Could I speak with you for a minute?" she asked.

Marielle looked up at her again, then motioned a finger in the direction of the TV. "Turn that thing down," she said loudly.

Rachel lowered the volume, then pulled a straight-back chair from beneath a small desk and sat down near the older woman.

"My name is Rachel Huber." She studied the woman's face, hunting for any light of recognition at the Huber name, but she could find none.

"Rachel Huber," the woman repeated.

"My grandfather was a friend of your father's."

Marielle's eyes remained blank, and Rachel continued.

"I'd like to talk with you about your property, if you're willing."

Marielle's eyes had drifted back to the TV again, although she couldn't possibly hear it. "She should buy a vowel," she said.

"I know you may be under some pressure to develop your land, but you don't have to. You can be the one to have the final say."

Marielle's eyes seemed to be attached to the TV by an invisible rubber band. Rachel wanted to take that boxy head and turn it toward her, hold it there. She was not even certain whether the old woman was listening to her. Or perhaps she heard her very well and was merely feigning a lack of interest. People were probably right when they said Marielle would speak only through her attorney.

"Maybe you don't realize the impact the development will have on Reflection," she said. She listed every cost to the quality of life she could think of, ending with the possibility of driving the Amish from the area.

"I'm listening to you," the woman said a few times as Rachel spoke, but she seemed transfixed by the silent picture of the game show.

Rachel finally stood up with a sigh. She reached over to turn up the volume on the TV. "Well, please think about what I've told you," she said. "You have a very beautiful piece of land. It seems a shame to destroy it."

Marielle's head suddenly darted up. "I have beautiful land, and it's mine," she said. "It says so in my Bible. The land thingy."

Rachel was not dealing with a lucid mind. "In your Bible?" she asked. Perhaps Marielle was religious. Maybe she was following the dictates of some Scripture in making the decision about her land.

"Yes." Marielle pressed the lever on the side of the chair and struggled to raise herself out of it. Rachel helped, her hand on the older woman's elbow. Marielle walked without difficulty to a dresser, where she pulled open a drawer and felt around beneath some neatly folded articles of clothing. "Here," she said, holding her hand out to Rachel.

Rachel put out her own hand, and Marielle dropped something into it. A key.

"It's in the Bible," the older woman said. "The land thingy."

"What is this the key to?" Rachel asked. "Is it to your house?"

Marielle shoved her gently toward the door. "*Wheel of Fortune* is my favorite," she said.

Rachel stood outside the door, looking in at Marielle absorbed once again in her program. She studied the key in her hand. Marielle either did not know what she was doing or knew entirely too well. Either way, the key had been given to her freely. She slipped it into the pocket of her pants and walked back down the hall.

The small front room was still empty, and Rachel noticed a phone on one of the end tables. She found the receptionist again and asked for permission to make a call, and she chewed her lower lip as she dialed the number for the church. She wasn't certain Michael would want to hear from her. She hadn't spoken to him since Friday night, when he'd called to tell her about his so-called support group—and that he didn't think they should see each other over the weekend. He'd planned to take Jason camping.

But surely he would want to know about this.

"You're *where*?" he said when she'd reached him.

"At the nursing home. They seemed pleased Marielle had a visitor. It was extremely easy to get in to see her."

"And she actually talked to you?"

"If you can call it that. She really seemed lost."

Michael sighed. "I'm sure her nephews are behind the whole thing. They're the ones who will benefit the most."

"Have you talked to them?"

Michael groaned. "Dozens of times. She has every right to develop her land, they say, and it will ultimately be good for the town. A lot of people honestly believe that. And I suppose there are some factions for whom that's the truth."

"She gave me what I think is the key to her house."

He was quiet for a minute. "The key to her house?" he repeated.

Rachel described the odd exchange, including Marielle's mention of the "land thingy" in the Bible. "She gave the key to me of her free will. I think we should go check out her cottage."

Michael laughed. "Oh, right. I always wanted to see the oven she shoved little kids into."

"Well, she's not shoving anyone in there these days." Rachel sounded brave, although the thought of making her way through those deep woods filled with horror stories from her childhood was not enticing.

"What would be the point?' Michael asked. "What would we be looking for?"

"I don't know," Rachel said. "Maybe she's marked a passage in her Bible that would help us understand why she's taking this stance. Then we could use it to dissuade her. Maybe."

"Seems far-fetched."

"I guess you're right."

Silence filled the line for a moment, and Rachel ran her fingers over the keypad of the telephone. She wasn't ready to let him go yet. "How was the camping trip?" she asked.

"It was fun." He sounded tired.

"And have you recovered from your support group yet?"

"They meant well," he said. "And I know they're right. I'm denying it backwards and forwards, but the truth is I have a problem. It might not be quite as juicy as some of them think, but it's a problem nonetheless."

"What can I do, Michael?" she asked. "What can I do that would be of the most help to you?"

"Besides going back to San Antonio?"

She said nothing, hurt.

"I'm sorry, Rache. You know that's not what I want. I'm just frustrated, in a lot of ways. I have to think things through, and you cloud my head."

She wondered if she could still think of herself as a good, honorable person. She wanted Michael. She would do nothing to encourage it, nothing to harm his marriage or his career, but she wanted him all the same.

"Do you still want to go to Washington with Gram and me on Friday?"

"Are you kidding? That's the only thought that's keeping me sane right now. Knowing I'll be with you on Friday night. Away from here. If only I didn't have to bring my conscience along with me, I'd have a great time."

"What about Jace?" she asked.

"He'll stay at the Pelmans'. He's going with them to some computer show in Lancaster on Saturday."

The receptionist poked her head in the door. "Your car vindows up yet?" she asked. "Going to make dawn any minute."

"They're up," Rachel said, stifling a giggle.

"What's that?" Michael asked.

"The receptionist said it's going to 'make dawn' soon." She looked out the window at the darkening sky and thought of her grandmother. "I'd better go, Michael. I want to get back to Gram before the storm hits. It's not raining there yet, is it?"

"Uh-uh. But it's looking ugly out."

"Okay. I've got to run."

"Rache," he said. "It's good to hear your voice. Are you doing all right?"

"Pretend I'm in San Antonio, Michael." She smiled, feeling just for an instant stronger than he was. She hung up before she could say she missed him.

Helen had been looking forward to this time all day long. Rachel had been with her throughout the morning, and much as she loved her granddaughter's company, today she wanted her out of the house. Her wrist was fine—well, almost—and the piano was calling her. She'd played several times in secret over the past few days, and now she could not wait to sit down at the instrument again.

She was not shy about playing for others. That was not it. She simply needed the time alone with the piano, the way lovers who've suffered a long separation need their privacy. So as soon as Rachel pulled out of the driveway, Helen took her seat at the keys and lost herself in the music.

This was when she most appreciated Peter's insistence on wall-to-wall windows in the house. She felt as if she were playing in the forest, swallowed up in green. The sunlight, filtered through the trees, formed a delicate ash-colored filigree of light across the open piano lid.

She felt close to Hans, sitting here. She could almost picture him at the other piano, a lock of dark hair slipping over his forehead as he stormed across the keys, dueling with her piano as they played. His face would be glistening when they'd finished, and she would be breathless. For a long time she'd thought that was as close as they would ever come to making love.

Friday night she would see him from her seat in the concert hall at the Kennedy Center. Should she have made some excuse to stay home? She still could. She could feign illness. But how could she stay away from a concert filled with Huber works? She would simply have to endure watching Hans play. She had endured tougher things in her life.

She finished one piece and immediately began another, this one slow and sweet. Her pleasure in playing was back in full force. Over the past year or so she had lost her excitement, not only for the piano but for everything else in her life as well. She recalled her willingness to die after being struck by lightning. Now, though, everything seemed touched with golden light. She owed Rachel for this fresh start, she knew. Rachel and her attention and caring and silly games. She should never have allowed the distance to exist between herself and her granddaughter for so long. They had missed out on too many years together.

She could not shake the feeling, though, that her pleasure and Rachel's were conversely related. Rachel had been so happy at finding Michael again, but her love for him had nowhere to go. The girl did not complain, but Helen saw the sadness in her eyes, the tightness in her cheeks that told her the smile she wore was wider than the smile she felt inside. Ah, yes. Piano or no piano, Helen had a new reason for living. Her dear granddaughter needed her comfort and counsel in a way no one had needed her for a very long time.

Rachel pulled the car into the driveway as the first few drops of rain were beginning to dot her windshield. She turned off the ignition and slipped her keys into her pants pocket. She heard them clink against Marielle Hostetter's key, and she shook her head with a laugh. Probably the key to her room at the nursing home.

Stepping out of the car, she heard the far-off rumble of thunder and something else—the sound of a piano coming from the house. She cocked her head to listen. Was it a recording? It had to be. The music was so clear and lively and loud. But she knew all of Gram's CD's by heart now, and this piece was not familiar.

Something told her not to go inside. She walked slowly around the side of the house until she could see in the rear windows, and what she saw made her gasp, hand to her throat. Gram was at the piano, her arms and shoulders pumping feverishly. Rachel's gentle, octogenarian grandmother was attacking the piano, with extraordinary results. Not missing a note, as far as Rachel could tell.

Gram came to the end of that piece and quickly started another, this one teasing in its pace: slow, then fast, then slow again. Rachel leaned against the wall of the house, listening, the rain light on her face. The theme quickly developed, and by the second time it wafted through the open windows, Rachel felt its warmth and longed to hear it repeated over and over again.

The rain was more insistent now, the thunder closer. Through the trees, she saw a pulse of light. She walked around the house again and climbed quietly onto the porch. She was about to reach for the knob of the screen door when a violent clap of thunder shook the floor of the porch. She heard her grandmother make a sound, like a moan, and the music abruptly ceased.

Rachel pushed open the door to meet Gram's frantic eyes. The hands that had only seconds before played the piano with strength and confidence now trembled as they pressed against her cheeks, and Rachel wordlessly pulled her grandmother into her arms.

23

Becky's car was parked in front of the Lutheran church. Hooray. Becky had missed aerobics class both Friday and Monday, and Rachel wasn't sure she could face this group of women one more time without her friend's presence.

All was not well in the class, and she knew she was the cause. She'd been alone among strangers during the past two sessions, and without Becky there, she could more clearly see the lines of battle. A few women—two actually—had been kind to her; others had gone out of their way to avoid her. They'd talked about one woman named Ellie who had dropped out of the class, and although no one said it in so many words, Rachel felt certain that she was being held responsible for the loss. After both classes, she'd made excuses—offered only to herself, since no one asked her—to avoid changing in the ladies' room. She hadn't known if she could bear the silence, or the forced kindness, or the whispers behind her back.

She was beginning to be seen in almost supernatural terms, she thought—a demonic temptress come back to seduce the man who wanted to save Reflection. She'd come back to bring harm to the town once again. She wanted to have a T-shirt made up that read I'M WILLING TO TALK ABOUT IT. If someone would confront her directly, she thought she could handle it. The subtlety of people's dislike put a lock on her tongue. Where she'd once talked to anyone on the street or in the shops, she now avoided meeting the eyes of strangers and did not speak until spoken to. Despite the conciliatory bag of tomatoes, the words of the man at the farmers' market were the last thing she heard each night before she fell asleep.

The class was already in its casual formation when she walked into the gym. Becky glanced at her but didn't acknowledge her wave, and Rachel felt an immediate sense of dread. She's merely preoccupied, she told herself. Don't panic.

In the ladies' room after class, she positioned herself close to her friend. "Missed you the past week," she said. "How've you been?"

"All right." Becky's attention was focused on the task of buttoning her blouse.

"Any chance you have time to get something to eat?"

"Not tonight."

Becky was clearly angry. There was a taut line to her jaw, a sharpness to her movements, and when she left the ladies' room, it was with a general "bye" to everyone in the room.

Rachel quickly stuffed her workout shoes into her gym bag and ran after her, catching up with her on the stairs.

"Wait a minute, Becky. Please."

Near the top of the stairs, Becky turned to face her, and Rachel recoiled from the look of hostility on her face.

"What's going on?" Rachel asked.

Becky waited until a few of their classmates had passed between them on the stairs. When they were alone again, she dropped her gym bag on the floor and folded her arms. "What's going on is that I'm pissed off, that's what."

"At me?"

"Yes, at you. I feel as though you used me. You played on my sympathy."

"I don't understand."

"Look, Rachel. I'm sorry for what happened with you and Luke. And I still don't blame you for it, like some people do. I was feeling bad at first about the way some people were treating you. But I'm a friend of Katy's, and I was quite honestly disgusted when I found out you were going after Michael."

So that was it. "I'm not going after anyone," Rachel said. "Come on, Becky. You know Michael and I go back forever. We're friends. That's it. Doesn't it make sense that I'd be spending time with him this summer?"

"I've heard you're much more than friends, and it infuriates me. Katy's going to hear about it from someone, and she's going to be hurt by it. She's living in some dump in Russia, and Michael's here entertaining his testosterone. I thought he was above that." She shook her head in exasperation. "He and Katy had the best marriage in this whole damn town. I don't know what's gotten into him. Except you. You seem to have no respect whatsoever for the fact that he's married."

"You're—"

"Look, I admit I'm supersensitive to infidelity. My husband cheated on me, and it just about killed me when I found out, but—"

"Becky, listen to me! No one's cheating on anyone. We are not romantically involved. If anyone tells Katy that we are, then they're the person responsible for hurting her. Not Michael. Not me."

Becky looked away from her, toward the foyer.

"Why are you so set on believing the worst?" Rachel asked.

"Because it's your word against the word of people I've known for a long time. And the truth is, I don't know you at all. I knew you once, but you could be a . . . a sociopath now, for all I know. Besides, Michael's walking around with guilt all over his face." She picked up her bag again and walked into the foyer of the church.

Rachel followed her with a sense of defeat. There was nothing more she could say. Becky was going to believe whatever she wanted to, and she couldn't change it.

"You're wrong about us," she said as they stepped outside. "I can't prove it to you, but as long as you have no proof to the contrary— and I know you can't possibly—then I wish you'd give me the benefit of the doubt."

"I wish I could, too, Rachel." She waved at a woman who was standing by her car. "I'll be right there," she called, and Rachel had the sinking realization that in a few minutes Becky and the woman would be talking about her.

She held back as Becky caught up with her friend, then slowly headed toward her car where it was parked in front of the small brick chapel across the street. Her eyes were on the Mennonite church next door. The last place you should go, Rachel, she told herself. The very last place.

She was nearly to her car when she saw the light on in Michael's basement office. With a glance over her shoulder, she turned and walked quickly toward the rear of the church. The welcome cover of darkness fell around her.

She looked through his office window. His back was to her. There were half a dozen books spread out on his desk, and he was writing something, his hand busy on the yellow legal pad.

She hesitated a moment before knocking on the glass. He looked up, and the smile came to his face so quickly that she laughed. He didn't speak, but as he rose from his desk, he nodded in the direction of the building's rear entrance.

She walked around to the basement door, and he met her there, standing in the doorway, not inviting her in.

"Sorry." She hugged herself. "I have no right to be here, but I'm upset and it just feels like I should be able to see you if I want to."

"Yeah, it does," he agreed. "What's upsetting you?"

"I just had a run-in with Becky."

He glanced behind him, and she wondered if anyone else was around.

"Let's take a walk," he said, stepping out into the darkness. "Come on."

They walked toward the path around the pond, quickly, silently, and she knew they were in hiding. She felt both her body and his relax when they reached the woods.

"So," he said, "tell me about Becky."

She described the conversation, and he groaned. "Where is this stuff coming from? This town must be hard up for a good piece of gossip."

"She said your marriage is the best in town."

Michael snorted. "If mine's the best, I'd hate to see the worst." He caught her arm and pulled her low as an overhanging branch suddenly appeared in the darkness.

"I'll call Becky," he said. "Set her straight."

"Don't bother on my account." Rachel ducked to avoid another branch. "I figure my reputation can't get much worse. But maybe you should talk to her for your own sake." She looked up at the trees and let out a sigh. "I don't know how I'm ever going to make Chris

understand what's going on here," she said. Chris had called that
morning to say he could come on the twenty-eighth and stay for a
week, and she was both delighted and unnerved by the thought of
having her son here with her.

They were walking on the far side of the pond, where the woods
surrounding the path were so thick that even at midday it would feel
like evening. At eight-thirty it was very dark. Neither of them spoke,
as if some hidden being might overhear them. Rachel shuddered.
They were on what had been the scariest part of the path when they
were kids. They could not be far from Marielle's cottage back here.

"I still have that key Marielle Hostetter gave me."

Michael glanced at her. "I can't believe she gave it to you." He
reached above his head and snapped off a twig. "Let's do it," he said.

"Do what? See if it fits her house?"

"Sure."

"Oh, right. I wouldn't walk through these woods in broad daylight
when I was an immortal teenager," she said. "I'm not about to do it
now."

"Come on." He nudged her arm.

She looked at him through narrowed eyes but could not read his
face in the darkness. "Are you serious?"

"Uh-huh."

"It's too dark. We'll get lost."

"I have a flashlight in my office. Wait here for me, and I'll go get it."

She darted a look over her shoulder. "I'm not waiting here," she
said. "I'm coming with you."

They walked back to the church, and she stood in the shadows
outside while he got the flashlight and a compass. They made their
way back up the path in silence, and when they reached the spot
where they'd turned around, Michael shined the light into the woods.

"I don't see a path," he said, "but look here." He pointed the light
toward an area where the brush seemed thinner, newer. "I think we
can get through. You game?"

"Sure." She feigned courage. She did not remember him being this
much braver than she.

Michael led the way, and it was slow going as he walked with the
flashlight in one hand, his other arm outstretched to catch branches

before they slapped him in the face. The woods were eerie, quiet, the only sound the crackling of twigs beneath their feet. It was a minute before she noticed the fireflies. They were high above them, silently blinking in the trees like pale yellow stars. Rachel stopped walking. "Look up," she said.

Michael turned off his flashlight, and for a moment they stood mesmerized by the lights. "Late in the summer for them," he said.

"I don't think I've ever seen so many in one place."

He tugged on her shoulder to start her walking again. "I remember your father used to take the little lightbulbs off them."

"What?" She had no memory of that at all. "Why would he have done that?"

"I don't remember his reasoning, but I know we'd catch a bunch in a jar and take them to him, and he'd do his surgery."

"That's barbaric." Her memories of her father—of both her parents—were already too muted and thin. The last thing she wanted to do was taint them with stories of depravity.

She reached for the flashlight. "I'll lead for a while," she said. "If you can promise me we're going in the right direction."

He held the compass into the beam of light. "We know the cottage is east of where we started out. We'll just keep walking east. And we're on a legitimate path now, don't you think?"

He was right. It was narrow and overgrown, but there was no doubt that someone had at one time cut this path through the trees.

They plodded on in silence. From somewhere high above them, an owl hooted, sending a shiver up Rachel's arms. She stopped in the middle of the path, realizing she no longer heard Michael's steps behind her. Turning around, she saw nothing but empty forest in the beam of the flashlight.

"Michael?"

"Bat woman!" He grabbed her from behind, and she jumped in the air. She spun around to face him, annoyed she'd fallen for his old childhood stunt.

"God, don't *do* that." She laughed.

His arms were still around her, the pressure of them light, barely there, and she rested her hands on them, flashlight dangling from her fingers. His eyes were locked with hers; there was no smile on his face, and for a moment neither of them spoke. Above them the owl hooted.

"You were wrong to come to the church tonight," he said, "and I was wrong to open the door to you."

"I know." She felt the slight contraction of the muscles in his arms beneath her hands. He was dangerously close.

He lifted one hand to her cheek, and she closed her eyes at the touch of his fingers. She could remember feeling that hand on her breast long ago. She could still remember the warmth, the tenderness in his touch, and that's what she was thinking about as he pressed his lips to hers. He kissed her softly, without any of the fever that was mounting in her body.

The darkness was disorienting. She felt dizzy when he touched her lower lip with the tip of his finger, when he opened her mouth that way, then leaned forward to kiss her again, deeply this time, and she felt the tension beginning to rise in his body as well. The hunger.

He wrapped his arms around her, and she pressed her head against his shoulder, stunned by her tears. After a minute, he spoke softly in her ear. "Why is it," he said, "that right now I feel no guilt?"

She tried to measure her own guilt and found it nearly absent. "Neither do I," she said.

She heard his sigh, muffled against her ear. "I feel so damned *human* these days. Weak-willed. And the worst part is, I can't seem to pray anymore. It scares me."

She hugged him harder. She thought he was shivering.

"You're shaking," he said, and she realized it was her own body that was trembling.

"I just want you so badly," she said.

He rubbed her arms, as if he could somehow still her tremor. "I want you, too. You know that, don't you?"

She nodded against his chest.

"And I'm crazy to play at it when we can't have it. I'm not willing to make love to you, Rachel, when there's no hope of anything more than that."

She was willing, though. It would be wrong. It would be the worst thing she'd ever done in her life, but right now she was willing. "I wish you weren't so strong," she said.

He laughed, pulling away from her. "If I were strong, I wouldn't be standing here in the dark with my arms around you."

She let go of him, and they began walking up the path again in silence.

Rachel could not recall ever having seen Marielle's cottage, but she sketched a quick picture of it in her imagination. A small living room, a tiny cramped kitchen, and one bedroom, the double bed miraculously made up with clean white sheets.

Damn Katy Esterhaus. Damn the Mennonite church.

"There it is." Michael caught her shoulder and pointed to their right.

Rachel shined the flashlight into the woods to illuminate the small, ramshackle, and thoroughly unthreatening cottage. The shutters hung askew; the shingles on the roof were in shreds. The chances of finding a clean bed inside seemed minuscule. Good.

"Incredible that she could live in this little shack all these years at the same time that she owned this valuable piece of land," Rachel said.

They walked toward the front door. Michael tried the knob, but it was locked. Rachel slipped the key from her pocket and inserted it into the keyhole. It was an easy fit. It turned with a satisfying *click*.

"I don't believe it," Michael said.

She glanced at him, shrugged, and stepped over the threshold.

Michael tried a wall switch, and a tiny living room suddenly appeared in front of them. "She didn't have the electricity turned off," he said.

The room was cluttered with nondescript furniture, old, moth-eaten blankets, and a few hundred copies of *Reader's Digest*.

"So now that we're here," Michael asked, "what are we hoping to find?"

"The Bible, for starters," Rachel said. She looked around her at the grimy blankets and magazines. "What a firetrap."

Michael sat down on a hassock and began rooting through a bookshelf. "I'll start in here," he said.

Rachel walked down a narrow hallway, past the door to the kitchen, which was as tiny and unappealing as she'd imagined it, to the small bedroom at the rear of the cottage. There was indeed a double bed, stripped, the striped ticking of the mattress yellowed and stained.

A wooden cross hung askew on the wall above the bed, and a dresser, caked with dust, stood against the wall. Rachel rummaged through the dresser's nearly empty drawers, finding a few balled-up articles of clothing, nothing else. The drawer of the small night table was empty.

Discouraged, she stood in the center of the room, hands on her hips. "Have you found anything?" she called into the hallway.

"A great article in a 1972 *Reader's Digest* about this blind guy who walked clear across the country with his two dogs."

"Michael!" She laughed.

"Seriously. It's inspirational."

She shook her head and opened the door to a deep closet. A few empty wire hangers were clumped together at one end of the rod, and yet another old blanket was bundled onto the shelf above her head. She was about to close the door when something caught her eye. Something dark stuck out from the shelf below the blanket.

She had to stand on her toes to reach it. It was definitely a book. She tugged at it, and the blanket fell over her head as the book landed in her arms. It was thick and leather-covered. Marielle Hostetter's Bible.

She tossed the blanket over the footboard as she sat down on the bed, the Bible on her knees. Now what? She opened the front cover. Someone had scrawled a family tree on the inside pages, the ink a faded purple. She found Marielle's name. The younger of two children, with no offspring of her own.

Leafing through the pages, she was disappointed to see no markings that might help them understand the old woman's thinking. Well, it had been a far-fetched idea, after all.

She was about to close the book when she thought to look inside the back cover. A folded sheet of onionskin paper slipped to the floor. She picked it up and lay it flat on the bed, and what she read forced her to read it through a second time.

"Michael!" she called. "Come here."

She was reading it a third time when he appeared in the doorway to the bedroom.

"I found the Bible," she said, "and this was inside it."

She handed him the thin sheet of paper. He began reading it, and she watched the blood leave his face as he understood its meaning.

24

Michael drove ahead of Rachel on the way to Helen's, glancing in his rearview mirror from time to time, trying to catch Rachel's eye, trying to get answers to the questions running through his head. On the seat next to him lay the precious sheet of paper they had found in the Hostetter Bible—the thoroughly bizarre codicil to Peter Huber's will. How had it come to be there? Was it legal? Did Helen know about it? And who was Karl Speicer? Nothing made sense.

He wished Rachel were sitting next to him so they could talk about it, puzzle it out. Just as well, though. He could not be with her. The walk through the woods had been pure temptation. Each time he saw her, he was playing with fire. If a member of his congregation came to him seeking counsel about a similar situation, he would have no hesitation in telling him or her to avoid the person.

But what if that person was your oldest, most precious friend?

He had barely come to a stop in front of Helen's house when Rachel was at his car window.

"I've been thinking," she said. "Maybe we shouldn't just lay this on her. She seems a lot stronger lately, on a physical level at least, but I don't know how this might affect her."

Michael gingerly lifted the sheet of paper from the seat and got out of the car. "We have to talk to her, Rache." There was no way he could keep their discovery from Helen.

She nodded reluctantly. "Gently, though. I have a bad feeling about it. It's so strange."

"Well." He took her arm and started toward the porch steps. "Let's go see if we can get some answers."

They found Helen reading in the library. She looked up when they walked into the room, a broad smile on her face.

"Michael!" she said. "It's good to see you."

He bent low to kiss her cheek. "Good to see you, too, Helen." He knew her happiness was linked to seeing him together with Rachel. Helen had a keen sense of how the universe should be ordered.

Rachel pulled the ottoman in front of her grandmother's chair and sat down. "We have to talk to you, Gram," she said. "We found something."

Helen frowned. "Found something?" she repeated.

Michael sat down on the sofa. "Rachel went to see Marielle Hostetter a few days ago," he began.

Helen turned her frown in Rachel's direction. "You did?" she asked.

Rachel nodded, and Michael continued. "For some reason we couldn't figure out, Marielle gave Rachel the key to her house. She said something about a 'land thing' being in her Bible. We went to her house tonight and found the Bible, and inside there was an addendum to Peter's will."

He glanced at Rachel, hoping she wasn't upset at him for plowing ahead this way, but her expression was one of apprehension rather than objection. He held the codicil out to Helen, but she drew back from it, the smile gone from her face.

"Shall I read it to you?" he asked.

"I think I know what it says," Helen said.

He exchanged a quizzical look with Rachel before he began reading.

"'The land which I inherited from my parents, bounded by the town limits of Reflection on the north, Colley Road on the east, Spring Willow Pond to the south, and Main Street to the west, has been home to the Hostetter family for generations,'" he read. "'Marielle Hostetter may continue to live on that land until her death, at which time the property shall pass to her heirs, or she may dispose of the land as she sees fit, and retain the proceeds from any sale. The foregoing will be void, however, if my last work, *Reflections*, is delivered, and publicly critiqued by, Karl Speicer. If that condition is met, the property will be made a gift to the town of Reflection, to be preserved as parkland, and Marielle Hostetter shall instead receive any royalties resulting from the sale of that work.'"

Michael was still astonished by the unorthodox message, although this was the fourth time he'd read it. He looked at Helen, whose face was nearly the same shade of gray as her hair.

"I remember that part of Peter's will, yes," she said quietly.

She'd known about this chance to save the land and said nothing? Michael was about to speak, and none too kindly, when Rachel sent him a look of warning.

She wrapped her hand around Helen's. "Are you all right, Gram?" she asked. "Is this upsetting you?"

"I'm all right."

"This Karl Speicer," Rachel continued. "He's the pianist we'll be seeing Friday night, isn't he?"

Michael was surprised. He had not made that connection.

Helen didn't answer. She was staring into the darkness outside the library window. "Peter's been dead ten years," she said, "and I'd truly forgotten about that part of his will. But to answer the question I'm sure you're both dying to ask, there is no piece called *Reflections*."

"Wait a second." Michael stood up from the sofa, frustrated. "Back up, please, Helen. First of all, the land was Huber land?"

"It was in Peter's family for a long, long time—generations—and he inherited it from his parents. Which means it is not mine. I have no say over what happens to it. Do you understand that?"

They nodded like admonished children.

"But why would he leave it to Marielle?" Rachel asked.

"Because he took pity on her. Peter was a caring, generous person. His family had allowed hers to live in that cottage for as long as anyone could remember, so everyone always assumed the land was Hostetter land. And now it is. There's nothing we can do about it."

"But if he took pity on her, why didn't he simply say she could live there until she died and have the land convert to parkland after her death?" Michael asked.

Helen looked out the window again, and Michael feared she was going to cry.

Rachel squeezed her grandmother's hand. "We don't have to talk about this right now if you don't want to, Gram," she said.

"Peter had his ways," Helen said, looking from Rachel to Michael. "He had his reasons for doing things that sometimes didn't make sense to other people," she said.

"Do they make sense to you?" Rachel asked.

She nodded. "Knowing Peter, yes. I understand his thinking perfectly."

Michael sat down again, resting the sheet of paper on his knees. "Is this addendum legal?" he asked.

"Yes. It's legal."

"The music must exist if he refers to it," Michael said. "Where could it be? Could this Karl Speicer have it? Why would Peter have wanted the music to go to him?

Helen eyed him with forced patience. "Which question do you want me to answer first?"

"Why Karl Speicer?"

"Karl is a pianist, and yes, he's the pianist performing at the Kennedy Center Friday night. He's very old—my age—by now. I can hardly believe he's still performing, although . . ." Her voice trailed off, and she looked into the distance for a moment before returning her attention to Rachel and Michael. "He was a good friend of Peter's," she said. "He loved playing his works."

"Could he have a copy of the music?"

Helen laughed, and he and Rachel glanced at each other. What was so funny? "No," Helen said. "We would certainly know about it if he did."

"Why would Peter make what happens to the land contingent on Karl Speicer seeing that particular piece of music?" Michael asked.

"I told you, Michael, Peter had his own reasons for doing things. I can't explain them."

"Gram." Rachel covered both her grandmother's hands with her own. "Where can we look for the music? Where might it possibly be?"

"*Nowhere.*" She was beginning to sound impatient. "I looked after Peter died, Rachel, and it's been ten years. If it existed, I would have found it by now."

"Maybe it's tucked away somewhere, though. I don't know—beneath the floorboards or something. Maybe we could find it and take it to Washington with us on Friday and give it to Karl Spei—"

"No, no, no, no!" Helen shook her head furiously. "Rachel. Michael. You *must* leave this alone!" Quick tears appeared in the older woman's eyes. They scared Michael but not as much as they seemed to rattle Rachel. She leaped up to put her arms around the older woman.

"Gram, sweetheart, it's all right," she said. She looked at Michael above her grandmother's head.

Helen raised her arms to cast off Rachel's embrace. "You have to promise me you won't try to talk to him," she said. "Not Friday night or ever. Promise?"

Rachel stood next to him. "I promise," she said.

"Michael?" The older woman looked for his answer.

He nodded reluctantly. "All right," he said, reaching for her hand. "And I'm sorry we upset you."

Helen took his hand briefly, then dropped hers limply into her lap. "I'd like some privacy now," she said.

Michael looked at Rachel. "I should go," he said. "I have to pick Jace up from his youth group."

Rachel nodded. "I'll walk you out." She touched her grandmother's shoulder. "I'll be back in a minute, Gram."

They were quiet until they reached his car. "What do you make of all that?" he asked.

She shook her head. "I have no idea."

"The last thing I want to do is hurt Helen," he said, "but if that music exists, we've got to find it."

Rachel sighed. "Do you think the attorney might know something about it? The one who drew up the will?"

"Well, it's certainly worth a try. Sam Freed drew it up, and I know him pretty well. I'll give him a call tomorrow." Maybe Sam could explain Peter's reasoning, if nothing else.

Rachel leaned against his car. "I had a terrible thought while we were talking to Gram," she said. The porch light caught the wide gray of her eyes, and he remembered kissing her in the woods. He wanted to kiss her again.

"What's that?"

"Well, does this make any sense to you? That my grandfather would leave that valuable a chunk of land to Marielle Hostetter?"

"It's the craziest thing I've ever heard, but none of this makes any sense to me."

"Gram is acting so strange about it," Rachel said, "and I don't want to push her on it. She's too fragile. But do you think there's any chance that Marielle could have been more to my grandfather than just a woman who lived on his land?"

Michael almost laughed. "First of all, she's more than twenty years younger than Peter. And secondly, Peter was very intellectual. A woman like that would have held no interest for him whatsoever."

"That's not what I was thinking." Rachel covered her mouth with her hand. She was nearly laughing herself, and he smiled without knowing what he was smiling about. "I'm sure this is ridiculous," she continued. "The product of an overactive imagination. But what if Marielle is his daughter?"

"Pardon?"

"Maybe Marielle's mother had an affair with my grandfather. Maybe that's why she killed herself. Because my grandfather wouldn't leave Gram. And Gram knows it all, but doesn't want to tell us. It would explain everything."

It would—everything except the strange contingency—but it seemed preposterous. He also didn't like to think of Peter tomcatting around the neighborhood. "Even if that were the case, which seems a little extreme, it's moot. We don't really need to know the explanation. We just need to find the music and then persuade Helen to let us talk to this Speicer guy."

Rachel looked toward the house. "I should go in to her," she said. "She's not herself."

He caught her hand before she could walk away. "Rachel?"

The gray eyes grew even wider, waiting.

"I love you." He felt safe enough, in control enough, to say those words out loud. "I don't know what to do about it, but I do."

She smiled. "I love you, too," she said. She gave him a hug, pulling away before it could become anything more than that, and he watched her walk toward the house.

* * *

Helen was in her bedroom when she heard the creak of the screen door and knew Rachel was back inside. Quickly she closed and locked her bedroom door. She needed another minute to herself. Needed to still her trembling. She felt dizzy and lay down on the bed, drawing in long, slow breaths. She heard Rachel's knock on the door.

"I'm resting, Rachel," she said. Closing her eyes, she listened to the resigned retreat of her granddaughter's footsteps.

She lay that way for a few more minutes, then opened her eyes again.

Peter, Peter, why couldn't you have left well enough alone?

He was trying to control things from the grave. She knew he was doing it for her, in his misguided way. But he should have known she would never agree to carry out his wishes. She couldn't do it ten years ago, and she couldn't do it now.

25

"Well, it's about time." Sam Freed sat on the edge of his desk and studied Rachel and Michael with a smile. "I was wondering how long it would take someone to figure out that the land under dispute is really Huber land."

The attorney was nearly seventy, Rachel knew, but she would have guessed him to be ten years younger. He looked very fit and lean, and he was impeccably dressed in a gray suit and blue tie.

"Do you have any idea where the music is?" she asked.

Sam raised his eyebrows in surprise. "I always assumed Helen had it."

"She claims not to," Michael said.

"Hmm." Sam shook his head. "You've got yourselves a mystery, then."

"Could my grandfather have had a safe-deposit box?" Rachel asked. "Somewhere he might have kept valuable papers?"

"If he did, I never knew about it."

"And this addendum is legal?" Michael pointed to the sheet of paper on Sam's desk.

"Oh, perfectly legal," Sam said. He touched the paper with the tips of his fingers. "I thought it was an odd contingency, but I knew Peter well enough to trust that he had a good reason for it. What that reason was, though, I haven't a clue." He looked at his watch and stood up. "I'm sorry to have to cut this short, but I have another appointment to get to." He ushered them toward his office door. "Wish I could be of more help to you, and I sure hope you can find that music somewhere. Ursula's been trying to convince me I could have a spanking new office in that building they plan to raise up by the pond, but frankly I'd rather have this old place and keep Reflection just the way it is."

On the street outside the law office, Michael took off his glasses and rubbed his eyes. "I don't think we'd better tell Helen we saw Sam," he said.

"No." Rachel agreed. "And I don't think we should push her about the will or the music right now, either." In the two days since they'd told her about the will, Gram had seemed withdrawn and preoccupied, occasionally a little impatient and snappish. Even the sweet, belated ears of Silver Queen from the garden failed to get her attention, and the fresh flowers Rachel had arranged throughout the house went unnoticed.

Michael slipped his glasses on again, nodding. "It's going to be frustrating tonight, though," he said, "seeing Karl Speicer at the Kennedy Center and not being able to talk to him. What if he has the music? Maybe we could—"

"We can't, Michael," she said. "We promised."

"All right." He let out a sigh. "I'm going to my office for a few hours. I'll pick you and Helen up around three, all right?"

"Yes." She touched his arm lightly. "I'm glad we had a few minutes alone," she said.

He smiled at her, then turned around and headed in the direction of his church. It was a moment before Rachel noticed the woman across the street, the man in the parked car at the corner, the two teenage girls coming out of the deli, and she realized that she and Michael had had no time alone after all.

She rode in the backseat of Michael's car on the drive to Washington, while her grandmother sat in the passenger seat next to him. It would be a two-hour drive, and Rachel wanted Gram to be comfortable. The older woman had moved slowly as she'd climbed into the car, her face pale and grim, and even now there was a brittle, nearly palpable anxiety about her.

Rachel watched as the countryside gave way to office buildings and industry. There had been little conversation so far on the drive, the few attempts feeble. She met Michael's eyes in the rearview mirror from time to time and thought she detected in them the same apprehensive excitement she felt at being with him, away from Reflection, away from everyone.

"When's the last time you heard any of Peter's music performed live?" Michael asked her grandmother.

It was a moment before Gram answered. "I don't think I've been to a live performance since before he died," she said. "Ten years, at least." She turned her head to look back at Rachel. "What pieces did you say they're performing tonight?" she asked.

"*Patchwork* and *Lionheart* and the Second Concerto." Rachel repeated information she had given her grandmother four times already.

They reached Washington at five-thirty and checked in at their hotel, Rachel and her grandmother in a room with two queen-sized beds, Michael in a single room next door. They were short on time and so began dressing immediately. Rachel had bought a dress the day before, in Lancaster, where no one would recognize her or talk about her after she'd left the store. The dress was short and black, cut low in back, and she grinned at her reflection in the mirror above the hotel dresser.

"Help me with this, Rachel?" Gram asked as she emerged from the bathroom. She was wearing a simple royal-blue dress and holding a strand of pearls to her throat. She looked taller, more striking than Rachel had ever seen her.

"That dress looks stunning on you." Rachel reached for the pearls and fixed the clasp at the back of her grandmother's neck.

"I need to sit down," Gram said, once the pearls were secure.

She sat down in one of the room's two wing chairs and shut her eyes. Rachel bit her lip as she studied her grandmother's face. The older woman was pale, pasty. Her white hands clutched the arms of the chair. She looked as full of fear as she would in the middle of a storm. Was she going to be all right? Perhaps they should have brought the wheelchair.

Rachel put on her makeup in the bathroom and was walking back into the bedroom when she noticed Gram surreptitiously transferring the little bag of herbs from her purse to her beaded evening bag. She pretended not to notice, but her heart ached for her grandmother. Poor thing. It had to be some superstition that made her captive to that little plastic bag. She always wanted those herbs with her. Rachel busied herself at the dresser, but she could see that Gram's hands were still trembling as they fastened the clasp on the handbag.

They joined Michael in the hotel lobby and took a cab to the Kennedy Center, and the three of them were quiet as they rode the elevator up to the rooftop restaurant.

"You ladies look beautiful," Michael said once they'd been seated at a table by the windows.

"Thanks." Rachel smiled at him.

She and Michael ordered full dinners, but Gram wanted only soup. She ordered the crab bisque, and Rachel watched her push her spoon through it, this way and that, bringing none of it to her lips. Michael looked across the table at Rachel, his eyes asking her what was wrong, and she shrugged.

They left the restaurant, Gram clutching her handbag, and waited by the bank of elevators for the ride down to the concert hall. Once off the elevator, Michael took each of them by the elbow.

"Well," he said, "I have a little surprise for you two tonight."

"What?" Rachel asked.

"You'll see." He winked at her.

In the massive foyer of the Kennedy Center, they picked up their tickets, then headed for the concert hall. When she'd called to order the tickets, Rachel had been disappointed to learn that the best available seats were in the very rear of the orchestra, so she was surprised when the usher led them toward the stage. She glanced at her stub. First row, smack in the center. She started to protest, then caught Michael's grin. So that was his surprise.

"How did you manage this?" she asked as they took their seats directly in front of the assembling orchestra. She sat between him and her grandmother.

Michael squeezed her arm. He seemed very happy tonight, more relaxed than she'd seen him since her arrival in Reflection. "Couple of phone calls," he said. "Didn't know I had such clout, did you?"

"I have a feeling it isn't you who has the clout," Rachel whispered, her lips close to his ear. She smelled the soft woody scent of his aftershave and wanted to snuggle up to him, lean her head against his shoulder. She resolutely wrapped her hands around the arms of her chair instead. "Did you tell them Helen Huber would be here?" she asked.

He smiled. "They would have put us *on* the stage if they could have."

Rachel read the program while waiting for the concert to begin. The biographical material on her grandfather was familiar, and she felt a chill of pride as she read about his accomplishments and awards. She leaned over to ask Gram a question about the article but realized that her grandmother was engrossed in the biography of Karl Speicer. Rachel turned the page and began reading about Speicer herself.

He was born in 1911, the article stated, and he lived in New York City with his wife of forty-four years, Winona. He had been a long-time friend of the composer, and he had a passion for Huber music. *Any competent pianist can demonstrate the technical brilliance of a Huber composition*, the biographer had written, *but Karl Speicer reaches deep into the heart and soul of the composer's work.*

The concert opened with *Patchwork*. The conductor was a woman Rachel had never heard of before, but it was apparent from the first chords of the music that she was a Huber fan herself. And Karl Speicer was an extraordinary presence. His thick, silver hair was striking against the black and white of his tuxedo. He was quite tall and slender, and he displayed a wired sort of energy as he bore down on the piano. During the slower parts of the music he lifted his face, eyes closed, to the heavens, and Rachel thought to herself: Karl Speicer does indeed love this music.

By the third movement she feared she would no longer be able to bear the lump in her throat. She did not know what images other people in the audience saw as they listened to *Patchwork*, but she pictured the threatened view from Winter Hill, and her grandfather at the piano in the house at Reflection, lost in concentration as his fingers worked their magic on the keys. She breathed through her mouth to stave off the tears. Michael knew, though. He took her hand and held it on her knee, his touch firm and warm, and the gesture only served to intensify her emotions.

She heard the slightest sniffle from her grandmother, and she took

Gram's hand in her free one. The older woman's fingers might have been carved from stone, they felt that cool and unyielding. Rachel ran her thumb over the back of her grandmother's hand to warm it.

When the piece ended, Karl Speicer was heartily applauded, returning to the front of the stage several times to accept the adulation. He did not walk like an old man; there was no hesitancy in his gait. He nodded toward the orchestra with an easy, handsome smile and left the stage for the last time as the lights came on for the intermission.

Michael leaned forward in his seat so that both Rachel and Gram could hear him. "Now, be prepared," he said. "After the intermission, the conductor's going to acknowledge the two of you."

"What do you mean?" Rachel asked.

"You know," Michael said. "She'll introduce Helen as Peter's wife and you as his granddaughter, and you'll stand up and—"

"I'm sorry, but no," Gram said abruptly. "I can't stay for the rest of the concert. I need to leave." She stood up and began backing away from her seat.

Rachel and Michael glanced at each other.

"No reason for the two of you to go," Gram said. "I'll get a cab back to the hotel and—"

Michael was on his feet, reaching across Rachel toward the older woman, catching her by the arm. "What is it, Helen?" he asked. "Are you ill? Dizzy?"

"Yes," she said, "I'm not feeling at all well. I'm so sorry." She glanced toward the emptying stage.

"We'll all go," Rachel stood up between them.

"No! I don't want to ruin—"

"Nonsense, Helen," Michael said. "We got to hear *Patchwork*, and I don't know about the two of you, but that was beautiful enough to last me a year or so. It's been a long day. Let's go back to the hotel and relax." He glanced toward the stage. "I'll let someone know we had to leave so they don't try to acknowledge you."

Rachel nodded at him, grateful for his caring.

Gram did not say another word until the three of them were back in her hotel room. By then, though, the color had returned to her face. "Now, I'm tired," she said. "I'm going straight to bed, but I'm sure you two would like to stay up and talk, so you just go on and sit in Michael's room for a while."

Michael laughed. "Helen, you're incorrigible."

Rachel felt more relief than amusement. Her feisty grandma was suddenly back. "I don't want to leave you if you're not feeling well," she said. "I'll stay with you a while. We can watch TV or—"

"No, you're not staying with me. I'm fine now."

"You're sure, Helen?" Michael asked.

"I'm absolutely fine."

"You seemed so upset, though," Rachel said. "Did we make a mistake bringing you here?"

Gram smiled. "No, of course you didn't." She ran her hand over the surface of her beaded handbag. "It's just that even something very beautiful can occasionally be too much to bear."

Rachel nodded. That she could understand. She kissed her grandmother good night, then followed Michael out into the hall. Closing the door behind her, she folded her arms across her chest.

"Not in your room, Michael," she said. "I have to tell you right now, I have no willpower tonight. When you held my hand at the concert, you might as well have been making love to me."

He nearly grinned at her, and she waited, hoping he would invite her in anyway. But he shook his head.

"You're right," he said. He looked up and down the empty corridor. There was a loveseat at one end, facing a broad window. "How about down there?" he asked.

They walked toward the loveseat and sat down. The view from the window was of a moonlit Washington, the dome of the Capitol visible in the distance.

"Pretty view," Rachel said.

"You think Helen's okay?" Michael asked.

"She seemed much better once we got out of the Kennedy Center." Rachel sighed. "I don't know what to make of her lately."

"She scared me in there," Michael said. "I thought we were going to have to take her out on a stretcher."

"Mmm. I know." She craned her neck, trying to pick out the White House from the myriad of buildings stretched out below them. "Do you remember our senior trip to Washington?" she asked.

He laughed, slipping his arm around her shoulders. "How could I forget it."

Their entire senior class had ridden the bus to D.C. and slept dormitory-style at the Y. She remembered little of the sights and a lot of the sneaking around. She and Luke had made love in the Y's furnace room.

"I remember the night you girls got drunk and—"

"I was not drunk."

"Okay. Some of you were, though. And you raided the guys' dorm."

"I remember that." She laughed. "Becky Frank threw up."

"In my bed."

"In *your* bed? I thought she was sitting on Luke's when it happened."

"No, it was mine . . . well, wait a second." He made a face. "You know, sometimes I can't separate my experiences from Luke's. I've always teased Becky that it was my bed, but now that you mention it, I'm not so sure."

Rachel thought of Becky and the aerobics class. She'd missed tonight's class by coming to Washington, just as Michael was missing his support group. It had been a relief for her to have a legitimate out.

"I don't think I'm going back to the aerobics class," she said.

"Oh, Rache, are you sure? You were really enjoying it."

"Yeah, when I thought I had a friend there. But the pleasure's outweighed by the discomfort now. "

"That's a shame. We'll have to take some more bike rides. I can use the exercise myself."

She tried to picture the two of them riding their bikes around town again, but the image wouldn't take shape. It was hard to imagine being able to relax with him out in the open.

Michael grew quiet, and she had the feeling that he, too, was trying to picture the impossible. "Maybe in Gettysburg," he said. "It's a great place to ride, and it's far enough from Reflection to be safe." Then he sighed and squeezed her shoulder. "Can we talk seriously for a minute?" he asked.

"Of course."

"Well, please don't let this scare you, but I've been trying lately to imagine a life with you. And that means a life without Katy or my church, and probably even more limits on my already limited time with Jace."

The thought didn't scare her so much as relieve her. She did not want to be alone in that fantasy any longer.

"I know the problems are nearly insurmountable," he continued, "even if I set aside the whole church-and-Katy issue. You and I live two thousand miles apart, to begin with. But I have to look at the possibility. Examine it. I can't live with myself unless I do."

"I'm glad you are," she said. "I think about it, too."

"What do you want, Rachel?" he asked. "I mean, with regard to me. I need to know. Please be very honest."

She drew in a long breath. "It wouldn't be fair for me to tell you," she said.

"For right now, forget about what's fair."

"I want *you*," she said. "I want to be with you. Take pictures with you and cook with you and go on long bike rides through the countryside with you. And I want to travel with you. See Norway together." She was speaking quietly, slowly. "I can be myself with you," she said. "I love our shared history. I love that you know me well enough to finish my sentences for me. I love the bond we have. I love that incredible feeling that your happiness matters to me as much as my own."

He smiled as she spoke. "'The soul of Jonathan was knit with the soul of David,'" he quoted, "'and Jonathan loved him as his own soul.'"

"Yes," she said, pleased. "That's it. And what I wish is that you and I could be together for the rest of our lives. But as long as I'm wishing, I have to add that I wish it wouldn't cost you anything." She knew it would cost him too much.

"Well." Michael stretched his long legs out in front of him. "What I want is not so different. I want you, of course—I guess that goes without saying at this point. And I want us to be able to do all those things together that you want us to do. But I also want not to hurt my wife, or my son, or my congregation, or my ability to be a minister."

Rachel said nothing. Yes, she would cost him far too much.

"I've thought of going to the elders with this," he said. "Or at least to Lewis Klock."

"Why to the elders?"

"Because I'm accountable to them, and I need their support. They're all good people, all on solid spiritual ground, and my own spiritual ground is quaking a bit these days. I'm closest to Lewis, of course, and he's a very fair person. A reasonable person. I've turned to him for other things since I've been a minister. Lesser things. And I know I need help with this." He touched her cheek. "I'm struggling, Rache."

"I know you are," she said softly.

"But if I talk to Lewis, I know what he'll say—not to see you at all. And I can't do it. And once he and I talk, he'll be watching me." He shook his head with a sigh. "People in my congregation have come to me over the years with similar problems, and I have to admit now that I never understood what they were going through. I wanted to tell them to grow up, to recognize what was important in their lives. I never realized it wasn't that simple."

"No, it's not," she said with a smile. "I know I'm not an evil person, yet I'm longing to do evil things with you."

He laughed. "Thanks for refusing to come into my bedroom tonight."

"You're welcome."

"We would have been okay, though. I don't want us to have a physical relationship if it's going to be temporary. I don't want to cross that line until I feel firm in my decision about us." The laugh again. "Though it's easy to say that when I'm sitting here feeling rational. But look at what happened in the woods the other night. I was lost. I wanted to toss you down on the leaves and devour you right there."

"I would have loved it."

He hesitated. "You could do this, couldn't you?" he asked quizzically. "Make love without the promise of something long-term between us?"

"Yes, I could," she admitted. "But I love that you can't." She shifted on the seat until she was facing him. "I want what's best for you, Michael," she said seriously. "And I realize that might not be me."

He shook his head. "Even if you disappeared tomorrow, your presence has raised too many questions for me to go back to my old life unchanged." He ran his hand over her knee, and the brief touch left her wanting more. "I've had to admit to myself how hollow my marriage is," he said. "I can see now that there's a gap in my life. I've filled it with religion and work to avoid having to really look at it."

She pulled her legs onto the loveseat and leaned over to hug him. "No matter what happens," she said, "I'll always be there for you. I'll always be your friend."

"I hope so," he said.

They were quiet as they sat nestled together, watching the moon make its way across the city sky.

It's in his hands, Rachel thought. The decision was Michael's, and she had to be prepared for it to go either way. She was not sure she was worthy of all he'd have to give up, but for the first time since her return to Reflection, she felt the seductive pull of hope.

26

There was tension in the church. Lily felt it the moment she stepped through the door. The people milling around in the foyer seemed more subdued than usual, and there weren't many smiles. She and Ian slipped through the crowd and found their favorite seats close to the center of the sanctuary.

"He'll talk about the rumors, don't you think?" she whispered to Ian. "Michael always addresses things head-on."

"I wouldn't bank on it this time around," Ian said.

She'd wondered if Michael had talked about the rumors in his support group. She'd known better than to ask Ian. Ian was a slave to confidentiality, a quality for which she admired him, although she'd never mastered it herself. From what he'd just said, though, she doubted that Michael had shared much about what was going on with him and Rachel.

Those rumors were starting to scare her, and she knew she wasn't alone. That's what she was feeling in the church this morning. Fear and doubt and anger hung in the air. It was not the first time she'd felt that mix of emotions in the congregation.

Whenever it was common knowledge that a church member had strayed or was grappling with his or her faith or expressing doubts, everyone felt it. It threatened them all. This church was a community. That was what she loved best about it, but it also made one person's problem everyone's problem.

She fidgeted and yawned her way through the singing and

announcements. Ian squeezed her knee, whispered in her ear. "Gotta get to bed earlier, kiddo," he said.

She'd been up late training Mule and Wiley for Thursday night's ASPCA charity show, and those dogs were nowhere near ready. But that was not the reason she was tired. Even after she'd gone to bed, she couldn't sleep. There were too many thoughts rolling around in her head, and each time she'd close her eyes, almost drift off, she'd picture Mr. Holt. Or Jenny. Or she'd see a blur of blood and torn camouflage clothing. She could see the drawings hanging in the school hallway, drawings other children had made of those who had died. She remembered the thousands of flowers people had brought to the school, laying them out on the front lawn in solemn observance of what had happened. She could even recall the planting of the weeping cherries and the memorial services and the funerals. She remembered those events as if she'd attended them, even though she had not. Her mother had not allowed it. Lily had not even attended the service for her sister.

She'd finally gotten out of bed the night before and sat on the living room floor, staring out the window, surrounded by the dogs. The memories were overpowering these days, and they took her more in the direction of guilt than sorrow. Sometimes it hurt to know too much, to know things others didn't. The responsibility was too great.

She wished she could talk to Ian about it. He was aware of her agitation but not of its source. She'd told him what she knew about Katy. He thought that was where her conflict was coming from, and she allowed him to hold on to that illusion.

Michael stood to begin his sermon, and Lily felt her body tense against the hard pew. He began talking about the value of friendship, and she could not believe her ears. A sermon on friendship? Now? He was copping out on them.

She was so disappointed in him that she ached. There was more anger around her now. It felt like a thousand fragile panes of glass, ready to splinter and break apart. Michael knew what they were all thinking. He *had* to. Yet he was ignoring their concerns.

We need your reassurance, Michael, she thought. *We don't need to know you're a saint. Just let us know you're aware of the problem. You're working on it.*

Her mind wandered, and she looked around her. Everyone else's eyes were riveted on the minister. She spotted Kirby Cash, Arlena's husband, sitting a few pews away from her. She'd heard Arlena was out of the hospital finally. That was good. The last thing Rachel needed was Arlena's blood on her hands.

Ian suddenly nudged her back to attention.

". . . grew up here," Michael was saying. "And when I was a child, I was quite friendless and very isolated. For whatever reason, I was not seen by my peers as having many redeeming qualities and was, in fact, ignored or berated by many of them. I was, as most unhappy people come to be, preoccupied with myself and my own trials and tribulations. But then two other children befriended me. They treated me with respect and kindness; they valued my opinions and my company. When I was no more than seven, they helped shape me into the adult I am today. Those children were Luke Pierce and Rachel Huber."

He paused only briefly, but it was long enough to hear the uneasy stirring of the congregation.

"Each time I reach out to one of you in comfort or compassion," Michael continued, "I am doing what those two children taught me to do. Each time I reach outside myself to help another person, I give thanks to Rachel and Luke. They taught me how to care about my fellow human beings."

He slipped into Scripture then, so easily that his listeners barely noticed the shift, and drew his sermon to a close.

Lily sat quietly when the service was over. People looked at one another as they rose from the pews, their faces hard to read. The tenor of emotion in the church had changed, but its new form did not yet have clarity. There was no single focus, but it didn't matter. All Lily cared about was that, in his own way, Michael had addressed the real issues after all.

27

Ursula Torwig sat across her desk from the young female reporter the Lancaster paper had sent over. Roslyn somebody, her name was. She'd called an hour earlier, telling Ursula she wanted to talk with her about the Hostetter project.

Twist my arm, Ursula had thought with a grin. She could not get the woman over to her office fast enough.

As soon as Roslyn stepped through her door, Ursula knew the type of person she was dealing with—one of those young, ambitious, blood-hungry reporters. Roslyn had probably been weaned on tabloid television shows and no doubt rued the fact that she was working for a small-town newspaper. She would want something juicy to get the notice of her superiors. Ursula would give her the best she had.

Rosyln pulled a notepad out of her briefcase. "It seems that there's a good deal of controversy over the Hostetter project," she began. She was an unattractive young woman. Her nose looked as if it had been broken and badly set; her eyes were too small for her face.

"Oh, that's been overplayed," Ursula said with a smile. "And it seems to be fading away. Michael Stoltz—he's the preacher of the Mennonite church in town—tried to rally opposition against the Hostetter project, but his leadership's been weakened considerably in recent weeks, and that sort of movement is really only as strong as its leader." Her cousin's charisma and credibility were marvelously strained these days.

"You mean, since Rachel Huber's return to the area."

Good. Roslyn had said it for her. "Well, let's just say that his concentration and good judgment seem to be a little off lately. I understand that he spent this past weekend in Washington, D.C., with her, so"—she shrugged—"who can say?"

Roslyn's hungry little eyes lit up. "You're sure of that? They were in Washington together?"

"I thought everyone knew about it," Ursula said innocently, although she knew that very few people had been privy to that information.

The reporter scribbled a few words on her pad.

"Well, let me show you the plans for the Hostetter development," Ursula said, reaching into her desk. "I want to reassure you and your readers that we've studied the impact of this development from every angle. If anyone still has concerns about it, we can address them at the hearing on September sixth."

She spread the drawings flat on her desk, turning them so Rosyln could get a good look. "Please let people know they can stop by my office anytime to review the plans and the various impact studies," she said. "Anytime at all. I'm sure anyone who examines the situation will reach the same conclusion I have—that this is exactly the sort of controlled growth Reflection needs. Our economy needs it, and our community needs it. And it will be a very attractive addition, completely in sync with the flavor of the town."

Roslyn lifted her eyes from the plans. "What about the Amish and other plain sects who are concerned about increased traffic and—"

Ursula cut her off with a wave of her hand. "If this were agricultural land under consideration, land that the Amish could farm, I would never allow it to be developed in this way. We must protect our farmland at all costs. That's why the Hostetters' development of their property is such a priceless gift. Here's a piece of land, already smack in the middle of town, completely separate from farmland, just crying out to be carefully, tastefully developed and incorporated into the town itself. And the Hostetters are willing to do that. What an opportunity we have!"

She had effectively shut Roslyn up. The reporter quietly jotted

down a few more notes before slipping her pad into her briefcase
again and standing up. Ursula stood as well, and as she walked Roslyn
to the door, she glanced through her window to see the new building
as clearly as if it already existed. She could even pick out her office
window.

28

"Dad?" Jason stood in the doorway of the study. "Can I talk to you when you get off the phone?"

Michael was sitting at his desk, on hold with National Public Radio. Drew was going to California on business the following day, and all the calls to the media about the hearing had suddenly fallen on Michael's shoulders. It had taken him more than an hour to get through to NPR, but he saw the clouded look in Jason's eyes and the way the boy shifted from one foot to the other, and he hung up the phone.

"Have a seat, Jace," he said.

Jason dropped onto the sofa but said nothing.

"What's up?" Michael prompted.

Jason looked at him from the corner of his eye, his head facing the window. The morning sun etched white rectangles of light on his glasses. "The kids at camp are saying things about you," he said.

So, the gossip had even reached the computer camp. "Are they?" he asked. "And what are they saying?"

"They said that old teacher who let the kids die is your girlfriend."

The look on Jason's face was one of guileless confusion, and Michael was suddenly furious at himself for not somehow protecting his son from the rumors. He should never have kept so much of his renewed friendship with Rachel a secret from Jason. How could he explain it to him now without looking as though he'd been hiding something?

He leaned forward, elbows on his knees. "I'm aware that people are talking about me," he began. "I'm sorry the rumors have reached your ears. But they *are* rumors, Jace, that's all. The teacher, Rachel Huber, was one of my closest friends when I was your age. You know my old house on Water Street?"

Jason nodded.

"Well, Rachel's family lived there, too. So we were very, very good friends." He knew his son could not easily relate to that concept. Even in his youth group Jason spent most of his time with the adult leaders. "She's here for the summer, and I've gone on a bike ride with her and . . . " He'd seen the paper that morning. He didn't know how Ursula had found out about the trip to Washington, but he supposed that piece of information had better come from him rather than from the kids at camp. "I went with her and her grand- mother to a concert in Washington on Friday night. Her grandmo—"

"You're cheating on Mom." Jason's cheeks were red and he shrank back on the sofa, as if he had said too much and expected Michael to strike him—something Michael had never done. No doubt Jason was repeating words he'd heard from the kids at camp.

Michael shook his head. "No, I'm not, Jace. Mom even knew Rachel when we were kids," he added, as though that would some- how make everything all right. "We all grew up together."

"Everyone says you're a sinner."

Michael sighed. "We've talked about this before," he said. "About how it doesn't matter what other people think, right? What matters is—"

The doorbell rang, and he glanced toward the hall in frustration. He leaned forward again and rested his hand on Jason's knee.

"I don't care what other people think," he said. "What matters to me is what *you* think."

Jason got to his feet. The rectangles of light in the boy's glasses dis- appeared, giving Michael a clear view of the anger in his eyes.

"I think you shouldn't go on bike rides and have a good time with some lady when Mom's away, no matter if you used to be friends or not," Jason said. He walked into the hall, turning in the direction of his room.

"Jace, wait." Michael stood to follow him, but the doorbell rang again, and he turned in the direction of the living room instead. He didn't know what else he could say to Jason anyway. He feared the boy believed the words of his peers over those of his father.

Walking toward the door, he could see the black car parked out on the street and he groaned. Lewis Klock. He'd been serious about possibly talking with Lewis about his dilemma, but he had the feeling the choice was about to be taken out of his hands.

"Morning, Michael," Lewis said when he opened the door.

"Good morning, Lewis. Come in."

He led the elder into the study.

"Is Jason at home?" Lewis asked as he sat down on the sofa.

"Yes, in his room."

"Then perhaps we'd better close the door."

Michael shut the study door with a mounting sense of dread—and resignation. Maybe he'd been weakened by his discussion with Jason, or maybe he was finally ready to ask for help, but for whatever reason, he knew he was going to be completely honest with his old mentor.

"You went to Washington, D.C., this weekend with Rachel Huber?" Lewis asked when Michael had taken his seat at the desk again.

Michael nodded. "Yes. But it wasn't as Ursula implied."

Lewis listened quietly as he described the trip to D.C. The older man seemed to have nothing to say once Michael had finished talking, but Michael knew Lewis was simply waiting to hear more, encouraging it with his silence.

"I love her, Lewis," he said finally. "It's not her fault in any way. She's done nothing intentionally to make that happen, but her being here has raised many, many doubts in me, both about my marriage and my faith."

He told Lewis about the pull of the past he shared with Rachel, and about the lure of a future sure to be filled with joy and love. Although he tried, he could not keep the enthusiasm out of his voice, and he was struck by the selfishness in his words. He waited for the elder to chastise him, but he should have known better. That was not Lewis's style. Lewis listened to him with patience and a seeming lack of judgment. Then he quietly began telling the story of David and

Bathsheba, unnecessarily, since that particular Scripture had been creeping uncomfortably into Michael's mind for a couple of weeks now.

"David lusted after Bathsheba," Lewis said, "and he slept with her despite her married status, sorely displeasing the Lord."

Michael listened to the story with gritted teeth. His mind was on Jason as he waited out the inevitable conclusion of the tale.

"David confessed his sin, and the Lord took it away. 'But because you have made the enemies of the Lord show contempt,'" Lewis quoted forcefully, "'the son born to you will die.'" He went on to describe the loss of the couple's infant son, while Michael sat in a pained silence.

"Temptation is everywhere," the elder said, more gently now. "The fact that this is the first time you've even noticed it speaks well of you, but it also makes it harder for you, because you have no experience in dealing with it. And you need to deal with it openly, Michael. You're surrounded by a congregation that loves you and will support you."

"Only if I'm willing to do what they want me to do," Michael said.

"I don't have to spell out the consequences you'll be facing if you don't, do I?"

"No. I'm fully aware of what I'm up against."

"We have to keep in touch on this, Michael."

"Yes," Michael said. That was what he feared. He stood up to walk the elder to the door.

"And Michael?" Lewis turned around to face him. "Whatever happens, remember that God is forgiving even when institutions and the people who run them are not."

He was struck by the man's compassion. He did not feel worthy of it, and he closed the door behind the elder wishing he could be that sort of spiritual leader, that sort of human being.

Throughout the day Michael made numerous attempts to talk with Jason again, but his son would not budge from the security of his computer screen. Even when he got into Michael's car to go to the ASPCA charity show that night, Jason was silent and sullen. He sat in the backseat while Michael picked up Drew, and the three of them headed for the junior-senior high school.

"Do I have to sit with you?" Jason asked as they neared the school.

Drew laughed. "God forbid, Jace," he said.

Michael looked at his son's tormented adolescent visage in the rearview mirror. "Want us to let you off out front so no one has to know you came with us?"

Jason made a sound of disgust and slumped back into the seat.

"Oh, the agony of being twelve," Drew said quietly.

"Tell me about it." Michael turned into the parking lot of the high school, thinking about Drew's son, Will. Before Rachel came to town, he'd simply forgotten about that loss. Now he wondered how Drew tolerated seeing him with Jason, seeing other fathers and sons together. He supposed that after twenty years he'd gotten used to it.

Michael glanced in the rearview mirror again to see Jason looking out the window. He followed Jason's gaze to the sidewalk, where a group of kids were walking and laughing together. He understood his son's dilemma instantly. Should he sit in the safe, but uncool, company of his father and Drew, or try to join a group of kids who would probably not welcome him?

"Seriously, Jace," he said, foot on the brake, "do you want me to let you out?"

"Yeah. Okay." Jason sounded like he was agreeing to his own execution. He opened the car door and stepped out.

"We'll be somewhere on the left side, if you want to come sit with us," Michael said through the open window, but Jason did not acknowledge hearing him as he walked toward the group of youngsters. For an instant Michael saw the group through his son's eyes. He could almost see the imaginary line drawn around their territory, the line that would keep the members safely inside while keeping Jason out. Michael quickly put his foot to the gas pedal. He did not want to see their reaction to Jason's attempt to join them. He wasn't ready to relive that pain.

"You put your heart and soul into raising them," Drew said as Michael pulled into a parking space in the packed lot, "and then they don't want a thing to do with you."

"It's a phase." Michael turned off the ignition. "Only supposed to last ten or fifteen years." He glanced around the lot, knowing but not quite willing to admit to himself that he was looking for Rachel. He felt undeniably better for his confession to Lewis, but the talk with the elder had worked no miracles when it came to his desire to see his old friend. He knew that Rachel was coming with Helen tonight, and he would have to ignore her. The rumors were too thick to fuel them any more than they had to, and the interview with Ursula had to be fresh in everyone's mind. It certainly was in his. He was angry at his cousin. It was going to be hard to be here tonight, with everyone in town thinking that he and Rachel had indulged in a clandestine rendezvous over the weekend.

"You know, I still don't get how Ursula knew about D.C.," Michael mused as they got out of the car. He chuckled. "You're the only person I told. You sure you're not sleeping with my cousin?"

Drew frowned at him. "I hope you don't seriously think I would do something like that."

There was surprising hurt in his voice, and Michael regretted having said anything. Drew was sensitive about the fine line he walked between protecting the land and developing it.

"Of course not," Michael said. "I was joking."

They started walking across the parking lot toward the school. "Looks like Lily's going to rake in a few bucks for her cause," Michael said.

"Have you seen her husband perform before?" Drew asked. Ian's magic act was the benefit's main draw.

"A couple of times." Michael remembered a party a few years ago when Ian pulled a parrot from Katy's hair. He'd seen a side to Katy that night that he'd never seen before. She'd been almost flirtatious with Ian, obviously pleased that he had plucked her from his audience to help with his tricks. She'd thrown herself into his act with abandon, and Michael had watched her, wondering where she'd been hiding the frivolous side of herself for so many years.

He felt an odd jolt when he walked into the auditorium. This was where the Reflection Day observance was held each year, and he wondered how many other people walking into the room were greeted with the memory of the last Reflection Day, or the one before that. He had to remind himself that the town had turned out for a pleasurable event this time. That was the way it should be.

The high school was old—it had been old back when he'd attended it—but the auditorium had been modernized fifteen years ago. Its lines were sleek, and the walls were a pale blue. The curtains on the stage were navy blue, and the overall effect was appealing. Kids filled the rear of the auditorium, where they could talk and act up without being under the scrutiny of their parents. He did not see Jason, but he hoped he was among them.

"Over there." Drew nodded to the corner of the auditorium, and Michael was surprised to see Ian and Jason standing together, deep in conversation.

"Wonder what that's all about?" Michael said.

He and Drew walked toward the front, where there were still some empty seats. Michael cringed when he saw they would have to pass Ursula on the way. She was standing at the edge of the aisle, bending over, talking to a few of her seated constituents. She stood up as she saw them approaching.

"Hi, Michael. Drew." She smiled as though she had not just done her best to slander Michael and hurt his cause.

Michael wanted to ask his cousin where she'd gotten her information, but instead he and Drew nodded polite hellos and continued walking. He was not about to let her know how she had gotten to him.

They found seats in the fourth row, and it wasn't until they had settled into them that he spotted Rachel and Helen. The two women were sitting in the row in front of him, ten or eleven seats down. Michael had a clear view of Rachel's profile. Obviously she knew he was there as well, because after a few minutes she turned her head to smile at him. He winked in return.

"There's Rachel," he said to Drew.

Drew looked in her direction. "Where? Oh, the woman with Helen?"

"Uh-huh." He could feel Drew assessing her. He was certain she'd pass his scrutiny, although he did not particularly care one way or another. He could no longer see her with any objectivity. She looked good to him, that was all he knew. She was losing the weight that seemed to annoy her, and her hair reflected the lights from the ceiling high above them.

"So, how are things going with her?" Drew asked. "How was the infamous D.C. trip?"

Michael sighed. "We remain careful friends."

"Are you trying for sainthood or what?" Drew laughed.

Michael shook his head. "You need to have pure thoughts to be a saint. My actions might be noble, but my thoughts are going to hang me."

"I can see you two together," Drew said. "I can see you writhing on that big old sofa in your den."

"Get off it, Drew," Michael said, but he could see it, too. "I think you need a woman of your own. You're a little overinvolved in this fantasy."

"I've probably had a woman more recently than you have," Drew said smugly.

Michael looked at him quizzically. He hadn't heard Drew talk about a woman for a long time.

"I could give you some lessons in discretion," Drew offered.

He might need them. Despite his talk with Lewis, the more he thought about changing his life to include Rachel, the more seduced he felt by the fantasy. Yet the obstacles—those he could see and touch, like Jason and Katy and the church, as well as those intangibles that gnawed at the edges of his heart—were overwhelming.

Drew began reading the program, but Michael could not shift his gaze from Rachel. Anyone watching him would know that his sitting apart from her was not a matter of choice.

Helen leaned over to whisper something in her granddaughter's ear. Telling her secrets? he wondered. He had the feeling Helen had more than one. He had known Peter Huber well. Peter had been sharp-witted up until the end. He would not have alluded so specifically in his will to music that did not exist. Did Helen know where that coveted piece of music was? As soon as Rachel thought Helen could handle it, he would question her about it again. They had only two weeks left until the hearing. And he'd heard that the bulldozers would be flattening the forest within a few days after the vote.

Michael's attention was suddenly stolen from Rachel and Helen by Jacob Holt's entry into the auditorium. Jacob headed toward one of the few empty seats up front only to be intercepted by Lily. She sprang from her own front-row seat, grabbed him by the arm, and pulled him toward the edge of the stage. She began talking to him intently, her face close to his, gesturing with her hands. There was color in her cheeks, and her usual smile was missing. Holt listened to her for a moment, then responded with a word or two and a shake of his head. He broke away from her and headed toward the empty seat only to have her grab his arm again. Michael watched in perplexed fascination.

Finally, Jacob Holt said something that ended the conversation, something assertive, firm. Lily closed her mouth into a tight line and let go of his arm. She watched him walk to his seat.

Michael turned his head toward Rachel to find her eyes on him. She was looking at him as if to ask, "What was that all about?" He shrugged in response and shifted his concentration to the program in his lap, smiling to himself, happy with that two-second interaction with the woman who was turning his life upside down.

Rachel had been afraid to attend the charity program. She was growing increasingly reclusive, and the article in that morning's paper had done nothing to enhance her comfort in public. She'd felt herself clinging to her grandmother as they'd walked through the hallway on the way to the auditorium, as if she felt safe only under the umbrella of Helen's protection. And that protection seemed invincible. People liked Helen Huber. They greeted her warmly, commenting on how well she looked, how lucky she had been to survive the lightning. Rachel listened, nodding and smiling, staying close to Gram's side until they had reached their seats.

They were sitting two rows behind Lily. Rachel had considered approaching her former student to say hello, but the thought filled her with fear, and not only for herself.

The last time they'd been out together, at the farmers' market, Lily had suffered for it. Rachel did not want to put her in that position again. By now she wouldn't be surprised if Lily was ready to turn away from her as others had.

She could feel Michael's presence behind her, though she tried to keep her furtive, backward glances to a minimum. It was difficult. She wanted to see his son, too. Jason was supposed to be with him tonight, but Michael was flanked by adults on either side. One of them, the man in the green Hawaiian-print shirt, she guessed to be his friend Drew.

Celine Humphrey sat several seats to her left. Rachel had called the elder the day before, asking if it was time to start working on the Rwanda supplies, and it had been obvious from Celine's response that the work had already begun. "But you're welcome to come help us on Saturday," she'd said. "We'll be sorting through the donations."

Rachel had said she would be there. She felt no encouragement from Celine and certainly no warmth, but she was determined to become involved in spite of her.

Lily took the stage at seven-thirty. "I'd like to welcome everyone to the first annual ASPCA benefit variety show!" she said.

A huge black dog bounded out from the side of the stage and came to a neat heel at Lily's side, and the audience applauded and whistled.

"This is Mule," Lily said. "I found him at the ASPCA four years ago and rescued him just before he was about to be put to sleep." She scratched the dog behind his ears. "Between ten and twelve million dogs and cats are euthanized—that means killed—in the United States each year, and another ten million die from abuse and neglect." Lily rattled off a few more statistics and encouraged responsible pet ownership as well as support for the shelter. Then she took on a more jovial tone. "Enough of the serious stuff," she said. "Our first act tonight is the Pembroke Dog Training Club's junior program."

A group of kids filed onto the stage, heeling—or attempting to heel—all manner of dogs. They demonstrated basic obedience training, and by the end of the exhibition, Rachel was longing for her own dog. She hoped Chris was giving Phoenix a lot of attention.

Following the young dog trainers was a routine by a local senior citizens club, describing the joys of pet ownership through song and dance. Watching them, Gram was near tears with laughter. It was Lily's dog show, though, that had everyone rolling on the floor. It was impossible to know if Lily had trained the five dogs to misbehave so spectacularly or if they were simply as rebellious as their trainer. Rachel laughed so hard her cheeks hurt.

Finally, the stage was darkened, and mysterious music filled the auditorium. Everyone fell silent, waiting. When the lights came up, Ian Jackson stood in the center of the stage, dressed in black pants and a black turtleneck. His straight black hair was tied back in its ponytail. He looked the part of a magician, Rachel thought, and as he launched into his act, she knew he was well seasoned in that role. He pulled eight white doves from a small purple basket, balanced silver balls in midair, and made long red streamers leap across the stage. Then he said, "I need a helper. Who can help me out up here?"

The kids in the rear of the auditorium waved their hands wildly, yelling, "Me, me!" A few of them were on their feet, a couple on their chairs.

"Back there." Ian pointed. "Jason Stoltz. Come on up here, Jace."

Rachel winced when she heard the moan of stunned disappointment from the rear. "Why him?" one of the kids asked, too loudly.

Jason walked up the aisle toward the stage, looking none too happy about being the chosen one. He was Michael through and through. Michael at twelve. The gawky slenderness brought tears to Rachel's eyes. She wished she could get to know him.

Jason stood awkwardly at Ian's side while a young woman wheeled out a large crate, painted sky blue and dotted with gold stars.

"Well, Jace," Ian said, patting the lid of the box. "Do you ever feel as if you'd like to disappear?"

Jason laughed. "Yeah."

"Like right about now?"

The audience chuckled, and Jason nodded. "Yeah," he said again.

"Well, hop up in here, and I'll see if I can help you out."

Jason climbed onto a footstool and into the box. Ian closed the lid on him and fastened it with a clasp. Rachel grimaced at the thought of being confined in that tiny space. She didn't dare turn around to look at Michael.

"Some people say that magic is nothing more than sleight of hand or mere legerdemain." Ian spoke with a cocky confidence as the woman turned the box around and around in circles on the floor. "But *I* believe there really is such a thing as pure, unadulterated, genuine, bewitching *magic*." He dismissed the woman to the side of the stage and, with a great flourish, opened the box. It was empty.

The audience gasped its appreciation. Some people applauded.

"Hey, Michael," Ian called out from the stage, "are you wondering if you're going to get your son back?"

People turned to look at Michael, and Rachel did not miss the opportunity to do so herself. He was grinning.

"I have faith," Michael said.

"The preacher has faith," Ian said. "And . . . it's either magic or a miracle!" He pointed toward the rear of the auditorium. Everyone turned to see Jason walking through the rear door. The applause thundered, and Jason was laughing as he walked up to the stage.

"How on earth . . ." Gram said.

"Amazing." Rachel applauded.

Ian put his arm around Jason once the boy had reached his side. "You're not a twin, are you, Jace?" Ian asked him.

"No." Jason shook his head. He was wearing Michael's grin.

"Dynamite," Ian said. "You go on back to your seat now. And you can be my assistant anytime."

Ian ended his routine with a few more tricks, and Lily took the stage again to thank everyone for coming. When the houselights came on, Rachel and her grandmother got to their feet and filed slowly out of their row.

"What a knockout haircut!"

Rachel turned to see Lily approaching her. The younger woman had made her exclamation so loudly that most of the people around them stopped to stare, and Rachel knew she was blushing as the young hairdresser gave her a hug. Lily was a trip, thumbing her nose at Reflection's judgmental few.

"It was a super show," Rachel said.

"How'd he make Jason disappear like that?" Gram asked.

Lily shrugged. "It's *magic*, Helen."

The three of them chatted for a few minutes, although Rachel found it difficult to concentrate on the conversation. Michael and Drew were in her line of vision. They were talking with a man and woman on the other side of the auditorium, and they were laughing. It was good to see that smile on Michael's face.

"Well, I gotta run," Lily said. She drew Rachel into another embrace, surprising her when she whispered into her ear. "There's something I want to tell you," she said. "Call me tomorrow." She pulled away abruptly and leaned over to kiss Gram's cheek. "Hey, Helen," she said, "you watch out for those old lightning bolts, okay?"

"I will," Gram promised. "You can count on it."

Lily moved away to another group of people, leaving Rachel to wonder what she wanted to talk to her about.

She glanced across the auditorium to see Michael looking at her. He waved, an act of bravery in this crowd, and she returned the gesture. That was as much of him as she'd be able to have tonight.

29

"Your son is beautiful," said Rachel.

Michael leaned back on the sofa and smiled into the phone. "Thanks. He did look kinda good up there tonight, didn't he?" He'd been surprised when Ian called Jason up to the stage. Ian must have given Jason some sort of instructions earlier, but Michael still saw his own trepidation mirrored in his son's eyes. It had gone well, though. "He even refused a ride home. Wanted to walk with some of the kids."

"That's great."

"Gives me some time alone with you, finally."

"Well, if you can call this time alone."

He laughed. "Frustrating, tonight, wasn't it?"

"An understatement. It was hard to be that close to you and not be able to talk to you."

"Where are you right now?"

"In the library, sitting in the fake-leather chair, sipping a cup of Earl Grey. Gram's gone to bed. I have the house to myself."

"Wish I were there with you." He let the words out, unwise though they may have been.

"I wish you were, too. It was so nice the other night, sitting with you on that loveseat in the hotel."

"With Ursula's hidden camera over our shoulders."

"Well, even if she had one, we didn't do anything we need to be ashamed of."

"True." But he knew that didn't matter. The article had done him irreparable damage. He thought of telling her about that morning's conversation with Jason and his visit from Lewis, but he didn't want to mar the warmth and comfort he was feeling just then.

"Lily told me to call her tomorrow," Rachel said. "She said there's something she wants to tell me. Do you have any idea what it might be?"

He heard the screen door open and the click of Jason's key turning in the lock. "She probably wants to convert you," he said. "Thinks you'd make a good Mennonite."

Rachel responded, but he didn't hear her. His eyes were on his son, who had walked in the door and was trying to hurry past him.

"Jace?" he said. "Come here."

With a resigned sigh, the boy turned to face him, and Michael sucked in his breath. There was a bruise on his cheek, near his eye, and blood was crusted under his nose. Someone had beaten him up.

"I've got to go," he said to Rachel. "I'll call you later."

He hung up the phone, then stood to slip his arm around his son's shoulders. "Let's get you cleaned up," he said, walking with him toward the kitchen. He wouldn't push Jason for details. Not yet. One thing at a time.

In the kitchen, Jason was quiet as Michael tended to his injuries. They were simple wounds, but Michael found himself wishing Katy were home. Some people thought Katy could heal children with her touch alone.

"Where are your glasses?" he asked.

"Broken."

"Do you still have them?"

Jason pulled the glasses from his pants pocket. One lens was completely missing. Michael took them from his hand and set them on the kitchen counter. Jason was lucky he hadn't lost an eye.

He filled the ice pack and instructed Jason to hold it to his cheek. "Now," he said, sitting down across the table from him. "Tell me what happened."

"I don't want to talk about it," Jason muttered. His lips were tight as he stared at the table.

The phone rang, and Michael ignored it. He would let the machine pick it up.

"I remember looking something like this once upon a time," he said. "Right down to the broken glasses." It had happened to him only once. After that, people knew that anyone who hurt him would have to answer to Luke.

Jason did not raise his eyes from the table, and Michael knew he didn't care whether his father had been through this or not. Maybe he shouldn't press him to talk about it.

"Mark Matthews said you were fucking her," Jason suddenly blurted out. He looked at Michael, and Michael could see in his son's face the anger that had been there this morning. "Rachel Huber," Jason added, as if Michael might not get it. "I was walking home with Patrick Geils, and Mark came up and said that. So I hit him. And then he hit me back."

Michael leaned back in his chair and looked at the ceiling. Jason had gotten himself beaten up defending his honor. "Are you wondering if what he said is true?" he asked.

"You said this morning you're just friends." There was an edge of cynicism in his voice. "You're acting so weird lately, I don't know. But I don't think you'd actually do something like that."

"You're right. I wouldn't. People like gossip, Jace, and I'm sorry you've gotten caught in the middle of it. You can't control it. I can't, either. We just have to live our lives the way we think is best."

"You were talking to her on the phone when I came in, weren't you?" he accused.

"Yes."

Jason made a look of disgust and winced, pressing the ice pack harder to his cheek. "I wish she'd never come here," he said. "I hate her."

"You don't even know her, Jace. That's not fair."

He knew he was skirting the real issues. If he were doing a good job of this conversation, he would ask Jason what he was afraid of. He'd try to help him get to the bottom of that fear and exorcise it. But he was afraid to hear his son's inevitable answer to that question—that Rachel could somehow derail his family. Michael would not be able to offer him easy reassurance to the contrary.

"Listen to me, Jace, please," he said. "I've been trying to figure out some questions for myself lately. Mainly some things about my faith.

I'm not certain what answers I'll find, but I can assure you that the one thing that will never change is how much I love you. That's something that will never, ever change, no matter what. So you're right if you think I'm acting different lately. I am. But please don't pin the blame for that on Rachel."

"I want to call Mom."

"Why?" he asked, alarmed. He had not mentioned to Katy that Rachel was still in town, much less that he'd been spending time with her. If she heard it first from Jason, it would look as if he'd been hiding the fact. Which, of course, he had been.

"To talk to her," Jason said. "Do I need some kind of special reason?"

"All right," Michael said. "Let's see if we can get through."

They tried for half an hour, but there was no answer, and Jason went to bed sulking.

Michael checked the answering machine after Jason was in bed. Sammi Carruthers, the chairperson of the board of supervisors, had left a message telling him that the date of the hearing had been changed from September 6 to August 29, the following Monday, four short days away. It felt like some sort of plot. Drew was not even due back from California until the first.

It was very late, but he tried calling Drew anyway. He got his machine, the message already changed to say that he would be "away from the phone for a week." He would call Drew's travel agent in the morning and find out where he could reach him. Maybe there was a chance he could come home in time for the hearing.

He'd said he would call Rachel back, but for the first time he was not anxious to talk to her, and he waited until he got into bed before dialing Helen's number. Rachel answered quickly.

"I hesitated calling this late," he said. "Didn't want to wake Helen up."

"I don't think you did. I'm still in the library, sitting by the phone. I was afraid you weren't going to call back. Is everything all right?"

"Not really." He told her about Jason's fight for his honor. He told her every detail of their conversation, as well as the gist of the conversation from that morning.

She was quiet for a moment, and when she spoke, her voice sounded tired. "I haven't done anyone much good by being here, have I?" she asked. "Except maybe Gram, and she really doesn't need my help any-more."

He had to admit she was right. Her being in town had stirred up painful memories of an old tragedy, turned good people into anxious gossips, and raised a conflict in him he happily could have gone his whole life without experiencing.

"None of this is your fault," he said. "Remember that."

"You're very upset," she said.

"Yes, I am," he said. "I'm upset that my actions have caused Jace so much grief."

"I'm so sorry, Michael."

"Not your fault," he said again.

They spoke a few minutes longer. He told her about his need to get in touch with Drew. He tried to shift his thoughts from Jason to the hearing, but when he hung up the phone, all he could think about was David and Bathsheba, and the son they'd lost as punish-ment for their weakness.

30

Rachel called Lily at Hairlights at exactly nine the following morning. Lily asked if she could get away for lunch, and she agreed but then pictured eating with her former student in one of the few restaurants in town and was immediately reminded of their farmers' market outing.

"Do you think we could we meet outside of town?" she asked.

"How about the Hearthside Restaurant?" Lily suggested. "It's in Bird-in-Hand—not too far away, but far enough."

As soon as Rachel stepped into the homey Hearthside Restaurant, she spotted Lily waiting for her at a corner table near the windows. She crossed the room and took a seat opposite the younger woman.

Lily handed her a menu. "I'm having the turkey and Swiss," she said.

"I'll have the same." She set the menu aside without looking at it. She wasn't here for the food.

They ordered their sandwiches, then Rachel smiled. "That was a great show last night," she said.

"It went well, didn't it?" Lily grinned.

"Yes. And that was a sweet thing Ian did for Jason Stoltz." She thought of telling Lily what had happened to Jason on his way home from the show but changed her mind. She didn't want Lily to think it had anything to do with Jason being in Ian's act.

"Yeah." Lily looked like a woman in love. "Ian does a lot of sweet things. And we made tons of money, too. Everyone was really generous." She cocked her head to the side. "Poor Rachel. You've seen too much of the ugly side of people here. You don't know the truth—that Reflection is truly a generous, caring town."

Rachel heard the mild defensiveness in her tone. "I believe that," she reassured her. "I know people's reaction to me is unusual."

Lily looked down at the table and ran a finger over the handle of her knife. "I have stewed and stewed about this," she said, raising her eyes to Rachel's. "But I think that if I were in your position, I would want to know."

Rachel tensed. "Know what?"

Lily took in a deep breath. "I have a funny job, Rachel," she said. "You wouldn't believe the information I get, unsolicited, from my clients. I know more about what goes on here than the mayor does."

Rachel thought of the newspaper interview with Ursula Torwig and wondered what more Lily could possibly know.

Lily hurried on. "Please forgive me if this is none of my business. It *is* none of my business. But I have to tell you."

"You're already forgiven, whatever it is," Rachel said. "You've been kinder to me than anyone in town."

Lily leaned back in her chair. "I know that Katy and Michael have been having problems for quite a while. Most people think they're terrific together, and everyone thinks highly of them. Well, people aren't so sure about Michael right now, but at least in the past both of them were truly respected. But I do the hair of a couple of Katy's friends, and I know things are not exactly blissful between them. And I also know you care a lot for Michael."

"He's a dear friend."

"And it's none of my business if he's more than that."

"He's not." Rachel felt her cheeks redden, and Lily quickly broke in.

"I don't care," she said. "Well, actually, I *do* care in a selfish sort of way, because I want Michael to be the strong leader in my church that he's always been and I want people to listen to him when he says we can save the land if we work together. But if I think about what *Michael* might need rather than what *I* need, then I wish the two of you *were* more than friends. I adore him, and he deserves better than Katy."

Rachel tried not to take pleasure in her words.

"Okay. So here goes." Lily blew out her breath. "Katy's pregnant," she said. "At least I know for a fact that she was pregnant when she left for Russia."

Pregnant? Rachel felt the smile slip from her face. Did Michael know? How far along was she? And she had to be forty-two, at least.

The waitress set their sandwiches on the table, and Rachel and Lily locked eyes, waiting out the intrusion.

"Are you certain?" she asked when the waitress had walked away.

"Yes, I'm sure. One of my clients works in her O.B.'s office, and she, of course, had no right in the world to tell me, and I, of course, have no right to pass it on, but here I am. She was about two months along when she left, I think."

"I don't think Michael knows." Surely he would have told her if he did.

"No, I don't think so, either. She didn't plan to tell him before she left for Russia. At least my client said that Katy was upset about it—being pregnant—because her marriage was on shaky ground to begin with. She was scared and crying in the O.B.'s office. She wanted her and Michael to use the separation as a time to think things through. She didn't want the pregnancy to cloud the process."

"But it *does* cloud it, whether she wants it to or not," Rachel protested. "It's not fair to keep that kind of information from your husband." Her hands were trembling, and she lowered them to her lap. She was about to lose something that had never been hers to begin with. Michael would not turn his back on a pregnant wife, a new baby. And she wouldn't want him to. "Do you think she might have an abortion over there?" she asked, although she was certain she already knew the answer.

Lily shook her head. "Some Mennonites could do it, but I don't think Katy is one of them."

Rachel tried to smile. "Well, actually, I think this will help Michael see things a little more clearly. Poor guy's been kind of . . . conflicted lately."

"I know," Lily said. "And I'm sorry, Rachel. I can see this has really shaken you up, but I thought you should know. I get the feeling you and Michael—well, if you're trying to make any decisions, I think you need to be aware of all the facts."

"I appreciate it," Rachel said. She looked at her untouched sandwich, her appetite shot. "Anything else you think I ought to know?" She was joking, but Lily's sober expression made her tense up again. "Lily?"

"Not a thing," Lily said. "That's the only Stoltz family gossip I can think of."

She could not do this, she thought as she drove home from Bird-in-Hand. She could no longer blithely fantasize about having something other than friendship with Michael while Katy was pregnant. It was bad enough to consider harming their marriage as it was, but with Katy expecting and upset? No. No way. She felt sick that she even had considered it. She'd believed—even delighted in—the descriptions of Michael's wife as a cold and noncommunicative woman. But the Katy that Lily described sounded like a frightened woman who badly needed her husband. Damn it.

She thought of Michael's words in the hotel in D.C. He'd been thinking about them, about the possibility of their having a future together, and she knew it could never be. He'd been very distressed last night, telling her about Jason. For the first time, he'd sounded as if he didn't want to talk to her, and she could hardly blame him. She was a threat to him and his family, a threat to this entire town. She was the demonic temptress after all.

She pulled into the driveway in front of her grandmother's house but did not get out of the car. Closing her eyes, she leaned back against the seat and thought about what she had to do. Chris was due to arrive in two days. She would have to call him, head him off. Suggest he meet her somewhere else for a few days' vacation. How far could she get in two days? Or maybe she could pick him up at the airport and they could drive to Philadelphia, spend a few days there together. Or go up to New York. Chris had never been there. Then she could take her time driving back to San Antonio. She pressed her fingertips to her temples. There was too much to figure out right now.

She went in and found her grandmother at the piano.

"Gram." She sat down on the other piano bench. "Do you feel strong enough to be left alone?"

Gram looked at her in surprise. "Left alone?"

"Yes. You're getting around well. We could put a chair in the little hallway where you feel safe in case it storms, and—"

"Has something happened?"

Rachel shook her head. "No, but I have to go," she said. "I'm hurting Michael. His son was beaten up because some kids think Michael and I are having an affair. His son hates me without even knowing me. And Lily told me that Katy's pregnant. I can't stay here. . . . " Her voice broke, and Gram moved quickly from her bench to Rachel's. She put an arm around her granddaughter's shoulders.

"I'm perfectly fine to be left alone," Gram said, "but I don't want you to go. Does Michael know you're thinking of it?"

"Not yet. I'm going to pack and be ready to leave before I call him so he can't change my mind." It would be far too easy for him to dissuade her if she called him now. She did not have nearly as much to lose as he did. "If I'm gone, he'll be able to focus on his family again. And his church. He'll regain everyone's respect."

"When will you go?" Gram still had her arm around Rachel's shoulders, and it felt good and warm.

"In the morning." She pressed one of the piano keys so lightly it didn't make a sound.

"You can't leave that quickly."

"I have to. I'm so sorry to rush off, Gram. I've loved having this time with you. But I'm afraid if I stay one more day, I'll end up staying one more month, and I don't want to . . ." She thought of the tired quality to Michael's voice on the phone the night before. "I think that deep down he'll be relieved if I go. It will make things easier on him."

"Well." Gram lowered her arm and folded her hands in her lap. "Let's you and me have a nice dinner together tonight, at least."

"All right," Rachel said. "And thanks for being so understanding."

She spent the afternoon packing and trying to reach Chris, who was either not home or not answering the phone. She went about her work with a calculated numbness. At least now she would know Michael's whereabouts. She would know where to send Christmas cards, the news of the year. She was immensely glad they had not "crossed the line," as he had called it—that she could leave with no more guilt than she'd brought with her.

By suppertime she had her closet emptied and one packed suitcase standing by the bedroom door. The smells from the kitchen were enticing. Gram had made couscous and vegetables. Rachel set the table, and when she took her seat across from her grandmother, she saw tears in the older woman's eyes. She reached across the table and squeezed her hand.

"Oh, Gram, I'm sorry." She had a sudden idea. "Why don't you come with me?" she asked. "Just for a visit. A few weeks. You'll get to meet Chris, and you'll love San Antonio. "

"That's not it." Gram drew her hand away to wipe her eyes with her napkin.

"What is it then?"

Gram shook her head. "It's been hard for me, watching you with Michael," she said. "I believe so strongly that you two were meant to be together. You're soul mates, like I said."

"Yes, we are, but—"

"And I know it's my own life I'm trying to relive through you. I know that. I see myself reflected in you, and I see a second chance. You could do what I didn't have the courage to do."

"Gram, what are you talking about?"

Gram looked at her hard, her eyes clear now. "I want to tell you something," she said. "Something about my own life. There was a man named Hans. He was very special to me, and I loved him deeply, but I lost him. I never should have lost him. And you never should lose Michael again."

31

Hans visited Reflection often, three or four times each year, even when Peter was traveling. Peter knew of these visits. He even seemed aware of the bond between Helen and Hans, and he told her more than once how glad he was that the two of them had become friends.

Hans never arrived without an armload of gifts: puzzles and books for Peter, intriguing food from around the world for Helen, toys for Johnny. Johnny in particular looked forward to his visits, because Hans was full of adventure. He took the boy to Hershey Park or canoeing or skating. And he and Helen went on long walks together. She was a daily walker, enjoying that time for herself, but having Hans with her intensified everything she saw and felt. When weather permitted, they often ended up in the tree house, two adults acting and feeling like children. During the long gaps between his visits, Helen talked to Hans in her mind, sharing her thoughts with him until she could no longer separate what she had actually told him from what she only wished she were able to tell.

She was twenty-nine years old in 1940 when Hans spent a full week with her during one of Peter's many foreign trips. It snowed for most of the week, and she and Hans and Johnny spent much of their time trudging happily on their snowshoes through the quiet white world above Reflection. The three of them spent their days building forts and snowmen, but it was the nights Helen treasured most, after Johnny was in bed. The nights were filled with music and conversation. And something else, something she could not easily admit to herself: a desire that was new to her, a mix of pleasure and pain.

She and Hans played the pianos together each night. They played with that ecstatic fury she came to recognize as a form of sublimation. She was filled with love as she played, for the music as well as for the man sitting on the other side of the black sea from her, and when they had finished a piece she often felt overcome with emotion, occasionally laughing, more often fighting tears.

She experienced her body in a new way around Hans. Until then, her body had been something of a shell, a vehicle to get her from one place to another. But she was suddenly aware of the fullness of her breasts, the hunger in them when she was close to him. She wanted him to touch her, and when he'd take her hand to help her up a snowy slope or over a frozen brook, she felt the warmth of that touch for an hour or more. And always, during that week, she felt the emptiness inside her that dear Peter could never hope to fill.

She tried, in a very conscious way, to enjoy the time with Hans without dwelling on what she couldn't have. Still, sometimes at night she woke up crying, the source of her tears no mystery to her.

The night before Peter's return, Hans sat with Helen on the floor of the library after Johnny had gone to bed. They sipped wine and watched the dying embers of the fire as they listened to Rachmaninoff's Second Concerto on the record player. When the piece was over Hans took her hand.

"You and I are two of a kind, you know that, don't you, Helen?"

There were threads of flame moving from his hand through her body. She felt the heat in her cheeks, her throat.

"Yes," she said.

"I adore Peter," Hans continued, "so this is hard for me to say, but I must. I love you, and I find that there is no other woman I want to be with as much as I do you. Peter leaves you alone so much—I would take you with me."

Her mouth was dry. "It's my choice that I don't go with him much of the time," she said.

Hans did not seem to hear her. "I watch the two of you," he said. "Obviously there's a deep attachment between you. Peter respects your opinions. He defers to you often and seems to listen to your suggestions about his work. But it's all so . . . intellectual. So cerebral. And you have such *passion* inside you, Helen." He tightened his hand around hers. "I catch glimpses of it when we're together. But most of the time, it's locked up in here." He touched the tips of his fingers lightly to her breast.

He was right, but until this week she had never known it. She and Peter were passionate about music and politics, but never about each other. Not the way Hans meant. She had not realized she was missing anything until then.

She had never felt closer to anyone in her life than she did to Hans, and for a moment she thought she might tell him everything. She clutched his hand with both of hers. She steadied her breathing and opened her mouth to let the words out, but they wouldn't come. It would mean a betrayal. But more than that, it would change things in a way she wasn't ready to change them. She doubted she ever would be ready.

He waited a moment for her to speak, and when she didn't, he continued. "What I'm saying to you is that I love you. Deeply. I seem incapable of caring this way about another woman. I compare them all to you. And I know you love me, don't you?"

"Yes."

"Then will you marry me, Helen? Will you ask Peter for a divorce and marry me?"

She imagined having a life with Hans. She could listen to him play the piano every day, travel with him, enjoy a passionately physical relationship that was missing for her now. But it could never happen. She and Peter had a symbiosis, pure and simple. Neither of them could exist without the other. And she owed Peter more than she could say.

She shook her head slowly. "I can't do that," she said. "I'm committed to him."

"Do you love him?"

"Yes." She did. She told Hans how Peter had saved her and her family from poverty. "If it weren't for Peter, I'd be scrubbing toilets," she said.

"I didn't know about any of that." Hans smiled slowly, sadly. "But I still think Peter's an extraordinarily lucky man. And he doesn't deserve you. Fond though I am of him, and much as I can appreciate what he did for you, he just simply doesn't." His voice was rising. "You should be with a man who can love you wholly," he said fervently. "Peter takes you for granted. He . . ."

She saw his anger and knew where it was coming from. Leaning forward, she touched his arm. "I know about Peter," she said softly. "I know that he is not completely faithful to me."

Hans looked at her in surprise. "Do you know . . . ?" He let his question trail off.

"Yes." She nodded.

"And yet still you want to stay with him?"

"Yes. It's true that ours isn't a marriage based on passion, but there are other things equally as important. I have Peter's love and respect. I have his honesty. And trust, and friendship. I have more than you can know, dearest Hans. I love you both, but he is my husband."

She went to bed that night filled with pain and longing, knowing she had set the boundaries for their relationship and in so doing had killed her most treasured fantasies.

Peter returned the following day, and that night the three of them sat in the living room listening to a new recording of a recent Huber work, *Lionheart*, performed by the Boston Symphony Orchestra. Helen found the music unbearably beautiful. She lay on the carpet, eyes shut as she listened, filled with the peace of having the two men she cared about close to her. Toward the end of the music, she looked over at her husband. He was watching her, tears in his eyes.

"I love you," Peter mouthed, and she remembered why she was with him.

After they went to bed that night, Peter lay awake humming a melody, a slight variation on the second theme of a new composition. He wanted her to listen to it, to comment. She did, suggesting a change of her own, which he scratched down on a piece of paper he kept on the night table. She watched him as he wrote, his profile barely visible in the moonlight. He was a very handsome man. The twist of love she felt in her chest as she watched him was real. Still, as they lay down together, as he lightly kissed her temple and bid her good night, the cool fingers of regret pinched her heart, and she knew she would have to live with that feeling for the rest of her life.

32

Rachel had grown sluggish in her packing. She pulled things from her dresser drawers and folded them with leaden hands. She'd been shaken by Helen's story about the pianist. Shaken that after all these years her grandmother still suffered such deep regret over the man she'd felt so close to and had to give up. Helen's voice had trembled as she talked about him, and Rachel had listened with the empathy of a woman who understood that pain, but the story would not make her stay. It only served to double her sadness. She hurt now for her grandmother as well as for herself.

"What do you think you're doing?"

She turned from the dresser to see Michael standing in her doorway, and she could not deny that her distress at seeing him there was edged with relief.

"Gram called you," she said.

"Yes. I was about to leave for the support group, but she rescued me." He gave her a rueful smile. "Second week in a row I'm missing."

She lifted a stack of jeans from the dresser. "Well, to answer your question, I'm going to leave, before either of us gets in too deep."

"We're already in too deep."

She dropped the jeans on the bed. "Michael, I've brought nothing but harm to you," she said. "I've hurt your son, I've turned your congregation against you, threatened your marriage, practically wrecked your career, and just about destroyed your credibility in the land fight."

He leaned against the doorjamb, arms folded across his chest. "Well, aren't you a powerful little thing?" he said. "That's all bull, Rachel. You haven't done a thing. Some *kids* hurt my son, and some unforgiving people have spread rumors. *I'm* the biggest threat to my marriage, and what happens to my career is entirely in my own hands. You have done nothing wrong. All you've done is be my friend, and I've needed that."

He walked over to where she was standing by the bed and put his arms around her. He held her tight, and she locked her arms around his back. "Were you planning on letting me know you were going?"

"Of course. I couldn't have left without saying good-bye."

"I don't want you to go," he said. "Please, Rache. Please stay."

She pulled away and sat down on the bed. "I have to tell you something," she said. "You need to know that Katy was pregnant when she left."

"Katy was *what*?"

"Lily Jackson told me. She heard it from one of her customers. Katy was about two months pregnant when she left, but she didn't want you to know because she didn't want it to affect whatever decisions the two of you made about your marriage."

His face was white. "I think Lily heard some misinformation."

"She sounded very sure. She said she heard it from a woman who worked in Katy's obstetrician's office. Katy was upset and crying, she said."

He shook his head, sitting down next to her, a dazed expression on his face.

"So you see why I have to leave?" she asked. "You need to focus on Katy right now, not on me. Not on us."

His face was ghostly. "Rachel," he said, "after we had Jason, Katy had an ectopic pregancy and then a couple of miscarriages, and her doctor finally said she shouldn't attempt to have any more children."

Rachel tried unsuccessfully to follow him. "I don't—"

"Let me finish." He stopped her with his hand on hers. "So I had a vasectomy. That was in 1985."

She looked down at his hand where it rested stiffly on her own and let reality sink in. "Could it have reversed itself?" she offered.

"After nearly ten years? I doubt it. And even if it did—" He shook his head. "The truth is, Katy and I haven't made love in months." He stood up and walked over to the window. "I have to think this through," he said. "Think clearly. This is secondhand stuff. Maybe Lily got her facts wrong. Or maybe her customer got Katy mixed up with someone else." He wasn't mentioning a more obvious explanation. Rachel did not dare.

"That could happen, I suppose," she said.

"I'm going to call Lily," he said. "May I use your phone?" He reached for the phone on the night table just as it began ringing.

Rachel picked up the receiver. It was a travel agent, calling for Michael.

"I gave her the number here. Sorry." He took the phone from her hand. "Doris?" he said into the receiver. "Thanks for getting back to me. Do you know where Drew is staying in California?"

Whatever the travel agent said drained any remaining color from Michael's face. "I didn't know that, no," he said. "I must have heard him wrong." He brushed a hand across his forehead, his fingers shaking. "And do you have a hotel for him there?" He hesitated a moment, turning to look at Rachel. "All right, thank you." He hung up the phone, then rested his hand on her shoulder, but he couldn't seem to speak. His eyes were riveted on the floor.

"Michael?" Her heart began to race. "What's wrong?"

After a long pause, he raised his eyes to hers. "She asked me where I ever got the idea that Drew was in California," he said. "She told me he's in Moscow."

"In Moscow?" It took her a moment to understand. "Oh, Michael. Surely you don't think—"

"And he's not in a hotel," he added flatly. "He's staying with a friend."

33

Rachel rose slowly from the chair in Gram's library. Turning off the light, she looked out into the yard toward the road, but she couldn't see Michael. He'd wanted to be alone, and she knew he was out there somewhere, walking and thinking.

So it was Drew's baby Katy was carrying. Obviously, Katy and Drew had calculated, plotted, and schemed behind Michael's back, and Rachel was angry with both of them. She was glad Michael had wanted some time to himself. The hurt and confusion in his face were hard for her to bear.

There was a movement in the darkness, and she leaned closer to the window. It was just the leaves of the bamboo, blowing in a breeze.

She walked into the kitchen, glad Gram had gone to bed early. She did not want to have to explain to her what had happened. She made herself a cup of tea, then sat down at the table in the darkness.

After a few minutes she heard Michael's step on the front porch, then the door creak open.

"I'm in here," she called softly.

He stepped into the dim light of the kitchen. She could barely see his face.

"Can I get you some tea?"

"No." He sat down across the table from her and let out a sigh. "I don't like the way I feel," he said.

"I can only imagine," she said. "I've never really been betrayed. There's been plenty of pain in my life, but not in that form. It must feel horrible."

Michael was quiet, staring at the dim image of his hands on the table. "He betrayed me to Ursula, too. I'm sure of it. He's been telling her things. How else would she have known about the trip to D.C.? He hasn't been on the side of the land fight at all. He's been a mole, using me every way he could. How can he live with himself?"

They sat in the stillness of the kitchen, talking, for more than an hour.

"So many clues I missed," Michael said. He sorted through them all, and she listened as he put together the picture of deception.

"I don't know how I'm going to handle this, Rachel," he said finally, "but I've decided I don't need to figure it out right now." He looked at her across the table. "Can I stay here tonight?"

What exactly did he mean? "What about Jace?" she asked.

"He's spending the night at Patrick's. He has a bona fide friend, it seems."

"That's good." She smiled uncertainly. Did he want to stay in the guest room, or . . . ?

He read her mind. "What I want, if you're okay with it, is to climb into your bed and hold you all night long."

She nodded, trying not to think about his neighbors, peering out their windows, watching for him to return home. "That's what I want, too," she said.

She found a new toothbrush in the cupboard beneath the bathroom sink and set out fresh towels for him. He came into the bathroom, moving like a man who had been stabbed in the heart by someone he trusted, and she knew they would not make love that night. Lovemaking was not what he needed.

She put on a cotton nightshirt and got into bed. When he came into the bedroom, he had stripped down to his boxers, and she tried not to stare at the body, at once familiar yet different. He was broader, slightly heavier than he'd been years ago. She remembered well the symmetrical pattern of hair on his chest. She remembered how, when they'd swim in the river at Katari, that hair would lie in a dark, tempting streak, disappearing beneath the waistband of his trunks. The desire she felt looking at him now, however, was far more than a memory.

Not what he needs, she reminded herself. Tonight she would simply shield him, comfort him. She reached her arms up toward him, and he smiled as he got into the bed next to her.

He turned off the lamp on the night table and pulled her close. Her head was on his shoulder; she could feel the smoothness of his skin against her cheek. They lay in a comfortable silence for many minutes before either of them spoke.

"I'm sorry, Michael," she said finally.

"I feel responsible for letting him into the fight against the Hostetter project. People warned me against him, but I was so convinced he was . . . honorable. I'm worried now that he's hurt us badly."

"You're a trusting person. I love that in you."

"It's going to be very difficult to forgive him."

How could he possibly? "And what about Katy?" she asked. He had barely mentioned her role in all of this.

"Katy I can forgive with relative ease," he said.

"Why?" she asked.

"How can I be angry with her? She's only doing what I wish I were doing. What I've been doing in my head since the day you arrived."

"But you *didn't* do it."

"Right. She has more guts than I do. I can't blame Katy for figuring out that our marriage was an empty shell long before I did."

"Whew," she said. "I'm not sure I could be so understanding."

He stroked her hair, rested his palm against her cheek. "Thank God you're still here," he said. "I need you."

"You were upset with me last night, though. After Jace got beat up. I figured things had finally gotten to the point where I was more trouble than I was worth. And I would have understood that completely."

"No," he said quickly. "Just then I was feeling very protective of my son. But I need your friendship. He'll have to accept that."

She ran her hand lightly down the length of his back, then pulled herself closer to him. "It's funny," she said. "This is so comfortable. I feel as though we've been together like this a million times before."

"I know."

Sleep was creeping into his voice, and she held him as he drifted off, knowing she would sleep very little herself. She didn't want to. She wanted to feel him next to her, all night long.

She must have dozed off toward morning, because she felt herself rising from sleep as Michael stroked her face with his fingers. For a long time she didn't open her eyes, didn't move. She didn't want to interrupt the delicious touch of his fingertips on her cheeks and chin, forehead and eyelids. When she finally did open her eyes, he was smiling at her, his face barely visible in the flimsy dawn light filtering through the curtains. She smiled back, and he leaned down to kiss her.

He did not kiss like a minister. His kiss was gentle, yes, but insistent and deep and exploratory, and she wrapped her arms around his neck. Her body rose toward his, searching for more.

"Rache," he whispered, his voice husky. He sat back on his heels, motioning to her to sit up, and when she did, he drew off her shirt, then gently pressed her shoulders toward the bed again. But he did not kiss her. Instead, he sat next to her, the sheet drawn down to her hips, and stroked the tips of his fingers over her body. If it had been any other man, she would have pulled the sheet up, squirming with discomfort under his scrutiny. But she had no doubt that what she saw in Michael's eyes was love, and she closed her own eyes and let him touch her, let him make love to her in that slow, tantalizing fashion.

His hands grazed the sides of her breasts until she wanted more. He traced languid circles around her nipples with his tongue, his breath warm against her skin. She pulled him to her, but he extracted himself from her embrace to stand up and take off his shorts. When she reached for him again, it was with real hunger.

So long, she thought, sinking her fingers into his hair. So long since anyone had made love to her. He knelt between her legs and stretched over her, the touch of his skin against hers a temptation. Slowly, he kissed her lips, her throat, her belly. She gripped the pillow behind her head and raised her hips to him. She felt the soft touch of his mouth and tongue on the inside of her thighs, and she moaned as he turned his head to ease her craving.

The world behind her eyelids glowed fiery red, and she arched her back, clutching the edges of the pillow until suddenly he was inside her—or very nearly so, his movements teasing and shallow until she lifted herself up against him, begging for more. She thought he laughed as he rolled onto his back, taking her with him, and she pressed her greedy hips down on him, over and over and over again until her body bucked with the force of her orgasm. He didn't let her stop though. He held her tightly against him, moving with her until he came himself, with a cry and a shudder. Only then did she think of her grandmother, sleeping on the other side of the wall. Could she hear them? Probably not. If Gram had heard, she would have applauded.

She leaned down to kiss him. They were both breathing hard, a thin wash of perspiration between their bodies, and although she tried to hold them back, her tears came, and she let her body sink onto his as she wept against his shoulder.

"It's all right," he said, turning his head to kiss her eyes.

She knew he was crying, too, or close to it. She could hear it in his voice.

It was another minute before she rolled onto her side, and they lay still together, arms entwined, his lips soft against her forehead.

When he spoke again, his voice was light. "What is that suitcase doing by the door?" he asked.

She opened her eyes to see the packed suitcase waiting by the bedroom door. "I don't remember." It seemed like weeks since she had packed it.

He suddenly drew in a breath and tightened his grip on her. "I can't lose you again, Rachel," he said. "I won't."

She tried not to think of the impossibilities laid out in front of them. "I'm afraid I come with a very high price tag," she said.

"I'll pay for quality."

She stroked her hand across his chest with a sigh. "I just wish . . ." She didn't know where to begin. She wished that he were not a Mennonite minister, that he were not married, that Jason knew her and adored her, that the town forgave her. "I wish—"

"I know," he said, and she knew that he understood completely.

34

That morning they took a leisurely walk through the woods surrounding the house. Rachel felt safe being with him within the confines of her grandmother's ten acres. They found the tree house Gram and Hans had built. It was little more than a platform now, but they leaned a ladder against it and sat beneath the canopy of leaves while Rachel told Michael the story of her grandmother's lost love.

When they returned from the walk, they loaded their bicycles onto Rachel's car and drove to Gettysburg, where they biked incognito along the roads surrounding the battlefields, stopping occasionally to munch on fruit and talk.

They agreed to put off any decisions, to live one day at a time for as long as they could. That was fine. Rachel feared that any decisions they might come to would put an end to their being together at all. Neither of them wanted to talk about the future or to acknowledge the fact that, more than ever, they feared being seen together in public. Although everything had changed between them, nothing had changed in the eyes of Reflection.

Michael went home in the late afternoon, and Rachel, bravely, went to the church to help sort through the donated clothes and blankets scheduled to be sent to the refugee camps. Celine was there, along with two other women. The four of them worked in one of the rooms in the basement, sorting the items on long tables. Rachel worked quietly, listening to the women talk among themselves. They had little to say to her. One of the women talked about her college-aged son, and Rachel considered telling them that Chris was arriving the following day, but they did not seem interested in including her in their conversation, and she kept her thoughts to herself.

Celine talked about the small camps the Mennonites were operating in Zaire. The volunteers were building latrines and shelters, she said, and providing support, both physical and emotional. A few volunteers were escorting people back into Rwanda. Rachel could picture the scene vividly, the people and the need. But she couldn't bring herself to share the images with the other women in the room. She was aware of her guilt. She had slept with their minister. She was no longer innocent.

Michael returned to Gram's house for a few hours that night, but he was clear that he didn't want to make love. "I have to deliver a sermon in the morning," he said, by way of explanation. He and Rachel were sitting on the porch swing, sipping tall glasses of iced tea. "I'm going to talk about forgiveness again, even though I addressed that topic a few weeks ago. This time it's for me, though. I'll be preaching to myself as much as to anyone."

She took a few sips from her tea before responding. "You mean, you feel as though you need to forgive yourself for what you've done?" she asked.

"What? Oh, no." He slipped an arm around her. "I know that what you and I did would be considered a grievous offense in the eyes of my congregation, and I'm still certainly . . . conflicted about us. But I'm through with the guilt. I have nothing to forgive myself for."

The words relieved her. "So you're talking about your desire to forgive Katy and Drew."

"My *need* to forgive them," he said. "Forgiveness is the only way to put an end to suffering. It's not the same as condoning what they did. It's not a denial that something hurtful occurred. But it's a way to be done with it, once and for all."

She knew he was talking about Katy and Drew, but she was thinking of herself and Reflection.

"It's freeing for all concerned," she said.

"Exactly." He lifted her chin with the tips of his fingers and kissed her, his lips cool from the tea. "And now I've got to get home to my son."

* * *

Chris was the first passenger off the plane at the Harrisburg airport, and Rachel could not get her arms around him fast enough. His hug was brief but enthusiastic.

"You're getting skinny," he said as he let go of her.

"Yeah, well, I've been working on it," she said, pleased.

He had a carry-on suitcase, his laptop computer, and some sort of electronic keyboard. "I'm traveling light," he said. "I hate waiting around for luggage." He sounded as though he traveled often, and although she knew that wasn't so, his words added to her sense of him as someone she no longer really knew. It had been only six weeks since she'd seen him, but the distance she felt from him these days had little to do with time or geography.

She wanted to get reacquainted with her son before sharing him with anyone else, and so she'd told Gram she planned to take him out to dinner on their way home from the airport. Excited though Gram was to meet her great-grandson, she supported Rachel's idea. Gram had been very agreeable this weekend, ever since she'd spotted Michael emerging from Rachel's bedroom on Saturday morning.

Rachel carried the computer in its soft-sided case as they walked toward the exit of the airport and out to the car. They said little, and she wondered how she was going to make Chris understand all that was going on in her life.

"So, this is the Pennsylvania Dutch country," Chris said as they began driving through the patchwork of farms.

"Is it like you imagined?"

"I feel like I've been here, you've got so many picture books around the house."

She did. Every time she saw another coffee-table book containing pictures of this part off the world, she bought it.

"Oh, cool!" Chris's eyes widened as he spotted a horse and buggy on the road ahead of them, and Rachel made a conscious effort to forgive his touristlike gawking.

"Remember, this is their home and you're a visitor, Chris. They just want to go on about their business."

"I know that." He sounded annoyed, and rightfully so. She had told him about the Amish, read him stories from the time he was very small. Chris was a stranger to Reflection but not to the ways of its people.

"Tell me about your summer," she said, carefully passing the buggy. To his credit, Chris did not even turn his head to look at the driver.

"It's been the best summer of my life," he said. He launched into a description of the band, how good they'd gotten, how successful their gigs had been. They had a female vocalist now, and one of the guys was writing some music of his own. They'd be playing one of the new songs for the first time at a party when he got back.

It was as if she'd unleashed his tongue, and she knew he could talk about the band all day if she were willing to listen. Her arms stiffened on the steering wheel.

"Look, Mom——" He suddenly interrupted his own chatter. "I was serious about not going back to school. I know you've been hoping I'd change my mind, but it's definite. I mean, registration for classes is next week, and I'm not going."

She opened her mouth, but he rushed ahead to block her attack. "I'm learning so much more about music by playing it with the band. Maybe I'll go back someday. Probably I will, so don't freak out. But right now, this is what I really want to do. And I can make some money at it. It's not like I'm just loafing around."

Rachel couldn't speak. She had the terrible and overwhelming feeling that his life was over, that he was about to ruin it. "We can talk more about it over the next few days," she said.

"Well, we can talk about it, but it's not going to change my mind," he said.

They were quiet as they drove. Rachel's head filled with images of Helen's house, of the inescapable music, the pianos, the books about composers. Chris would have a week in that house. A smile formed on her lips, and she tried to keep it in check.

Turning onto Farmhouse Road, she wondered how much of a tour to give Chris on his first day in town—and how much she should tell him. She decided to begin with Winter Hill to show him the breathtaking, almost aerial view of Reflection.

Once she'd reached the peak of the hill, Rachel pulled the car to the side of the road, as she had done on her own nearly six weeks earlier.

"Awesome!" Chris said as they got out of the car.

Rachel smiled. He'd always had a sense of wonder, an appreciation of everything. She'd forgotten that about him. She and Phil had taken his scout troop to the Grand Canyon when he was ten, and while the other boys roughhoused and spit pieces of hot dogs at one another and told dirty jokes, Chris had sat awestruck on the edge of the canyon, by himself, for over an hour. She had talked to Phil about it, a little worried that he was not like other kids.

"That's right, he's not," Phil had said. "He's extremely special."

She saw a shadow of that same awe in her son now, and she stepped next to him on the crest of the hill.

"This is the view that inspired your great-grandfather to write *Patchwork*," she said.

"I can believe it," he said. "It's like this incredible example of what God and man can do when they work together, you know?"

She put her hand on his back. She had never heard Chris mention God before; he'd grown up in a rather God-deprived home. But his description of the scene in front of them was perfect.

She pointed toward Huber Pond, where the reflection of the Mennonite church lay still and clear in the water. "There's probably going to be a change soon, though," she said. She told him about the proposed development of the land adjacent to the pond. "There's going to be a hearing tomorrow night, and we're hoping a lot of people will come to make their wishes known. It may be too little too late to do any good, though."

Chris shook his head as though personally wounded by the thought of harming that patch of green. "Greed," he said. "People don't think, sometimes. They just go after the money."

They drove through town, following the same route she had taken when she'd first arrived. She showed him the triplex where she and Luke and Michael had grown up and the statue of Peter Huber, which he said gave him goose bumps. She loved this boy, this young man. She wished he were not so intent on throwing his future away.

She had planned to take Chris to a restaurant outside of Reflection for dinner, but he spotted the Brahms Café on their drive through town, and she knew they were doomed. Inside the café, they were seated in the same booth she and Michael had shared. Although there were only a few vegetarian items, it took Chris a long time to decide what to order, because he had to read the descriptions of all the entrees to see how they related to the composers after which they were named.

While he was studying the menu, Rachel said, "Your great-grandmother loves this game where I play a few notes from a classical piece on the CD player and then she guesses what it is and who wrote it. You could probably give her a run for her money."

Chris smiled at her. "You know, I still love classical music, Mom. Don't get scared or anything that I'm gonna limit myself. I love the music I'm playing with the band, but I know where my roots are."

She nodded. She wouldn't push him. She just might push him away from the music he was meant to study.

Chris decided on the Puccini Pasta; Rachel, the Chicken Verdi. They closed their menus and waited for the waitress to take their order, but the woman—the same one who had waited on her and Michael—steadfastly walked past their table, looking straight ahead as if they weren't there. Rachel had no doubt that she herself was the cause of the poor service. The waitress tossed her blond ponytail and began taking the order of a table of diners who had arrived after them.

"We were here before them," Chris said to Rachel. "She acts like she can't even see us." He raised his hand when the waitress walked away from the newcomers' table. "Excuse me?" he said. "We've been waiting a long time to give our order."

The waitress wore a sullen expression as she walked toward their table. She said nothing as they gave her their orders, nothing as she turned and headed toward the kitchen.

"I thought you said this part of the country was so friendly," Chris said, too loudly. "She's a bitch."

"Shh," she admonished. She looked down at the table, then up at her son. "Chris, I have some things to tell you. Some things about me, and about your father, and about why that waitress is treating us like she wishes we would disappear."

Chris frowned. "What are you talking about?"

Rachel rapped her fingertips lightly on the table. "I don't know where to begin," she said. "And I don't know that now, when we're trying to enjoy a meal, is the time to do it."

"Well, you've gotta tell me now that you've started," he said. "So either tell me here, or let's cancel dinner and go outside."

She looked at him for a moment, then rose and approached the waitress. "Please cancel our orders," she said, turning away before she could see the expression on the woman's face. She looked at Chris, nodded toward the door, and he rose to follow her out of the restaurant.

It was a relief to be outside. Rachel stood on the sidewalk and looked toward the circular park in the center of town. "Let's walk over to the park," she said.

They walked the block to the park in silence, and once they'd reached the circle of green, she pointed to one of the weeping cherries.

"See these cherry trees?" she asked. "They were planted here around the time I left. There are ten of them."

"Is that significant?" he asked.

"Yes, it's significant."

They walked through the wooded circle until they came to the memorial. She sat down on the bench, and he joined her.

"What's that?" He pointed to the graceful wall of stone.

"That's part of what I'm going to tell you about. I should have told you long ago, I guess, but I never knew how, and I didn't want to harm your father's memory. But you can't be here and not know the truth."

Chris waited, and she felt his apprehension as well as her own in the still air around them.

She began talking. She told him about Luke going off to Vietnam, while she and Michael went to Rwanda. He had heard her mention Michael before, but she knew he had no real image of who Michael was and what he had meant to her. Even now she could not comfortably tell Chris how she had loved Michael back then, only that their friendship had been deep and caring. She told him about the change that had taken place in Luke during the war, how different he had been when he returned. She skipped the part about the inflammatory letter from Michael but described Luke's bizarre visits to the school. Chris frowned as the plot thickened.

"I'm not sure I want to hear more," he said when she described

Luke's fascination with his weapons. "He didn't hurt anyone, did he?"

She nodded. "Yes, honey, he did."

Chris looked at the memorial. "Hurt, as in killed?" His jaw was tight.

"Let me finish." She told him about her last day in the classroom, about seeing Luke outside the window, about trying to stop him from entering the school. "But I couldn't," she said. "I missed him somehow, and—"

She stopped talking as Chris stood up and walked toward the memorial. She stayed on the bench, her eyes on his back as he read the plaque.

It was a minute before he spoke. "These were all children?" he asked without turning around.

"Yes. My students."

"He shot them?" His shoulders looked rigid.

"No," she said. "It was a grenade. People here are angry with me because they think I should have been able to protect the children from him. But by the time I got back to the classroom after trying to head him off, it was too late. He was killed in the explosion himself."

"God, what a shit!" Chris turned to face her. "If he wanted to take himself out, why didn't he just do it at home? Why did he have to take a bunch of little kids with him?"

Rachel got to her feet. "He—"

"Phil was my real father anyhow," Chris said.

Rachel reached him and put her arm around him, squeezing his shoulder. "No, honey. That's not fair. Phil was a wonderful father to you, but your biological father was an equally wonderful man."

"Oh, yeah, right." Chris's eyes were red.

"He was. He was a good man who was injured in a bad war. He'd been wounded just like those guys who came back with one leg missing. Only his injury was inside him. You couldn't see it."

"Ten little kids." He pulled away from her and sat down on the bench again, head lowered to his knees. "I feel sick. I'm glad you didn't tell me this while we were eating 'cause I would've puked. I feel like puking. God, how'd they ever let you in a classroom again?"

"Phil did it. He had faith in me."

He looked up at her. "You're a good teacher, Mom."

"Thanks." His words meant more to her than all of the awards she'd won put together.

"I think you should leave this asinine town if they can't see it wasn't your fault."

She sat next to him again. "Well, remember you're hearing my side of the story," she said. "If you were hearing it from the mother of one of those children, it would sound very different. And that waitress? Who knows? Maybe she's the sister of one of the children. The relatives are everywhere, and even after twenty-one years, they still hurt."

He shook his head wordlessly.

"Well, honey, there's more," she said. "That's the worst of it. But other things are going on here."

"I don't think I want to know."

She told him about the land situation and finding the codicil to her grandfather's will. She told him about the missing music, and he was fascinated.

"Have you looked everywhere?" he asked. "A Huber piece no one's ever heard? You've got to find it!"

"I wish we could, but either it no longer exists or it's hidden away so well it doesn't matter."

And then, carefully, she told him about Michael.

"He might just be using you," he suggested with the simple perspective of a twenty-year-old male. "His wife's out of town, so he's lonely."

"They are essentially separated." She stretched the truth, then decided she needed to tell him more to clarify the picture. "He's also learned that she's been having an affair with one of his close friends."

"God, this town is full of cutthroat people." He shook his head. "You know what, Mom? I don't think I like this place."

She smiled. "I do. As a matter of fact, I love it, and I need very badly to make peace with it somehow." She stood up, reaching her hand toward him. "Let's get something to eat and then head up to Gram's," she said. "She's anxious to meet her great-grandson."

35

Michael could not shake the eerie, irrational, and thoroughly wonderful feeling that he was sitting in Helen's kitchen with Luke Pierce. Rachel had cooked an early, prehearing supper for the four of them, and Michael could barely take his eyes from the young man's face. Chris had Luke's features, Luke's height, Luke's voice. More than anything, though, he had Luke's way of moving, his mannerisms. The way he used his hands when he talked. The way he opened his eyes wide when he listened. Michael had to keep reminding himself that Chris was *not* Luke, that it was not fair to try to make him into Luke. Yet, when he'd met the boy an hour ago, he'd felt a surge of love that still had not left him.

His fascination with Luke and Rachel's son was not the only reason he could barely touch his supper. He was anxious about the hearing, especially now that he knew that Drew's dealings within the business community had probably been designed to harm rather than help the fight against the Hostetter development.

He'd arranged for Jason to spend the night with his new friend, Patrick, again, so at least he did not have that worry on his mind. Jason could not stop talking about Patrick, conversation so alien in the Stoltz household that it was going to take some getting used to. At least having a buddy seemed to have taken the boy's mind off Katy. He hadn't mentioned trying to call his mother again.

"You haven't touched your corn bread, Michael," Helen said.

"Or his beans or chicken," Rachel added. "A little uptight about tonight, huh?" She touched his arm, and he felt the warmth of her fingertips on his skin. When would they have the chance to make love again? Their relationship had a time-limited feel to it, as if he'd only be free to love her until his conscience caught up to him again.

He smiled at her. "Just a tad."

"You said the Amish will be there tonight?" Chris asked.

Michael speared a green bean with his fork. "Some of them. They rarely get involved in this sort of thing, but this hearing is important enough that they're willing to come and show their opposition to the development."

"You're driving several of them, aren't you?" Helen asked.

"Uh-huh. Most will come in their buggies, but I'll be driving a few and so will some other members of the church."

"I don't get it," Chris said. "They won't drive themselves, but it's okay for them to go in someone else's car?"

"Right." Michael set down his fork again. "They can't own a car or have a driver's license, but their economic survival has come to depend on them being more mobile. So if they can ride with others, or take a taxi, they can keep up with the rest of the world economically without giving up their traditional values."

"Can I go to the hearing?" Chris asked.

"Sure you can, if your mother will let me steal you away." He looked at Rachel, who smiled.

"He's all yours."

"As a matter of fact," Michael added, "how would you like to help me with the transportation? With picking up some of the Amish and taking them over to the bank building?"

Chris's eyes lit up, their shape and sparkle the same as Luke's. It gave Michael a chill.

"Yeah!" Chris said. "But I don't have a car."

"You can use mine," Rachel said.

"Aren't you coming, Mom—no, I guess you wouldn't be." He answered his own question as Rachel shook her head. Obviously he had a good grasp of her dilemma.

"That'll be a big help, especially since Drew's not around." He gave Rachel a wry look. Then he was jarred by a memory. He turned to

Chris. "Your father used to hire himself out to the Amish as a driver, remember that, Rache?"

Rachel nodded, but Chris groaned. "I don't think I want to hear any more about my father," he said.

Michael wanted to erase the pain and disappointment in the young man's eyes. "Your father was the best friend anyone could ever ask for," he said.

Chris didn't reply, but he looked as if he wanted to hear more, and so Michael continued. "He was very popular, but not like so many kids you think of who are popular at everyone else's expense. You know, who think they're above it all."

Chris nodded.

"He cared about people, no matter who they were or where they came from. I was the runt of the class, for example, either ignored or teased by other kids—"

"It wasn't *that* bad," Rachel interrupted.

"You weren't inside my skin," Michael said seriously. "But Luke treated me like I was every bit as valuable a person as he was. Your mom treated me the same way. The three of us were inseparable. We'd ride our bikes out to the quarry and explore caves, or play in the woods around the pond. The woods that are about to be demolished."

"Or you three would come up here and play in the crick," Helen added.

"That's right," Rachel said. "We'd fish or skate or swim up here."

"Luke was smart, too," Michael continued. "And he looked so much like you. So much." He felt a lump form in his throat, and Rachel reached across the corner of the table to rest her hand on his. He liked the openness of the gesture.

"That's what Mom says," Chris said. "I can't get it out of my head, though, about those kids. What he did."

"He was a casualty of the war, Chris. Believe me, the guy who went over there was a different person from the guy who came back. Luke was one of the most extraordinarily kind people I've ever known. You know what he did for me one time? For my family?"

Chris waited, hope in his eyes that Michael could somehow erase the terrible images coursing through his head.

"My dog had to be put to sleep. We were fourteen, I guess?" Michael looked at Rachel for confirmation, and she nodded. "My father was out of town, and my mother was so upset that she couldn't bear to take Cleo to the vet. And I was pretty useless myself. So Luke took Cleo for us, and he sat on the floor holding her, talking to her and comforting her, while the vet gave her an injection."

"Wow," Chris said softly, and Michael thought of another example of Luke's compassion.

"One time we were cruising around Lancaster. It was about five in the evening, wintertime and very cold. We went past a bus stop, and this old woman was hunched over, waiting for her bus. We drove on, went about our business, and about half an hour later, we drove by that same bus stop again, and there was that same woman. Luke couldn't stand it. He stopped the car and got out. He asked her if we could give her a ride someplace."

"I remember you telling me about that." Rachel smiled.

"Did she accept?" Chris asked.

Michael shook his head. "No. I guess she thought freezing to death was a better risk than getting into the car with two teenage boys. But I wanted you to know what kind of person your father was. He wasn't the man in that classroom. That man had a mental illness that was not his fault. He was a patriot and thought he should fight for his country. He did what he thought was right."

"He followed his beliefs," Helen added. "You can't ask a person to do more than that."

"When he came back, he was different," Michael said, "and no one realized how serious the problem was until it was too late."

Chris's eyes were red, and Michael hoped he had not gone too far. He looked at his watch. "Well, listen," he said. "We'd better get going. We have a lot to do before the hearing. You ready?"

Chris nodded and stood up.

"Oh!" Rachel said. "I forgot about the box in the attic, Chris. There's memorabilia, pictures of your father and some other things. Would you like to see—" The expression on her face changed suddenly. Michael saw her shoot a glance at Helen, then she stared at him.

"What is it?" he asked.

She shook her head. "I just thought of something. It's nothing, really. I'll bring the box down tonight, and you can sift through it tomorrow if you like, Chris."

"Okay."

Michael looked at Chris. "You ready?" he asked again.

Chris rested his crumpled napkin on the table and stood up. "Yeah. You'll have to tell me where to go and everything."

Michael stood himself. "Well, for now you can follow me over to the church. We'll get organized with the other drivers and then make our pickups." He looked at Helen and Rachel. "Wish us luck," he said. "I hope we can pack the place."

"Me, too." Rachel walked them to the door, handing Chris her car keys. "Drive carefully," she said.

"Yes, Mom," Chris said with mock annoyance.

The air outside was still thick with the heat of the day as Michael and Chris walked toward their cars. "I'm glad you want to do this," Michael said. He felt nearly overwhelmed with happiness, walking next to Luke's son.

"I just have one question," Chris said. "How do I explain who I am to the people I'm picking up?"

"Ah." Michael understood. "You can tell them you're Helen Huber's great-grandson. It probably doesn't matter. Most of the Amish don't hold anything against your mother, but everyone knows who Helen is, and they like her."

Chris got behind the wheel of Rachel's car and rolled down the window. He smiled up at Michael. "Thanks for the stuff about my father," he said. "It helped."

Michael gave Chris's arm a squeeze where it rested on the window. "I'm glad," he said, and as he walked toward his own car, he thought to himself that he would never let this young man or his mother out of his life again.

36

"Holy moly," Ian said as he and Lily pulled into the crowded parking lot behind the Starr and Lieber Bank building. "It's gonna be a hot time in the old town tonight."

Lily lifted her gaze from the dog collar she was mending in her lap to the parking lot and its strange combination of automobiles and gray-topped buggies. "Looks like the Amish are out in force," she said.

"And the media, too." Ian pointed to several vans parked alongside the rear of the building. Lily recognized the logo for a Philadelphia television station on the side of one of them. Good. They would have plenty of coverage.

"We'll have to park on the street." Ian turned out of the parking lot and began hunting for a spot.

They parked two blocks from the bank, and once they reached the side door of the bank's meeting room, they knew they had arrived far too late to find a seat. People were already standing along the back wall of the room.

"We'll have to stand," Ian said. "How about right here?" He pointed to the side wall near the door.

It didn't look as though they had much choice. They pressed their backs against the wall, and the space on either side of them quickly filled with other latecomers. The room was hot and airless, and Lily noticed all the windows were open. She wiped perspiration from her forehead with her fingers. "The air-conditioning must not be working," she said to Ian.

"No joke," Ian replied.

Lily studied the wilting crowd. She saw many of her neighbors, many longtime citizens of the area. Marielle Hostetter's two nephews sat in the front row, perspiring in their suits and ties. And there were strangers, two dozen or more. Reporters from newspapers and radio and television. A few of them milled around, holding video cameras.

The Amish had congregated mainly in the seats in the rear of the room, or standing along the back wall. The men looked hot in their tan shirts and black waistcoats, holding their straw hats in their hands or on their knees. The women chatted quietly with one another. No doubt this was an opportunity for them to catch up with neighbors they had not seen in a long time. Three Old Order Mennonite women, in their print dresses and starched head coverings, sat in the seats directly in front of Lily. The mix of people pleased her. The town was well represented in all its diversity.

The six members of the board of supervisors were assembling behind a long table at the front of the room. Their faces were grim, their expressions a little shell-shocked. They kept their eyes on the cameras, whispering to one another.

"I don't think they anticipated this kind of turnout," Lily said to Ian.

"Uh-uh." Ian glanced toward the rear door. "There's Michael," he said.

Lily turned to see the minister in the doorway, but it was the young man standing next to him that made her hand fly to her mouth.

"Oh, my God, Ian." She gripped the sleeve of her husband's shirt.

"What?"

She squeezed her eyes shut and pressed her cheek to his shoulder. "It's Luke Pierce."

"Where? That guy with Michael?"

"Yes." She kept her eyes tightly closed.

"He's a teenager, Lily. Not to mention that Luke Pierce is dead."

She looked at the man again. Ian was right, of course. Luke Pierce would be in his forties by now, but his youthful image had been kept alive over the years in photographs seen occasionally on TV or in the paper. Closing her eyes again, she saw the inside of her second-grade

classroom, turned upside down. Glass everywhere, shreds of camouflage cloth, a small hand jutting out from underneath an overturned
desk. She moaned. The air in the meeting room was too thick, too
fetid to breathe.

Without a word, she stepped past her husband and through the
side door of the room into the hallway. Pushing open the exit doors,
she walked out onto the sidewalk.

And then she was fine. She sat down on the curb and let her heartbeat settle back to normal.

She didn't turn around when she heard the door open and shut
behind her. "Hey, Lily, girl." Ian sat down next to her, his arm around
her shoulders. "What's this all about?"

"Sorry," she said. "It was just too hot in there. And that guy." She
shuddered. "He must be Rachel Huber's son. I remember her saying
he was coming for a visit. But he is the spitting image." She shook her
head. "No kidding, Ian. That's exactly what Luke Pierce looked like."

"Must feel kinda freaky."

"That's an understatement. Whew." She put her head down on her
knees. "I think I can go back in now. I just wish it weren't so stifling
in there."

"You sure you want to go in? Why don't you go get a Coke or
something down at the Brahms and cool off?"

"Nah." She shook her head and stood up. "He's not Luke. I can
deal with it."

But much of the meeting was lost on her. Luke Pierce's son stood
against the opposite wall of the room, directly across from her and
Ian, and she could not steal her eyes from him for more than a second
or two no matter how hard she tried to concentrate on the dour-
faced board sitting up front. Someone at the end of the table was
standing, reading from a fat sheath of papers bound in a blue cover.
He was some sort of sewage expert, and she listened only long
enough to hear him say that the development would pose no problem for the town before she found herself staring at Luke's son again.

She turned her attention to the slides someone was showing on a
screen at the front of the room. They were artist's renderings of the
proposed development. The office buildings were actually quite
attractive, but they simply swallowed up Spring Willow Pond. They'd

look great someplace other than Reflection. The *houses*, though. Ticky-tacky. Only a handful of models, and they all looked basically alike to her. They lined the curved, treeless streets of the Hostetter development, bumping right up against the Amish-Mennonite cemetery and Jenny's grave. The audience buzzed, and she knew what they were saying and thinking. The beautiful forest was about to be transformed into a plastic, sterile landscape.

Luke Pierce's son stood with his arms folded. He looked as if he were listening intently. He turned his head once, and she could see the wisp of hair at the nape of his neck. What would old Luke have made of *that*? she wondered.

Another expert read from a soil study, and Lily realized she was not the only person in the audience with her eye on the stranger. Otto Derwich sat a few seats away from her, his head turned in the young man's direction, and Lily guessed that he was absorbing no more of the technical information on erosion than she was. Otto whispered something to his wife, who batted his words away with a jerk of her hand.

Sammi Carruthers, one of the two women on the board, began talking about the importance of controlled growth. Ian sighed loudly, then whispered in her ear, "The Hostetters have the board in their back pocket, wouldn't you say?"

"All right," Sammi said, resting her notes on the table in front of her. "The board will now open the floor to anyone who wishes to express their opinions on the project."

Michael, who'd been standing near the front of the room, raised a sheath of papers in his hand. "I have several petitions opposing the Hostetter development that I would like to present to the board," he said. "They represent not only the general citizenry and the business community, but the Amish and other plain sect groups as well."

"Who don't vote, so who cares?" Ian whispered to her. She knew the sentiment was not his own but rather what he guessed was going through the minds of the board members.

Michael handed the petitions to Sammi Carruthers and took his place at the side of the room again. Lily watched his face for a moment, wondering if Rachel had told him about Katy's pregnancy.

Will Gretch stood up and talked about the increased load the development would mean for the fire department. It would lead to higher taxes, he said, and the audience stomped its feet in protest.

"I have a question," Ian said loudly when the din had died down. "I'd like to know what connections the members of the board of supervisors have to the building industry."

Lily held her breath while the board sat in stunned silence, and several people in the audience laughed. Then one of the men on the board spoke up.

"That's irrelevant to the task of this hearing," he said.

"Right," Ian said with a grin. He leaned back against the wall again, arms folded. He'd made his point. Probably every member on the board stood to benefit economically from the Hostetter development, and probably every member of the audience knew it. Everyone knew that Sammi Carruthers's husband, for instance, was a roofer.

There were a few more comments and questions from the increasingly antagonistic audience. Then Michael raised both his arms to get everyone's attention.

"Will all those who are opposed to the Hostetter project please stand?" he asked.

Only the Amish were hesitant about getting to their feet, and after a few awkward seconds, even they rose to join the vast majority of the audience. Not everyone stood, true, but it was hard to see those who were still seated, so dwarfed were they by the forest of unhappy citizens.

"Thank you," Michael said. "You may sit down now."

It wasn't until everyone started to take their seats again that Lily saw Jacob Holt near the rear of the room. And that's when the old principal saw Luke Pierce's double. Holt stopped halfway into his seat, his hand gripping the back of the chair in front of him. He lowered himself slowly, then turned his head to look at Lily, and she knew he was not finished with September 10, 1973, any more than she was. She held his gaze until the old man turned his head away, and in that instant she made a decision. She could not wait for Jacob Holt to do something about the past. She would have to do it herself. *Find a way to end the suffering.* That's what Michael had said in yesterday's impassioned sermon.

"Well," Sammi Carruthers said, obviously wrapping things up, "we appreciate your input here tonight, and we'll certainly be taking all your concerns under consideration as we think about the proposal this week. We will be voting on it Tuesday night, September sixth. Whatever the outcome, I can assure all of you that the board has Reflection's future at heart."

People rose from their seats, and Ian leaned his head toward her. "Want to mill around? Talk to some people?"

Lily shook her head. "No. It's too hot. And I want to talk to you, alone," she said.

Something in her voice made him raise his eyebrows, and she averted her eyes. She was going to tell Ian everything. She was going to ask him what he thought she should do, and as they made their way from the room, it was more than the heat that made her perspire.

37

The air-conditioning did not quite reach the attic, and Rachel's shirt stuck to her back as she dug into the box. Downstairs, Gram was at the piano, playing a piece Rachel had never heard before. "An obscure Huber creation," Gram had told her when she'd asked. She'd waited until her grandmother was deep into the music before slipping up the stairs.

Her hands tightened around the old Beatles albums. Yes, this was the right box. She closed it up again and set it at the top of the stairs to take down for Chris. Then she walked over to the other side of the attic, ducking under the slant of the open-beamed ceiling. She found her grandparents' box where she'd left it, the box she'd accidentally opened when she first arrived. She took out the photographs and journals and laid them carefully on the floor next to her. Then she began looking through the sheets of music, which had meant nothing to her the last time she'd seen them.

She glanced at the titles. There seemed to be two copies of each work, in two distinct handwritings, one sloppier than the other, with dozens of directive notes—*the violins must go head to head with the piano here*—scratched into the margins. They had to be her grandfather's early drafts.

It was at the very bottom of the box, a thick chunk of paper set inside a tan folder. The typed label on the front of the folder read *Reflections*. Rachel sat back against the wall with a smile.

She looked at the folder in her hand, opened it, and leafed through the thick stack of music. Would her grandfather have left the piece here, in the bottom of a box of music, or had Gram hurriedly packed these things and never noticed it? Perhaps she'd simply forgotten about it.

The piano stopped, and she cocked her head to listen for it to begin again. When it did not, she rose to her feet and turned out the attic light. She carried the box of memorabilia downstairs, along with the tan folder and the treasure inside it.

Light poured through the open door of the library. She took the box into Chris's room first, setting it on the dresser next to his computer. Then she carried the folder into the library.

Gram was reading, but she glanced up when Rachel walked into the room.

"Look what I found," Rachel said. She held the folder out in front of her and saw the color leave her grandmother's face.

"I didn't say you could look through my personal belongings," Gram said without touching the music.

"I'm sorry." Rachel lowered the folder to her side. "When I first arrived and was looking through the boxes, I accidentally opened one of yours first and noticed there was music inside it. I remembered it tonight and thought I should check it out, just in case. Forgive me, Gram. I thought you'd be pleased that I found it."

"No." Gram looked down at her book again. "I'm not pleased."

Rachel hesitated before speaking again. "You've known all along, haven't you?" she said. "You knew where this was."

"It doesn't matter."

"Gram." Rachel sat down on the ottoman. "I don't understand. This doesn't make any sense. I know you want to save that land as much as anybody. All we have to do now is get this music to that pianist and we're—"

"We are not sending the music to anyone." Gram slammed her book closed. "Not to anyone!"

She stared at her grandmother until the older woman had to avert her eyes.

"It's not negotiable, Rachel," Gram said. "And that's final. So you might as well put the music back where you found it."

"I can't do that."

"I don't expect you to understand my reasons," Gram said, "but I do expect you to honor my wishes. That music belonged to my husband, so it's mine now, and I will decide what's done with it. We should burn it. I should have burned it long ago."

Rachel clutched the folder to her chest. She would not let her grandmother get her hands on it.

Gram stood up. "I should have let you go back to Texas," she said.

Rachel's eyes stung as she watched her grandmother start for the door. Gram stopped, resting her hand on Rachel's shoulder. "I'm sorry," she said. "I didn't mean that. This is all just very disturbing to me."

They didn't speak for the rest of the night, and Rachel kept the folder with her, looking at the handwritten music inside it every once in a while. It was almost midnight and Gram was in bed by the time she heard the two cars pull into the driveway. She met Michael and Chris on the porch.

"How did it go?" she asked, turning on the porch light. She could tell by Michael's expression that he was not happy.

"The people don't want the development," Chris said. "Michael told everyone who was against it to stand, and practically the whole room stood up, but it doesn't seem to matter."

"He's right." Michael sat down on the porch swing with a sigh, and Rachel sat next to him, the folder on her lap. "The board seems to have its mind made up. They really don't care what the little guys think, I'm afraid."

"It was so cool, though, Mom." Chris sat down on the top step. "I mean, I met so many people. So many Amish. They were really nice, but you could tell they weren't used to that kind of meeting—not that I was, either." He grinned.

"The place was packed to the rafters," Michael said. "People stood out in the hall."

"And there was no air-conditioning," Chris added.

"Oh, no." She thought of her hour in the heat of the attic.

"There were lots of reporters, lots of cameras," Michael said. "NPR was there, and the *Wall Street Journal*. One thing we got was good coverage. I don't think it's going to make a difference, though." His gaze fell to the folder on her lap, and she saw his expression change as he made out the typed word on the label. "What the . . . ?"

It was her turn to grin. She handed the folder to him. "You won't believe this," she said. She described finding the music and Gram's reaction.

"That's it?" Chris asked. "That's *Reflections*?"

Rachel nodded.

"Can I see it?" Chris asked, and Michael handed the folder over to him. He set the music on the floor of the porch so that the light hit it, then began leafing through it with concentration, head bobbing slightly, one hand keeping time on his thigh.

"I'll talk to Helen," Michael said. "Maybe she just doesn't understand how this can save us. What do you think the problem is?"

"I have no idea." Rachel shrugged. "Maybe she wants to hold on to this piece herself as her last remembrance of her husband. Although she did say she should have burned it."

Michael shook his head. "Weird."

"Can I play it?" Chris asked. "Can I use the piano?"

Rachel was longing to hear the music, but she shook her head. "We'd better wait until you ask Gram, since she's being so strange about it. And I don't want to wake her up with the piano."

Chris returned his attention to the music, clearly mesmerized.

Michael got to his feet. "I'm going to go," he said.

She wished he would stay, but she was not certain how Chris would react, and she knew that was Michael's reason for leaving.

"Can I take this to my room with me?" Chris asked. "I want to finish it."

"All right." Rachel stood up herself.

"Good night, Chris," Michael said. "I enjoyed your company tonight."

"Yeah, me, too," Chris said. "See you tomorrow?"

"Sure." Michael gave Rachel a quick hug, and she reluctantly let him go.

She was in bed when she was startled by the knock on her window. At the second knock, she laughed out loud.

Naked, she got up and opened the window for him. "You used to throw stones," she whispered as she unfastened the screen.

"Well, you slept upstairs back then," he said, climbing over the sill.

They would wake one another that way, the three of them. They'd sneak out of their houses and go exploring in the middle of the night. Their mothers would compare notes the following day on how lazy and tired their kids were all the time.

"And you slept in your jammies back then." Michael stepped into the room and pulled her into his arms for a kiss. His clothes felt cool and soft against her bare skin. "I've missed touching you," he said.

She began unbuttoning his shirt, and in minutes she had him undressed and stretched out beneath her on the bed. He let her make love to him as he had to her a few nights before—slowly, dragging it out, as if making up for all the years of lovemaking that had been lost to them. They lay naked together afterward, the moonlight on their bodies. Despite the air-conditioning, it was too hot for the covers.

"Your son is terrific," Michael said. He was stroking the backs of his fingers along her side.

"You were so good with him," she said. "Thanks for asking him to go with you tonight."

"He was a big help."

She could see Chris's face at the kitchen table, the hope in his eyes as he listened to the stories about his father. "I love him too much," she said.

"Impossible."

"I do," she said. "It makes me so afraid of losing him. I've lost too many people. Two husbands, my parents. I lost you, in a different way."

He hesitated. "Are you afraid of losing me again?"

"Yes."

He pulled her closer, but she knew he could offer her no reassurance that that wouldn't happen. She clutched him tightly, pressing her face against his chest to breathe in his scent.

"It's understandable that you'd fear losing Chris, but it's unfounded," he said. "Really."

"He's so much like Luke, though," she said.

"Yes. I couldn't stop looking at him tonight. He's Luke, through and through."

Rachel felt the lump form in her throat. "He's like the Luke you were describing tonight. Beautiful and kind and loving. But he's getting to that age where Luke changed."

"It won't happen."

She began weeping, and for the first time she realized the fear had been inside her all along. "He wants to quit school. He wants to play full time in his band."

"He has a passion. Let him follow it."

She sat up. "But I'm afraid it will be the beginning of the end," she said. "He'll change. Maybe the mental illness is there, beneath the surface, just waiting for something to trigger it."

Michael reached up to touch her cheek. "There's no Vietnam right now, Rache. And Chris is not Luke."

She studied his face for a moment. His expression was serious. There was love in his eyes, and she lay down again, pulling close to him. She would not think about Chris any longer tonight. She would not think about all she had to lose.

Helen lay in her bed, staring at the ceiling as she had been for the past couple of hours. She knew Michael was in the house. She'd heard him at Rachel's window, and it warmed her heart to know they were together.

She had not felt this sort of love for other human beings in so very long. She would look at her granddaughter and her beautiful great-grandson and be filled with an almost foreign sense of joy and caring. But that joy was tinged with sorrow, because she knew she was a disappointment to them. They thought she was being selfish and unreasonable, and there was no way she could make them understand. Rachel and Chris were both too young to know that integrity and love and sacrifice could be more important than a simple piece of land.

She thought of Peter often these days. She'd known him better than anyone, known his kind heart and his compassion. And she'd known all too well the core of self-doubt that had festered inside him.

She rolled onto her side and closed her eyes. The land would be developed or not, she thought. And Rachel and Chris would either love her or loathe her. She would do nothing to change either outcome—not because she couldn't, but because she knew in her heart that the path she had chosen was the honorable one.

38

Rachel was reading about Rwanda in the two-day-old issue of the Sunday *Times* when Chris walked into the kitchen.

"Is Gram up yet?" he asked as he sat down across the table from her. He plucked a bran muffin from the open tin and took a bite.

"Not yet." She knew he was anxious to get his great-grandmother's permission to play *Reflections* on the piano.

"I was up practically all night," Chris said, "but I didn't get to look through that box of pictures and stuff yet."

He'd been up all night studying the music, she thought. She watched his face as he chewed his muffin. He looked like a perfectly happy, healthy twenty-year-old. Her fears of the night before seemed silly in the light of day.

"Well," Chris said casually, eyes on his muffin, "was Michael sneaking around last night for my sake or Gram's?" A small smile played at the corners of his mouth.

Rachel caught her breath, let it out. "Yours," she said.

"Tell him he doesn't need to do that. It's okay. As a matter of fact, I think it's cool you two are together."

Rachel felt the color in her cheeks. "Thank you," she said. "It's very difficult, though, Chris. He and I don't feel as though we're doing anything wrong, but the rest of the world might. His congregation definitely would. It's not a very good situation."

"Yeah, I know, but you told me once to do what feels right to me and not worry about what the rest of the world thinks. You should do the same."

Had she actually said that to him? She did not recall.

Chris stood up, wolfing down the last of his muffin as he grabbed another. "There's something really weird about that music," he said as he headed toward the living room.

"What do you mean, 'weird'?"

He shrugged. "I don't know. Not sure. But I can't wait to play it. Call me when Gram gets up, okay?"

"I will," she said.

She returned her attention to the paper after Chris left the room, forcing herself to face the new pictures from the refugee camps. The cholera-stricken children looked dazed and flat, lifeless versions of the children she'd taught. At least she was finally doing something to help—not much, but it was better than nothing.

"Good morning." Helen walked into the room.

"Hi." Rachel folded the paper and carried her teacup to the sink. "Can I get you something for breakfast?" she asked.

"No, this will be fine," Gram said as she sat down at the table and pulled a bran muffin from the tin. Rachel took the jar of marmalade from the refrigerator and handed it to her.

"I'm sorry we fought last night, Rachel," Gram said. "I love you very much. But I ask you to please respect my wishes regarding the music."

Rachel sat down. "I want to, Gram, but it's hard when I don't understand the position you've taken. Especially when the stakes are so high." She picked up a crumb from the table with the tip of her finger and dropped it onto a napkin. "I told Michael I found the music. I know he wants to talk with you about it."

"He can talk to me until his lips are blistered, I'm not going to bend."

"If you could tell me why, Gram." She leaned toward her grandmother. "The bulldozers are set to roll as soon as the board casts its vote, and everyone knows the vote is nothing more than a formality at this point. Everyone—"

"Gram?" Chris appeared at the door to the kitchen. "May I play *Reflections* on the piano? Please?"

Gram studied his face as if she might find her answer there, and Rachel saw the love in the older woman's eyes. Gram would not be able to resist her great-grandson's request.

"When I'm done with my breakfast and out the door, you may," Gram said. She looked at Rachel as Chris disappeared from the doorway. "I'm going into town this morning," she said. "I need to return those library books and get some more."

"Do you want me to take you?"

"No, thank you. I feel up to the drive, and I'd just as soon be by myself today." She narrowed her eyes at her granddaughter. "I trust you'll keep that music in the house?" she asked.

"I won't do anything with it without your okay," Rachel answered.

Chris was at the piano the instant Gram left the house. Rachel sat in the chair by the window, sipping a cup of tea, listening. He played smoothly, humming the orchestral parts, playing the piece as if he'd performed it many times before. Most likely he had, in his head, throughout the night. Already there was emotion in the playing, passion, and she tightened her hands around her cup. It had been a while since she'd heard him play anything classical. Chris had inherited something powerful from his great-grandfather, no doubt about it.

It was a long piece, with very few places that gave Chris pause. It was only near the end of the second movement that Rachel realized she would not have recognized the composition as a Huber. There was something different about it. And the middle of the third movement was, as Chris had said, weird. The notes spilled on top of one another without harmony. She thought of those artists who threw paint on a canvas with no method to their madness.

When he finished playing, Chris turned to face her. She could see the glistening of perspiration on his forehead. He was smiling.

"Nice, isn't it?" he asked.

She nodded. "You play beautifully."

He picked up a sheet of the music and looked at it. "It's different, though. Different from his other stuff."

"I thought so, too. Though I really couldn't say in what way."

"This third movement is downright bizarre."

"It was a little . . . cacophonous there for a while."

"Good word, Mom!" He looked impressed, then began leafing through the music again. "I don't think I could ever memorize that passage," he said. "This climax"—he played a few notes—"leads to a fortissimo unison on the B-A-C-H theme. Then he starts this weird six-page cadenza with a statement of the main theme in the bass, F major. But after that, he goes right into new material. It's like some-one else wrote these few pages."

Rachel laughed. "If you say so, sweetie. You lost me somewhere around the fortissimo bit."

"He must have been experimenting," Chris said. "Maybe that's why this piece was special to him. This is my favorite part." He played the theme from the first movement. It was lovely. "Awesome," he said.

"It's beautiful," she agreed.

"I want to put this into my computer. I have a really cool music program. Maybe I can adapt some of this to my band."

She nearly vetoed the idea; she'd just told Gram she would not let the music leave the house. But she wanted *Reflections* in Chris's computer. She wanted it someplace other than in that tan folder, where it could be burned or lost or thrown away. "Put it in the computer," she said. "But you'll need Gram's permission to use any of it publicly."

"Right." His voice told her that he would worry about that later. He jumped up from the piano bench and raced off to his room. Michael was right—Chris had a passion.

She spent the afternoon in the basement of the church, with Celine and the same two women she'd worked with the last time. Members of the congregation had assembled and donated health kits and layettes, and Rachel packed them into boxes to be shipped to the Mennonite Central Committee in Ohio. From there, the supplies would go to the camps.

The women worked quietly, and Rachel figured that she was the damper on their conversation. They thanked her for her help, but she was certain they wished she hadn't joined them.

"Did you see the pictures from the camps in the *New York Times* this Sunday?" she ventured to ask when they'd been working for over an hour.

The women did not answer her right away, and Rachel chewed the inside of her cheek in the silence.

"I didn't," Celine said finally. "I don't get the paper."

The other women shook their heads without looking up from

their work, and Rachel waited a moment before speaking again. "Does the Mennonite Central Committee require a volunteer to be a Mennonite?" She told herself she wanted the answer to that question merely out of curiosity, nothing more.

"No, but they'd have to be a member of some church," Celine said. "And they have to be screened."

Would they ever take a Unitarian? she wondered.

She returned home at six. There were two messages from Michael on the answering machine, the first telling her that he would be working with the youth group on the Reflection Day presentation that night and would not get to see her again until the following day. The second message was for Gram, merely asking her to return his call.

She found her grandmother on her knees in the garden, pulling weeds from around the tomato plants. "Did you call Michael back?" she asked.

Gram looked up, shading her eyes from the sinking sun with her hand. "Does a cat go into a doghouse?" she replied.

Rachel felt a flash of impatience. She turned and walked back to the house before she could say anything she might regret.

She found Chris still in his room, sitting on the bed, bent over his laptop computer. "Pasta for dinner?" she asked.

"I'm not hungry." He barely looked up from the computer screen. "Maybe later."

She made pasta for herself and Gram, and they ate in silence. She didn't know what to say. Her grandmother's stubborn selfishness was starting to irritate the hell out of her.

"I'm tired," the older woman said when they'd finished dinner. "I get tired too easily these days."

"Well, you've had a very full day," Rachel said. "A trip to town. All that work in the garden."

Gram nodded. "I think I'll go to bed early. Read a little."

Rachel felt helpless as she watched her grandmother leave the room. There was nothing she could do. She could not make her return Michael's call or force her to send the music to Karl Speicer. Gram had all the power in this situation.

She cleaned up the kitchen, wishing she could see Michael, wishing her son would come out from the cave of his room. She was fighting a pang of loneliness when she heard Chris's bedroom door open. In a moment he stood at the door of the kitchen. He looked ashen, ill, and she set the dish towel down on the counter.

"Are you all right?" she asked.

"You won't believe this, Mom. I . . . " He shook his head. "There's a code in the music. A cipher."

She did not understand what he meant. "A cipher?"

"Some composers put messages in their music—although not usually this elaborate. This is . . ." He shook his head again.

"You mean, Grandpa put a message in his music? He says something?"

"He says something unbelievable."

"What?"

"Come here."

She followed him into his room.

"Sit here."

She sat next to him on his bed, and he put the computer on his knees.

"It's only in this one section," he said. "You know, where it all sounded so weird?"

She nodded.

"He was trying to tell us something with that B-A-C-H theme. See, the Germans know B flat as B, and B as H. So where he has A-D-D-A-B-E-A-D, he's really saying 'add ahead' and what he really means—and believe me it took me about a millennium to figure this out—is to keep adding more alphabet. He does it twice. He already had A through H. Then he tells us to add I through P by using the next higher octave, then Q through X by going even higher. So he's got nearly the whole alphabet to work with, but that's why the music sounds so bizarre here. He didn't really care about the music, although he pads it with a few things, but he was primarily interested in getting his message across."

He had lost her again. "So what does he say?" she asked.

"Well, like I said, he padded it with some superfluous stuff, but when you take all that out and add some punctuation and some y's in the right places" —he hit a few keys on the computer— "here's what you're left with." He set the computer on her lap, and she read the message on the screen aloud.

"My dear Karl, this is my finest work. Yet you may listen to it and wonder how I can say that. You must believe me, this is my finest creation. But it doesn't approach Helen's poorest."

Rachel looked at Chris. "What does that mean?"

"Keep reading."

"All the work passed off as mine was, in reality, Helen's." Rachel read the line again, chilled. *"Didn't you ever guess?"* she continued. *"Helen was good at protecting me, but I thought you, of all people, would one day figure it out. I believe the world should know the truth. When you receive this work, I will be dead, and I ask you to make this fact known—that Helen Huber is one of this country's finest composers, that her husband, though a man of integrity despite this one major transgression, was a fraud. I composed a great deal, dear friend, but none of my work ever reached the public ear. I was no competition for my wife. The piece you hold in your hands now is the only work of mine you have ever seen, and you will know as you listen to it that I'm telling the truth."*

Rachel looked up from the computer. "This is ridiculous," she said. She thought of the institution that was her grandfather. She thought of all the music the world knew as his. "For some reason he wanted Gram to have some fame after he was gone. Or maybe he felt sorry for her because she'd been a composition student, too, and she essentially gave it up to marry him."

"Mom, he's telling the truth," Chris argued. "I was confused by this piece. I thought maybe he was in a different creative phase or something, and that's why it was so stylistically different. But it makes sense now. He wrote this"—he held up the music from his desk—"and Gram wrote everything else."

"How could he . . . why would she allow . . . ?"

"I don't know," Chris said, "but that statue down by the pond? That should be Gram standing there in bronze, not Peter Huber."

Rachel still could not grasp the obvious truth. Was this why her grandmother did not want Karl Speicer to see *Reflections*? Did she know or suspect a cipher in the music and want to protect her husband and his secret forever? Or did she simply know that this piece would not be as good as her own, that it would serve only to tarnish her husband's memory?

Suddenly she thought of the music in the box in the attic. "Come with me, Chris," she said.

He followed her into the attic. They opened the box and pulled out the sheets of yellowed music. Quickly, the two different hand-writings made sense.

"She'd create it," Chris said, holding up one copy of a sonata. "And he'd copy it over in his own writing." He held up a second manu-script of the same piece, the handwriting neat and clean. "Maybe he'd change it a little here and there, but basically it was hers. Look here in the margins. These are her notes to him." He read one of them. "Remember, you're moving toward the climax of the cadenza," she'd written.

They went through two more boxes, until there was no doubt left in Rachel's mind that her grandparents had engaged in a lifelong ruse. For what reason, she couldn't guess. But Helen Huber was indeed one of the country's finest composers.

Rachel awakened to the sound of the piano in the morning. At first she thought Chris was playing again, but once she entered the living room, she discovered it was her grandmother. She stood next to the piano until Gram finally looked up, her hands coming to rest on the keys.

"Gram." Rachel folded her hands on the ebony lid of the piano. "Please play me something you wrote yourself. Play me one of your compositions."

Gram looked perplexed. "What do you mean?" she asked.

Rachel flattened her palms on the lid. They were sticky with per-spiration. "Chris made a discovery last night," she began. "He found that Grandpa had put a coded message in the music of *Reflections*." She spoke very slowly, deliberately.

A swatch of color formed on her grandmother's cheeks, and the older woman lowered her hands from the keys to her lap.

"Then Chris and I went upstairs in the attic, and—I know this was against your wishes and I'm sorry—we looked through the boxes of music. Please, Gram," she pleaded, "play me something. Play me the piece you've written that you love the best."

Gram looked at her a long time before finally lifting her hands to the keys once more. The opening notes of *Patchwork* filled the room, and Rachel sat down in the chair by the window to listen to her grandmother play her masterwork.

"You know I studied composition with him," Gram said.

"Yes." They were sitting in the wing chairs in the library, and Rachel was relieved that Gram finally seemed ready to talk.

"But my ambitions were tempered by the times," Gram continued. "I often felt torn between what I wanted as an artist and what I wanted as a woman, which was to be a supportive wife and mother. Also, there were precious few successful female composers."

Rachel shook her head. "I'm still stunned, Gram."

"I would submit work, and it would receive no recognition whatsoever. Then Peter decided to enter a competition. He tried to persuade me to enter it with him, but I was so discouraged by the poor reception of my work that I decided against it. Peter thought my compositions were excellent, and he was angry that they were being ignored on the basis of my gender. At any rate, the competition involved the submission of three separate works over the course of a year. Peter worked very hard on his first submission, but he could not get it to fall together properly by the first deadline. He was so distraught. On a whim, I suggested he submit one of my pieces, just to qualify for the contest. He did so, under his own name, of course, and with my blessing, and the judges thought it was extraordinary." Gram smiled to herself. "It was not bad, and I had a good laugh when they said Peter was in first place after that initial round.

"He continued working on his own piece and turned it in as his second submission. The judges were anxiously waiting for it, and they were very disappointed. They advised him to return to the style of the first piece. This second, they said, lacked the warmth and heart and mystery of the first." Gram shook her head. "I'm afraid they were right. Technically, Peter was a master at composition, but he couldn't seem to instill his work with much emotion. He worked on a third piece, but as the deadline for submission rolled around, he knew it was no good. He and I had a long talk one night. We stayed up the entire night, and we made a decision. We entered into a pact. I would give him another composition for the competition. We both knew that if it was well received, we would be starting a ruse that had no end. And the piece was indeed well received—well enough to cancel out the lackluster reception for his second submission and enough to propel him to a national standing."

"But why didn't you claim what was rightfully yours?" Rachel asked. "Show the bastards who rejected you as a female what fools they were."

"It would have ruined both of us at that point to admit to our . . . duplicity," Gram said. "Neither of us would have had a chance for a successful career. And the ruse served us both very well. I loved composing. I had no desire for the travel and other responsibilities and supposed benefits that went along with fame, while Peter thrived on that end of things. While he was away, I'd write music. When he returned, he'd take what I had written and make minor adaptations to it. The thing that was hardest for him, though, were the accolades, because he knew they were not truly meant for him. That's why he always refused to appear publicly to receive them. But his fame and his reputation gave him the opportunity to have influence and power, and because I fully agreed with his political leanings, I felt I was doing something for the greater good, freeing him up that way. Plus, I had the personal satisfaction of hearing and seeing my work performed by the finest musicians in the world." She shook her head again. "I didn't need public recognition, Rachel. It's always been enough for me to know in my heart that what I created touched people. I have no need for them to know that I did it."

"Didn't you feel any resentment?"

"Not at all. Peter sometimes struggled with the humiliation, but I would encourage him. I made sure he knew that I was content with my role. And I truly was. We stepped into a trap of sorts, I guess. The price of stepping out again was too high for both of us." She tapped her fingers on her lips and looked out the window. "He felt such guilt, though. In the last few years of his life, he'd occasionally talk about letting the world know the truth, but I couldn't bear the thought of him being an object of scorn and ridicule. When I read the codicil to his will and saw that he wanted Karl Speicer to have the music, I knew he was up to something.

"You knew about the cipher?"

"I guessed. He and Hans were fascinated by ciphers. They'd sit up here for hours trying to work them out. But I vowed Hans would never—"

"Hans?" Rachel asked. Gram had to be confused. "The music was to go to Karl Speicer. Hans was your . . . friend, wasn't he? The man you—"

"Karl and Hans were one and the same," Gram said. "I always called him Hans."

Rachel's mind raced, trying to put together a puzzle when she knew she lacked too many of the pieces. "He was the pianist we saw then? That was Hans, the man you—"

Gram nodded.

"Oh, Gram, that concert must have been so painful for you."

"Yes," Gram said. "It was."

She remembered reading in the biographical article on Karl Speicer that he'd been married for forty years. "I can understand it would be uncomfortable for you to have to contact him," Rachel said. "But I could do it for—"

"No," Gram said adamantly.

"I really think it's time you took credit for your work," Rachel argued.

"No one will know, ever."

"Forgive me, Gram, but you're being selfish. Maybe Karl—Hans—won't even notice the cipher. Chris had to use his computer to figure it out."

"Hans could do it."

"Maybe we could take out the part with the cipher, and—"

"No. I won't allow it."

"But, Gram, it means so much to Reflection. So many people are going to be hurt if—"

Gram suddenly began to cry, and Rachel leaned forward, alarmed.

"I won't do it, Rachel," Gram said. "I'm sorry, but I won't. Please just burn the folder. Forget you ever saw it."

"But Peter *wanted* Hans to see it."

"No, he didn't," Helen argued. "If he had wanted Hans to see it, he would have given it to him himself. This was merely Peter's way of assuaging his guilt. He knew that the land would be valuable to the town someday. If he had truly wanted the world to know the truth, he would have found a surer way than leaving the decision in my hands. Peter knew I would never allow his reputation to be tarnished. He'd lose all his awards. The Peace Prize, for heaven's sake. They'd all be taken from him. How could I allow that?"

Rachel was exasperated. "Why do you still feel such a need to protect him? He's been dead ten years. What does it matter at this point?"

The older woman shook her head, fist pressed to her mouth. Tears ran over the pale curve of her knuckles. She did not speak for nearly a minute, and Rachel could not decide between trying to comfort her or allowing her privacy.

After a minute, Gram straightened her shoulders and drew in a breath. "We've come this far, you and I," she said quietly. "Maybe if I tell you the rest of it, you'll finally be able to understand."

39

The boundaries Helen had set in place when she refused to leave Peter for Hans lasted for ten years. "I learned to take comfort in the structure and safety of those constraints," she told Rachel. "But the day after my fortieth birthday, everything changed."

She eyed her granddaughter. Rachel sat in the wing chair, her hands folded in her lap, listening, waiting.

"It was 1950," Helen continued, "and Peter was in Europe. John— your father—had dropped out of college, where he'd been a music major, to marry your mother. The truth was, John had no feel for music. Peter and I had tried to make it part of his life, but . . ." She shrugged. "John had one driving interest, and that was Inge, your mother. The two of them were living in a tiny apartment in town, and I worried about them constantly. Inge was already pregnant with you, and John was working as a custodian in an office building in Lancaster, something that just about killed Peter."

"A custodian?" Rachel looked surprised. "I never knew that."

Helen nodded. There was a great deal Rachel didn't know about her father. "And your mother was working as a waitress. I have to admit they were good together, though, your parents, and I really couldn't fault John for putting his family ahead of any career he might have had.

"Anyway, it was very late on the day after my birthday, and I was building a fire right here in the library when I heard a footstep on the porch. I went to the door, and there was Hans. His face was white as the snow on the ground, and he was very upset. He told me to call the rescue squad, that there'd been an accident at the bottom of Winter Hill between a buggy and a truck. Then he left to go back down there."

She remembered standing numbly at the door for a moment, trying to determine whether Hans had been an apparition. Then she'd dialed the operator to connect her to the police, grabbed a flashlight, and ran out to her car. It had been so dark that night that the snow layering the ground had looked like a blanket of ashes.

"The road was as icy and slick as I've ever seen it," she said, and I knew just what had happened. It wasn't the first time. You know where Fisher Lane crosses Farmhouse Road at the bottom of the hill?"

Rachel nodded.

"Well, the buggies used Fisher Lane a great deal in those days, and crossing Farmhouse Road was not ordinarily dangerous, because that section of the road was rarely used. But if an automobile happened to be coming down the hill at the same time a buggy was trying to cross . . . well. A collision was inevitable."

"I can imagine," Rachel said.

The night had been so horribly, thickly black that Helen had been nearly on top of the accident before she saw it. "The buggy was overturned in the snow at the side of the road," she said, "and a small truck was parked on the shoulder, twenty or so yards away. I found Hans on the other side of the buggy. He was taking off his coat and draping it over a young girl lying in the snow." She could still see the images vividly. "The girl's leg was broken, and someone lay next to her, covered by a shawl of some sort. I remember reaching for the corner of the shawl, and Hans catching my hand. He whispered, 'It's her mother' to me, and I knew that the woman was dead and he didn't want the girl to know." Hans had treated that young girl so tenderly, calling her 'dear,' smoothing her hair from her face, trying to keep her warm.

"The girl told us her father had been in the buggy with her, and Hans went looking for him. He found the father, and I went over to see if I could help, but the man was dead. Hans was kneeling over him, crying." She remembered Hans's frantic search for a pulse, his fingers probing the man's neck. She had knelt next to him and touched his arm, telling him there was nothing more he could do.

"The rescue-squad people thought Hans was one of the victims, he was so distraught," Helen continued. "I was afraid to let him drive back to the house, but he insisted he was all right. I kept my eyes on his headlights in my rearview mirror all the way up the hill."

Helen felt lost in the memory, and she was grateful to Rachel for not pushing her to hurry.

"Back at the house," Helen continued, "I put on a pot of coffee, and then my knees gave out. I guess the reality of what had happened finally caught up with me, and I had to sit down. When Hans walked into the room, though, I stood up again and put my arms around him." For a moment Helen thought she was going to cry at the memory of that embrace, but the threat of tears passed quickly. "He held on to me for a long time," she said. "Then he said, 'Life is too damn short. We waste time as if we're going to live forever. We pass up opportunities. We neglect what's truly important to us.'

"I knew exactly what he was talking about," she said to Rachel. "And I took his hand and led him in here to the library, and we lay down right here on this rug"—she pointed to the plush oriental carpet in front of the hearth— "and we stayed there all night long."

She and Hans spent the night in a quiet embrace, talking little, communicating in a way that required neither words nor action. And sometime close to dawn, their friendship shifted, slowly and naturally, to something more.

Helen leaned toward her too-quiet granddaughter, suddenly self-conscious. "I told you about the accident so you could understand that we were weakened. I doubt very much we ever would have become lovers if that accident hadn't happened."

Rachel nodded. "I understand," she said.

"Those next two days, though, were the best of my life," Helen said, sitting back again. "Two days that will live in my heart forever. I felt no regret whatsoever, but as the hours passed and I knew that soon Hans would leave and Peter would be coming home, I began to feel a terrible sadness. I couldn't bear the thought of going back to my life with Peter. I loved him dearly, but suddenly I realized that I could have much more than that. And then, out of the blue, Hans told me that he'd met a woman. Winona."

"That's his wife's name, isn't it?" Rachel asked.

"Yes, but you're jumping ahead."

"Sorry." Rachel clamped her lips shut again.

"We were sitting up in the tree house, and he told me what a fine person Winona was. A teacher, I remember. He said he didn't love her, but he cared about her, and he was going to marry her . . . unless I would reconsider leaving Peter and marrying him. I felt like he'd socked me in the stomach, telling me about Winona, and so I said yes, I'd marry him."

"You *did*?"

"Yes, I did. I'd been blinded by those wonderful few days together, I guess, and I thought Peter would accept my decision." She cocked her head at her granddaughter. "It's a bit difficult to explain our marriage to you," she said. "Peter had many affairs, Rachel, but he was open about them all, and I recognized his need and tolerated it."

Rachel shook her head. "I just don't get why—"

"You will," Helen interrupted her. "Be patient." She shifted in her seat. "So, anyhow, I knew we'd have a lot of details to work out because of the"—she smiled—"strange working arrangement we had, but I felt certain Peter would understand about Hans. And he did. It's just that understanding sometimes isn't enough."

Rachel was frowning, and Helen wondered if her story was making any sense at all to her.

"I couldn't tell Peter right away when he got back," she said. "That seemed too blunt. But after a couple of days I told him that Hans and I had been in love for many, many years, and that we had finally become lovers, and that I wanted to be free to marry him."

Rachel looked pale. "What did he say?"

"He was shocked but very calm. He said he loved me enough to want me to be happy, and that if I needed a divorce to be happy, he would grant it. Later that night, though, I found him hiding in his study—the room that's now your room—weeping, and I realized he was devastated. He didn't want to let me see it, because he truly did not want to stand in my way. But once I knew how hurt he was, I couldn't—"

"But he'd had affairs!" Rachel challenged. "He'd hurt *you*."

"And that's just what he said. He suddenly realized what it had been like for me all those years. He couldn't bear the thought of me being with someone else, and he knew I must have felt the same way and had simply never let on about it.

"I could not cause him pain, Rachel." She knew she sounded almost apologetic. "I could not. And so when he asked me for another chance to be a better husband, when he promised to give up his affairs and commit himself to me totally, I couldn't turn him down. And he never did have another affair. Never."

"What did you tell Hans?"

"I told him I couldn't marry him, and that he must never come to visit us again. They were the hardest words I've ever had to get out of my mouth, but I knew he couldn't come here any longer. The temptation would have been too great, and the pain of having him that close to me would have been unbearable." She knotted her hands together in her lap. "I became very depressed once I'd cut Hans out of my life, though. Melancholia, they said I had. And of course I couldn't write any music."

Rachel gasped. "Peter Huber's dark period," she said, citing the phrase that was commonly used to describe those dry years.

"That's right," Helen said. "Peter Huber's dark period, when he was caring for his sick wife. You were born during that time. I don't think I was able to be a very attentive grandma back then."

"You've made up for it since, Gram," Rachel assured her. "And so, Hans let you go?" she asked. "Just like that?"

"After I told him what I'm about to tell you, he did."

Rachel's frown deepened. "There's more?" she asked.

"Yes, there's more." Helen plowed ahead before she could stop herself. "I told you about all the things Peter did for me. How he helped my family and paid for me to go to school. How he got my father the best specialists."

Rachel nodded.

"Peter was generous to a fault, and this . . . damned cipher is his generosity run amok." She shook her head. "Do you remember I said I had a wild streak when I was young?"

"Yes."

"And remember I told you that Peter and I were never soul mates?"

"Uh-huh."

"We were friends, that's all. He was a kind and attractive and interesting man who thought I had talent, and he tried to do everything in his power to give me the opportunity to develop it. But we never actually dated. Never."

Rachel shook her head in confusion.

"I dated all sorts of other men, though. And I do mean all sorts. And I drank more than I should have, too. I was even a smoker."

Rachel's smile seemed uncertain.

"And it got me into trouble. One day I went on a train ride with a boy from a nearby college. We were alone in one of the cars, drinking, and we got very drunk. I was a virgin, of course, but I let him . . . do some things, and then I wasn't able to stop him. These days I guess you call it date rape."

"Oh, Gram," Rachel said. "That must have been terrible."

"Well, I didn't know about date rape. What I knew is that I was drunk and let a boy go too far with me. Of course I never heard from him again. I was ashamed and embarrassed. And I was also pregnant."

"Oh, no."

Helen eyed her granddaughter closely, but she could see that Rachel still had not put the pieces of the story together.

"I couldn't tell my family, of course," she said. "I couldn't tell anyone, except Peter, on whom I'd come to lean whenever anything went wrong. Peter cried for me, he was so upset. And he said he would marry me and take responsibility for my child. He told—"

"What?" Rachel was on the edge of her chair. "Are you saying . . . was that my father you were pregnant with?"

"Yes."

"Then Grandpa is not my grandfather?"

"Not by blood. But in his heart he was. And no one would ever have guessed he wasn't your father's father. He told my family the baby was his. He raised John as his own, and there was never a more loving daddy. He continued teaching me about composition on his own time, since I could no longer attend school."

She leaned forward and rested her hand on Rachel's. "Do you see now why I couldn't leave him? Couldn't hurt him? Do you understand why, even now, I won't bring harm to his memory?"

Rachel sat back in the chair. She looked tired and defeated.

"Yes," she said. "I think I finally do."

40

Michael worked in his office on Wednesday morning, barely able to concentrate. There were too many interfering thoughts vying for his attention, too much looming over him. To begin with, Drew was due back the following night. What would he say to him? And what would he say to Katy the next time he spoke to her? He was not looking forward to either of those conversations. He would have to think them through carefully.

And in less than a week the board would put the Hostetter project to its final, inevitable vote, and next Friday morning the bulldozers would begin leveling the woods surrounding Spring Willow Pond. All the while Helen held the solution in her stubborn hands. He would have to talk to her tonight, plead with her to relinquish that music.

He was thinking about what words he would use to convince her when his phone rang.

"Michael Stoltz," he said into the receiver.

"Hi." It was Katy.

He closed his eyes at the sound of her voice. So much for careful preparation.

"Hi, Katy." He was tempted to ask her if she'd had a nice little vacation. No. He would not play games with her. Yet he did not feel ready to blurt out all he knew.

"Michael," she said, and he was surprised by the rasp of tears in her voice. "I'm going to come home early."

Come home early? He sat up straight. "You sound upset," he said.

"I need to see you. I miss you and Jace. I think I'm . . . I'm just not doing very well."

He felt a stab of worry. His tough, armor-coated wife did not talk this way. "Katy," he said, "I know about you and Drew."

Several seconds of silence filled the line. "I . . . What do you mean?" she asked finally.

"I mean, I know he's been over there. I know you two have been together. I know you were seeing him before you left, although I don't know how long it was going on. And I know you're pregnant."

She was crying. "I'm sorry, Michael. I've made a mess out of things. I can't believe what I've done. How did you . . . I didn't ever want you to know, to be hurt by it. I wanted it to be between me and God."

He had to work to keep his voice calm and controlled. "How could I not be hurt by it, Katy? Drew was pretending to be my best friend. He pretended to care about stopping the Hostetters."

"I think he was sincere about that. He—"

"Oh, Katy, dream on! Drew's a con artist, a manipulator."

She said nothing.

He picked up a paper clip and began twisting it out of shape with his fingers. "How serious is it?" he asked. He wanted it to be serious.

"It's not," she said. "It never was, and it's over. Completely over. I was crazy. I didn't know what I was doing."

It was his turn to remain quiet. None of the responses he could think of would be charitable. He held the phone between his ear and shoulder, using both hands to straighten the paper clip into a long, kinked piece of wire.

"He told me Rachel Huber's still there," Katy said.

"Yes."

"He said you're seeing her."

"We're old friends, you know that."

The tears again. "Are you sleeping with her?" Her voice cracked on the last word.

He dropped the paper clip into the wastebasket under his desk. "Let's not talk about this over the phone," he said.

"Oh, Michael."

He shut his eyes.

"I'm coming home. In a week, I hope. As soon as I can get out of here."

"Katy . . . how far along are you?"

"I'm not pregnant."

"I heard you were."

"Who told you that?"

"Doesn't matter."

She hesitated a moment. "I was," she said.

"You had an abortion?" He would believe anything of her at this point.

"Miscarriage."

He leaned his elbows on the desk. "I don't know what to say. Do I say I'm sorry? I don't know the rules of etiquette for this sort of situation." He heard the sarcasm in his voice and was annoyed with himself for it.

"I don't blame you," she said. "I know I've made a terrible mistake, Michael. But I need you. And I love you. Please remember that. I'll be home in a few days, and I'll make it up to you. We can start over. See a counselor. I'll do anything. And please tell Jace I love him, all right?"

"Katy . . . be safe," he said. "Be careful."

He felt sick when he hung up the phone. He sat quietly for a few minutes, then left his office and walked upstairs to the sanctuary, where he sat down in one of the pews to wait for the comfort of his church, the comfort of prayer, to wash over him. But comfort was elusive this morning. It had been elusive for a while.

Prayer used to fill him with peace, no matter how difficult the trials he was facing. Prayer calmed him, gave him direction. The choices in his faith, while not always easy or simple, were clear: a Mennonite should seek to emulate the life of Christ. He'd been doing a poor job of that lately, and his praying this morning seemed hollow and hypocritical. He could muster no remorse for his sin. He could muster no love for his enemy.

So Katy wanted to save their marriage. He had never heard her sound so full of pain and remorse. Never so vulnerable, and his heart ached for her. It had been easy to put her feelings aside when she seemed to have none. This morning, though, her needs and fears were so near the surface, so thoroughly human, that he could not turn his back on them. Was he meant to sacrifice his happiness for the sake of his wife and son? For the sake of his congregation? Or did one man have the right to set his needs above those of so many others?

Rachel met him outside when he arrived at Helen's that night.

"We need to talk before you come in," she said, grabbing his arm and leading him toward the woods. He glanced back at the house, wondering what was going on inside, what had occurred that put the urgency in Rachel's hand on his arm, the red in her eyes.

He let her lead him toward the woods without a word, and only when they were in the shelter of the forest did she loosen her grip on him.

"What's going on?" he asked.

"Can we sit up there?" She pointed toward the floor of the old tree house, and he nodded.

He followed her up the ladder and took his seat next to her, legs hanging over the side of the platform.

"Oh, Michael," she said. "I don't know where to begin. I guess with the cipher."

"The cipher?"

"Yes." She proceeded to tell him about Chris unearthing an encoded message in *Reflections*, and Michael could not mask his shock.

"*No*," he said. "Helen? You're saying that Helen wrote all that music?"

"Yes." She explained how Helen and Peter had joined together in their lifelong duplicity, and Michael shook his head.

"So this is why she doesn't want the music to go to that Speicer guy? He'll crack the code, and then everyone will know?"

"Yes, but that's only part of it." She told him about the rape, and about Peter marrying Helen and raising her son as his own. She told him about Helen and Hans, and he found the story unbearable in its inevitable conclusion. He listened to every word without interruption. Rachel had tears in her eyes by the time she had finished.

"So . . ." Michael said, "the pianist we saw with the symphony in Washington was once Helen's lover?"

"Yes," Rachel said. "She hadn't seen him in over forty years."

He shook his head. "No wonder she was so upset that night." He looked up at the dark canopy of the old oak above them. "But I still think it's time she got her due. I think she—"

"No," Rachel interrupted him. "I understand completely how she feels. It would be like me bringing public disgrace to Phil's memory after all the things he did for me."

He closed his eyes and tried unsuccessfully to put himself in Helen's place. Then he sighed. "All right," he said. "I have to let go of this. I have to accept that the development's going to happen and move on."

"She equates us—you and me—with her and Hans," Rachel said. "Star-crossed lovers. That's why she wants us to be together so badly. It's as though she can live out what she wanted to do through me. My poor grandmother. It would be as if you and I made a firm decision to be together and then Katy begged you to take her back."

He couldn't speak. He put his arms around her and buried his head in the hollow between her throat and shoulder.

"Michael?" There was concern in her voice, and something else. Trepidation?

"Katy called this morning," he said.

"Oh."

He drew away from her and looked into her eyes. They had not lost their redness from telling him Helen's story. "She's coming home early," he said. "Next week. She says it's over with Drew. She was very upset and contrite. She wants to see a counselor with me, make our marriage work."

Rachel studied his face for a moment before looking away from him, and he suddenly felt guilty for having begged her to remain in Reflection when she'd wanted to return home.

Rachel reached out to the tree branch in front of them and broke off a twig. "And what do *you* want?" she asked.

"I want to do what's right," he said. "I just don't know what that is anymore."

She ran the twig slowly across the back of his hand. "And I want you to do what's right, too," she said softly. "My only fear is that what's right for you might not be right for me."

He nodded. His fear was the same.

He pulled her close again, knowing that, for now, all they could do was hold each other. There was nothing else to say.

Michael sat in his car in front of Drew's house at ten o'clock the following night. Drew had told him he'd be getting in—from California—around nine, and Michael didn't know if that was the time of his arrival at the airport or the time he expected to be home. So he'd been waiting for over an hour by the time Drew's car finally appeared on the street. Drew did not seem to notice him as he pulled into the driveway. Michael got out of his car and walked up the driveway to meet him.

Drew got out of his own car and opened the trunk. He looked up when he heard the crunch of Michael's shoes on the gravel driveway, and the light from the street lamp caught the surprise in his face. He looked away quickly, back to the trunk, reaching in for one of his suitcases.

"Hey, Michael. Didn't expect to see you here." He set the suitcase on the ground. "You all set for the hearing?"

"I know you've been with Katy," Michael said.

Drew opened his mouth as if to protest, then seemed to think better of it. "How did you find out?"

"Doesn't matter. But I'm very angry. You betrayed me. I trusted you completely."

"Look." He shut the trunk. "You should know some things. First of all, it's over with Katy and me."

He wanted to ask exactly how long it had gone on. What did it matter, though? Did he really want to know?

"She was going through some sort of midlife thing," Drew continued. "She was not very happy with herself, or with you, or with her life in general. She needed something you weren't giving her."

Michael winced, fearing there was truth in that accusation. He'd failed Katy somehow.

"Being over there gave her time to think things through, and she came to the conclusion that she doesn't want to screw up her marriage. So it's over. And I know you've had some complaints about her in the past, but I think now she'll do anything to make things work with you."

"Sounds like you were using her. Taking advantage of her unhappiness, her weakness."

"Oh, please." Drew smirked. "We were using each other. We were grown-ups. We knew what we were doing."

"Were you sleeping with Ursula, too?" Michael asked.

"Not for a while. Not since I've been seeing Katy."

Michael kept a lock on his surprise. He had not been serious with that question.

"Do you have a conscience, Drew?"

Drew sighed. "Certainly not as refined and perfected as yours. You're so honorable all the time, aren't you? It's made me sick. It's been so . . . *refreshing* to hear you talk about wanting to get inside of Rachel Huber's jeans. So refreshing to hear you sound like a flesh-and-blood man instead of some sort of saint. But you know"—Drew pointed a finger in Michael's face—"I was getting pretty sick of listening to you talk about how hung up you are on the . . . fucking bitch who's responsible for taking my son's life. Did you ever think about that? What that felt like to me, hearing you go on about what a wonderful person she is?"

Michael felt himself color, embarrassed that he'd exposed so much of his interior to a man who had been mocking him—*hating* him, it seemed—behind his back. He could imagine all in a flash the conversations Drew had had with Ursula about him and Rachel, and he suddenly felt sorry for his onetime friend. How terrible to have no clear sense of right and wrong, of good and evil.

"I don't think we have any more to say to each other," Michael said. He began backing away from the car. "I hope someday you can find a way to be happy without harming other people at the same time."

Drew's mouth curved into a sneer. "You self-righteous bastard," he said.

Michael turned and walked down the driveway, got into his car. Maybe Drew was lucky to have no conscience. He felt a little envious. He knew only too well the difference between right and wrong. It was choosing between them that was the hard part.

41

"You want to do *what*?" Celine Humphrey's reaction to Rachel's proposal was so startled and disbelieving that Rachel nearly laughed into the phone.

"I want to go to Zaire as a Mennonite volunteer," she repeated. "My background in Rwanda with the Peace Corps should be a plus. I'm nearly fluent in French, and my Kinyarwanda should come back to me. I know the people. I understand the culture." She'd made up her mind the night before to see whether she could volunteer, and an odd peace had settled over her ever since making that decision.

"Well, you are a surprise, Rachel," Celine said.

"Am I?" Rachel asked the question rhetorically. She worried that Celine, whose dislike for her was obvious, might try to stand in her way.

"Yes, indeed you are, and I don't pretend to understand you," the elder said. "But I do believe your interest in helping out in the refugee camps is entirely sincere. It will be tough on such short notice, but I'll do all I can to help you through the screening. You'll have to get your medical clearance quickly, though, and a hideous number of inoculations."

"That's fine." Rachel felt relieved.

"All right," Celine said. "I'll get right to work on it, then. And God bless you, Rachel."

It was Rachel's turn to be startled. "Thank you," she said, and she hung up the phone with a smile.

* * *

She took Chris to the airport the following day, and she was pleased when Gram agreed to come along for the ride. She did not feel comfortable leaving her alone. Gram seemed to have aged a year in the past few days, ever since telling Rachel the truth about her marriage and the sad ending to her relationship with Karl Speicer. Apparently there had been nothing cleansing, nothing freeing in that telling. Instead, Gram seemed weighed down by the memories. She leaned on Rachel, clung to her, and Rachel worried that her grandmother was sinking into the sort of depression she'd experienced after cutting Hans from her life.

She worried, too, about how her grandmother would react to her decision to go to Zaire. She'd already spoken to Chris about it, and although he'd initially expressed surprised concern, he encouraged her to go. She would talk to Gram about it on the way back from the airport. And then she would have to tell Michael.

Chris leaned forward from the backseat as Rachel approached the crest of Winter Hill. "I want to see the church reflected in the pond one last time," he said.

They reached the crest of the hill, but they could not see the pond at all.

"Something's in the way," Rachel said. She squinted into the distance. Their view was blocked by something yellow, big, and bulky, like a trailer or a Dumpster.

It wasn't until they reached the center of town that they could make out the obstacles to their view: bulldozers, backhoes, and trucks littered the lawn around the western end of the pond, poised and ready for their attack on the forest.

"I don't believe it," Chris said with the naiveté of someone young enough to still trust in the system. "How can they be here already? The vote's not till Tuesday night."

"It's a fait accompli," Rachel said. "The Hostetters obviously have no doubt how the vote's going to go."

"That's disgusting." Chris slouched down in the seat, and Rachel saw his look of dismay in her rearview mirror.

"I feel sorry for Michael," Chris said. "His church shouldn't have to sit in the middle of a bunch of office buildings."

Rachel wished Chris would stop talking about the development. She glanced at Gram, whose eyes were on the small militia surrounding the pond but whose face remained impassive. Rachel gently squeezed the older woman's hand. She didn't want her grandmother to feel responsible for this. She didn't want Gram to think she blamed her.

She felt sorry for Michael, too. Not only because of what was about to happen to the setting for his church but for the dilemma he was in, the crisis he was facing in his family and his faith. It was a crisis in which she played too great a role.

She was going to lose him, one more time. She'd heard it in his voice when they'd sat in the tree house the other day. He wanted to do the right thing. She knew what that was. They both did.

The road blurred in front of her, and she quickly shifted her thoughts to other things. She did not want to cry with Chris and Gram in the car.

"Are you excited about your gig tonight?" she asked her son.

"Yeah, sort of," Chris said. "The band needs a lot of work, though."

It was the first negative thing she'd heard him say about the band.

"And Mom? I was wondering if I could call the piano tuner and have her come out?"

Yes, she thought with a grin. She hadn't heard him play their own piano in far too long. "Of course," she said. "Good idea."

"Gram?" Chris leaned forward again, this time to talk to his great-grandmother.

"I was wondering something about *Reflections*."

Rachel knew what he was going to say, and she held her breath as Gram turned her head toward the backseat.

"I was wondering if I could, like, adapt a little of it for my band," Chris said. "Some of the themes. I know that might be asking too much."

"I'd like you to do that," Gram said. "Send me a tape so I can hear what you did with it."

"Cool," Chris sat back again, a broad smile on his face.

She and Gram said good-bye to Chris curbside at the airport. Rachel hugged him hard.

"I'm so glad we had this week together," she said. "I loved having you around."

"Me too, Mom." He glanced at Gram, then whispered in Rachel's ear. "Take care of yourself over there, okay?"

Rachel nodded, letting go of him, and Chris immediately drew his great-grandmother into a hug. "Bye, Gram," he said. "I love you."

"I love you, too," Gram said, and there was a small but beautiful smile on her lips.

"I won't tell anyone the truth about you," Chris said, "but I'm very proud to be your great-grandson."

Rachel couldn't stop her tears this time. She had a terrific son.

She waited until they were a few miles from the airport before telling Gram her plans.

"I'm seriously considering going with the Mennonites to Zaire to work in the refugee camps," she said, glancing at the older woman. "I would have to leave in a couple of weeks, though, and I'm concerned about leaving you alone right now."

Gram was quiet. After a minute, she said, "You're trying to get yourself away from Michael so he can make a decision without you being a factor in it."

"No," Rachel said, although she knew that was part of it. A small part, though. She wasn't running away from Reflection this time. "No, I want to do this for myself. It felt right the second I thought of it. Regardless of what decisions Michael makes, I'm still going. There were people I loved in Rwanda, and it tears me up to see what's happening over there. I speak the language. I'm a little rusty, but it'll come back to me."

"How long will you be gone?" Gram's voice sounded tight.

"A few months. But I won't go if you still need me, Gram."

"It's dangerous there."

"I'm not afraid. I only wish I could leave *before* Reflection Day." She smiled to herself. Reflection seemed more dangerous to her than Zaire.

She stole a look at her grandmother and saw the sheen of tears in the older woman's eyes. "Oh, Gram," she said, "will you be all right?"

"I'll be fine." Gram reached out to touch Rachel's hand on the steering wheel. "I'll just miss you terribly, that's all."

"I'll miss you, too." She sighed. "I love Reflection, Gram. It's my hometown. But I haven't brought it anything but pain by coming back. I need to do something that makes me feel good about myself again. I need to do something that helps somebody."

"I understand."

They drove the rest of the way home in silence, and Rachel knew that the hardest part of her decision was still ahead of her. Telling Chris and Gram had been easy. Telling Michael would be something else.

42

A hand on his shoulder.

Michael rolled over in the darkness, struggling to pull himself back from sleep.

Katy sat on the edge of the bed next to him, her blond hair lit up from the light in the hallway. She moved her hand from his shoulder to her lap, as though she didn't dare touch him any longer. He could see her cheeks were wet.

"Please forgive me," she said.

"I do." He touched his fingers to her cheek. "Did you take a cab from the airport?"

She nodded.

"Why didn't you call me to pick you up?"

"I didn't want to bother you."

She buried her face in her hands, and he felt sorry for her. He rested his hand on her knee while she cried.

"I felt like a part of me was missing," she said finally, raising her head again. "No excuse, I know. But I worked hard to become a doctor and to become a success in my career. I wanted a child, and I had a child. It all just didn't feel like enough to me anymore. That's trite, I suppose. I felt like a doctor and a mother and a wife. And I guess I still needed to feel like a *woman*. Like an attractive woman."

"I'm sorry if I didn't make you feel that way."

"I think we've been together so long that we've started taking each other for granted," she said.

"Probably, yes." He felt remarkably calm.

"Then all of sudden, Drew was there, paying me compliments, looking at me like he . . . wanted me. I was terribly weak. I thought I was a smart person—"

"You're a brilliant person."

"Then how could I do such a stupid thing?"

Michael sighed. "Affairs of the heart seem to defy intelligence and reason," he said. He was living proof of that.

"I want things to work out for us," she said. "They have to, Michael. We have too much to lose."

He sat up in the bed, leaning back against the headboard. "I don't think we can base staying together on our fear of what we have to lose," he said.

She sucked in her breath. "*Michael*. What about your ministry? You can't seriously be telling me you would throw that away? And we'd be shunned if we split up. It'd be subtle, sure, but it would be there all the same. You know that."

"Yes, I know."

Katy tugged idly at the edge of the blanket. "It's Rachel, isn't it?" she asked.

He shook his head. "No. Not entirely."

"You've always loved her."

"I've always cared very deeply about her." He thought of the incident at the after-game party when he was thirteen, of Katy turning her back on him, of Rachel coming to his rescue. "Do you remember that time when we were kids and I scored the winning point for the opposing team in basketball?" he asked her.

She looked at him blankly and shook her head. "I don't want to see her," she said. "I just . . . I feel humiliated. And ashamed. I assume she knows about me and Drew? And I'm jealous."

"You may not see her at all," he said. "She's leaving for Zaire in a couple of weeks."

He'd seen Rachel briefly on Labor Day, when they'd slipped—unnoticed, he hoped—into the high school to use the darkroom. She'd told him there, in the darkness, as they watched images of the countryside emerge before their eyes. Celine had pulled some strings to allow her to go, she'd said. Her plans had stunned him into silence, but only for a moment. It made sense for her to go, and it was important to her. He had heard the resolve in her voice. The peace. He was glad that at least one of them had come to a decision of sorts.

"Zaire?" Katy asked. "She's not going with the church, is she?"

He nodded, and Katy looked out the window.

"She's moved right into my life, hasn't she? Into my town, my church. And my husband's bed, I assume?"

"Katy."

"Do you love her?"

"Yes."

"Do you love me?"

"I feel a strong commitment to you, Katy."

Katy closed her eyes and stood up. She ran the fingers of both hands through her hair. "Everyone hates her, Michael," she said. "Drew said the whole town despises her."

"Rachel is not the issue here."

She leaned against the wall. "I don't want to talk about this any-more," she said.

Typical Katy, he thought. Any real meat in a conversation, anything remotely difficult, and she tuned out.

"What's happening with the Hostetter project?" she asked.

"The vote was last night." He had watched the board sign, seal, and deliver permission to the Hostetters to destroy the land. "They start work Friday."

She let out an exasperated sigh. "Everything's falling apart." She turned to the window and toyed with the lock for a moment before looking over at him again. "Can we do something together tomor-row?" she asked. "The three of us? Take Jace to Hershey Park, maybe?"

"Yes," he said. He wanted to do that, to give tomorrow to his fam-ily.

"Good." She tried to smile, then added, almost shyly, "I'm really tired, Michael. Where do you want me to sleep?"

He could not sleep with her, not when he'd been so recently with Rachel. Could he ever—would he ever want to—sleep with Katy again?

"You stay here." He got out of the bed, reaching for his robe. "I'll sleep in the guest room."

The bed in the guest room was not made up, but he didn't care. He lay down on the spread and covered himself with a blanket. It didn't matter where he tried to sleep tonight. Between the confusion in his mind and the turmoil in his heart, he knew he would not be able to sleep at all.

43

Rachel awakened with a sense of doom she could not place. She stared at the ceiling, trying to determine the reason for the gray shroud hanging over her. Then suddenly, she had it: It was Friday, ground-breaking day for the Hostetter Project. By the end of the day, acres of trees would be felled, the earth around them would be torn and raw, and the vision of Reflection so many held dear would be gone forever. Soon the Amish and Mennonites would be sharing their cemetery with tract houses. A few hundred more cars would snake their way between the buggies and spook the horses. Glossy, glassy office buildings would block the reflection of Michael's church in the pond, and the forest that had been her playground as a child would be flattened and transformed into one hundred houses and four hundred people.

She got out of bed, wincing when her foot hit the floor. Her hip ached where she'd gotten a few of the shots for her trip. Her arm was even stiffer. She dressed quickly, then left a note for Gram. *Running errands,* she wrote. She was certain where she was going but not yet sure what she would do once she got there. She had an idea, though—a bizarre idea that she feared was the product of a hazy, not-quite-awake mind.

It was nearly eight o'clock by the time she reached the center of town, and she could see that a crowd had already formed in the street in front of the pond. Yellow plastic tape had been stretched along the sidewalk, separating the crowd from the Hostetter property. The bulldozers and trucks and backhoes were planted on the grass, lined up next to a slender dirt road someone had cut through the lawn, from street to forest, over the past couple of days. The blunt noses of the vehicles were pointed at the trees, ready to charge.

Rachel pulled her car to the side of the road, across the street from the crowd. She could see Celine Humphrey and Becky Frank among the throng. She spotted Lily, sipping from a mug, and Marge eating what looked like a doughnut. Sixty or seventy people, she guessed, and more were arriving by the minute, talking among themselves, pointing toward the woods.

Michael's car cut through the crowd and turned into the narrow driveway next to the Mennonite church on the opposite side of the pond. In another minute he walked out front, joining the other bystanders. Rachel wished she could talk to him. Katy was back, that much she knew. He'd called her to let her know and to tell her he'd planned to spend yesterday with her and Jason. That was good, she'd told herself. He needed to experience fully what he had come so close to giving up.

She lost him in the thickening crowd, and she could not see Lily anymore, either. Or Becky. How long should she wait? Her pulse thrummed in her hands where they rested in her lap.

It was eight-thirty when one of the workmen got into a bulldozer and turned the engine over, and that's when Rachel drew in a deep breath and got out of her car. She made her way, gently but resolutely, through the crowd, aware of the flurry of whispers that followed her progress. Without a moment's hesitation, she stepped over the yellow tape and walked toward the dirt road.

"Hey, lady!" one of the men called out to her. "Ma'am! You can't go there."

She feigned deafness, only turning around in the road once she'd reached the bulldozer, which looked very large, very menacing, this close up. She glanced at the crush of people in the street. They had fallen utterly silent, and Rachel felt the color in her cheeks. She was making a spectacle of herself.

The crowd began to chatter again, and there was excitement in the sound. She folded her arms across her chest as one of the workmen approached her.

"You've got to move, lady," he said. "We're ready to start work here."

"Then you'll have to roll over me to start it," she said.

"Oh, come on, lady." He scowled. "We don't have time for the heroics. They're gonna cart you away, you know that? Either jail or the asylum. Come on now, let's go." He reached out to take hold of her arm.

"Don't touch me." She jerked away from him, giving him a look that had lawsuit written all over it, and he backed away.

"Hey! Huber!" A male voice hollered from behind the yellow ribbon. She spotted a man in a gray suit standing at the edge of the crowd, making a megaphone with his hands. She didn't recognize him. "You're an outsider, Huber," he called. "What the hell right do you have to interfere with what's going on here?"

A few people in the crowd cheered him, but others—by far the majority—booed and hissed.

"We're calling the police," one of the workmen shouted to her. The guy in the bulldozer had turned the engine off and was lighting a cigarette.

She saw movement in the center of the crowd, and in a moment Michael stepped over the yellow tape. Was he coming to talk her out of this? When he reached her, he merely winked at her, took her hand, and stood a short distance away from her. With their arms outstretched, their two-man blockade effectively bisected the road.

"Oh, *shit*," said the workman. "Look, you two, we're just here to do our job. I don't know what your problem is with the situation here, but we're getting paid to knock down these trees, and that's what we're going to do. It's legal. It's our right. So get the hell out of our way."

One of the other workmen added, "The cops have been called."

Michael leaned over to speak quietly to her. "What do you want to bet this will be the slowest police response in history? They all love this place as much as we do."

Rachel smiled at him. She hoped he was right.

Michael nodded toward the crowd. "Check it out," he said.

Rachel looked toward the gathering to see Lily stepping over the yellow tape. Lily set her mug down on the sidewalk and marched along the dirt road until she reached them. She was grinning as she took Michael's hand, leaning forward to talk to Rachel.

"Cool idea, Rache!" she said.

Then someone tore the tape. In an instant, at least half the crowd moved en masse down the hill, and Rachel could not help laughing. Each person linked up with them on Michael and Lily's side, as if Rachel's hand might burn them. She stepped farther and farther to her left, until she was right up against one of the backhoes. It was Sarah Holland, the clerk from the bookstore whose face had been scarred in Rachel's classroom, who finally took her hand and gave her a smile.

"Let's make it a triple line," one of the men said, and people regrouped until a boisterous clot of humanity blocked entrance to the forest, and for the moment anyway, Reflection was safe.

Helen turned on the television to check the weather, a habit she'd gotten into ever since the storm that had changed her life. She realized quickly that some major news story had broken, and she struggled to make sense of the images on the screen. There were dozens of people and a couple of bulldozers. She spotted the Mennonite church and the forest behind it. A protest at Spring Willow Pond, a reporter said. The blockade had been started by Rachel Huber. Once Helen recovered from her shock, she watched the rest of the broadcast with tears in her eyes.

By afternoon, a Harrisburg station had picked up the story. The newscaster spoke about Rachel's past in Reflection. He showed horrible old pictures of the demolished wing of the Spring Willow Elementary School. He showed old high school photos of Rachel and Michael, and Luke. He talked about the nonresistance of a Mennonite, how potentially devastating the Hostetter development had to be for it to move a Mennonite minister to action.

The police had been called hours earlier, a second reporter said from the scene, and were only now beginning to make arrests. It didn't matter. The workmen had already given up for the day. Too late to start, they said.

Helen smiled. Tomorrow was Saturday. Reflection would have a two-day reprieve.

She sat on the sofa, her eyes on the television, her mind on Peter. She gnawed her lip as she watched her granddaughter being led away from the pond by a police officer. Rachel and Michael had taken the risk, Helen thought. They'd put the past aside for the sake of the future. She could do at least as much.

At two o'clock she walked into the library. She lifted the phone to her ear and dialed the information number for New York City.

"I'd like the number for a Speicer," she said, sitting down. "Karl Speicer."

44

Helen brewed a pot of peppermint tea and drank it slowly, cup after cup, trying to calm her nerves. Hans had said he would rent a car at the Harrisburg airport and arrive at her house sometime between two and three. It was nearly three now.

She'd had to leave a message on an answering machine for him the day before. His voice had surprised her with its strength, had brought tears to her eyes with its familiarity. It was different, yes—forty-three years had made a difference. But even though the speaker did not identify himself, she had known whose voice she was hearing.

She had first apologized for calling, telling him she would not do it if it were not absolutely necessary. She told him only that he needed to come to Reflection, that it was urgent. She had something for him from Peter. "Please, Hans," she begged, "you must come." She hung up, kicking herself for sounding so desperate. What if Winona were the one to pick up the messages from the answering machine?

Hans called back late last night, so late that she feared the phone would awaken Rachel—or that he might not call at all. He did not sound at all distressed by her call, but rather pleased. Still, she felt edgy talking to him and did not allow him to draw her into conversation once she had his perplexed commitment to come.

She'd gotten Rachel out of the house, asking her to stay away, to spend the night elsewhere. "I want to get used to being alone while you're still close enough to call," she'd told her.

Rachel had looked surprised for a minute before responding. Then she smiled, shaking her head. "You're still trying to push Michael and me together, aren't you?" she'd asked.

Helen had shrugged noncommittally. It didn't matter what Rachel thought. She just didn't want her granddaughter around while Hans was here, not until she knew how this situation was going to turn out.

At ten after three she heard a car on the gravel driveway. The muscles in her legs shook as she stood up. She felt as if something were expanding inside her chest, that it was going to explode soon, spill out of her. She walked out onto the porch. It was cool outside, the weather almost autumnlike, and she hugged herself as she watched Hans get out of the white rental car.

He was half the pianist from the Kennedy Center and half the man from her memory. She had forgotten how tall he was. He was slimmer than she remembered, and he was wearing glasses. She walked down the porch steps, and he shut the car door and smiled, walking toward her, holding out his arms. She sank into his embrace, as if she were falling, and felt the strength in his body. Leaning wordlessly against him, she was finally able to whisper only one thing.

"I was struck by lightning," she said, and then she began to cry.

She helped him settle into the room that Chris had used. In the past, he had always stayed in Rachel's room, with its wonderland of books, but he seemed quite content with the smaller space, and he stared out the window toward the thick greenery of the woods for several minutes before beginning to unpack.

She sat on the bed and watched him with a longing she had never expected to feel again. "Thank you for coming," she said, over and over, and he replied that he had stayed away far too long.

Once his clothes were hung up and put away, she offered him an early dinner.

"Do you still take walks?" he asked.

"Yes, though not with quite the energy I used to have."

"Can we go for one before dinner? Is the tree house still there?"

"In part." She smiled.

They set out on the walk. She told him about her injuries and about Rachel coming to help her. He told her that Winona was in a nursing home.

"Alzheimer's," he said. "She doesn't know who I am anymore, but I guess we were lucky that she didn't develop it until five or six years ago. So many people get it when they're young."

"You had a long marriage together." Helen did not want to think about how he had filled all those years they had been apart.

They came to the tree house. Hans looked up at the splintered wooden platform and smiled. "We were young," he said. "How did we ever get up there?"

"Come here," she said, walking around the tree to where the ladder stood. "Are you game?"

He laughed and started up the ladder, quite nimbly, then reached down to help her up. They sat on the edge of the boards, legs dangling. She felt like a child.

"It's even more beautiful and peaceful than I remember it," he said. For a moment they were quiet, listening to the cicadas hidden in the forest. After a few minutes he turned to her. "Tell me why you called me here," he said.

"It can wait." Now that he was here, she wanted to savor the time before she told him.

Hans did not press her. He leaned his head back to breathe in the scent of the forest. "I had to give up performing a couple of years ago," he said. "I have a little bit of a tremor."

He held up his hand, but she could see no sign of shaking. Instead, all she could see was a hand she had once loved to hold, to feel against her skin.

"I occasionally perform all-Huber concerts, though. I've never lost my love for Peter's music."

"I've seen you perform recently," she said.

"Yes, I know," he said. "You were at the Kennedy Center."

Of course they had told him. "My granddaughter took me precisely because it was an all-Huber program. I didn't want to go, and she had no idea that the pianist was anyone special to me. I thought you were extraordinary."

"Why didn't you tell me you were coming?" he asked gently. "Why did you leave?"

"Too painful." She shook her head. "I had to get away."

"I'm so sorry, dear. I would have felt the same way, I'm sure." He touched her hand lightly, then took it fully in his own. "Winona and I had a good life together, but I never forgot you. I never lost my feelings for you."

How is it that pain can remain inside a person for so long, she wondered? It was as if her body had a memory for it, and when that memory was triggered, the pain returned in full force, with all its nuances and sharp, cutting edges.

She could not speak. Instead, she simply wept the tears she thought she'd emptied herself of so long ago. "I still remember sending you away," she said. "Watching you leave. My arms ached to hold you one last time." She lifted her arms in the air, and he caught them, locked them in an embrace.

"Trust at least, Helen," he said as he held her, "that you were never alone in your sorrow."

Once back in the house, she fed him supper, then brought out the folder containing *Reflections.* She explained the dire situation facing the town and the imminent development of the Hostetter land. She turned on the television, and they didn't have to wait long before seeing some of the footage from the day before. It showed the human blockade at the entrance to the woods. It showed an irate Ursula Torwig and Marielle Hostetter's red-faced nephews, along with a few police officers, who were trying to suppress their grins as they slowly made arrests.

"My granddaughter started the protest," she said. She could not keep the pride out of her voice.

She showed Hans the codicil. "Peter said the land would be preserved if you were given this, his last work, to critique."

He looked puzzled. "Why on earth? How odd." He stroked his chin with those long, beautiful fingers. "Why me? Why . . . and you waited so long to give this to me. It's down to the wire now, isn't it? You waited because—"

"Because I made up my mind forty-some years ago that you no longer existed for me and that I must no longer exist for you," she said. "I kept track, though. I knew Winona was still alive. I wouldn't dare interfere with your life. And because . . . well, I think you'll understand once you study the music."

He opened the folder, frowning mildly at the contents. Then he stood up and walked into the living room. She did not follow him but rather waited at the kitchen table, holding her breath. How long had it been since she'd heard Hans play the piano in her home? She listened as he felt out the warm and quiet theme in the first movement, the tense mystery of the second. He muddled through the tumultuous central passage of the third and closed with the splendid beauty that marked the final strains of that movement. Peter had had such talent. He never should have hidden behind hers.

An hour had passed by the time Hans returned to the kitchen, and she was still sitting at the table, the last notes of *Reflections* lingering in the air around her.

"Something very strange," he said. "I don't believe this is the right work." He set the open folder on the table and shook his head. "I mean, I see that he wrote *Reflections* here at the top, but it doesn't sound like a Huber. It doesn't *play* like a Huber. Though I like it. It's a lovely piece, although this third movement . . . ." He stared silently out the window, then looked at her. "There's a cipher in here, isn't there?" he said. "There's a cipher in that third movement."

"Yes."

"Do you know what it says?"

"Yes."

"And you're not going to tell me?"

She shook her head, and he closed his eyes, opening them again with a weak smile. "Ah, Peter, old friend." He chuckled. "I guess I have my evening's work cut out for me, then, don't I?"

She nodded, wondering if she should simply tell him. No. She would let the revelation proceed as Peter had wanted it to.

Hans was still up studying the music in the library while she watched the eleven o'clock news. The townspeople were vowing to return to the blockade again on Monday, and some of the students from the local colleges were promising to join them.

He was still up when she went to bed. She did not expect to sleep, did not even bother to turn off the lamp on her night table. But she must have dozed off, because she awakened to a shuffling in the hall outside her door. The door creaked open, and she sat up to see Hans walking toward her. He stopped in the middle of the floor. She read his face as easily as she used to, and in his features she saw shock and awe.

She drew back the covers, the empty side of her bed an invitation. He moved into it easily, and for the second time that day, she let herself sink into his arms.

45

Rachel's room in the bed-and-breakfast was large, with a canopy bed, floral bedspread and draperies, and broad windows overlooking a pasture. She'd checked in around five, when the pasture had been filled with black cows, some of them just a few feet from her window. She'd sat on the small antique sofa in her room, watching the cows for nearly an hour before taking herself out to dinner. Now she was on the sofa again, waiting for Michael. He would not be able to spend the night with her, but at least she would have him for a few hours. It was Saturday; she was leaving in less than a week, and Katy was home. This could very well be their last time together.

Gram had told her in no uncertain terms to stay away from the house tonight. She wanted to practice being on her own, she'd said, but Rachel guessed there was more to it than that. Gram had something up her sleeve. Whatever it was had lifted the older woman from her sulky, leaden depression to a state of agitation, and Rachel decided that was preferable. She would not interfere. She called the bed-and-breakfast in Elizabethtown, far enough from Reflection that with any luck her name would not be recognized when she made the reservation, and as far as she knew, it had not been.

Then she'd told Michael where she would be and left it up to him to decide whether he could spend some time with her. She was relieved when he said he would.

He arrived at seven-thirty, carrying red roses, a bottle of sparkling cider, and an ancient Kinyarwanda dictionary. She arranged the roses in the ice bucket while he poured the cider into glasses he found in the bathroom.

"If I'd been thinking, I would have brought some wineglasses with me," he said.

"No, this is perfect." She sat cross-legged on the bed, balancing the glass in her hand.

He sat down and leaned back against the headboard, then he reached out to touch his glass to hers. "To a safe, successful and personally rewarding journey to Africa," he said.

"Thank you." She took a sip, meeting his eyes over the top of her glass. "I'm so glad you came," she said.

He nodded. "I didn't lie to Katy, but I didn't tell her the truth, either. I just said I was going out. I knew she wouldn't ask. She wouldn't want to know."

"This must be difficult for her." She knew he felt no malice toward his wife for her betrayal. She doubted she could be so forgiving.

"Yes, I guess it is, although Katy's being typical Katy. She holds it all inside. Doesn't like to deal with anything painful or difficult. So I'm not really sure what's going through her head."

"You enjoyed Hershey Park with her, though," she said, annoyed with herself as the words left her mouth. He'd already talked to her about it; she did not need to bring it up again. She did not like the jealousy she felt when she thought about his being with his wife. She had no right to it.

"Rache," he said, "look—"

"I'm sorry, Michael. Really. I've tried not to say anything that—"

"Shh. I know." He grabbed her hand. "You've been terrific. And I've been doing a lot of thinking about my wife and son, and a lot of thinking about you. But, please . . . I don't want to talk about any of it tonight. Because if I talk about Katy, I won't be able to make love to you. And I want to." He shook his head. "I *have* to."

She stared at him for a moment, then set her glass on the night table and leaned toward him. "Good," she said. "Because I need you to."

With a grin, he set his own glass next to hers, then drew her head down for a kiss, long and deep and feverish. And she knew that, at least for the rest of the evening, Katy would be the farthest thing from his mind.

She had promised herself she would not cry, wanting the memory of their last time together to be good for each of them. She managed to keep her tears in check until he'd fallen asleep—or at least until she thought he was asleep. He heard her quiet crying, though, and he pulled her to him, wrapping his arms around her and holding her close.

"Whatever happens, I'm glad we had this summer together," he whispered.

"Mmm." She pressed her cheek against his chest, loving the way he smelled, missing his scent already.

"I don't want to leave you," he said.

But within an hour he was gone, home to his wife and son, and Rachel sat alone on the sofa again, watching the unhurried progression of moonlight across the pasture.

There was a strange car in the driveway when Rachel got home the following morning. As she stepped onto the porch, she heard laughter coming from inside the house. A man's laughter. Curious, she walked into the kitchen to find her grandmother and an elderly man sitting at the table, sipping coffee from mugs. The glow in Gram's face lit up the room, and the lanky, handsome gentleman's eyes crinkled with good humor. It was a moment before she recognized him.

"Karl Speicer!" she gasped.

Gram smiled. "Rachel, I'd like you to meet Hans," she said.

Rachel moved forward as the pianist rose from his seat. She grasped his hand in hers. "You've come. Oh, Gram, you called him!" She let go of his hand to lean over and hug her grandmother. "Thank you!"

"Don't blame her for delaying so long," Hans said. He was very tall. "She had many reasons, all of them honorable."

"Yes, I know." She looked from one of them to the other. "Please sit down," she said, taking a seat at the table herself. "When did you arrive?"

"Late yesterday afternoon," he said, and Rachel thought she detected a blush in her grandmother's cheeks. She knew the look well. Gram was with the man she'd always loved, always wanted. They had spent the night together. No wonder she had wanted Rachel out of the house.

She wondered briefly about Hans's wife, Winona, but swept the thought from her mind. "Has he seen the music?" she asked.

"I have indeed," he said. "It was quite a shock to me, but after I thought about it, I wonder how I couldn't have known before. The passion of your grandmother's music—it's something I never could understand coming out of Peter."

She wanted to know what would happen next, but she knew she'd better sit tight. Gram could not be rushed. Nor did Hans seem particularly anxious to hurry things along.

"How wonderful that you and your grandmother have gotten to know each other again," he said chattily. "She told me you hadn't seen each other since you were fifteen."

"Yes." Rachel sat back in her chair, trying to relax. "My parents were apparently scandalized by the fact that she and my grandfather dared to help draftees stay out of Vietnam."

"Rachel," Gram said. "That was only part of it."

"What do you mean?"

Gram took in a breath. "Your father learned something about Peter that upset him greatly, and that's when he broke away from us."

"What did he learn?"

"It's about Peter and his relationship to Marielle Hostetter."

"Oh, no." She'd known all along, hadn't she? And Gram had said he'd been a philanderer. "Was Marielle actually Grandpa's daughter?"

Gram looked momentarily confused. Hans laughed, and she joined him a second later. "No, dear, that wasn't it." She sobered quickly. "No. Your grandfather was . . . well, these days I guess you'd call it bisexual."

Rachel sat back in her chair. "*Oh*," she said.

"I told you about Marielle's father, right? He was a painter?"

Rachel nodded.

"He and Peter were attracted to each other, both being artistic types and all. They spent a good deal of time together, and they were lovers." Gram spoke easily, as if this were something she had long ago made peace with. "And one day, Dolly—his wife—came home to find them together. She was a crazy woman. I guess many women would lose their sanity if they made that sort of sudden discovery, but Dolly already had half a screw loose. Anyway, Peter immediately left the house, but seconds after he left, Dolly got a handgun from the closet. She was aiming it at her husband when her daughter—Marielle—came out of nowhere and into the path of the bullet. I don't know if Dolly knew what she'd done or not. She was blind with rage, I understand, and she put the gun to her own head and pulled the trigger again."

"My God," Rachel said.

"When your grandfather found out what happened, he was wracked with guilt. It was his money that paid for Marielle's medical care, and he'd take her presents over the years. He wanted to be sure she would never be forced to leave that land as long as she was still living in the cottage. Anyhow"—Gram shifted in her chair—"your father always wondered about Peter's relationship to the Hostetters, finally coming to the same conclusion you'd reached—that Marielle might have been Peter's child. That's when we told him the truth. I think his original suspicion would have been more palatable to him. An affair with a woman John might have been able to understand. But the truth sickened him. He didn't want to be around us, and he was afraid for you to be around us, too."

She had a vivid recollection of her father referring to homosexuals as "perverts." "Daddy was a bit of a bigot, I'm afraid," she said.

"I never did understand that," Gram mused. "We raised him to be anything but."

Karl Speicer finished his coffee and set the mug on the table with a flourish. "Well, young lady," he said, changing the subject. "You must be wondering what I'm going to do with this music?"

"Yes, I am." She was relieved he was addressing the topic. The bulldozers were still at the pond, ready to begin knocking down trees the following day.

Hans smiled. At eighty-three he was a stunning man. She could easily imagine how attractive he would have been at forty.

"It's all taken care of," he said. "Helen has spoken to the attorney . . . what's his name?"

"Sam Freed," Gram said.

"And we're going to hold a press conference in a few hours. Your friend—" He looked at Gram again.

"Michael," she said.

"Your friend Michael is arranging it, and then the entire world will know the truth about Helen and Peter Huber. The attorney seems to think that will do the trick. Reflection should be safe."

"Wow." Rachel smiled. "You two have had a busy morning."

Hans and Gram exchanged looks and laughed like embarrassed teenagers, and Rachel guessed the business between them this morning had not been limited to saving Reflection.

46

"Are you ready?" Michael looked at the two men sitting on the other side of his office desk.

Sam Freed and Karl Speicer nodded solemnly.

"Yes, sir," Karl said. "Let's go face the music."

The three of them laughed at that and stood up.

Michael had agreed to escort the two men to the press conference. Helen and Rachel had wisely chosen to avoid the crowd and stay home. The conference would be televised. They wouldn't miss anything.

He led the men to the back door of the church basement. Outside, they walked around the path to the front of the church, and from there they could see the crowd gathered by the pond.

The street was clotted with vans, and men and women dodged among the crowd carrying video equipment. Local television crews and a variety of reporters had been covering the story for the past two days, but after receiving the call from Helen this morning, Michael had alerted the national media.

"We will be making an announcement of international significance to the music world," he'd said in his phone calls. Apparently, everyone had taken him seriously.

The police were everywhere. Michael called one of the officers over, and two others quickly appeared to escort them to the statue of Peter Huber in front of the pond. Once they had reached the statue, cameras clicked and microphones materialized from all directions.

Michael worried about the two elderly men being intimidated by the crush of people, but they did not seem at all disturbed. As a matter of fact, the two of them looked as if they were having a good time.

Sam Freed began speaking, and the crowd hushed.

"When Reflection's favorite son, Peter Huber, died ten years ago, he left a will with an odd addendum. No one other than his wife, Helen, myself, and the Hostetter family knew about it. The fact is that Mr. Huber was the owner, through inheritance, of the land that has come to be known as Hostetter land."

There was a wild buzz in the crowd. Michael caught sight of his cousin standing a few feet away. Ursula's mouth was open in disbelief.

Sam waited until the din had died down before speaking again.

"In his will, Mr. Huber specified that Marielle Hostetter be allowed to live on the land for as long as she wanted. After moving out of her cottage, the land would be treated as hers to dispose of as she saw fit. That is what has happened—Ms. Hostetter has chosen to develop the land. However, Mr. Huber made a contingency in his will. He stated that if his last musical work, a piece called *Reflections*, were presented to pianist Karl Speicer, the land would be made a gift to the town and the royalties generated by that work—which should be considerable—would go to Ms. Hostetter."

Again the buzz. Sam held up a hand for quiet.

"Until very recently," he continued, "that particular Huber composition could not be located. But it has been found, and Mr. Speicer is in receipt of it. And I will now turn the floor over to Mr. Speicer."

Michael tensed as the microphones shifted toward the older man. He hoped this would not be too much for Speicer but knew instantly he had nothing to worry about. It was obvious that the pianist was accustomed to public speaking. He had an odd, engaging accent and a dramatic flair in his presentation, dramatic enough to match the impact of what he was about to say.

"The Huber work, *Reflections*, was delivered to me last night," he said. "When I played it, I thought it might be a fake, because although it is, for the most part, a lovely piece of work, it was entirely different from Peter Huber's work in the past. The third movement in particular was quite choppy, and at first I was mystified by it. Then I recalled that, long ago, when Peter and I were close friends, we were fascinated by ciphers in music—codes that a composer might employ to add a message to his work. I realized that Peter had wanted *me* to see the work because he knew I would be able to unravel his cipher. And although it took me half the night, I have done so."

The crowd waited silently for him to continue.

"What I am about to say will stun the music world," he said, "as well as this beautiful town. But it must be said, and it should have been said long, long ago. Peter Huber is *not* the composer of the music we have come to treasure. Rather, his wife and Reflection's longtime resident, Helen Nolan Huber, is the creator of all the extraordinary works attributed to her husband."

There was a collective gasp from the crowd, and then the steady murmur of disbelief. Ursula's face was hideously contorted by anger.

The questions began. Karl detailed the complicated means by which he'd broken the music's code, but it was Sam's assertion that the pristine tract of land surrounding Spring Willow Pond was now a gift to the city and protected from any future development that drew the loudest cheers.

"The Hostetters will sue!" someone called out. It might even have been Ursula, but it didn't matter. Not a soul was listening.

Michael watched the coverage of the event on the news that night from the couch in his family room. Jason was in his room playing computer games with Patrick Geils, but Katy watched the news as well, sitting in front of Michael on the floor, her back against the couch. She was very tired, she said. Indeed, he'd noticed a sluggishness about her, an emptiness these past few days. She'd returned to her medical practice the day before and was having trouble keeping her mind on her work. Even though she'd been home for several days now, jet lag still seemed to be taking a toll on her.

They didn't speak as they watched the press conference unfold on the TV. Karl Speicer looked too old to be up there handling that crowd, but his voice was full of confidence, and his accent and sense of melodrama made Michael smile.

"The protest was started by Rachel Huber," the newscaster said after footage of the conference had been aired. The two pictures the news stations had been showing for three days now, the high school yearbook pictures of Rachel and himself, appeared on the screen. "Miss Huber was quickly joined by her childhood friend, minister of the Reflection Mennonite church, Michael Stoltz." The pictures remained on the air as the newscaster talked about Rachel's past in the town, a story people had to be tired of by now.

The pictures were mesmerizing. Side by side, he and Rachel looked like a couple, as if they were meant to be together. Katy must have noticed it, too, because she began to cry, quietly.

He touched her hair with his fingertips. "Katy?" he said.

She shook her head, and he knew she did not want to talk. He did not know if he should feel anger or relief. It no longer really mattered.

47

Despite the frivolity of the last twenty-four hours, Reflection Day found the town quiet and subdued. Storm clouds gathered in the sky, churches held special services, and shops and schools were closed.

At the last minute Rachel decided to join her grandmother and Hans—who was still in town and showing no sign of leaving—at the Reflection Day observance in the high school. After all, what could the townspeople do to her now? She was leaving on Friday. Besides, several people had called her, offering quiet apologies and gratitude for her role in saving the land.

She also wanted to see Michael's small band of Mennonite teenagers present their program. More precisely, she wanted to see Michael.

They were late and had to take seats in the last row of the auditorium. That was good, Rachel thought. Few people would notice her.

The stage was bare, except for the eight teenagers and Michael sitting in a row of chairs. At exactly two o'clock Michael stepped up to the dais, and the light chatter of the audience subsided.

"I would like to ask," Michael began, "that as you listen to our program this afternoon, you think about making this the final observance of Reflection Day."

A rush of whispering spread across the auditorium, and Rachel could not tell whether there was support or derision in the sound.

"It's been twenty-one years since the tragedy occurred at Spring Willow Elementary School," Michael continued. "And it is my belief—a belief I think many of you share—that it's time to let go of the destructive grief and move on."

He returned to his chair, and a short, frail-looking teenage girl stood up and walked to the dais. She had to stand on a box to reach the microphone. She read a poem she had written about the loss of the future when a child dies. Then a few other students read essays they had written on the same theme. Two boys read a poem in tandem about the toll war takes on its soldiers. Another had written about the strength of a solid community. The last girl read a story about a fictional town that held on so tightly to the past that it lost sight of its future.

Rachel's eyes stung as she listened to the young speakers, and a tight pain grew in her throat. It had been a mistake to come.

Finally, one of the boys who'd read the poem about war took his place in front of the dais again.

"Michael suggests that this be the last observation of Reflection Day," he read from a note card, "and with respect to those people who have suffered, the senior youth group of the Reflection Mennonite Church agrees. Teach us about the horrors of war, the value of life, and individual responsibility, and use September tenth, 1973, as an example of those things, but allow schools and shops to stay open, and allow us to let go of the past. We cannot afford to hold on to sorrow and anger and hatred any longer. Reflection's children deserve a better legacy than that. So we'd like to ask you to vote here today. It won't be binding of course. The town council has to make the final decision. But we can let them know what this audience has to say. So—"

A woman suddenly stood up from the third or fourth row of the auditorium. "Excuse me?" she asked.

The voice was familiar, and Rachel craned her neck to see. Lily.

"I'd like to say something to the audience before we have our vote, please," Lily said.

The student turned to look at Michael, who nodded, and Lily walked up onto the stage.

"I want to tell you something that happened on September tenth, 1973," she began, "something you don't already know." Lily wrapped her fingers around the edges of the dais. "I was a student in Rachel

Huber's classroom at that time, and I didn't get along very well with Ms. Huber. As many people could tell you, I didn't get along very well with anyone in authority back then. My sister, Jenny, was the compliant one. The good twin. I was the bad one. And although I'd only been in Ms. Huber's room for a few days, she and I had already butted heads numerous times. One of those times was on the morning of September tenth. I don't remember what it was about; all I know is that I was angry with her."

Lily looked anxious and pale, Rachel thought. Her usual boisterous self-confidence was entirely missing.

"At some point that morning, Ms. Huber suddenly told us we had to go sit on the floor of the cloakroom," Lily continued. "We were to take books with us, or something to color, and we had to move fast. It was a game, she told us. She hurried us back there, made sure we were all sitting, and told us to stay there until she returned. Everyone believed the part about it being a game—even me—but because I was angry with her, I wasn't going to go along with it."

Lily hesitated, looking down at the dais, and Rachel gripped the edge of her seat. She noticed someone quietly walking up the steps of the stage. Was it Jacob Holt? Yes. When he reached the stage, he stood off to one side, close to the curtains, his arms folded as he listened.

"I got up and left the cloakroom," Lily said, "and I walked into the empty classroom. Ms. Huber was nowhere to be seen, so I decided to take off. But the door was locked." She looked hard at the audience. "*Yes*," she said, "*Rachel Huber locked that door*. She did all she could think of to do to protect us in the few seconds she had to come up with a plan. The door was easy to unlock from the inside, though, so I unlocked it and walked out into the hall. And . . . " Lily's voice suddenly cracked. She coughed, regaining her composure. "Luke Pierce was standing right in front of me," she continued. "Jacob Holt was running down the hall toward us. And the rest you know. But I needed to set the record straight. Rachel locked the door. I unlocked it. I was only seven, and too terrified to tell anyone what I'd done. I thought I killed my sister and my classmates. But I'm not seven now. And Rachel's not twenty-three. And no one should judge either of us by our past mistakes."

Jacob Holt had walked closer to her, and Lily did a double take when she noticed him. He touched the young woman's shoulder and took her place behind the dais. Lily slipped back next to Michael, who stood up to give her his chair. Someone brought out a tenth chair, but he stood behind it rather than sit down again.

"That took a lot of courage, Lily," Jacob Holt said into the microphone. "And you've given me courage as well." He looked out at the audience. "Lily has made a confession," he said, "but she knows more than she is saying, and now I have to finish the story for her. I have to make a confession of my own."

The audience was utterly still. Rachel exchanged a look of confusion with her grandmother.

"At least Lily can use the excuse that she was only seven years old at the time of the tragedy," he said. "My only excuse was my own confusion and self-preservation. I thought I would take all of this to my grave with me"—he shook his head—"but with what's gone on in Reflection these past few months, I cannot. I see how people treat Rachel Huber. She's the scapegoat for our grief and misery. I see we have never let go of the past, and I agree wholeheartedly with Michael Stoltz that we must."

Someone in the row in front of her turned to look at Rachel. Rachel kept her eyes riveted on the stage.

"On September tenth, 1973, a terrible tragedy occurred in Spring Willow Elementary School, and I am guilty of lying about that tragedy." The rustle of whispers filled the auditorium again. "I've said publicly that, several days before the incident occurred, I told Rachel Huber that I planned to call the police to have her husband locked up. I wish to God that I'd been that aggressive in my handling of the situation, but I was not. I simply shared my concerns about that young man with Rachel. I told her I would consider calling the police if he set foot on school grounds again, and she said she would do all she could to keep him away. That was it, but I twisted the truth to save my own skin. Yet that's not the worst thing I did." Holt seemed suddenly overcome by emotion. He bowed his head for a moment before lifting it once more to continue, and Rachel realized she was holding her breath.

"I saw Luke Pierce from my office window," Holt said. "He looked as if he was out for blood. When I realized he had entered the school,

I left my office and ran down the hall after him. By the time I got to Rachel Huber's classroom, I found the door open, little Lily Wright in the hallway, and Luke just inside. He had pulled the pin on a grenade he was holding, and he hollered, 'Where is everybody? Where's Rachel?' He was crying, and I knew that he meant to kill himself in front of his wife." Holt leaned forward, elbows on the dais. "I truly believe that's all he wanted—to kill himself in front of Rachel—not to hurt a bunch of kids. I tried to get the grenade from him. Please understand, I thought Rachel had taken the kids and fled the classroom. It never occurred to me that she had them hidden away back there in the cloakroom. When I finally managed to pull the grenade from his hand, I threw it as far from us as I could—through the open door of the cloakroom. Luke screamed at me. 'My God, there's kids back there!' and he ran after the grenade, I'm sure in the hope that he could throw himself on it to try to save those kids. Of course, he was not able to."

Rachel stared numbly at the stage. Luke had tried to *save* the children. He had died trying. She didn't bother to wipe away her tears, and they were warm on her cheeks. Gram took her hand.

"It wasn't until all the screaming started that I realized what I had done," Holt continued. "What *Luke* had done, because in my mind I quickly began to believe the story I later told the police—that it was Luke who threw that grenade." Holt made a loud swallowing sound into the microphone.

"I have no right to ask for your forgiveness," he said. "Instead, I ask you to forgive Rachel Huber, who, at a very young age and newly home from the Peace Corps, was suddenly forced to deal with a deranged husband who had been ruined serving his country. This community did very little to help her with that. The one thing that should be obvious to all of us by now is that holding on to hate and anger exacts too great a price. We have our land back, secure and safe, in large measure owing to Rachel, but do we deserve it? Does a town that cannot forgive truly deserve to hold on to the beauty it's been blessed with? In many ways, we're still stuck back in 1973. Forgiveness is the only thing that can move us forward and make our town whole again."

The audience sat in stunned silence as Jacob Holt climbed down the stairs and returned to his seat. Rachel could hear sniffling. Gram handed her a tissue, and she wiped her eyes.

Michael rose slowly from the row of chairs on the stage. His voice when he reached the dais was thick with emotion. "My friend Luke Pierce was no murderer," he said. "He suffered in the war, fighting for what he thought was right. He brought back invisible scars from that battle. But in his last moment of sanity, he tried to save the children in that cloakroom.

"And my friend Rachel Huber is no accomplice to murder," he continued. "She was as much a victim as our children were. So I ask you, in the name of forgiveness, to lay this sad chapter to rest. Not forgotten, but allowed simply to take its place in our town's history. Let's make this the final observance of Reflection Day. Please stand up if you agree."

It seemed to Rachel that nearly everyone rose to their feet, including Gram and Hans. She was slow to rise herself, uncertain whether she should be allowed to vote, but a woman from the row in front of her turned around, reaching over to pull her up by the shoulder, and she squeezed the stranger's hand with a grateful smile.

48

The kids from the youth group had done a terrific job. Michael congratulated them, thanked them heartily, and then escaped to his church. After managing that huge audience and its myriad of surprises, he wanted some time to himself.

He'd imagined those last few minutes of Luke's life many times before, always taking comfort in the fact that, in the end, his old friend had not been lucid, not truly aware of what was going on around him. But apparently that had not been the case. Luke had had one last agonizing moment of sanity when he'd realized the children were in danger. The thought of him suffering that moment of awareness was nearly too much for Michael to bear.

He had the church to himself, and he sat in a pew near the front. He closed his eyes, and the welcome quiet filled him like something tangible, something he could pull into his heart.

Thank you, Lord, for giving Lily and Jacob such courage. And please give me the courage to do what I know I have to do. I've been dishonest, I know.

In the past few weeks, he'd often felt abandoned by God, but he sensed his presence here, inside him now.

Give me the courage to be honest with you, and with myself. And please help my son understand. Help me be a good father to him.

Keep Rachel safe on her journey. She's not much of a believer, but she's an excellent person. Some of your best work.

He finished praying but sat with his eyes closed a few minutes longer, drinking in the silence. Then he stood up and walked downstairs to his office. He had some phone calls to make.

It was nearly ten by the time he got home that night, and Katy met him at the kitchen door.

"Jace is terribly upset," she said. "He can't sleep. He says that every time he closes his eyes, he sees Luke Pierce and the grenade."

Katy and Jace had sat in the front row of the auditorium during the Reflection Day program, and Michael had been aware of his son's rapt attention while Lily and Jacob were speaking.

He walked down the hall to Jason's bedroom, Katy close behind him. Jace was sitting up in bed, the light on behind him and a book in his hands.

"Can't sleep?" Michael sat down on the bed. Katy leaned against the edge of the desk.

"I'm not tired," Jace said. "I just wanted to read awhile."

"We heard some shocking things today, huh?"

Jace shrugged.

"I think a lot of people will have trouble sleeping tonight," Michael said. "People thought they knew exactly what happened that day at Spring Willow School, and now suddenly they know it wasn't that way at all. Gives people a lot to think about."

"Lily and Mr. Holt were very brave," Katy said, and Michael nodded.

Jace lowered his book to his lap. "Now everyone all of a sudden thinks Rachel Huber's okay," he said. "I still can't stand her."

Michael was about to protest, but Katy beat him to it. "You've never even met her, Jason," she said.

"I just think she messed things up." He shot Michael a look.

"Well, you know, Jace," Michael said, "sometimes things have to be messed up before they can be made better. Sometimes it helps to shake things up a bit."

Jason scowled. "That's stupid," he said.

"I don't think so."

"Things are messed up with you and Mom, aren't they? Are they going to get better?"

Michael looked at Katy. She was biting her lower lip.

"Yes," Michael said, "things are going to get better, but it will take some time, and the end result may not be exactly what you would like it to be."

"What do you mean?" Jace looked at him suspiciously.

"Mom and I have a lot of talking to do. We have to figure out what to do about our mess."

Jason closed his book and set it on the nightstand. "Well, figure it out soon, okay?" he asked. Then he rolled onto his side, facing the wall.

Michael touched his shoulder. "We'll try," he said, standing up.

Katy leaned over to kiss her son's cheek. "Good night, honey," she said.

They walked in silence into the family room. Michael wished Jason could somehow be spared the problems between them.

Katy sat down on the couch. "I was proud of you today," she said, "watching you up there with those kids. Up till now, no one's ever had the guts to say, 'Let's be done with this.'"

"Thanks," he said. "I thought the kids were wonderful."

"I was watching you and thinking, 'What did I ever see in Drew?'" She wrung her hands in her lap. "I just don't know how I could have done what I did. It seems like some other woman did it, not me."

He sat down at the far end of the couch. "I've forgiven you, Katy," he said. "When are you going to forgive yourself?"

She shook her head. "I don't know. I felt guilty the whole time I was involved with Drew, but I couldn't seem to stop myself. I was operating on pure emotion, for the first time in my life. And it was too much for me. I wasn't used to it. I let it get the better of me. I know you've always wanted me to be a more emotional person, but I think I instinctively knew it was a part of myself I had to keep in check."

He listened to her carefully. It wasn't like Katy to talk about herself this way.

"Mennonite schools shelter you from so much," she said. "I was never really allowed to be myself growing up. To express myself or think about what I needed. And even when I started going to public schools, it was so ingrained in me . . . " She lifted her hands in the air a few inches and dropped them in frustration. "I was never really allowed to be *myself*, Michael. I never had a single second of rebellion."

"Until now."

"Yes. I've always been so logical. So *rational*—"

He laughed. "That you are, Katy."

She looked hurt. "And I know that's bothered you, but it's who I am, and I'm comfortable that way. I think a logical, rational person is just as valuable to society as someone who operates on emotion all the time. Maybe even more so."

He nodded. "You're probably right."

She brushed her hair away from her face. "So what do we do about our mess, Michael?" she asked.

"I think we need to separate." There. The words had slipped out easily.

Katy lowered her eyes quickly to her hands. It was a minute before she spoke. "You're going to lose—"

"I know what I'm losing. This isn't a decision I've come to lightly."

She smoothed the tip of her thumb across the nail on her index finger, over and over again. "I feel like I deserve to lose you after what I've done," she said. Her nose was red.

"Come here." He patted the sofa next to him, and she scooted over. He put his arm around her. "My decision has very little—nothing, in fact—to do with what happened between you and Drew."

"I know you haven't really been happy in our marriage," she said, her voice thick. "You've always seemed very satisfied in other parts of your life, but not with me."

"Can you honestly say you've been happy with me?" he asked.

"Early on I was." She studied her fingernail. "In recent years, no. But I knew we were an odd match from the start. It just seemed very important to stay together. The cost of splitting up was—and still is, I think—way too high. I know that, if we put our individual happiness first, splitting up is the right thing to do. But I'd be willing to put my own happiness on a back burner, for Jace's sake. For the sake of the church."

"I'm not willing," he said firmly. "It's dishonest. The worst hypocrisy, the worst lie I can imagine."

She was quiet a minute. Her tears had stopped, and he felt the stiffness in her shoulder beneath his hand. She'd always felt that way, he realized with a jolt. Always that stiff, cool stoniness in her body.

"You never actually told me how far things have gone between you and Rachel," she said finally.

He was not sure how to respond. He did not want to hurt her. "How much do you want to know?" he asked.

"The truth."

"Rachel and I have had a friendship this summer," he said. "We were attracted to each other, but we didn't act on that attraction until I learned about you and Drew."

Katy groaned, looking up at the ceiling. "I'm a fool," she said.

"It doesn't matter, Katy," he said. "The physical side of my relationship with Rachel is almost immaterial. My connection to her goes way beyond that. It's a stronger bond than I've ever had with anyone, except maybe Luke."

"I resent her," Katy said irritably. "I always have. Even when we were teenagers. I knew even then that you adored her. And I do remember that time you were asking about the other day. That time after the basketball game. But I'm ashamed of it. I'd just started public school then, and I was trying so hard to fit in, which I never actually did, I guess. But I was trying, nevertheless, and if I'd aligned myself with you in that instance I thought I'd be dead socially forever. I'm sorry."

"It was a long time ago," he said, though his words sounded hollow. He could forgive her the most recent transgression, but for some reason her role in that incident would always haunt him. "Rachel was the catalyst for all this," he said, "but she's not the cause. There's a difference."

"She's definitely going to Rwanda?"

"Zaire. Yes."

"Are you upset that she's leaving?"

"No. It's going to be very good for her, and it will be good for me to have the time on my own. I need to think and pray." He sighed. "And, I guess, to look for a new place to live . . . and a new job."

She shifted away from him on the couch and pounded her fist on her thigh, her first show of anger. He imagined there was more where that came from. "How can you possibly give this all up?" she asked.

"I have to, or I'll be of no use to anyone."

"I'm so *angry* with you," she said. "And with myself. We should never have let things get out of hand this way. *I'm* not ready to give everything up, Michael."

"I won't go on living a lie," he said. "The lie might please you and it might please the church, but it doesn't please God. That much I'm sure of."

She lowered her head, taking in a few long breaths. When she raised her eyes to him again, they were red. "I'm afraid," she said softly. "Of the unknown. Of all we have to go through."

"Katy," he smiled at her, "do you realize that tonight is probably the first time you've ever talked to me about how you feel about anything?"

"I know," she said. "But it's too late, isn't it?"

"Yes," he agreed, taking her hand. "It's way too late."

49

Michael found all five of the elders waiting for him in the smaller of the church meeting rooms. Lewis Klock looked up when he walked through the door, then nodded at the one empty chair in the circle, next to Celine.

Celine gave him a questioning smile as he took the seat.

Michael looked around the circle. He could not bear the mixture of hope and worry that lined Lewis's face, or Jim Rausch's troubled frown. Samuel Morgan and Ed Flynn, sitting rigid as statues, were even less comforting to behold, and Celine rubbed an imaginary spot on her skirt with the tip of her index finger.

"Thanks for agreeing to meet with me on such short notice," Michael began. "I felt that it was important for me to address this issue without delay."

Lewis, Celine, and Jim nodded, but Ed and Samuel maintained their stoic reserve. Ed folded his hands neatly on his knees.

"I need your prayers, brothers and sister." Michael wanted to get directly to the point. "Katy and I have decided to end our marriage."

Lewis let out his breath and leaned back in his seat, a resigned look on his face.

Celine touched Michael's hand. "Oh, Michael," she said, "I'm sorry."

Ed clucked his disgust. "'He must not be a recent convert, or he may become conceited and fall under the same judgment as the devil,'" he quoted.

"Michael," Jim leaned toward him. "Is this a mutual decision between you and Katy?"

Michael looked at the ceiling, as though he might find the answer in the acoustic tiles. "Katy and I both recognize that our marriage is not a good one," he said slowly. "I know we've given the appearance of being a happy and contented couple, but that's all it's been—an appearance. It was too painful and too frightening to admit to the problems, so I guess we kept them hidden, from ourselves as well as from others." He would not tell them about Katy's relationship with Drew. Her infidelity was only a symptom of a disease they both shared.

"Katy would be willing to stay in our marriage for the sake of our son and the church." He shook his head. "But I can't do that. I can't continue to preach honesty and openness when all the while I'm living a lie."

"Wasn't fair to *you* that they ordained you," Ed said. "You grew up with worldly values. A zebra can't change his stripes."

Michael willed the elder's patronizing comments to roll off his back.

"Where exactly does Rachel Huber fit into all of this?" Samuel asked.

He'd known the question was coming. The answer was easy. "Rachel's responsible for changing many things in Reflection recently," he said, "but she's not responsible for ending my marriage. I fully admit to you that I love her deeply, that I would like eventually to have a loving and permanent relationship with her. Her presence has forced me to take a hard look at my marriage, to recognize that it is an empty shell."

"Convenient," Ed muttered.

Michael ignored him. "Even if Rachel were to go back to San Antonio and swear she would never see me again, I would still end my marriage."

Lewis sat up straight, the kindness in his wise old eyes a sudden refuge of warmth in the room. "I'm sorry about your decision, Michael," he said gently, "and I know you're aware that such a decision carries enormous consequences."

"Yes," he said.

"You were right to bring this to us right away," Lewis continued. "I'll take care of Sunday's sermon. Will you come and address the congregation during the sharing period?"

Michael nodded, but for the first time since the meeting had begun, his throat threatened to close up on him. He would be in the pews on Sunday. Lewis would be in the pulpit.

Lewis studied him for another moment before bowing his head. "Let us pray," he said as they lowered their heads. "Heavenly father, Michael needs your love and guidance right now, and we need your wisdom to know how to handle this situation. Please show us your will in this matter, and give our entire congregation strength and tolerance. Amen."

"Amen." Michael whispered his response, and Lewis looked at him again.

"The elders will need to meet privately for a while, Michael," he said. "We must pray together and ask God to help us in our decision."

Michael rose from his seat. He knew what their decision would be. He was ready for it. "I'll be at home this evening," he said. "You can reach me there."

If anyone said good-bye to him as he left the room, he didn't hear them. He walked down the hall and up the stairs and was about to leave the church when he changed his mind. Instead, he walked into the sanctuary and sat down in one of the rear pews. He needed some time to himself: time to grieve all he was about to lose and to celebrate all he was about to gain.

50

From her seat on the porch swing Rachel watched Michael's car pull into the driveway and come to a stop in front of the garden. She knew where he'd been, and as she walked down the porch steps to meet him, the tension that had been with her all afternoon threatened to break loose.

The muscles in his face were set and unsmiling, and he said nothing as he pulled her into an embrace. She held him tightly, aware that he was drawing strength from her and wanting to give him all she could.

After a long moment, they pulled apart.

"Do you want me to cancel the trip to Zaire?" she offered. "I feel like you need me around right now."

"Yes, I need you," he said, "but no, I don't want you to cancel your trip. I want you to go." His eyes told her that he meant it.

"Tell me what happened," she asked.

They walked up the stairs to the porch and sat down on the swing, and he told her in detail about his meeting with the elders.

"What do you think they'll do?" she asked.

"I know exactly what they'll do," he said. "They'll notify the bishop, and my ordination will be pulled—sometime this week, I would guess. Only I plan to step down voluntarily from my ministry tonight." His voice was flat, but sure and steady, and Rachel knew his mind was made up.

"It seems like such an extreme response," she said. "To lose a good minister."

He slipped his arm around her shoulders. "I can't be a good minister without the trust and confidence of my congregation," he said. "I can still be a good Mennonite, though. I always will be. That's portable, like prayer. Something no one can ever take away from me."

"What will you say to the congregation on Sunday?" She could imagine how painful that church service was going to be for him.

"I'll be brief," he said. "I'll tell them that Katy and I are separating, and that I'm leaving the ministry. I'll say I'm sorry for any discomfort I've caused them over the past couple of months, and I'll ask everyone to continue to welcome Katy and Jason. Katy and Jace are going to need the support of their church community more than ever."

Rachel swallowed a bitter retort. "It bothers me that you have to shoulder all the responsibility for the end of your marriage," she said.

"The decision is mine." Michael brushed a strand of hair from her cheek. "Regardless of anything Katy did."

Rachel rested her head on his shoulder. "Will people blame me?" she asked.

"Does it matter?"

No. She knew it didn't. There would always be people who could not forgive her. But she had found her own peace.

Michael ran the back of his fingers softly across her shirt where it covered her breast. "I told Katy that the physical side of our relationship was insignificant," he said with a smile in his voice. "I lied."

She closed her eyes to let his touch fill her up. "Yeah." She spoke quietly. "I think you did."

"When you get back, I'll have my own place, and we can be freer."

She loved the idea. "That will give me something to look forward to," she said, then she snuggled closer to him. "I already miss you." She did, but she had no regrets over her decision to leave. Being apart from Michael didn't scare her at all. Twenty-one years and thousands of miles had done nothing to diminish their bond. Time and distance could not harm it now, either.

"How do you say 'soul mates' in Kinyarwanda?" she asked.

Michael stared at the ceiling of the porch. It took him a minute to respond. *"Inshuti?"* he suggested.

"Hmm." She was not certain of the translation, but the word sounded soft and satisfying to her ears. *"Inshuti,"* she said, and she settled easily into the comfort of his arms.

Epilogue

EIGHT MONTHS LATER

The curtain-call bells were ringing as Helen and Rachel left Hans's dressing room in the Kennedy Center. Helen slipped her arm through her granddaughter's for the walk down the corridor toward the concert hall. "He has such focus," she said to Rachel. "Couldn't you see him pulling in while we were talking? Withdrawing from us as he's preparing to perform? I remember seeing him do that any number of times in the old days."

"Yes," Rachel agreed. "He looked as if he was trying to hold in his energy until he gets onstage."

Helen smiled to herself. It was that energy, that unbridled, out-of-control side of Hans that had always attracted her, that attracted her still.

They turned to walk through the concert-hall door, to the right of the stage.

The orchestra was tuning up, the chaotic frenzy of sound exciting to Helen's ears.

"Michael's already there." Rachel nodded toward the front row, and they walked toward him to take their seats. Michael hadn't joined them in Hans's dressing room because he wanted to call Jason before the concert. Helen knew he didn't like to let a day go by without some contact with his son.

It was May 6, the debut performance of the slightly doctored cadenza for *Reflections*. She and Hans had spent several joy-filled months over the winter secluded in her house, collaborating on a new version of the third movement. They tried to remain true to Peter's vision of the piece as a whole, and they were able to create new variations on the theme from parts of the cipher so that, at least symbolically, the message Peter had embedded in the music would remain.

She'd talked to Hans about the anguish she'd experienced in letting the world know the truth about Peter.

"Don't you see?" Hans had responded. "Peter wanted all of this to happen. He knew the addendum to his will would force you to see me. He was granting us permission to finally be together."

It was an aspect of Peter's intentions she had not considered. She wasn't certain Hans's interpretation was accurate, but the thought comforted her all the same.

Hans had been most fascinated by the music Helen had written since Peter's death, music she had created and tucked away. She'd had no outlet for it; Peter Huber could hardly have composed from the grave. But Hans was thrilled by the music, and he was making it his own. He was planning to play a couple of those compositions that evening as encores.

Michael leaned forward from his seat. "Feeling a little better than the last time we were here, Helen?" he asked.

"Lord, yes." *She* felt fine, but she was still a little worried about Michael. He'd been depressed the past few months as the loss of his ministry caught up with him. But things were turning around for him now, and she felt confident he would be all right. Rachel didn't seem concerned in the least.

"He just needs to feel worthwhile again," Rachel had said to her. "Everything will fall into place come September."

She was probably right. Only the day before, Michael had signed a contract to begin teaching theology at the college in Elizabethtown in the fall, and he was joining a pastoral-counseling practice in a few weeks. Rachel would be teaching learning-disabled kids in Lancaster come September, and the two of them would be married in October, once Michael's divorce was final. They would also be the godparents of Lily and Ian Jackson's baby, due in August. And they were building a house on Helen's land, on the other side of the woods from her house.

Michael had been all set to join Rachel in Zaire in January. He'd had his inoculations and was already packed when the flooding hit California, and he knew the need was more urgent there. So off he went to Los Angeles with other Mennonite volunteers. Helen knew how anxious he had been to see Rachel, and she admired him immensely for that personal sacrifice. She wrote as much to Rachel. *I could never sacrifice my own desires for others in that way,* she'd written, and Rachel had written back, *You're joking, right?*

She supposed she *had* sacrificed a good deal over the years, but there was no longer any need to. She had all she could ever want now. Hans had arrived and never left, except for a few visits to his wife before Winona's death in early October. He and Helen had been married on Christmas Day. Rachel teasingly complained that they should have waited until her return in February so she could have attended the wedding.

"Sorry," Hans had said. "We're too old for a long engagement."

He'd hired someone to rebuild the tree house and surprised Helen with it as a wedding gift. He'd had two rocking chairs set inside the screened-in structure, and a long, curved staircase now led up to the door. Helen knew that the day would come when neither she nor Hans could get up those stairs, but for now it was one of their favorite places to sit and talk.

The conductor walked onto the stage, and the audience applauded. He smiled at his orchestra, then looked down at Helen with a nod before holding his hand out to welcome the pianist.

Hans strode across the stage with that familiar, commanding presence. He dove right into playing the dramatic opening passage of *Reflections*, and Helen played along with him in her mind.

Nearly an hour had passed by the time Hans and the orchestra had finished the piece, and the audience was quick to give the musicians a standing ovation. The conductor asked Helen to rise, and the applause thundered around her as she waved to the crowd. It was the first time she was being acknowledged as something more than the wife of an important man, she thought. The experience was surprisingly gratifying.

Hans joined them in the foyer during the intermission. "I think we should all enjoy a glass of champagne out on the terrace," he said.

Michael got their champagne—and his club soda—and they headed for the doors to the terrace. Only then did Helen notice the lightning. It flashed against the windows, and she had one moment of panic before she remembered the opine and Saint-John's-wort in her beaded handbag. She'd clipped fresh sprigs just that morning and wrapped them in plastic to bring with her on the trip. Now she clutched the handbag close to her side as she accompanied her husband through the doors.

The broad terrace stretched the entire length of the Kennedy Center, high above the Potomac River. It was not yet raining, but the air was charged with the approaching storm. Thunder grumbled in the distance, rising up in waves, and lightning turned the water of the Potomac silver. Helen felt her breathing sharpen, quicken, and she consciously worked to slow it down. Her palm was perspiring where it pressed against the handbag.

"I want to walk out to the edge," she said to Hans.

He looked surprised for only a second before nodding and taking her elbow, guiding her toward the far side of the terrace. The lights from a plane moved toward them through the darkness before slipping over their heads, and to their right Georgetown glittered in the sky and the river.

"All right, dear?" Hans asked, and she nodded, drawing in a few long, calming breaths.

Rachel and Michael stood a short distance away from them. Rachel pointed toward Georgetown, and Michael put his head back and laughed, the sound carrying like an echo above the river. Rachel glanced over at them and said something to Michael before walking toward Helen and Hans.

"Are you all right out here, Gram?" she asked. "Would you rather be inside?"

"I'm absolutely fine," Helen said with an assurance she was beginning to feel in her bones.

Rachel smiled at her. "Good for you," she said. She walked back to Michael and took his arm, and Helen watched with a sense of contentment as the younger couple began to stroll down the terrace.

The lightning grew fiercer, surrounding her and Hans with arrhythmic splashes of white light, and the thunder settled into a constant, deep-throated rumbling. Helen lifted her face to the sky as the first tentative raindrops fell. As if he knew she needed to take this fearless stand against the storm, Hans waited quietly at her side.

"It's a beautiful storm," Helen said, and she meant it. Her love of treacherous weather was being reborn inside her. The river suddenly lit up like a long, sinewy pool of mercury. "Look at that!" she exclaimed with childish delight, and Hans chuckled.

In the next flash of lightning, the buildings and spires of Georgetown were abruptly altered, washed in silver, transformed into something entirely new—the way the lightning had transformed her, transformed all of them.

It was raining harder. "We should go in, Helen," Hans said. "I need to get backstage. Can you tear yourself away?"

She nodded, reluctantly turning her back on the storm to walk with him across the terrace. She was a new woman as she crossed the grand foyer, calm and brave and invulnerable as she listened to her husband play a piece she'd written only a year ago. And it wasn't until the end of the piece, when she reached into her handbag for a tissue to blot her tears, that she discovered something she had probably known all along: she had left her herbs at home.

About the Author

Diane Chamberlain is the award-winning author of six previous novels, including *Brass Ring, Fire and Rain,* and *Keeper of the Light.* She lives in Vienna, Virginia.